The raging elements—uncontrollable torrents and massive approaching glaciers—were not the only enemies in Alaska at the turn of the century.

Charlatans and confidence men undermined the efforts of honest developers with shady promotion schemes.

Eastern coal mine interests formed pressure groups to prevent the harvest of Alaskan coal, and obtained a shipping monopoly to California and the Hawaiian islands that completely cut out the potential supply from the North.

The United States government itself violated its contracts with Alaska more flagrantly than England had hamstrung her colonies.

It took a determined man to confront the odds against civilizing the fledgling territory, but Murray O'Neil had the strength to fight—and the devoted support of most of his men. . . .

THE IRON TRAIL

An epic of early Alaska

THE
IRON
TRAIL

Rex Beach

A COMSTOCK EDITION

SAUSALITO • CALIFORNIA

SBN 0-89174-022-8-225

First Printing: March 1972
Second Printing: February 1977

Printed in the United States of America

COMSTOCK EDITIONS, INC.
3030 Bridgeway, Sausalito, CA 94965

CONTENTS

In the struggle to build Alaska's first railroad, and in the rush for gold, it wasn't so much the men who were seeking a fortune as the men who wanted the challenge who were drawn to the North. The challenge was the building it, or the finding it, more than the having it.

The greatness which Rex Beach captures in *The Iron Trail* is that the uniqueness of Alaska, its geological and climatic conditions, the impossibility of the odds, is what has drawn greatness out of the men in the Great Land.

"Alaska the Unknown" of sixty years ago is still "Alaska the Unknown" today. It may take another fifty years before America in general has any grasp of the realism that is here; the dimensions, the variety, the constrasts. If you have sailed in the magnificent beauty of the Fjords of Southeastern Alaska and compared them with the isolation and desolation of the Arctic flatlands in the north, you understand.

The story Rex Beach tells is essentially true, although the names of the characters, cities, rivers, and glaciers are drawn from his imagination. The real "Irish Prince" was Michael J. Heney, the builder of Alaska's first railroads— the White Path and Yukon, and the Copper River and Northwestern. The latter, around which this story is told, ran from the Port of Cordova to Kennecott. Challenging the destructive power of the Miles and Childs Glaciers, Heney built his famous line up the Copper River, a daring feat which beat the competition to the coal and copper fields of the interior.

Written in the romantic style of the turn of the century, this book is an engrossing yarn of heroes, villains and adventure. Yet it is relevant today because it deals with the opening of the Arctic, a saga which has only begun.

Sixty years ago the railroad was seen as the key to Arctic development. Today it is still the key. Though old-fashioned as it comes, it is as modern and as necessary as tomorrow. The iron trail is still the best way to open the Arctic for conservation and for the greatest enjoyment of people.

Walter J. Hickel
Anchorage, Alaska
1971

I *In which the Tide Takes a Hand*

The ship stole through the darkness with extremest caution, feeling her way past bay and promontory. Around her was none of that phosphorescent glow which lies above the open ocean, even on the darkest night, for the mountains ran down to the channel on either side. In places they overhung, and where they lay upturned against the dim sky it could be seen that they were mantled with heavy timber. All day long the *Nebraska* had made her way through an endless succession of straits and sounds, now squeezing through an inlet so narrow that the somber spruce trees seemed to be within a short stone's-throw, again plowing across some open reach where the pulse of the north Pacific could be felt. Out through the openings to seaward stretched the restless ocean, on across uncounted leagues, to Saghalien and the rim of Russia's prisonyard.

Always near at hand was the deep green of the Canadian forests, denser, darker than a tropic jungle, for this was the land of "plenty waters." The hillsides were carpeted knee-deep with moss, wet to saturation. Out of every gulch came a brawling stream whipped to milk-white frenzy; snow lay heavy upon the higher levels, while now and then from farther inland peered a glacier, like some dead monster crushed between the granite peaks. There were villages, too, and fishing-stations, and mines and quarries. These burst suddenly upon the view, then slipped past with dreamlike swiftness. Other ships swung into sight, rushed by, and were swallowed up in the labyrinthine maze astern.

Those passengers of the *Nebraska* who had never before traversed the "Inside Passage" were loud in the praises of its picturesqueness, while those to whom the route

1

was familiar seemed to find an ever-fresh fascination in
its shifting scenes.

Among the latter was Murray O'Neil. The whole north
coast from Flattery to St. Elias was as well mapped
in his mind as the face of an old friend, yet he was
forever discovering new vistas, surprising panoramas,
amazing variations of color and topography. The mysterious rifts and passageways that opened and closed as
if to lure the ship astray, the trackless confusion of islets,
the siren song of the waterfalls, the silent hills and glaciers and snow-soaked forests—all appealed to him strongly, for he was at heart a dreamer.

Yet he did not forget that scenery such as this, lovely
as it is by day, may be dangerous at night, for he knew
the weakness of steel hulls. On some sides his experience
and business training had made him sternly practical and
prosaic. Ships aroused no manner of enthusiasm in him
except as means to an end. Railroads had no glamour
of romance in his eyes, for, having built a number of
them, he had outlived all poetic notions regarding the
"iron horse," and once the rails were laid he was apt
to lose interest in them. Nevertheless, he was almost poetic in his own quiet way, interweaving practical thoughts
with fanciful visions, and he loved his dreams. He was
dreaming now as he leaned upon the bridge rail of the
Nebraska, peering into the gloom with watchful eyes.
From somewhere to port came the occasional commands
of the officer on watch, echoed instantly from the inky
interior of the wheelhouse. Up overside rose the whisper
of rushing waters; from underfoot came the rhythmic
beat of the engines far below. O'Neil shook off his mood
and began to wonder idly how long it would be before
Captain Johnny would be ready for his "nightcap."

He always traveled with Johnny Brennan when he
could manage it, for the two men were boon companions. O'Neil was wont to live in Johnny's cabin, or on
the bridge, and their nightly libation to friendship had
come to be a matter of some ceremony.

The ship's master soon appeared from the shadows—
a short, trim man with gray hair.

"Come," he cried, "it's waiting for us."

O'Neil followed into Brennan's luxurious, well-lit quarters, where on a mahogany sideboard was a tray holding decanter, siphon, and glasses, together with a bottle of ginger ale. The captain, after he had mixed a beverage for his passenger, opened the bottle for himself. They raised their glasses silently.

"Now that you're past the worst of it," remarked O'Neil, "I suppose you'll turn in. You're getting old for a hard run like this, Johnny."

Captain Brennan snorted. "Old? I'm a better man than you, yet. I'm a teetotaler, that's why. I discovered long ago that salt water and whiskey don't mix."

O'Neil stretched himself out in one of Brennan's easy chairs. "Really," he said, "I understand why a ship carries a captain. Now of what earthly use to the line are you, for instance, except for your beauty, which, no doubt, has its value with the women? I'll admit you preside with some grace at the best table in the dining-salon, but your officers know these channels as well as you do. They could make the run from Seattle to Juneau with their eyes shut."

"Indeed they could not; and neither could I."

"Oh, well, of course I have no respect for you as a man, having seen you without your uniform."

The captain grinned in thorough enjoyment of this raillery. "I'll say nothing at all of my seamanship," he said, relapsing into the faintest of brogues, "but there's no denying that the master of a ship has many unpleasant and disgusting duties to perform. He has to amuse the prominent passengers who can't amuse themselves, for one thing, and that takes tact and patience. Why, some people make themselves at home on the bridge, in the chart-room, and even in my living-quarters, to say nothing of consuming my expensive wines, liquors, and cigars."

"Meaning me?"

"I'm a brutal seafaring man, and you'll have to make allowances for my well-known brusqueness. Maybe I did mean you. But I'll say that next to you Curtis Gordon is the worst grafter I ever saw."

"You don't like Gordon, do you?" O'Neil queried with a change of tone.

"I do not! He went up with me again this spring, and he had his widow with him, too."

"His widow?"

"You know who I mean—Mrs. Gerard. They say it's her money he's using in his schemes. Perhaps it's because of her that I don't like him."

"Ah-h! I see."

"You *don't* see, or you wouldn't grin like an ape. I'm a married man, I'll have you know, and I'm still on good terms with Mrs. Brennan, thank God. But I don't like men who use women's money, and that's just what our friend Gordon is doing. What money the widow didn't put up he's grabbed from the schoolma'ams and servant-girls and society matrons in the East. What has he got to show them for it?"

"A railroad project, a copper-mine, some coal claims—"

"Bah! A menagerie of wildcats!"

"You can't prove that. What's your reason for distrusting him?"

"Well, for one thing, he knows too much. Why, he knows everything, he does. Art, literature, politics, law, finance, and draw poker have no secrets from him. He's been everywhere—and back—twice; he speaks a dozen different languages. He out-argued me on poultry-raising and I know more about that than any man living. He can handle a drill or a coach-and-four; he can tell all about the art of ancient Babylon; and he beat me playing cribbage, which shows that he ain't on the level. He's the best-informed man outside of a university, and he drinks tea of an afternoon—with his legs crossed and the saucer balanced on his heel. Now, it takes years of hard work for an honest man to make a success at one thing, but Gordon never failed at anything. I ask you if a living authority on *all* the branches of human endeavor and a man who can beat me at 'crib' doesn't make you suspicious."

"Not at all. I've beaten you myself!"

"I was sick," said Captain Brennan.

"The man is brilliant and well educated and wealthy. It's only natural that he should excite the jealousy of a weaker intellect."

Johnny opened his lips for an explosion, then changed his mind and agreed sourly.

"He's got money, all right, and he knows how to

spend it. He and his valet occupied three cabins on this ship. They say his quarters at Hope are palatial."

"My dear grampus, the mere love of luxury doesn't argue that a person is dishonest."

"Would *you* let a hired man help you on with your underclothes?" demanded the mariner.

"There's nothing criminal about it."

"Humph! Mrs. Gerard is different. She's all class! You don't mind her having a maid and speaking French when she runs short of English. Her daughter is like her."

"I haven't seen Miss Gerard."

"If you'd stir about the ship instead of wearing out my Morris chair you'd have that pleasure. She was on deck all morning." Captain Brennan fell silent and poked with a stubby forefinger at the ice in his glass.

"Well, out with it!" said O'Neil after a moment.

"I'd like to know the inside story of Curtis Gordon and this girl's mother."

"Why bother your head about something that doesn't concern you?" The speaker rose and began to pace the cabin floor, then, in an altered tone, inquired, "Tell me, are you going to land me and my horses at Kyak Bay?"

"That depends on the weather. It's a rotten harbor; you'll have to swim them ashore."

"Suppose it should be rough?"

"Then we'll go on, and drop you there coming back. I don't want to be caught on that shore with a southerly wind, and that's the way it usually blows."

"I can't wait," O'Neil declared. "A week's delay might ruin me. Rather than go on I'd swim ashore myself, without the horses."

"I don't make the weather at Kyak Bay. Satan himself does that. Twenty miles offshore it may be calm, and inside it may be blowing a gale. That's due to the glaciers. Those ice-fields inland and the warm air from the Japanese Current offshore kick up some funny atmospheric pranks. It's the worst spot on the coast and we'll lose a ship there some day. Why, the place isn't properly charted, let alone buoyed."

"That's nothing unusual for this coast."

"True for you. This is all a graveyard of ships and there's been many a good master's license lost because of half-baked laws from Washington. Think of a coast like this with almost no lights, no beacons nor buoys; and yet we're supposed to make time. It's fine in clear weather, but in the dark we go by guess and by God. I've stood the run longer than most of the skippers, but—"

Even as Brennan spoke the *Nebraska* seemed to halt, to jerk backward under his feet. O'Neil, who was standing, flung out an arm to steady himself; the empty ginger-ale bottle fell from the sideboard with a thump. Loose articles hanging against the side walls swung to and fro; the heavy draperies over Captain Johnny's bed swayed.

Brennan leaped from his chair; his ruddy face was mottled, his eyes were wide and horror-stricken.

"Damnation!" he gasped. The cabin door crashed open ahead of him and he was on the bridge, with O'Neil at his heels. They saw the first officer clinging limply to the rail; from the pilot-house window came an excited burst of Norwegian, then out of the door rushed a quartermaster.

Brennan cursed, and met the fellow with a blow which drove him sprawling back.

"Get in there, Swan," he bellowed, "and take your wheel."

"The tide swung her in!" exclaimed the mate. "The tide— My God!"

"Sweet Queen Anne!" said Brennan, more quietly. "You've ripped her belly out."

"It—was the tide," chattered the officer.

The steady, muffled beating of the machinery ceased, the ship seemed suddenly to lose her life, but it was plain that she was not aground, for she kept moving through the gloom. From down forward came excited voices as the crew poured up out of the forecastle.

Brennan leaped to the telegraph and signaled the engine-room. He was calm now, and his voice was sharp and steady.

"Go below, Mr. James, and find the extent of the damage," he directed, and a moment later the hull began to throb once more to the thrust of the propeller. Inside the wheelhouse Swan had recovered from his panic and repeated the master's orders mechanically.

The second and third officers arrived upon the bridge

now, dressing as they came, and they were followed by the chief engineer. To them Johnny spoke, his words crackling like the sparks from a wireless. In an incredibly short time he had the situation in hand and turned to O'Neil, who had been a silent witness of the scene.

"Glory be!" exclaimed the captain. "Most of our good passengers are asleep; the jar would scarcely wake them."

"Tell me where and how I can help," Murray offered. His first thought had been of the possible effect of this catastrophe upon his plans, for time was pressing. As for danger, he had looked upon it so often and in so many forms that it had little power to stir him; but a shipwreck, which would halt his northward rush, was another matter. Whether the ship sank or floated could make little difference, now that the damage had been done. She was crippled and would need assistance. His fellow-passengers, he knew, were safe enough. Fortunately there were not many of them—a scant two hundred, perhaps—and if worse came to worst there was room in the life-boats for all. But the *Nebraska* had no watertight bulkheads and the plight of his twenty horses betweendecks filled him with alarm and pity. There were no lifeboats for those poor dumb animals penned down yonder in the rushing waters.

Brennan had stepped into the chart-room, but returned in a moment to say:

"There's no place to beach her this side of Halibut Bay."

"How far is that?"

"Five or six miles."

"You'll—have to beach her?"

"I'm afraid so. She feels queer."

Up from the cabin deck came a handful of men passengers to inquire what had happened; behind them a woman began calling shrilly for her husband.

"We touched a rock," the skipper explained, briefly. "Kindly go below and stop that squawking. There's no danger."

There followed a harrowing wait of several minutes; then James, the first officer, came to report. He had regained his nerve and spoke with swift precision.

"She loosened three plates on her port quarter and she's filling fast."

"How long will she last?" snapped Brennan.

"Not long, sir. Half an hour, perhaps."

The captain rang for full speed, and the decks began to strain as the engine increased its labor. "Get your passengers out and stand by the boats," he ordered. "Take it easy and don't alarm the women. Have them dress warmly, and don't allow any crowding by the men. Mr. Tomlinson, you hold the steerage gang in check. Take your revolver with you." He turned to his silent friend, in whose presence he seemed to feel a cheering sympathy. "I knew it would come sooner or later, Murray," he said. "But—magnificent mummies! To touch on a clear night with the sea like glass!" He sighed dolefully. "It'll be tough on my missus."

O'Neil laid a hand upon his shoulder. "It wasn't your fault, and there will be room in the last boat for you. Understand?" Brennan hesitated, and the other continued, roughly: "No nonsense, now! Don't make a damned fool of yourself by sticking to the bridge. Promise?"

"I promise."

"Now what do you want me to do?"

"Keep those dear passengers quiet. I'll run for Halibut Bay, where there's a sandy beach. If she won't make it I'll turn her into the rocks. Tell 'em they won't wet a foot if they keep their heads."

"Good! I'll be back to see that you behave yourself." The speaker laughed lightly and descended to the deck, where he found an incipient panic. Stewards were pounding on stateroom doors, half-clad men were rushing about aimlessly, pallid faces peered forth from windows, and there was the sound of running feet, of slamming doors, of shrill, hysterical voices.

O'Neil saw a waiter thumping lustily upon a door and heard him shout, hoarsely:

"Everybody out! The ship is sinking!" As he turned away Murray seized him roughly by the arm and thrusting his face close to the other's, said, harshly:

"If you yell again like that I'll toss you overboard."

"God help us, we're going—"

O'Neil shook the fellow until his teeth rattled; his own countenance, ordinarily so quiet, was blazing.

"There's no danger. Act like a man and don't start a stampede."

The steward pulled himself together and answered in a calmer tone:

"Very well, sir. I—I'm sorry, sir."

Murray O'Neil was known to most of the passengers, for his name had gone up and down the coast, and there were few places from San Francisco to Nome where his word did not carry weight. As he went among his fellow-travelers now, smiling, self-contained, unruffled, his presence had its effect. Women ceased their shrilling, men stopped their senseless questions and listened to his directions with some comprehension. In a short time the passengers were marshaled upon the upper deck where the life-boats hung between their davits. Each little craft was in charge of its allotted crew, the electric lights continued to burn brightly, and the panic gradually wore itself out. Meanwhile the ship was running a desperate race with the sea, striving with every ounce of steam in her boilers to find a safe berth for her mutilated body before the inrush of waters drowned her fires. That the race was close even the dullest understood, for the *Nebraska* was settling forward, and plowed into the night head down, like a thing maddened with pain. She was becoming unmanageable, too, and O'Neil thought with pity of that little iron-hearted skipper on the bridge who was fighting her so furiously.

There was little confusion, little talking upon the upper deck now; only a child whimpered or a woman sobbed hysterically. But down forward among the steerage passengers the case was different. These were mainly Montenegrins, Polacks, or Slavs bound for the construction camps to the westward, and they surged from side to side like cattle, requiring Tomlinson's best efforts to keep them from rushing aft.

O'Neil had employed thousands of such men; in fact, many of these very fellows had cashed his time-checks and knew him by sight. He went forward among them, and his appearance proved instantly reassuring. He found his two hostlers, and with their aid he soon reduced the mob to comparative order.

But in spite of his confident bearing he felt a great uneasiness. The *Nebraska* seemed upon the point of diving; he judged she must be settling very fast, and wondered that the forward tilt did not lift her propeller out of the water. Fortunately, however, the surface of the sound was like a polished floor and there were no swells to submerge her.

Over-side to starboard he could see the dim black outlines of mountains slipping past, but where lay Halibut Bay or what distance remained to be covered he could but vaguely guess.

In these circumstances the wait became almost unbearable. The race seemed hours long, the miles stretched into leagues, and with every moment of suspense the ship sank lower. The end came unexpectedly. There was a sudden startled outcry as the *Nebraska* struck for a second time that night. She rose slightly, rolled and bumped, grated briefly, then came to rest.

Captain Brennan shouted from the bridge:

"Fill your life-boats, Mr. James, and lower away carefully."

A cheer rose from the huddled passengers.

The boiler-room was still dry, it seemed, for the incandescent lights burned without a flicker, even after the grimy oilers and stokers had come pouring up on deck.

O'Neil climbed to the bridge. "Is this Halibut Bay?" he asked Captain Johnny.

"It is. But we're piled up on the reef outside. She may hold fast—I hope so, for there's deep water astern, and if she slips off she'll go down."

"I'd like to save my horses," said the younger man, wistfully. Through all the strain of the past half-hour or more his uppermost thought had been for them. But Brennan had no sympathy for such sentiments.

"Hell's bells!" he exclaimed. "Don't talk of horses while we've got women and children aboard." He hastened away to assist in transferring his passengers.

Instead of following, O'Neil turned and went below. He found that the water was knee-deep on the port side of the deck where his animals were quartered, which showed that the ship had listed heavily. He judged that she must be much deeper by the head than he had imagined, and that her nose was crushed in among the rocks. Until she settled at the stern, therefore, the case was not quite hopeless.

His appearance, the sound of his voice, were the signals for a chorus of eager whinnies and a great stamping of hoofs. Heads were thrust toward him from the stalls, alert ears were pricked forward, satin muzzles rubbed against him as he calmed their terror. This blind trust made the man's throat tighten achingly. He loved animals as he loved children, and above all he cared for horses. He understood them, he spoke their language as nearly as any human can be said to do so. Quivering muscles relaxed beneath his soothing palm; he called them by name and they answered with gentle twitching lips against his cheek. Some of them even began to eat and switch their tails contentedly.

He cursed aloud and made his way down the sloping deck to the square iron door, or port, through which he had loaded them. But he found that it was jammed, or held fast by the pressure outside, and after a few moments' work in water above his knees he climbed to the starboard side. Here the entrance was obstructed by a huge pile of baled hay and grain in sacks. It would be no easy task to clear it away, and he fell to work with desperate energy, for the ship was slowly changing her level. Her stern, which had been riding high, was filling; the sea stole in upon him silently. It crept up toward him until the horses, stabled on the lower side, were belly-deep in it. Their distress communicated itself to the others. O'Neil knew that his position might prove perilous if the hulk should slip backward off the reef, yet he continued to toil, hurling heavy sacks behind him, bundling awkward bales out of the way, until his hands were bleeding and his muscles ached. He was perspiring furiously; the commotion around him was horrible. Then abruptly the lights went out, leaving him in utter blackness; the last fading yellow gleam was photographed briefly upon his retina.

Tears mingled with the sweat that drained down his cheeks as he felt his way slowly out of the place, splashing, stumbling, groping uncertainly. A horse screamed in a loud, horribly human note, and he shuddered. He was sobbing curses as he emerged into the cool open air on the forward deck.

His eyes were accustomed to the darkness now, and he could see something of his surroundings. He noted numerous lights out on the placid bosom of the bay, evidently lanterns on the life-boats, and he heard distant voices. He swept the moisture from his face; then with a start he realized his situation. He listened intently; his eyes roved back along the boat-deck; there was no doubt about it—the ship was deserted. Stepping to the rail, he observed how low the *Nebraska* lay and also that her bow was higher than her stern. From somewhere beneath his feet came a muffled grinding and a movement which told him that the ship was seeking a more comfortable berth. He recalled stories of explosions and of the boiling eddies which sometimes accompany sinking hulls. Turning, he scrambled up to the cabin-deck and ran swiftly toward his stateroom.

II *How a Girl Appeared Out of the Night*

O'Neil felt for the little bracket-lamp on the wall of his stateroom and lit it. By its light he dragged a life-preserver from the rack overhead and slipped the tapes about his shoulders, reflecting that Alaskan waters are disagreeably cold. Then he opened his traveling-bags and dumped their contents upon the white counterpane of his berth, selecting out of the confusion certain documents and trinkets. The latter he thrust into his pockets as he found them, the former he wrapped in handkerchiefs before stowing them away. The ship had listed now so that it was difficult to maintain a footing; the lamp hung at a grotesque angle and certain articles had become dislodged from their resting-places. From outside came the gentle lapping of waters, a gurgling and hissing as of air escaping through the decks. He could feel the ship strain.

He acknowledged that it was not pleasant thus to be left alone on a sinking hulk, particularly on an ink-black night—

All at once he whirled and faced the door with an exclamation of astonishment, for a voice had addressed him.

There, clinging to the casing, stood a woman—a girl—evidently drawn out of the darkness by the light which streamed down across the sloping deck from his state-room. Plainly she had but just awakened, for she was clothed in a silken nightrobe which failed to conceal the outlines of her body, the swelling contour of her bosom, the ripened fullness of her limbs. She had flung a quilted dressing-gown of some sort over her shoulders and with one bare arm and hand strove to hold it in place. He saw that her pink feet were thrust into soft, heelless slippers—that her hair, black in this light, cascaded down to her waist, and that her eyes, which were very dark and very large, were fixed upon him with a stare like that of a sleep-walker.

"It is so dark—so strange—so still!" she murmured. "What has happened?"

"God! Didn't they waken you?" he cried in sharp surprise.

"Is the ship—sinking?" Her odd bewilderment of voice and gaze puzzled him.

He nodded. "We struck a rock. The passengers have been taken off. We're the only ones left. In Heaven's name where have you been?"

"I was asleep."

He shook his head in astonishment. "How you failed to hear that hubbub—"

"I heard something, but I was ill. My head—I took something to ease the pain."

"Ah! Medicine! It hasn't worn off yet, I see! You shouldn't have taken it. Drugs are nothing but poison to young people. Now at my age there might be some excuse for resorting to them, but you—" He was talking to cover the panic of his thoughts, for his own predicament had been serious enough, and her presence rendered it doubly embarrassing. What in the world to do with her he scarcely knew. His lips were smiling, but his eyes were grave as they roved over the cabin and out into the blackness of the night.

"Are we going to drown?" she asked, dully.

"Nonsense!" He laughed in apparent amusement, showing his large, strong teeth.

She came closer, glancing behind her and shrinking from the oily waters which could be seen over the rail and which had stolen up nearly to the sill of the door. She steadied herself by laying hold of him uncertainly. Involuntarily he turned his eyes away, for he felt shame at profaning her with his gaze. She was very soft and white, a fragile thing utterly unfit to cope with the night air and the freezing waters of Halibut Bay.

"I'm wretchedly afraid!" she whispered through white lips.

"None of that!" he said, brusquely. "I'll see that nothing happens to you." He slipped out of his life-preserver and adjusted it over her shoulders, first drawing her arms through the sleeves of her dressing-gown and knotting the cord snugly around her waist. "Just as a matter of precaution!" he assured her. "We may get wet. Can you swim?"

She shook her head.

"Never mind; I can." He found another life-belt, fitted it to his own form, and led her out upon the deck. The scuppers were awash now and she gasped as the sea licked her bare feet. "Cold, isn't it?" he remarked. "But there's no time to dress, and it's just as well, perhaps, for heavy clothes would only hamper you."

She strove to avoid the icy waters and finally paused, moaning: "I can't! I can't go on!"

Slipping his arm about her, he bore her to the door of the main cabin and entered. He could feel her warm, soft body quivering against his own. She had clasped his neck so tightly that he could scarcely breathe, but, lowering her until her feet were on the dry carpet, he gently loosed her arms.

"Now, my dear child," he told her, "you must do exactly as I tell you. Come! Calm yourself or I won't take you any farther." He held her off by her shoulders. "I may have to swim with you; you mustn't cling to me so!"

He heard her gasp and felt her draw away abruptly.

Then he led her by the hand out upon the starboard deck, and together they made their way forward to the neighborhood of the bridge.

The lights he had seen upon coming from the forward hold were still in view and he hailed them at the top of his voice. But other voices were calling through the night, some of them comparatively close at hand, others answering faintly from far inshore. The boats first launched were evidently landing, and those in charge of them were shouting directions to the ones behind. Some women had started singing and the chorus floated out to the man and the girl:

> Pull for the shore, sailor,
> Pull for the shore.

It helped to drown their cries for assistance.

O'Neil judged that the ship was at least a quarter of a mile from the beach, and his heart sank, for he doubted that either he or his companion could last long in these waters. It occurred to him that Brennan might be close by, waiting for the *Nebraska* to sink—it would be unlike the little captain to forsake his trust until the last possible moment—but he reasoned that the cargo of lives in the skipper's boat would induce him to stand well off to avoid accident. He called lustily time after time, but no answer came.

Meanwhile the girl stood quietly beside him.

"Can't we make a raft?" she suggested, timidly, when he ceased to shout. "I've read of such things."

"There's no time," he told her. "Are you very cold?"

She nodded. "Please forgive me for acting so badly just now. It was all so sudden and—so awful! I think I can behave better. Oh! What was that?" She clutched him nervously, for from the forward end of the ship had come a muffled scream, like that of a woman.

"It's my poor horses," said the man, and she looked at him curiously, prompted by the catch in his throat.

There followed a wait which seemed long, but was in reality of but a few minutes, for the ship was sliding backward and the sea was creeping upward faster and faster. At last they heard a shuddering sigh as she parted

from the rocks and the air rushed up through the deck
openings with greater force. The *Nebraska* swung slug-
gishly with the tide; then, when her upper structure had
settled flush with the sea, Murray O'Neil took the woman
in his arms and leaped clear of the rail.

The first gasping moment of immersion was fairly paralyzing; after that the reaction came, and the two began to
struggle away from the sinking ship. But the effect of the
reaction soon wore off. The water was cruelly cold and
their bodies ached in every nerve and fiber. O'Neil did his
best to encourage his companion. He talked to her through
his chattering teeth, and once she had recovered from the
mental shock of the first fearful plunge she responded
pluckily. He knew that his own heart was normal and
strong, but he feared that the girl's might not be equal
to the strain. Had he been alone, he felt sure that he
could have gained the shore, but with her upon his hands
he was able to make but little headway. The expanse of
waters seemed immense; it fairly crushed hope out of him.
The lights upon the shore were as distant as fixed stars.
This was a country of heavy tides, he reflected, and he
began to fear that the current was sweeping them out.
He turned to look for the ship, but could see no traces
of her, and since it was inconceivable that the *Nebraska*
could have sunk so quietly, her disappearance confirmed
his fears. More than once he fancied he heard an answer
to his cries for help—the rattle of rowlocks or the splash
of oars—but his ears proved unreliable.

After a time the girl began to moan with pain and terror, but as numbness gradually robbed her of sensation
she became quiet. A little later her grip upon his clothing
relaxed and he saw that she was collapsing. He drew her
to him and held her so that her face lay upturned and her
hair floated about his shoulders. In this position she could
not drown, at least while his strength lasted. But he was
rapidly losing control of himself; his teeth were clicking
loosely, his muscles shook and twitched. It required a great
effort to shout, and he thought that his voice did not carry
so far as at first. Therefore he fell silent, paddling with
his free arm and kicking, to keep his blood stirring.

Several times he gave up and floated quietly, but courage was ingrained in him; deep down beneath his con-

sciousness was a vitality, an inherited stubborn resistance to death, of which he knew nothing. It was that unidentified quality of mind which supports one man through a great sickness or a long period of privation, while another of more robust physique succumbs. It was the same quality which brings one man out from desert wastes, or the white silence of the polar ice, while the bodies of his fellows remain to mark the trail. This innate power of supreme resistance is found in chosen individuals throughout the animal kingdom, and it was due to it alone that Murray O'Neil continued to fight the tide long after he had ceased to exert conscious control.

At length there came through the man's dazed sensibilities a sound different from those he had been hearing: it was a human voice, mingled with the measured thud of oars in their sockets. It roused him like an electric current and gave him strength to cry out hoarsely. Some one answered him; then out of the darkness to seaward emerged a deeper blot, which loomed up hugely yet proved to be no more than a life-boat banked full of people. It came to a stop within an oar's-length of him. From the babble of voices he distinguished one that was familiar, and cried the name of Johnny Brennan. His brain had cleared now, a great dreamlike sense of thanksgiving warmed him, and he felt equal to any effort. He was vaguely amazed to find that his limbs refused to obey him.

His own name was being pronounced in shocked tones; the splash from an oar filled his face and strangled him, but he managed to lay hold of the blade, and was drawn in until outstretched hands seized him.

An oarsman was saying: "Be careful, there! We can't take him in without swamping."

But Brennan's voice shouted: "Make room or I'll bash in your bloody skull."

Another protest arose, and O'Neil saw that the craft was indeed loaded to the gunwales.

"Take the girl—quick," he implored. "I'll hang on. You can—tow me."

The limp form was removed from his side and dragged over the thwarts while a murmur of excited voices went up.

"Can you hold out for a minute, Murray?" asked Brennan.

"Yes—I think so."

"I'd give you my place, but you're too big to be taken in without danger."

"Go ahead," chattered the man in the water. "Look after the girl before it's—too late."

The captain's stout hand was in his collar now and he heard him crying:

"Pull, you muscle-bound heathens! Everybody sit still! Now away with her, men. Keep up your heart, Murray, my boy; remember it takes more than water to kill a good Irishman. It's only a foot or two farther, and they've started a fire. Serves you right, you big idiot, for going overboard, with all those boats. Man dear, but you're pulling the arm out of me; it's stretched out like a garden hose! Hey! Cover up that girl, and you, lady, rub her feet and hands. Good! Move over please—so the men can bail."

The next O'Neil knew he was feeling very miserable and very cold, notwithstanding the fact that he was wrapped in dry clothing and lay so close to a roaring spruce fire that its heat blistered him.

Brennan was bending over him with eyes wet. He was swearing, too, in a weak, faltering way, calling upon all the saints to witness that the prostrate man was the embodiment of every virtue, and that his death would be a national calamity. Others were gathered about, men and women, and among them O'Neil saw the doctor from Sitka whom he had met on shipboard.

As soon as he was able to speak he inquired for the safety of the girl he had helped to rescue. Johnny promptly reassured him.

"Man, dear, she's doing fine. A jigger of brandy brought her to, gasping like a blessed mermaid."

"Was anybody lost?"

"Praise God, not a soul! But it's lucky I stood by to watch the old tub go down, or we'd be mourning two. You'll be well by morning, for there's a cannery in the next inlet and I've sent a boat's crew for help. And now, my boy, lay yourself down again and take a sleep, won't you? It'll be doing you a lot of good."

But O'Neil shook his head and struggled to a sitting posture.

"Thanks, Johnny," said he, "but I couldn't. I can hear those horses screaming, and besides—I must make new plans."

III   *The Irish Prince*

As dawn broke the cannery tender from the station near by nosed her way up to the gravelly shore where the castaways were gathered and blew a cheering toot-toot on her whistle. She was a flat-bottomed, "wet-sterned" craft, and the passengers of the *Nebraska* trooped to her deck over a gangplank. As Captain Brennan had predicted, not one of them had wet a foot, with the exception of the two who had been left aboard through their own carelessness.

By daylight Halibut Bay appeared an idyllic spot, quite innocent of the terrors with which the night had endowed it. A pebbled half-moon of beach was set in among rugged bluffs; the verdant forest crowded down to it from behind. Tiny crystal wavelets lapped along the shingle, swaying the brilliant sea mosses which clung to the larger rocks. Altogether the scene gave a strong impression of peace and security, yet just in the offing was one jarring contrast—the masts and funnel of the *Nebraska* slanting up out of the blue serenity, where she lay upon the sloping bottom in the edge of deep water.

The reaction following a sleepless night of anxiety had replaced the first feeling of thankfulness at deliverance, and it was not a happy cargo of humanity which the rescuing boat bore with her as the sun peeped over the hills. Many of the passengers were but half dressed, all were exhausted and hungry, each one had lost something in the catastrophe. The men were silent, the women hysterical, the children fretful.

Murray O'Neil had recovered sufficiently to go among them with the same warm smile which had made him friends from the first. In the depths of his cool gray eyes was a sparkle which showed his unquenchable Celtic spirit, and before long smiles answered his smiles, jokes rose to meet his pleasantries.

It was his turn now to comfort Captain Johnny Brennan, who had yielded to the blackest despair, once his responsiblity was over.

"She was a fine ship, Murray," the master lamented, staring with tragic eyes at the *Nebraska's* spars.

"She was a tin washtub, and rusted like a sieve," jeered O'Neil.

"But think of me losing her on a still night!"

"I'm not sure yet that it wasn't a jellyfish that swam through her."

"Humph! I suppose her cargo will be a total loss. Two hundred thousand dollars—"

"Insured for three hundred, no doubt. I'll warrant the company will thank you."

"It's kind of you to cheer me up," said Brennan, a little less gloomily, "especially after the way I abandoned you to drown, but the missus won't allow me in the house at all when she hears I left you in pickle. Thank God the girl didn't die, anyway! I've got that to be thankful for. Curtis Gordon would have broken me—"

"Gordon?"

"Sure! Man dear, don't you know who you went bathing with? She's the daughter of that widow Gerard, and the most prominent passenger aboard, outside of your blessed self. Ain't that luck! If I was a Jap I'd split myself open with a bread-knife."

"But, fortunately, you're a sensible 'harp' of old Ireland. I'll see that the papers get the right story, so buck up."

"Do you think for a minute that Mrs. Brennan will understand why I didn't hop out of the life-boat and give you my place? Not at all. I'm ruined nautically and domestically. In the course of the next ten years I may live it down, but meanwhile I'll sleep in the woodshed and speak when I'm spoken to."

Murray knew that Miss Gerard had been badly shaken by her ordeal, hence he made no attempt to see her even after the steamer had reached the fishing-village and the rescued passengers had been taken in by the residents. Instead, he went directly to the one store in the place and bought its entire stock, which he turned over to the sufferers. It was well he did so, for the village was small and, although the townspeople were hospitable, both food and clothing were scarce.

A south-bound steamer was due the next afternoon, it was learned, and plans were made for her to pick up the castaways and return them to Seattle. At the same time O'Neil discovered that a freighter for the "westward" was expected some time that night, and as she did not call at this port he arranged for a launch to take him out to the channel where he could intercept her. The loss of his horses had been a serious blow. It was all the more imperative now that he should go on, since he would have to hire men to do horses' work.

During the afternoon Miss Gerard sent for him and he went to the house of the cannery superintendent, where she had been received. The superintendent's wife had clothed her, and she seemed to have recovered her poise of body and mind. O'Neil was surprised to find her quite a different person from the frightened and disheveled girl he had seen in the yellow lamplight of his stateroom on the night before. She was as pale now as then, but her expression of terror and bewilderment had given place to one of reposeful confidence. Her lips were red and ripe and of a somewhat haughty turn. She was attractive, certainly, despite the disadvantage of the borrowed garments, and though she struck him as being possibly a little proud and cold, there was no lack of warmth in her greeting.

For her part she beheld a man of perhaps forty, of commanding height and heavy build. He was gray about the temples; his eyes were gray, too, and rather small, but they were extremely animated and kindly, and a myriad of little lines were penciled about their corners. These were evidently marks of expression, not of age, and although the rugged face itself was not handsome, it had a degree of character that compelled her interest. His clothes were good, and in spite of their recent hard usage they still lent him the appearance of a man habitually well dressed.

She was vaguely disappointed, having pictured him as being in the first flush of vigorous youth, but the feeling soon disappeared under the charm of his manner. The ideal figure she had imagined began to seem silly and school-girlish, unworthy of the man himself. She was pleased, too, by his faint though manifest embarrassment at her thanks, for she had feared a lack of tact.

Above all things she abhorred obligation of any sort, and she was inclined to resent masculine protection. This man's service filled her with real gratitude, yet she rebelled at the position in which it placed her. She preferred granting favors to receiving them.

But in fact he dismissed the whole subject so brusquely that he almost offended her, and when she realized how incomplete had been her acknowledgment, she said, with an air of pique:

"You might have given me a chance to thank you without dragging you here against your will."

"I'm sorry if I seemed neglectful."

She fell silent for a moment before asking:

"Do you detest me for my cowardice? I couldn't blame you for never wanting to see me again."

"You were very brave. You were splendid," he declared. "I simply didn't wish to intrude."

"I was terribly frightened," she confided, "but I felt that I could rely upon you. That's what every one does, isn't it? You see, you have a reputation. They told me how you refused to be taken into the boat for fear of capsizing it. That was fine."

"Oh, there was nothing brave about that. I wanted to get in badly enough, but there wasn't room. Jove! It was cold, wasn't it?" His ready smile played whimsically about his lips, and the girl felt herself curiously drawn to him. Since he chose to make light of himself, she determined to allow nothing of the sort.

"They have told me how you bought out this whole funny little place," she said, "and turned it over to us. Is it because you have such a royal way of dispensing favors that they call you 'The Irish Prince'?"

"That's only a silly nickname."

"I don't think so. You give people food and clothes with a careless wave of the hand; you give me my life with a shrug and a smile; you offer to give up your own to a boatful of strangers without a moment's hesitation. I—I think you are a remarkable person."

"You'll turn my head with such flattery if you aren't careful," he said with a slight flush. "Please talk of something sensible now, for an antidote—your plans, for instance."

"My plans are never sensible, and what few I have are as empty as my pockets. To tell the truth, I have neither plans nor pockets," she laughed, "since this is a borrowed gown."

"Pockets in gowns are entirely matters of hearsay, anyhow; I doubt if they exist. You are going back to Seattle?"

"Oh, I suppose so. It seems to be my fate, but I'm not a bit resigned. I'm one of those unfortunate people who can't bear to be disappointed."

"You can return on the next ship, at the company's expense."

"No. Mother would never allow it. In fact, when she learns that I'm out here she'll probably send me back to New York as fast as I can go."

"Doesn't she know where you are?"

"Indeed no! She thinks I'm safely and tamely at home. Uncle Curtis wouldn't object to my visit, I fancy; at any rate, I've been counting on his good offices with mother, but it's too late now."

"I'm like you," he said; "I can't brook disappointment. I'm going on."

In answer to her questioning look he explained his plan of intercepting the freight-steamer that night, whereupon her face brightened with sudden hope.

"Can't I go, too?" she implored, eagerly. She was no longer the haughty young lady he had met upon entering the room, but a very wistful child.

"I'm afraid that's hardly—"

"Oh! If only you knew how much it means! If only you knew how badly I want to! I'm not afraid of discomforts."

"It's not that—"

"Please! Please! Be a real prince and grant me this boon. Won't you? My heart is set upon it."

It was hard to resist her imploring eyes—eyes which showed they had never been denied. It was hard for O'Neil to refuse anything to a woman.

"If your uncle is willing," he began, hesitatingly.

"He isn't my really uncle—I just call him that."

"Well, if Mr. Gordon wouldn't object, perhaps I can manage it, provided, of course, you promise to explain to your mother."

Miss Gerard's frank delight showed that she was indeed no more than a child. Her changed demeanor awakened a doubt in the man's mind.

"It will mean that you'll have to sit up all night in an open launch," he cautioned her.

"I'll sit up for a week."

"With the creepy water all about, and big black mountains frowning at you!"

"Oh, fiddle!" she exclaimed. "You'll be there if I get frightened." Rising impulsively she laid her hand on his arm and thanked him with an odd mingling of frankness and shyness, as if there could be no further doubt of his acquiescence. He saw that her eyes were the color of shaded woodland springs and that her hair was not black, but of a deep, rich brown where the sun played upon it, the hue of very old mahogany, with the same blood-red flame running through it. He allowed himself to admire her in silence, until suddenly she drew back with a startled exclamation.

"What is it?"

"I forgot—I have no clothes." Her words came with a doleful cadence.

"The universal complaint of your sex," he said, smiling. "Allow me to talk with your hostess. I'm sure she will let you walk out with your borrowed finery, just like Cinderella. You'll need a nice thick coat, too."

"But this is her very, very best dress."

"She shall receive, on the next ship, a big box all lined with tissue-paper, with the imprint of the most fashionable dressmaker in Seattle. I'll arrange all that by cable."

"You don't know how she loves it," the girl said, doubtfully.

"Come! Call her in. If I'm to be a prince you mustn't doubt my power."

Nor did the event prove him over-confident. Before he had fairly made known his request the good lady of the house was ready to surrender not only her best Sunday gown, but her fluttering heart as well. Murray O'Neil had a way of making people do what he wanted, and women invariably yielded to him.

IV *How a Journey Ended at Hope*

To Natalie Gerard the trip down the bay and into the sound that night was a wonderful adventure. She remembered it afterward far more vividly than the shipwreck, which became blurred in retrospect, so that she soon began to think of it as of some half-forgotten nightmare. To begin with, the personality of Murray O'Neil intrigued her more and more. The man was so strong, so sympathetic, and he had such a resistless way of doing things. The stories she had heard of him were romantic, and the superintendent's wife had not allowed them to suffer in the telling. Natalie felt elated that such a remarkable person should exert himself on her behalf. And the journey itself impressed her imagination deeply.

Although it was nine o'clock when they boarded the launch, it was still light. The evening was yellow with the peculiar diffused radiance of high latitudes, lending a certain somberness to their surroundings.

The rushing tide, the ragged rock-teeth which showed through it, the trackless, unending forests that clothed the hills in every direction, awed her a little, yet gave her an unaccustomed feeling of freedom and contentment. The long wait out between the lonely islands, where the tiny cockle-shell rolled strangely, although the sea seemed as level as a floor, held a subtle excitement. Darkness crept down out of the unpeopled gorges and swallowed them up, thrilling her with a sense of mystery.

When midnight came she found that she was ravenously hungry, and she was agreeably surprised when O'Neil produced an elaborate lunch. There were even thermos bottles filled with steaming hot coffee, more delicious, she thought, than anything she had ever before tasted. He called the meal their after-theater party, pretending that they had just come from a Broadway melodrama of shipwreck and peril. The subject led them naturally to talk of New York, and she found he was more familiar with the city than she.

"I usually spend my winters there," he explained.

"Then you have an office in the city?"

"Oh yes. I've maintained a place of business there for years."

"Where is it? On Wall Street?"

"No!" he smiled. "On upper Fifth Avenue. It's situated in the extreme southwest corner of the men's café at the Holland House. It consists of a round mahogany table and a leather settee."

"Really!"

"That's where I'm to be found at least four months out of every twelve."

"They told me you built railroads."

"I do—when I'm lucky enough to underbid my competitors. But that isn't always, and railroads aren't built every day."

"Mr. Gordon is building one."

"So I'm told." O'Neil marveled at the trick of fortune which had entangled this girl and her mother in the web of that brilliant and unscrupulous adventurer.

"Perhaps it will be a great success like your famous North Pass & Yukon Railway."

"Let us hope so." He was tempted to inquire what use Gordon had made of that widely advertised enterprise in floating his own undertaking, but instead he asked:

"Your mother has invested heavily, has she not?"

"Not in the railroad. Her fortune, and mine too, is all in the coal mines."

O'Neil smothered an exclamation.

"What is it?" she demanded.

"Nothing, only—are you sure?"

"Oh, quite sure! The mines are rich, aren't they?"

"There are no mines," he informed her, "thanks to our misguided lawmakers at Washington. There are vast deposits of fine coal which would make mines if we were allowed to work them, but—we are not allowed."

" 'We'? Are you a—a coal person, like us?"

"Yes. I was one of the first men in the Kyak fields, and I invested heavily. I know Mr. Gordon's group of claims well. I have spent more than a hundred thousand dollars trying to perfect my titles and I'm no nearer patent now than I was to begin with—not so near, in fact. I fancy Gordon has spent as much and is in the same fix. It is a coal matter which brings me to Alaska now."

"I hardly understand."

"Of course not, and you probably won't after I explain. You see the Government gave us—gave everybody who owns coal locations in Alaska—three years in which to do certain things; then it extended that time another three years. But recently a new Secretary of the Interior has come into office and he has just rescinded that later ruling, without warning, which gives us barely time to comply with the law as it first stood. For my part, I'll have to hustle or lose everything I have put in. You see? That's why I hated to see those horses drown, for I intended to use them in reaching the coal-fields. Now I'll have to hire men to carry their loads. No doubt Mr. Gordon has arranged to protect your holdings, but there are hundreds of claimants who will be ruined."

"I supposed the Government protected its subjects," said the girl, vaguely.

"One of the illusions taught in the elementary schools," laughed O'Neil. "We Alaskans have found that it does exactly the opposite! We have found it a harsh and unreasonable landlord. But I'm afraid I'm boring you." He wrapped her more snugly in her coverings, for a chill had descended with the darkness, then strove to enliven her with stories garnered from his rich experience—stories which gave her fascinating glimpses of great undertakings and made her feel personally acquainted with people of unfamiliar type, whose words and deeds, mirthful or pathetic, were always refreshingly original. Of certain individuals he spoke repeatedly until their names became familiar to his hearer. He called them his "boys" and his voice was tender as he told of their doings.

"These men are your staff?" she ventured.

"Yes. Every one who succeeds in big work must have loyal hands to help him."

"Where are they now?"

"Oh! Scattered from Canada to Mexico, each one doing his own particular work. There's Mellen, for instance;

he's in Chihuahua building a cantilever bridge. He's the best steel man in the country. McKay, my superintendent, is running a railroad job in California. 'Happy Tom' Slater—"

"The funny man with the blues?"

"Exactly! He was at work on a hydraulic project near Dawson the last I heard of him. Dr. Gray is practising in Seattle, and Parker, the chief engineer, has a position of great responsibility in Boston. He is the brains of our outfit, you understand; it was really he who made the North Pass & Yukon possible. The others are scattered out in the same way, but they'd all come if I called them." The first note of pride she had detected crept into his voice when he said: "My 'boys' are never idle. They don't have to be, after working with me."

"And what is your part of the work?" asked the girl.

"I? Oh, I'm like Marcelline, the clown at the Hippodrome—always pretending to help, but forever keeping underfoot. When it becomes necessary I raise the money to keep the performance going."

"Do you really mean that all those men would give up their positions and come to you if you sent for them?"

"By the first train, or afoot, if there were no other way. They'd follow me to the Philippines or Timbuctoo, regardless of their homes and their families."

"That is splendid! You must feel very proud of inspiring such loyalty," said Natalie. "But why are you idle now? Surely there are railroads to be built somewhere."

"Yes, I was asked to figure on a contract in Manchuria the other day. I could have had it easily, and it would have meant my everlasting fortune, but—"

"But what?"

"I found it isn't a white man's country. It's sickly and unsafe. Some of my 'boys' would die before we finished it, and the game isn't worth that price. No, I'll wait. Something better will turn up. It always does."

As Natalie looked upon that kindly, square-hewn face with its tracery of lines about the eyes, its fine, strong jaw, and its indefinable expression of power, she began to understand more fully why those with whom she had talked had spoken of Murray O'Neil with an almost worshipful respect. She felt very insignificant and purposeless as she huddled there beside him, and her complacence at his attentions deepened into a vivid sense of satisfaction. Thus far he had spoken entirely of men; she wondered if he ever thought of women, and thrilled a bit at the intimacy that had sprung up between them so quickly and naturally.

It confirmed her feeling of prideful confidence in the man that the north-bound freighter should punctually show her lights around the islands and that she should pause in her majestic sweep at the signal of this pigmy craft. The ship loomed huge and black and terrifying as the launch at length drew in beneath it; its sides towered like massive, unscalable ramparts. There was a delay; there seemed to be some querulousness on the part of the officer in command at being thus halted, some doubt about allowing strangers to come aboard. But the girl smiled to herself as the voices flung themselves back and forth through the night. Once they learned who it was that called from the sea their attitude would quickly change. Sure enough, in a little while orders were shouted from the bridge; she heard men running from somewhere, and a rope ladder came swinging down. O'Neil was lifting her from her warm nest of rugs now and telling her to fear nothing. The launch crept closer, coughing and shuddering as if in terror at this close contact. There was a brief instant of breathlessness as the girl found herself swung out over the waters; then a short climb with O'Neil's protecting hand at her waist and she stood panting, radiant, upon steel decks which began to throb and tremble to the churning engines.

One further task remained for her protector's magic powers. It appeared that there were no quarters on the ship for women, but after a subdued colloquy between Murray and the captain she was led to the cleanest and coziest of staterooms high up near the bridge. Over the door she glimpsed a metal plate with the words "First Officer" lettered upon it. O'Neil was bidding her good night and wishing her untroubled rest, then almost before she had accustomed herself to her new surroundings an immaculate, though sleepy, Japanese steward stood before her with a tray. He was extremely cheerful for one so lately awakened, being still aglow with pleased surprise over the banknote which lay neatly folded in his waistcoat pocket.

Natalie sat cross-legged on her berth and munched with the appetite of a healthy young animal at the fruit and biscuits and lovely heavy cake which the steward had brought. She was very glad now that she had disobeyed her mother. It was high time, indeed, to assert herself, for she was old enough to know something of the world, and her judgment of men was mature enough to insure perfect safety—that much had been proved. She felt that her adventure had been a great success practically and romantically. She wanted to lie awake and think it over in detail, but she soon grew sleepy. Just before she dozed off she wondered drowsily if "The Irish Prince" had found quarters for himself, then reflected that undoubtedly the captain had been happy to tumble out of bed for him. Or perhaps he felt no fatigue and would watch the night through. Even now he might be pacing the deck outside her door. At any rate, he was not far off. She closed her eyes, feeling deliciously secure and comfortable.

In one way the southern coast of Alaska may be said to be perhaps a million years younger than any land on this continent, for it is still in the glacial period. The vast alluvial plains and valleys of the interior are rimmed in to the southward and shut off from the Pacific by a well-nigh impassable mountain barrier, the top of which is capped with perpetual snow. Its gorges, for the most part, run rivers of ice instead of water. Europe has nothing like these glaciers which overflow the Alaskan valleys and submerge the hills, for many of them contain more ice than the whole of Switzerland. This range is the Andes of the north, and it curves westward in a magnificent sweep, hugging the shore for a thousand leagues. Against it the sea beats stormily; its frozen crest is played upon by constant rains and fogs and blizzards. But over beyond lies a land of sunshine, of long, dry, golden summer days.

Into this chaos of cliff and peak and slanting cañon, midway to the westward, is let King Phillip Sound, a sheet of water dotted with islands and framed by forests. It reaches inland with long, crooked tentacles which end like talons, in living ice. Hidden some forty miles up one of these, upon the moraine of a receding glacier, sits Cortez, a thriving village and long the point of entry to the interior, the commencement of the overland trail to the golden valleys of the Yukon and the Tanana. The Government wagon trail winds in from here, tracing its sinuous course over one pass after another until it emerges into the undulating prairies of the "inside country."

Looking at the map, one would imagine that an easier gateway to the heart of Alaska would be afforded by the valley of the Salmon River, which enters the ocean some few miles to the eastward of King Phillip Sound, but there are formidable difficulties. The stream bursts the last rampart of the Coast Range asunder by means of a cañon down which it rages in majestic fury and up which no craft can navigate. Then it spreads itself out through a dozen shallow mouths across a forty-mile delta of silt and sand and glacial wash. As if Nature feared her arctic strong-box might still be invaded by this route, she has placed additional safeguards to the approach in the form of giant glaciers, through the very bowels of which the Salmon River is forced to burrow.

In the early days of the Klondike rush men had attempted to ascend the valley, but they had succeeded only at the cost of such peril and disaster that others were warned away. The region had become the source of many weird stories, and while the ice-fields could be seen from the Kyak coal-fields, and on still days their cannonading could be heard far out at sea, there were few who had ventured to cross the forty-mile morass which lay below them and thus attempt to verify or to disprove the rumors.

It was owing to these topographical conditions that Cortez had been established as the point of entry to the interior; it was because of them that she had grown and flourished, with her sawmills and her ginmills, her docks, and her dives. But at the time when this story opens Alaska had developed to a point where an overland outlet by winter and a circuitous inlet, by way of Bering Sea and the crooked Yukon, in summer were no longer sufficient. There was need of a permanent route by means of which men and freight might come and go through all the year. The famous North Pass & Yukon Railway, far to the eastward, afforded transportation to Dawson City and the

Canadian territory, and had proven itself such a financial success that builders began to look for a harbor, more to the westward, from which they could tap the great heart of Alaska. Thus it was that Cortez awoke one morning to find herself selected as the terminus of a new line. Other railways propositions followed, flimsy promotion schemes for the most part, but among them two that had more than paper and "hot air" behind them. One of these was backed by the Copper Trust which had made heavy mining investments two hundred miles inland, the other by Curtis Gordon, a promoter, who claimed New York as his birthplace and the world as his residence.

Gordon had been one of the first locaters in the Kyak coal-fields, and he had also purchased a copper prospect a few miles down the bay from Cortez, where he had started a town which he called Hope. There were some who shook their heads and smiled knowingly when they spoke of that prospect, but no one denied that it was fast assuming the outward semblance of a mine under Gordon's direction. He had erected a fine substantial wharf, together with buildings, bunk-houses, cottages, and a spacious residence for himself; and daily the piles of debris beneath the tunnel entries to his workings grew. He paid high wages, he spent money lavishly, and he had a magnificent and compelling way with him that dazzled and delighted the good people of Cortez. When he began work on a railroad which was designed to reach far into the interior his action was taken as proof positive of his financial standing, and his critics were put down as pessimists who had some personal grudge against him.

It was up to the raw, new village of Hope, with its odor of fresh-cut fir and undried paint, that the freight-steamer with Natalie Gerard and "The Irish Prince" aboard, came gingerly one evening.

O'Neil surveyed the town with some curiosity as he approached, for Gordon's sensational doings had interested him greatly. He was accustomed to the rapid metamorphoses of a growing land; it was his business, in fact, to win the wilderness over to order, and therefore he was not astonished at the changes wrought here during his absence. But he was agreeably surprised at the businesslike arrangement of the place, and the evidence that a strong and practised hand had guided its development.

Even before the ship had tied up he had identified the tall, impressive man on the dock as the genius and founder of Hope, and the dark-haired, well-formed woman beside him as Natalie's mother. It was not until they were close at hand that the daughter made her presence known; then, unable to restrain herself longer, she shrieked her greeting down over the rail. Mrs. Gerard started, then stared upward as if at an apparition; she stretched out a groping hand to Gordon, who stood as if frozen in his tracks. They seemed to be exchanging hurried words, and the man appeared to be reassuring his companion. It looked very odd to O'Neil; but any suspicion that Natalie was unwelcome disappeared when she reached the dock. Her mother's dark eyes were bright with unshed tears of gladness, her face was transfigured, she showed the strong, repressed emotion of an undemonstrative nature as they embraced. Natalie clung to her, laughing, crying, bombarding her with questions, begging forgiveness, and babbling of her adventures. Their resemblance was striking, and in point of beauty there seemed little to choose between them. They might have been nearly of an age, except that the mother lacked the girl's restless vivacity.

O'Neil remained in the background, like an uncomfortable bridegroom, conscious meanwhile of the searching and hostile regard of Curtis Gordon. But at last his protégée managed to gasp out in a more or less coherent manner the main facts of the shipwreck and her rescue, whereupon Gordon's attitude abruptly altered.

"My God!" he ejaculated. "You were not on the *Nebraska?*"

"Yes, yes, yes!" cried Natalie. "The life-boats went off and left me all alone—in the dark—with the ship sinking! Mr. O'Neil saved me. He took me up and jumped just as the ship sank, and we were all night in the freezing water. We nearly died, didn't we? He fainted, and so did I, mummie dear—it was so cold. He held me up until we were rescued, though, and then there wasn't room in the life-boat for both of us. But he made them take me in, just the same, while he stayed in the water. He was unconscious when he reached the shore. Oh, it was splendid!"

O'Neil's identity being established, and the nature of his service becoming apparent, Curtis Gordon took his hand in a crushing grip and thanked him in a way that might have warmed the heart of a stone gargoyle. The man was transformed, now that he understood; he became a geyser of eloquence. He poured forth his appreciation in rounded sentences; his splendid musical voice softened and swelled and broke with a magnificent and touching emotion. Through it all the Irish contractor remained uncomfortably silent, for he could not help thinking that this fulsome outburst was aroused rather by the man who had built the North Pass & Yukon than by the rescuer of Mrs. Gerard's daughter.

As for the mother, she said little, and the few words she spoke to him were stiffly formal, but in the depths of her dazed, wide-open eyes he read a gratitude which affected him deeply.

A crowd was collecting round them, but Gordon cleared it away with an imperious gesture.

"Come!" he said. "This is no place to talk. Mr. O'Neil's splendid gallantry renders our mere thanks inane. He must allow us to express our gratitude in a more fitting manner."

"Please don't," exclaimed O'Neil, hastily.

"You are our guest; the hospitality of our house is yours. Hope would be honored to welcome you, sir, at any time, but under these circumstances—"

"I'm going right on to Cortez."

"The ship will remain here for several hours, discharging freight, and we insist that you allow us this pleasure meanwhile. You shall spend the night here, then perhaps you will feel inclined to prolong your stay. All that Cortez has we have in double proportion—I say it with pride. Cortez is no longer the metropolis of the region. Hope— Well, I may say that Cortez is, of all Alaskan cities, the most fortunate, since it has realized its Hope." He laughed musically. "This town has come to stay; we intend to annex Cortez eventually. If you feel that you must go on, I shall deem it a pleasure to send you later in my motorboat. She makes the run in fifteen minutes. But you must first honor our house and our board; you must permit us to pledge your health in a glass. We insist!"

"Please!" said Mrs. Gerard.

"*Do* come, your Highness," Natalie urged, from the shelter of the elder woman's arms.

"You're more than kind," said O'Neil, and together the four turned their faces to the shore.

V   *Wherein We See Curtis Gordon and Others*

Curtis Gordon's respect for his guest increased as they walked up the dock, for, before they had taken many steps, out from the crowd which had gathered to watch the ship's arrival stepped one of his foremen. This fellow shook hands warmly with O'Neil, whereupon others followed, one by one—miners, day laborers, "rough-necks" of many nationalities. They doffed their hats—something they never did for Gordon—and stretched out grimy hands, their faces lighting up with smiles. O'Neil accepted their greetings with genuine pleasure and called them by name.

"We just heard you was shipwrecked," said Gordon's foreman, anxiously. "You wasn't hurt, was you?"

"Not in the least."

"God be praised! There's a lot of the old gang at work here."

"So I see."

"Here's Shorty, that you may remember from the North Pass." The speaker dragged from the crowd a red-faced, perspiring ruffian who had hung back with the bashfulness of a small boy. "He's the fellow you dug out of the slide at twenty-eight."

"Connors!" cried O'Neil, warmly. "I'm glad to see you. And how are the two arms of you?"

"Better'n ever they was, the both av them!" Mr. Connors blushed, doubled his fists and flexed his bulging muscles. "An' why shouldn't they be, when you set 'em both with your own hands, Misther O'Neil? 'Twas as good a job as Doc Gray ever done in the hospittle. I hope you're doin' well, sir." He pulled his forelock, placed one foot behind the other, and tapped it on the planking, grinning expansively.

"Very well indeed, thank you."

O'Neil's progress was slow, for half the crowd insisted upon shaking his hand and exchanging a few words with him. Clumsy Swedes bobbed their heads, dark-browed foreign laborers whose nationality it was hard to distinguish showed their teeth and chattered words of greeting.

"Bless my soul!" Gordon exclaimed, finally. "You know more of them than I do."

"Yes! I seldom have to fire a man."

"Then you are favored of the gods. Labor is my great problem. It is the supreme drawback of this country. These people drift and blow on every breeze, like the sands of the Sahara. With more and better help I could work wonders here."

Unexpected as these salutations had been, O'Neil's greatest surprise came a moment later as he passed the first of the company buildings. There he heard his name pronounced in a voice which halted him, and in an open doorway he beheld a huge, loose-hung man of tremendous girth, with a war-bag in his hand and a wide black hat thrust back from a shiny forehead.

"Why, Tom!" he exclaimed. "Tom Slater!"

Gordon groaned and went on with the women, saying: "Come up to the house when you escape, Mr. O'Neil. I shall have dinner served."

Mr. Slater came forward slowly, dragging his clothes-bag with him. The two shook hands.

"What in the world are you doing here, Tom?"

"Nothing!" said Slater. He had a melancholy cast of feature, utterly out of keeping with his rotund form. In his eye was the somber glow of a soul at war with the flesh.

"Nothing?"

"I had a good job, putting in a power plant for his nibs"—he indicated the retreating Gordon with a disrespectful jerk of the thumb—"but I quit."

"Not enough pay?"

"Best wages I ever got. He pays well."

"Poor grub?"

"Grub's fine."

"What made you quit?"

"I haven't exactly quit, but I'm going to. When I saw you coming up the dock I said: 'There's the chief! Now he'll want me.' So I began to pack." The speaker dangled his partly filled war-bag as evidence. In an even sourer tone he murmured: "Ain't that just me? I ain't had a day's luck since Lincoln was shot. The minute I get a good job along you come and spoil it."

"I don't want you," laughed O'Neil.

But Slater was not convinced. He shook his head.

"Oh yes, you do. You've got something on or you wouldn't be here. I've been drawing pay from you now for over five minutes."

O'Neil made a gesture of impatience.

"No! No! In the first place, I have nothing for you to do; in the second place, I probably couldn't afford the wages Gordon is paying you."

"That's the hell of it!" gloomily agreed "Happy Tom." "Where are your grips? I'll begin by carrying them."

"I haven't any. I've been shipwrecked. Seriously, Tom, I have no place for you."

The repetition of this statement made not the smallest impression upon the hearer.

"You'll have one soon enough," he replied. Then with a touch of spirit, "Do you think I'd work for this four-flusher if you were in the country?"

"Hush!" O'Neil cast a glance over his shoulder. "By the way, how do you happen to be here? I thought you were in Dawson."

"I finished that job. I was working back toward ma and the children. I haven't seen them for two years."

"You think Gordon is a false alarm?"

"Happy Tom" spat with unerring accuracy at a crack, then said:

"He's talking railroads! Railroads! Why, I've got a boy back in the state of Maine, fourteen years old—"

"Willie?"

"Yes. My son Willie could skin Curtis Gordon at railroad-building—and Willie is the sickly one of the outfit. But I'll hand it to Gordon for one thing; he's a money-getter and a money-spender. He knows where the loose stone in the hearth is laid, and he knows just which lilac

bush the family savings are buried under. Those penurious
Pilgrim Fathers in my part of the country come up and
drop their bankbooks through the slot in his door every
morning. He's the first easy money I ever had; I'd get rich
off of him, but"—Slater sighed—"of course you had to
come along and wrench me away from the till."

"Don't quit on my account," urged his former chief.
"I'm up here on coal matters. I can't take time to explain
now, but I'll see you later."

"Suit yourself, only don't keep me loafing on full time.
I'm an expensive man. I'll be packed and waiting for you."

O'Neil went on his way, somewhat amused, yet undeniably pleased at finding his boss packer here instead of
far inland, for Slater's presence might, after all, fit well
enough into his plans.

"The Irish Prince" had gained something of a reputation for extravagance, but he acknowledged himself completely outshone by the luxury with which Curtis Gordon
had surrounded himself at Hope. The promoter had spoken of his modest living-quarters—in reality they consisted
of a handsome twenty-room house, furnished with the ele-
gance of a Newport cottage. The rugs were thick and richly
colored; the furniture was of cathedral oak and mahogany.
In the library were deep leather chairs and bookcases,
filled mainly with the works of French and German au-
thors of decadent type. The man's taste in art was revealed
by certain pictures, undeniably clever, but a little too
daring. He was undoubtedly a sybarite, yet he evidently
possessed rare energy and executive force. It was an
unusual combination.

The dinner was notable mainly for its lavish disregard
of expense. There were strawberries from Seattle, fresh
cream and butter from Gordon's imported cows, cheese
prepared expressly for him in France, and a champagne
the date of which he took pains to make known.

On the whole he played the part of host agreeably
enough and his constant flow of talk was really entertaining. His anecdotes embraced three continents; his wit,
though Teutonic, was genial and mirth-provoking. When
Mrs. Gerard took time from her worshipful regard of her
daughter to enter the conversation, she spoke with easy
charm and spontaneity. As for Natalie, she was intoxi-

cated with delight; she chattered, she laughed, she interrupted with the joyful exuberance of youth.

Under such circumstances the meal should have proved enjoyable, yet the guest of honor had never been more ill at ease. Precisely what accounted for the feeling he could not quite determine. Somewhere back in his mind was a suspicion that things were not as they should be, here in this house of books and pictures and incongruities. He told himself that he should not be so narrow-minded as to resent Gloria Gerard's presence here, particularly since she herself had told him that her friendship for Gordon dated back many years. Nevertheless, the impression remained to disturb him.

"You wonder, perhaps, why I have been so extravagant with my living-quarters," said Gordon, as they walked into the library, "but it is not alone for myself. You see I have people associated with me who are accustomed to every comfort and luxury and I built this house for them. Mrs. Gerard has been kind enough to grace the establishment with her presence, and I expect others of my stockholders to do likewise. You see, I work in the light, Mr. O'Neil; I insist upon the broadest publicity in all my operations, and to that end I strive to bring my clients into contact with the undertaking itself. For instance, I am bringing a party of my stockholders all the way from New York, at my own expense, just to show them how their interests are being administered. I have chartered a special train and a ship for them, and of course they must be properly entertained while here."

"Quite a scheme," said O'Neil.

"I wanted to show them this marvelous country, God's wonderland of opportunity. They will return impressed by the solidity and permanence of their investment."

Certainly the man knew how to play his game. No more effective means of advertising, no more profitable stock-jobbing scheme could be devised than a free trip of that sort and a tour of Alaska under the watchful guidance of Curtis Gordon. If any member of the party returned unimpressed it would not be the fault of the promoter; if any one of them did not voluntarily go out among his personal friends as a missionary it would be because Gordon's magnetism had lost its power. O'Neil felt a touch of unwilling admiration.

"I judge, from what you say, that the mine gives encouragement," he ventured, eying his host curiously through a cloud of tobacco smoke.

"'Encouragement' is not the word. Before many years 'Hope Consolidated' will be listed on the exchanges of the world along with 'Amalgamated' and the other great producers. We have here, Mr. O'Neil, a tremendous mountain of ore, located at tide water, on one of the world's finest harbors. The climate is superb; we have coal near at hand for our own smelter. The mine only requires systematic development under competent hands."

"I was in Cortez when Lars Anderson made his first discovery here, and I had an option on all this property. I believe the price was twelve hundred dollars; at any rate, it was I who drove those tunnels you found when you bought him out."

Gordon's eyes wavered briefly, then he laughed.

"My dear sir, you have my sincere sympathy. Your poison, my meat—as it were, eh? You became discouraged too soon. Another hundred feet of work and you would have been justified in paying twelve hundred thousand dollars. This 'Eldorado' which the Copper Trust has bought has a greater surface showing than 'Hope,' I grant; but—it lies two hundred miles inland, and there is the all-important question of transportation to be solved. The ore will have to be hauled, or smelted on the ground, while we have the Kyak coal-fields at our door. The Heidlemanns are building a railroad to it which will parallel mine in places, but the very nature of their enterprise foredooms it to failure."

"Indeed? How so?"

"My route is the better. By a rigid economy of expenditure, by a careful supervision of detail, I can effect a tremendous saving over their initial cost. I hope to convince them of the fact, and thus induce them to withdraw from the field or take over my road at—a reasonable figure. Negotiations are under way."

At this talk of economy from Curtis Gordon O'Neil refrained from smiling with difficulty. He felt certain that the man's entire operations were as unsound as his state-

ment that he could bring the Trust to terms. Yet Gordon
seemed thoroughly in earnest. Either he expected to fool
his present hearer, or else he had become hypnotized by
the spell of his own magnificent twaddle—O'Neil could
not tell which.

"Who laid out your right-of-way?" he asked with some
interest.

"A very able young engineer, Dan Appleton. An excellent man, but—unreliable in certain things. I had to let
him go, this very afternoon, in fact, for insubordination.
But I discharged him more for the sake of discipline than
anything else. He'll be anxious to return in a few days.
Now tell me"—Gordon fixed his visitor with a bland stare
which failed to mask his gnawing curiosity—"what brings
you to King Phillip Sound? Are we to be rivals in the
railroad field?"

"No. There are enough projects of that sort in the
neighborhood for the present."

"Five, all told, but only one destined to succeed."

"I'm bound for the Kyak coal-fields to perfect and
amend my surveys under the new ruling."

"Ah! I've heard about that ruling."

"Heard about it?" exclaimed O'Neil. "Good Lord!
Haven't you complied with it?"

"Not yet."

"You surely intend to do so?"

"Oh yes—I suppose so."

"If you don't you'll lose—"

"I'm not sure we can ever win."

"Nonsense!"

"I'm not sure that it's wise to put more good money
into those coal claims," said Gordon. "This ruling will
doubtless be reversed as the others have been. One never
knows what the Land Office policy will be two days at
a time."

"You know your own business," O'Neil remarked after
a pause, "but unless you have inside information, or a bigger pull in Washington than the rest of us, I'd advise you
to get busy. I'll be on my way to Kyak in the morning
with a gang of men." Gordon's attitude puzzled him, for
he could not bring himself to believe that such indifference was genuine.

"We have been treated unfairly by the Government."
"Granted!"

"We have been fooled, cheated, hounded as if we were a crowd of undesirable aliens, and I'm heartily sick of the injustice. I prefer to work along lines of least resistance. I feel tempted to let Uncle Sam have my coal claims, since he has lied to me and gone back on his promise, and devote myself to other enterprises which offer a certainty of greater profits. But"—Gordon smiled deprecatingly—"I dare say I shall hold on, as you are doing, until that fossilized bureau at Washington imposes some new condition which will ruin us all."

Remembering Natalie's statement that her own and her mother's fortunes were tied up in the mines, O'Neil felt inclined to go over Gordon's head and tell the older woman plainly the danger of delay in complying with the law, but he thought better of the impulse. Her confidence in this man was supreme and it seemed incredible that Gordon should jeopardize her holdings and his own. More likely his attitude was just a part of his pose, designed to show the bigness of his views and to shed a greater luster upon his railroad project.

It was difficult to escape from the hospitality of Hope, and O'Neil succeeded in doing so only after an argument with Natalie and her mother. They let him go at last only upon his promise to return on his way back from the coalfields, and they insisted upon accompanying him down to the dock, whither Gordon had preceded them in order to have his motor-boat in readiness.

As they neared the landing they overheard the latter in spirited debate with "Happy Tom" Slater.

"But my dear fellow," he was saying, "I can't lose you and Appleton on the same day."

"You can't? Why, you've done it!" the fat man retorted, gruffly.

"I refuse to be left in the lurch this way. You must give more notice."

Slater shrugged, and without a word tossed his bulging war-bag into the motor-boat which lay moored beneath him. His employer's face was purple with rage as he turned to Murray and the ladies, but he calmed himself sufficiently to say:

"This man is in charge of important work for me, yet he tells me you have hired him away."

"Tom!" exclaimed O'Neil.

"I never said that," protested Slater. "I only told you I was working for Murray."

"Well?"

"I hired myself. He didn't have anything to say about it. I do all the hiring, firing, and boosting in my department."

"I appeal to you, O'Neil. I'm short-handed," Gordon cried.

"I tell you he don't have a word to say about it," Slater declared with heat.

Natalie gave a little tinkling laugh. She recognized in this man the melancholy hero of more than one tale "The Irish Prince" had told her. Murray did his best, but knowing "Happy Tom's" calm obstinacy of old, he had no real hope of persuading him.

"You see how it is," he said, finally. "He's been with me for years and he refuses to work for any one else while I'm around. If I don't take him with me he'll follow."

Mr. Slater nodded vigorously, then imparted these tidings:

"It's getting late, and my feet hurt." He bowed to the women, then lowered himself ponderously yet carefully over the edge of the dock and into the leather cushions of the launch. Once safely aboard, he took a package of wintergreen chewing-gum from his pocket and began to chew, staring out across the sound with that placid, speculative enjoyment which reposes in the eyes of a cow at sunset.

Curtis Gordon's face was red and angry as he shook hands stiffly with his guest and voiced the formal hope that they would meet again.

"I'm glad to be gone," Slater observed as the speed-boat rushed across the bay. "I'm a family man, and—I've got principles. Gordon's got neither."

"It was outrageous for you to walk out so suddenly. It embarrassed me."

"Oh, he'd let me go without notice if he felt like it. He fired Dan Appleton this afternoon just for telling the truth about the mine. That's what I'd have got if I'd stayed on much longer. I was filling up with words and my skin was getting tight. I'd have busted, sure, inside of a week."

"Isn't the mine any good?"

"It ain't a mine at all. It's nothing but an excavation filled with damn fools and owned by idiots; still, I s'pose it serves Gordon's purpose." After a pause he continued: "They tell me that snakes eat their own young! Gordon ought to call that mine the Anaconda, for it'll swallow its own dividends and all the money those Eastern people can raise."

"I'm sorry for Mrs. Gerard."

Slater emitted a sound like the moist exhalation of a porpoise as it rises to the surface.

"What do you mean by that snort?" asked Murray.

"It's funny how much some people are like animals. Now the ostrich thinks that when his head is hid his whole running-gear is out of sight. Gordon's an ostrich. As for you—you remind me of a mud turtle. A turtle don't show nothing but his head, and when it's necessary he can yank that under cover. Gordon don't seem to realize that he sticks up above the underbrush—either that or else he don't care who sees him. He and that woman—"

"Never mind her," exclaimed O'Neil, quickly. "I'm sure you're mistaken."

Mr. Slater grunted once more, then chewed his gum silently, staring mournfully into the twilight. After a moment he inquired:

"Why don't you show these people how to build a railroad, Murray?"

"No, thank you! I know the country back of here. It's not feasible."

"The Copper Trust is doing it."

"All the more reason why I shouldn't. There are five projects under way now, and there won't be more than enough traffic for one."

Slater nodded. "Every man who has two dollars, a clean shirt, and a friend at Washington has got a railroad scheme up his sleeve."

"It will cost thirty million dollars to build across those three divides and into the copper country. When the road is done it will be one of heavy grades, and—"

"No wonder you didn't get the contract from the Heidlemanns—if your estimate was thirty million."

"I didn't put in a figure."

Tom looked surprised. "Why didn't you? You know them."

"I was like the little boy who didn't go to the party—I wasn't asked." The speaker's expression showed that his pride had been hurt and discouraged further questioning. "We'll hire our men and our boats to-night," he announced. "I've arranged for that freighter to drop us off at Omar on her way out. We'll have to row from there to Kyak. I expected to land my horses at the coast and pack in from Kyak Bay, but that shipwreck changed my plans. Poor brutes! After my experience I'll never swim horses in this water again."

An eleven-o'clock twilight enveloped Cortez when the two men landed, but the town was awake. The recent railway and mining activity in the neighborhood had brought a considerable influx of people to King Phillip Sound, and the strains of music from dance-hall doors, the click of checks and roulette balls from the saloons, gave evidence of an unusual prosperity.

O'Neil had no difficulty in securing men. Once he was recognized, the scenes at Hope were re-enacted, and there was a general scramble to enlist upon his pay-roll. Within an hour, therefore, his arrangements were made, and he and Tom repaired to Callahan's Hotel for a few hours' sleep.

A stud game was going on in the barroom when they entered, and O'Neil paused to watch it while Slater spoke to one of the players, a clean-cut, blond youth of whimsical countenance. When the two friends finally faced the bar for their "nightcap" Tom explained:

"That's Appleton, the fellow Gordon fired to-day. I told him I'd left the old man flat."

"Is he a friend of yours?"

"Sure. Nice boy—good engineer, too."

"Umph! That game is crooked."

"No?" "Happy Tom" displayed a flash of interest.

"Yes, Cortez is fast becoming a metropolis, I see. The man in the derby hat is performing a little feat that once cost me four thousand dollars to learn."

"I'd better split Dan away," said Tom, hastily.

"Wait! Education is a good thing, even if it is expensive at times. I fancy your friend is bright enough to take care of himself. Let's wait a bit."

"Ain't that just my blamed luck?" lamented Slater. "Now if they were playing faro I could make a killing. I'd 'copper' Appleton's bets and 'open' the ones he coppered!"

O'Neil smiled, for "Happy Tom's" caution in money matters was notorious. "You know you don't believe in gambling," he said.

"It's not a belief, it's a disease," declared the fat man. "I was born to be a gambler, but the business is too uncertain. Now that I'm getting so old and feeble I can't work any more, I'd take it up, only I broke three fingers and when I try to deal I drop the cards. What are we going to do?"

"Just wait," said O'Neil.

VI *The Dreamer*

Unobserved the two friends watched the poker game, which for a time proceeded quietly. But suddenly they saw Appleton lean over the table and address the man with the derby hat; then, thrusting back his chair, he rose, declaring, in a louder tone:

"I tell you I saw it. I thought I was mistaken at first." His face was white, and he disregarded the efforts of his right-hand neighbor to quiet him.

"Don't squeal," smiled the dealer. "I'll leave it to the boys if I did anything wrong."

"You pulled that king from the bottom. It may not be wrong, but it's damned peculiar."

"Forget it!" one of the others exclaimed. "Denny wouldn't double-cross you."

"Hardly!" agreed Mr. Denny, evenly. "You're 'in' a hundred and eighty dollars, but if you're sore you can have it back."

Appleton flung his cards into the middle of the table

and turned away disgustedly. "It's a hard thing to prove, and I'm not absolutely sure I saw straight, or—I'd take it back, fast enough."

Denny shrugged and gathered in the discarded hand. "You've been drinking too much, that's all. Your eyesight is scattered."

Appleton's face flushed as he beheld the gaze of the company upon him and heard the laughter which greeted this remark. He turned to leave when O'Neil, who had continued to watch the proceedings with interest, crossed to the group and touched Denny on the shoulder, saying, quietly:

"Give him his money."

"Eh?" The smile faded from the fellow's face; he looked up with startled inquiry. "What?"

"Give him his money."

In the momentary hush which followed, "Happy Tom" Sltaer, who had frequently seen his employer in action and understood storm signals, sighed deeply and reached for the nearest chair. With a wrench of his powerful hands he loosened a leg. Although Mr. Slater abhorred trouble, he was accustomed to meet it philosophically. A lifetime spent in construction camps had taught him that, of all weapons, the one best suited to his use was a pick-handle; second to that he had come to value the hardwood leg of a chair. But in the present case his precaution proved needless, for the dispute was over before he had fairly prepared himself.

Without waiting for O'Neil to put his accusation into words Denny had risen swiftly, and in doing so he had either purposely or by accident made a movement which produced a prompt and instinctive reaction. Murray's fist met him as he rose, met him so squarely and with such force that he lost all interest in what followed. The other card-players silently gathered Mr. Denny in their arms and stretched him upon a disused roulette table; the bartender appeared with a wet towel and began to bathe his temples.

Appleton, dazed by the suddenness of it all, found a stack of gold pieces in his hand and heard O'Neil saying in an every-day tone:

"Come to my room, please. I'd like to talk to you." Something commanding in the speaker's face made the engineer follow against his will. He longed to loiter here until Denny had regained his senses—but O'Neil had him by the arm and a moment later he was being led down the hall away from the lobby and the barroom. As Slater, who had followed, closed the door behind them, Dan burst forth:

"By Jove! Why didn't you tell me? I knew he was crooked—but I couldn't believe—"

"Sit down!" said O'Neil. "He won't pull himself together for a while, and I want to get to bed. Are you looking for a job?"

The engineer's eyes opened wide.

"Yes."

"Do you know the Kyak country?"

"Pretty well."

"I need a surveyor. Your wages will be the same that Gordon paid and they begin now, if it's agreeable."

"It certainly is!"

"Good! We'll leave at six o'clock, sharp. Bring your bedding and instruments."

"Thanks! I—This is a bit of a surprise. Who are you?"

"I'm O'Neil."

"Oh!" Mr. Appleton's expression changed quickly. "You're Murray—" He stammered an instant. "It was very good of you to take my part, after I'd been fool enough to—"

"Well—I didn't want to see you make a total idiot of yourself."

The young man flushed slightly, then in a quieter voice, he asked:

"How did you know I was out of work?"

"Mr. Gordon told me. He recommended you highly."

"He did?"

"He said you were unreliable, disloyal, and dishonest. Coming from him I took that as high praise."

There was a moment's pause, then Appleton laughed boyishly.

"That's funny! I'm very glad to know you, Mr. O'Neil."

"You don't, and you won't for a long time. Tom tells me you didn't think well of Gordon's enterprise and so he fired you."

"That's right! I suppose I ought to have kept my mouth

shut, but it has a way of flying open when it shouldn't. He is either a fool or a crook, and his mine is nothing but a prospect. I couldn't resist telling him so."

"And his railroad?"

Appleton hesitated. "Oh, it's as good a route as the Trust's. I worked on the two surveys. Personally I think both outfits are crazy to try to build in from here. I had to tell Gordon that, too. You see I'm a volunteer talker. I should have been born with a stutter—it would have saved me a lot of trouble."

O'Neil smiled. "You may talk all you please in my employ, so long as you do your work. Now get some sleep, for we have a hard trip. And by the way"—the youth paused with a hand on the doorknob—"don't go looking for Denny."

Appleton's face hardened stubbornly.

"I can't promise that, sir."

"Oh yes you can! You must! Remember, you're working for me, and you're under orders. I can't have the expedition held up on your account."

The engineer's voice was heavy with disappointment, but a vague admiration was growing in his eyes as he agreed:

"Very well, sir. I suppose my time is yours. Good night!"

When he had gone "Happy Tom" inquired:

"Now, why in blazes did you hire him? We don't need a high-priced surveyor on this job."

"Of course not, but don't you see? He'd have been arrested, sure. Besides—he's Irish, and I like him."

"Humph! Then I s'pose he's got a job for life," said Tom, morosely. "You make friends and enemies quicker than anybody I ever saw. You've got Curtis Gordon on your neck now."

"On account of this boy? Nonsense!"

"Not altogether. Denny is Gordon's right bower. I think he calls him his secretary; anyhow, he does Gordon's dirty work and they're thicker than fleas. First you come along and steal me, underhanded, then you grab his pet engineer before he has a chance to hire him back again. Just to top off the evening you publicly brand his confidential understrapper as a card cheat and thump him on the medulla oblongata—"

"Are you sure it wasn't the duodenum?"

"Well, you hit him in a vital spot, and Gordon won't forget it."

Late on the following morning O'Neil's expedition was landed at the deserted fishing-station of Omar, thirty miles down the sound from Cortez. From this point its route lay down the bay to open water and thence eastward along the coast in front of the Salmon River delta some forty miles to Kyak. This latter stretch would have been well-nigh impossible for open boats but for the fact that the numerous mud bars and islands thrown out by the river afforded a sheltered course. These inside channels, though shallow, were of sufficient depth to allow small craft to navigate and had long been used as a route to the coal-fields.

Appleton, smiling and cheerful, was the first member of the party to appear at the dock that morning, and when the landing had been effected at Omar he showed his knowledge of the country by suggesting a short cut which would save the long row down to the mouth of the sound and around into the delta. Immediately back of the old cannery, which occupied a gap in the mountain rim, lay a narrow lake, and this, he declared, held an outlet which led into the Salmon River flats. By hauling the boats over into this body of water—a task made easy by the presence of a tiny tramway with one dilapidated push-car which had been a part of the cannery equipment—it would be possible to save much time and labor.

"I've heard there was a way through," O'Neil confessed, "but nobody seemed to know just where it was."

"I know," the young man assured him. "We can gain a day at least, and I judge every day is valuable."

"So valuable that we can't afford to lose one by making a mistake," said his employer, meaningly.

"Leave it to me. I never forget a country once I've been through it."

Accordingly the boats were loaded upon the hand-car and transferred one at a time. In the interval O'Neil examined his surroundings casually. He was surprised to find the dock and buildings in excellent condition, notwithstanding the fact that the station had lain idle for several years. A solitary Norwegian, with but a slight suspicion of English, was watching the premises and managed to make known his impression that poor fishing had led the owners to abandon operations at this point. He, too, had heard that Omar Lake had an outlet into the delta, but he was not sure of its existence; he was sure of nothing, in fact, except that it was very lonesome here, and that he had run out of tobacco five days before.

But Dan Appleton was not mistaken. A two hours' row across the mirror-like surface of Omar Lake brought the party out through a hidden gap in the mountains and afforded them a view across the level delta. To their left the range they had just penetrated retreated toward the cañon where the Salmon River burst its way out from the interior, and beyond that point it continued in a coastward swing to Kyak, their destination. Between lay a flat, trackless tundra, cut by sloughs and glacial streams, with here and there long tongues of timber reaching down from the high ground and dwindling away toward the seaward marshes. It was a desolate region, the breeding-place of sea fowl, the hunting-ground for the great brown bear.

O'Neil had never before been so near the cañon as this, and the wild stories he had heard of it recurred to him with interest. He surveyed the place curiously as the boats glided along, but could see nothing more than a jumble of small hills and buttes, and beyond them the dead-gray backs of the twin glaciers coming down from the slopes to east and west. Beyond the foot-hills and the glaciers themselves the main range was gashed by a deep valley, through which he judged the river must come, and beyond that he knew was a country of agricultural promise, extending clear to the fabulous copper belt whither the railroads from Cortez were headed. Still farther inland lay the Tanana, and then the Yukon, with their riches untouched.

What a pity, what a mockery, it was that this obvious entrance to the country had been blocked by nature! Just at his back was Omar, with its deep and sheltered harbor; the lake he had crossed gave a passage through the guardian range, and this tundra—O'Neil estimated that he could lay a mile of track a day over it—led right up to the glaciers. Once through the Coast Range, building would be easy, for the upper Salmon was navigable, and its banks presented no difficulties to track-laying.

He turned abruptly to Appleton, who was pulling an oar.

"What do you know about that cañon?" he asked.

"Not much. Nobody knows much, for those fellows who went through in the gold rush have all left the country. Gordon's right-of-way comes in above, and so does the Trust's. From there on I know every foot of the ground."

"I suppose if either of them gets through to the Salmon the rest will be easy."

"Dead easy!"

"It would be shorter and very much cheaper to build from Omar, through this way."

"Of course, but neither outfit knew anything about the outlet to Omar Lake until I told them—and they knew there was the cañon to be reckoned with."

"Well?"

Appleton shook his head. "Look at it! Does it look like a place to build a railroad?"

"I can't tell anything about it, from here."

"I suppose a road could be built if the glaciers were on the same side of the river, but—they're not. They face each other, and they're alive, too. Listen!" The oarsmen ceased rowing at Dan's signal, and out of the northward silence came a low rumble like the sound of distant cannonading. "We must be at least twenty miles away, in an air line. The ice stands up alongside the river, hundreds of feet high, and it breaks off in chunks as big as a New York office-building."

"You've been up there?"

"No. But everybody says so, and I've seen glacier ice clear out here in the delta. They're always moving, too— the glaciers themselves—and they're filled with crevasses, so that it's dangerous to cross them on foot even if one keeps back from the river."

"How did those men get their outfits through in '98?" O'Neil queried.

"I'm blessed if I know—maybe they flew." After a moment Dan added, "Perhaps they dodged the pieces as they fell."

O'Neil smiled. He opened his lips to speak, then closed

them, and for a long time kept his eyes fixed speculatively in the direction of the cañon. When he had first spoken of a route from Omar he had thrown out the suggestion with only a casual interest. Now, suddenly, the idea took strong possession of his mind; it fascinated him with its daring, its bigness. He had begun to dream.

The world owes all great achievements to dreamers, for men who lack vivid imaginations are incapable of conceiving big enterprises. No matter how practical the thing accomplished, it requires this faculty, no less than a poem or a picture. Every bridge, every skyscraper, every mechanical invention, every great work which man has wrought in steel and stone and concrete, was once a dream.

O'Neil had no small measure of the imaginative power that makes great leaders, great inventors, great builders. He was capable of tremendous enthusiasm; his temperament forever led him to dare what others feared to undertake. And here he glimpsed a tremendous opportunity. The traffic of a budding nation was waiting to be seized. To him who gained control of Alaskan transportation would come the domination of her resources. Many were striving for the prize, but if there should prove to be a means of threading that Salmon River cañon with steel rails, the man who first found it would have those other railroad enterprises at his mercy. The Trust would have to sue for terms or abandon further effort; for this route was shorter, it was level, it was infinitely cheaper to improve. The stakes in the game were staggering. The mere thought of them made his heart leap. The only obstacle, of course, lay in those glaciers, and he began to wonder if they could not be made to open. Why not? No one knew positively that they were impregnable, for no one knew anything certainly about them. Until the contrary had been proven there was at least a possibility that they were less formidable than rumor had painted them.

Camp was pitched late that night far out on the flats. During the preparation of supper Murray sat staring fixedly before him, deaf to all sounds and insensible to the activities of his companions. He had lost his customary breeziness and his good nature; he was curt, saturnine, unsmiling. Appleton undertook to arouse him from this abstraction, but Slater drew the young man aside hurriedly with a warning,

"Don't do that, son, or you'll wear splints for the rest of the trip."

"What's the matter with him, anyhow?" Dan inquired. "He was boiling over with enthusiasm all day, but now —Why, he's asleep sitting up! He hasn't moved for twenty minutes."

Tom shook his head, dislodging a swarm of mosquitoes. "Walk on your toes, my boy! Walk on your toes! I smell something cooking—and it ain't supper."

When food was served O'Neil made a pretense of eating, but rose suddenly in the midst of it, with the words:

"I'll stretch my legs a bit." His voice was strangely listless; in his eyes was the same abstraction which had troubled Appleton during the afternoon. He left the camp and disappeared up the bank of the stream.

"Nice place to take a walk!" the engineer observed. "He'll bog down in half a mile or get lost among the sloughs."

"Not him!" said Slater. Nevertheless, his worried eyes folllowed the figure of his chief as long as it was in sight. After a time he announced: "Something is coming, but what it is or where it's going to hit us I don't know."

Their meal over, the boatmen made down their beds, rolled up in their blankets, and were soon asleep. Appleton and Tom sat in the smoke of a smudge, gossiping idly as the twilight approached. From the south came the distant voice of the sea, out of the north rolled the intermittent thunder of those falling bergs, from every side sounded a harsh chorus of water-fowl. Ducks whirred past in bullet-like flight, honkers flapped heavily overhead, a pair of magnificent snow-white swans soared within easy gunshot of the camp. An hour passed, another, and another; the arctic night descended. And through it all the mosquitoes sang their blood song and stabbed the watchers with tongues of flame.

"Happy Tom" sang his song, too, for it was not often that he obtained a listener, and it proved to be a song of infinite hard luck. Mr. Slater, it seemed, was a creature

of many ills, the wretched abiding-place of aches and
pains, of colics, cramps, and rheumatism. He was the
target of misfortune and the sport of fate. His body was
the galloping-ground of strange disorders which baffled
diagnosis; his financial affairs were dominated by an evil
genius which betrayed him at every turn. To top it all,
he suffered at the moment a violent attack of indigestion.

"Ain't that just my luck?" he lamented. "Old 'Indy's'
got me good, and there ain't a bit of soda in the outfit."

Appleton, who was growing more and more uneasy at
the absence of his leader, replied with some asperity:

"Instead of dramatizing your own discomforts you'd
better be thinking of the boss. I'm going out to look for
him."

"Now don't be a dam' fool," Slater advised. "It would
be worth a broken leg to annoy him when he's in one of
these fits. You'd make yourself as popular as a smallpox
patient at a picnic. When he's dreamed his dream he'll
be back."

"When will that be?"

"No telling—maybe to-night, maybe to-morrow night."

"And what are we going to do in the meantime?"

"Sit tight." Mr. Slater chewed steadily and sighed. "No
soda in camp, and this gum don't seem to lay hold of
me! That's luck!"

Darkness had settled when O'Neil reappeared. He came
plunging out of the brush, drenched, muddy, stained by
contact with the thickets; but his former mood had disappeared and in its place was a harsh, explosive energy.

"Tom!" he cried. "You and Appleton and I will leave
at daylight. The men will wait here until we get back."
His voice was incisive, its tone forbade question.

The youthful engineer stared at him in dismay, for only
his anxiety had triumphed over his fatigue, and daylight
was but four hours away. O'Neil noted the expression,
and said, more gently:

"You're tired, Appleton, I know, but in working for me
you'll be called upon for extraordinary effort now and
then. I may not demand more than an extra hour from
you; then again I may demand a week straight without
sleep. I'll never ask it unless it's necessary and unless I'm
ready to do my share."

"Yes, sir."

"The sacrifice is big, but the pay is bigger. Loyalty is all I require."

"I'm ready now, sir."

"We can't see to travel before dawn. Help Tom load the lightest boat with rations for five days. If we run short we'll 'Siwash' it." He kicked off his rubber boots, up-ended them to drain the water out, then flung himself upon his bed of boughs and was asleep almost before the two had recovered from their surprise.

"Five days—or longer!" Slater said, gloomily, as he and Dan began their preparations. "And me with indigestion!"

"What does it mean?" queried Appleton.

"It means I'll probably succumb."

"No, no! What's the meaning of this change of plan? I can't understand it."

"You don't need to," "Happy Tom" informed him, curtly. There was a look of solicitude in his face as he added, "I wish I'd made him take off his wet clothes before he went to sleep."

"Let's wake him up."

But Slater shook his head. "I'd sooner wake a rattle-snake," said he.

O'Neil roused the members of his expedition while the sky was reddening faintly, for he had a mind which worked like an alarm-clock. All except Appleton had worked for him before, and the men accepted his orders to await his return with no appearance of surprise.

With the first clear light he and his two companions set out, rowing up the estuary of the Salmon until the current became too swift to stem in that manner. Then landing, they rigged a "bridle" for the skiff, fitted their shoulders to loops in a ninety-foot tow rope, and began to "track" their craft up against the stream. It was heart-breaking work. Frequently they were waist-deep in the cold water. Long "sweepers" with tips awash in the flood interfered with their efforts. The many branches of the stream forced them to make repeated crossings, for the delta was no more than an endless series of islands through which the current swirled. When dusk overtook them they were wet, weary, and weak from hunger. With the dawn they were up and at it again, but their task became constantly more difficult because of the floating glacier ice, which increased with every mile. They were obliged to exercise the extremest caution. Hour after hour they strained against the current, until the ropes bit into their aching flesh, bringing raw places out on neck and palm. Hour after hour the ice went churning past, and through it all came the intermittent echo of the caving glaciers ahead of them.

Dan Appleton realized very soon whither the journey was leading, and at thought of actually facing those terrors which loomed so large in conjecture his pulses began to leap. He had a suspicion of O'Neil's intent, but dared not voice it. Though the scheme seemed mad enough, its very audacity fascinated him. It would be worth while to take part in such an undertaking, even if it ended in failure. And somehow, against his judgment, he felt that his leader would find a way.

For the most part, O'Neil was as silent as a man of stone, and only on those rare occasions when he craved relief from his thoughts did he encourage Dan to talk. Then he sometimes listened, but more frequently he did not. Slater had long since become a dumb draught animal, senseless to discomfort except in the hour of relaxation when he monotonously catalogued his ills.

"Are you a married man?" O'Neil inquired once of Dan.

"Not yet, sir."

"Family?"

"Sure! A great big, fine one, consisting of a sister. But she's more than a family—she's a religion." Receiving encouragement from his employer's look of interest, he continued: "We were wiped out by the San Francisco earthquake, and stood in the bread line for a while. We managed to save four thousand dollars from the wreck, which we divided equally. Then we started out to make our fortunes. It was her idea."

"You came to Cortez?"

"Yes. Money was so easy for me that I lost all respect for it. The town rang with my mirth for a while. I was an awful fool."

"Education!"

"Now it's my ambition to get settled and have her with me. I haven't had a good laugh, a hearty meal, or a Christian impulse since I left her."

"What did she do with her half of the fortune?"

"Invested it wisely and went to work. I bought little round celluloid disks with mine; she bought land of some sort with hers. She's a newspaper woman, and the best in the world—or at least the best in Seattle. She wrote that big snow-slide story for *The Review* last fall. She tells 'em how to raise eight babies on seven dollars a week, or how to make a full set of library furniture out of three beer kegs, a packing-case, and an epileptic icebox. She runs the 'Domestic Economy' column; and she's the sweetest, the cleverest, the most stunning—"

Appleton's enthusiastic tribute ceased suddenly, for he saw that O'Neil was once more deaf and that his eyes were fixed dreamily upon the cañon far ahead.

As the current quickened the progress of the little party became slower and more exhausting. Their destination seemed to retreat before them; the river wound back and forth in a maddening series of detours. Some of the float ice was large now, and these pieces rushed down upon them like charging horses, keeping them constantly on the alert to prevent disaster. It seemed impossible that such a flat country could afford so much fall. "Happy Tom" at length suggested that they tie up and pack the remaining miles overland, but O'Neil would not hear to this.

They had slept so little, their labors had been so heavy, that they were dumb and dull with fatigue when they finally reached the first bluffs and worked their boat through a low gorge where all the waters of the Salmon thrashed and icebergs galloped past like a pallid host in flight. Here they paused and stared with wondering eyes at what lay before; a chill, damp breath swept over them, and a mighty awe laid hold of their hearts.

"Come on!" said O'Neil. "Other men have gone through; we'll do the same."

On the evening of the sixth day a splintered, battered poling-boat with its seams open swung in to the bank where O'Neil's men were encamped, and its three occupants staggered out. They were gaunt and stiff and heavy-eyed. Even Tom Slater's full cheeks hung loose and flabby. But the leader was alert and buoyant; his face was calm, his eyes were smiling humorously.

"You'll take the men on to the coal-fields and finish the work," he told his boss packer later that night. "Appleton and I will start back to Cortez in the morning. When you have finished go to Juneau and see to the recording."

"Ain't that my luck?" murmured the dyspeptic. "Me for Kyak where there ain't a store, and my gum all wet."

"Chew it, paper and all," advised Appleton, cheerfully.

"Oh, the good has all gone out of it now," Slater explained.

"Meet me in Seattle on the fifteenth of next month," his employer directed.

"I'll be there if old 'Indy' spares me. But dyspepsia, with nothing to eat except beans and pork bosom, will probably lay me in my grave long before the fifteenth. However, I'll do my best. Now, do you want to know what I think of this proposition of yours?" He eyed his superior somberly.

"Sure; I want all the encouragement I can get, and your views are always inspiriting."

"Well, I think it's nothing more nor less than hydrophobia. These mosquitoes have given you the rabies and you need medical attention. You need it bad."

"Still, you'll help me, won't you?"

"Oh yes," said Tom, "I'll help you. But it's a pity to see a man go mad."

VII *The Dream*

The clerk of the leading hotel in Seattle whirled his register about as a man deposited a weather-beaten war-bag on the marble floor and leaned over the counter to inquire:

"Is Murray O'Neil here?"

This question had been asked repeatedly within the last two hours, but heretofore by people totally different in appearance from the one who spoke now. The man behind the desk measured the stranger with a suspicious eye before answering. He saw a ragged, loose-hung, fat person of melancholy countenance, who was booted to the knee and chewing gum.

"Mr. O'Neil keeps a room here by the year," he replied, guardedly.

"Show me up!" said the new-comer as if advancing a challenge.

A smart reply was on the lips of the clerk, but something in the other's manner discouraged flippancy.

"You are a friend of Mr. O'Neil's?" he asked, politely.

"Friend? Um-m, no! I'm just him when he ain't around." In a loud tone he inquired of the girl at the news-stand, "Have you got any wintergreen gum?"

"Mr. O'Neil is not here."

The fat man stared at his informant accusingly. "Ain't this the fifteenth?" he asked.

"It is."

"Then he's here, all right!"

"Mr. O'Neil is not in," the clerk repeated, gazing fixedly over Mr. Slater's left shoulder.

"Well, I guess his room will do for me. I ain't particular."

"His room is occupied at present. If you care to wait you will find——"

Precisely what it was that he was to find Tom never learned, for at that moment the breath was driven out of his lungs by a tremendous whack, and he turned to behold Dr. Stanley Gray towering over him, an expansive smile upon his face.

"Look out!" Slater coughed, and seized his Adam's apple. "You made me swallow my cud." The two shook hands warmly.

"We've been expecting you, Tom," said the doctor. "We're all here except Parker, and he wired he'd arrive to-morrow."

"Where's Murray?"

"He's around somewhere."

Slater turned a resentful, smoldering gaze upon the hotel clerk, and looked about him for a chair with a detachable leg, but the object of his regard disappeared abruptly behind the key-rack.

"This rat-brained party said he hadn't come."

"He arrived this morning, but we've barely seen him."

"I left Appleton in Juneau. He'll be down on the next boat."

"Appleton? Who's he?" Dr. Gray inquired.

"Oh, he's a new member of the order—initiated last month. He's learning to be a sleep-hater, like the rest of us. He's recording the right-of-way."

"What's in the air? None of us know. We didn't even know Murray's whereabouts—thought he was in Kyak, until he sounded the tocsin from New York. The other boys have quit their jobs and I've sold my practice."

"It's a railroad!"

Dr. Gray grinned. "Well! That's the tone I use when I break the news that it's a girl instead of a boy."

"It's a railroad," Slater repeated, "up the Salmon River!"

"Good Lord! What about those glaciers?"

"Oh, it ain't so much the glaciers and the floating icebergs and the raging chasms and the quaking tundra— Murray thinks he can overcome them—it's the mosquitoes and the Copper Trust that are going to figure in this enterprise. One of 'em will be the death of me, and the other will bust Murray, if he don't look out. Say, my neck is covered with bumps till it feels like a dog-collar of seed pearls."

"Do you think we'll have a fight?" asked the doctor, hopefully.

"A fight! It'll be the worst massacre since the Little Big Horn. We're surrounded already, and no help in sight."

O'Neil found his "boys" awaiting him when he returned to his room. There was Mellen, lean, gaunt and serious-minded, with the dust of Chihuahua still upon his shoes; there were McKay, the superintendent, who had arrived from California that morning; Sheldon, the commissary man; Elkins; "Doc" Gray; and "Happy Tom" Slater. Parker, the chief engineer, alone was absent.

"I sent Appleton in from Cortez," he told them, "to come down the river and make the preliminary survey into Omar. He cables me that he has filed his locations and everything is O.K. On my way East I stopped here long enough to buy the Omar cannery, docks, buildings, and town site. It's all mine, and it will save us ninety days' work in getting started."

"What do you make of that tundra between Omar and the cañon?" queried McKay, who had crossed the Salmon River delta and knew its character. "It's like calf's-foot jelly—a man bogs down to his waist in it."

"We'll fill and trestle," said O'Neil.

"We couldn't move a pile-driver twenty feet."

"It's frozen solid in winter."

McKay nodded. "We'll have to drive steam points ahead of every pile, I suppose, and we'll need Eskimos to work in that cold, but I guess we can manage somehow."

"That country is like an apple pie," said Tom Slater—"it's better cold than hot. There's a hundred inches of rainfall at Omar in summer. We'll all have web feet when we get out."

Sheldon, the light-hearted commissary man, spoke up. "If it's as wet as all that, we'll need Finns—instead of Eskimos." He was promptly hooted into silence.

"I understand those glaciers come down to the edge of the river," the superintendent ventured.

"They do!" O'Neil acknowledged, "and they're the liveliest ones I ever saw. Tom can answer for that. One of them is fully four hundred feet high at the face and four miles across. They're constantly breaking, too."

"Lumps bigger than this hotel," supplemented Slater. "It's quite a sight—equal to anything in the state of Maine."

O'Neil laughed with the others at this display of sectional pride, and then explained: "The problem of passing them sounds difficult, but in reality it isn't. If those other engineers had looked over the ground as I did, instead of relying entirely upon hearsay, we wouldn't be meeting here today. Of course I realized that we couldn't build a road over a moving river of ice, nor in front of one, for that matter, but I discovered that Nature had made us one concession. She placed her glaciers on opposite sides of the valley, to be sure, but she placed the one that comes in from the east bank slightly higher upstream than the one that comes in from the west. They don't really face each other, although from the sea they appear to do so. You see the answer?" His hearers nodded vigorously. "If we cross the river, low down, by a trestle, and run up the east bank past Jackson glacier until we are stopped by Garfield—the upper one—then throw a bridge directly across, and back to the side we started from, we miss them both and have the river always between them and us. Above the upper crossing there will be a lot of heavy rock work to do, but nothing unusual, and, once through the gorge, we come out into the valley, where the other roads run in from Cortez. They cross three divides, while we run through on a one-per-cent. grade. That will give us a downhill pull on all heavy freight."

"Sounds as simple as a pair of suspenders, doesn't it?" inquired Slater. "But wait till you see it. The gorge below Niagara is stagnant water compared with the cataract above those glaciers. It takes two looks to see the top of the mountains. And those glaciers themselves—Well! Language just gums up and sticks when it comes to describing them."

Mellen, the bridge-builder, spoke for the first time, and the others listened.

"As I understand it we will cross the river between the glaciers and immediately below the upper one."

"Exactly!"

He shook his head. "We can't build piers to withstand those heavy bergs which you tell me are always breaking off."

"I'll explain how we can," said O'Neil. "You've hit the bull's-eye—the tender spot in the whole enterprise. While the river is narrow and rapid in front of Jackson—the lower glacier—opposite Garfield there is a kind of lake, formed, I suppose, when the glacier receded from its original position. Now then, here lies the joker, the secret of the whole proposition. This lake is deep, but there is a shallow bar across its outlet which serves to hold back all but the small bergs. This gives us a chance to cross in safety. At first I was puzzled to discover why only the ice from the lower glacier came down-river; then, when I realized the truth, I knew I had the key to Alaska in my hands. We'll cross just below this bar. Understand? Of course it all depends upon Parker's verdict, but I'm so sure his will agree with mine that I've made my preparations, bought Omar and gathered you fellows together. We're going to spring the biggest coup in railroad history."

"Where's the money coming from?" Slater inquired, bluntly.

"I'm putting in my own fortune."

"How much is that? I'm dead to all sense of modesty, you see."

"About a million dollars," said O'Neil.

"Humph! That won't get us started."

"I've raised another million in New York." The chief was smiling and did not seem to resent this inquisitiveness in the least.

"Nothing but a shoe-string!"

"My dear 'Happy,' " laughed the builder, "I don't intend to complete the road."

"Then—why in blazes are you starting it?" demanded Slater in a bewilderment which the others evidently shared. "It's one thing to build a railroad on a contractor's commission, but it's another thing to build it and pay your own way as you go along. Half a railroad ain't any good."

"Once my right-of-way is filed it will put those projects from Cortez out of business. No one but an imbecile would think of building in from there with the Omar route made possible. Before we come to that Salmon River bridge the Copper Trust will have to buy us out!"

"That's language!" said "Happy Tom" in sudden admiration. "Those are words I understand. I withdraw my objections and give my consent to the deal."

"You are staking your whole fortune on your judgment, as I understand it," McKay ventured.

"Every dollar of it," Murray answered.

"Say, chief, that's gambling some!" young Sheldon remarked with a wondering look.

They were deep in their discussion when the telephone broke in noisily. Sheldon, being nearest to the instrument, answered it. "There's a newspaper reporter downstairs to interview you," he announced, after an instant.

"I don't grant interviews," O'Neil said, sharply. He could not guess by what evil chance the news of his plans had leaked out.

"Nothing doing!" Sheldon spoke into the transmitter.

He turned again to his employer. "Operator says the party doesn't mind waiting."

O'Neil frowned impatiently.

"Throw him out!" Sheldon directed, brusquely, then suddenly dropped the receiver as if it had burnt his fingers. "Hell! It's a woman, Murray! She's on the wire. She thanks you sweetly and says she'll wait."

"A woman! A newspaperwoman!" O'Neil rose and seized the instrument roughly. His voice was freezing as he said: "Hello! I refuse to be interviewed. Yes! There's no use—" His tone suddenly altered. "Miss Appleton! I beg your pardon. I'll be right down." Turning to his subordinates, he announced with a wry smile: "This seems to terminate our interview. She's Dan Appleton's sister, and therefore—" He shrugged resignedly. "Now run along. I'll see you in the morning."

His "boys" made their way down to the street, talking guardedly as they went. All were optimistic save Slater, whose face remained shrouded in its customary gloom.

"Cheer up, 'Happy'!" Dr. Gray exhorted him. "It's the biggest thing we ever tackled."

"Wait! Just wait till you've seen the place," Tom said.

"Don't you think it can be done?"

"Nope!"

"Come, come!"

"It's impossible! Of course *we'll* do it, but it's impossible, just the same. It will mean a scrap, too, like none of us ever saw, and I was raised in a logging-camp where fighting is the general recreation. If I was young, like the rest of you, I wouldn't mind; but I'm old—and my digestion's gone. I can't hardly take care of myself any more, Doc. I'm too feeble to fight or—" He signaled a passing car; it failed to stop and he rushed after it, dodging vehicles with the agility of a rabbit and swinging his heavy war-bag as if it weighed no more than a good resolution.

O'Neil entered the ladies' parlor with a feeling of extreme annoyance, expecting to meet an inquisitive, bold young woman bent upon exploiting his plans and his personality in the usual inane journalistic fashion. He was surprised and offended that Dan Appleton, in whom he had reposed the utmost faith, should have betrayed his secret. Publicity was a thing he detested at all times, and at present he particularly dreaded its effect. But he was agreeably surprised in the girl who came toward him briskly with hand outstretched.

Miss Appleton was her brother's double; she had his frank blue eyes, his straw-gold hair, his humorous smile and wide-awake look. She was not by any means beautiful! —her features were too irregular, her nose too tip-tilted, her mouth too generous for that—but she seemed crisp, clean-cut, and wholesome. What first struck O'Neil was her effect of boyishness. From the crown of her plain straw "sailor" to the soles of her sensible walking-boots there was no suggestion of feminine frippery. She wore a plain shirtwaist and a tailored skirt, and her hair was arranged simply. The wave in its pale gold was the only concession to mere prettiness. Yet she gave no impression of deliberate masculinity. She struck one as merely not interested in clothes, instinctively expressing in her dress her own boyish directness and her businesslike absorption in her work.

"You're furious, of course; anybody would be," she began, then laughed so frankly that his eyes softened and the wrinkles at their corners deepened.

"I fear I was rude before I learned you were Dan's sister," he apologized. "But you see I'm a bit afraid of newspaper people."

"I knew you'd struggle—although Dan described you as a perfectly angelic person."

"Indeed!"

"But I'm a real reporter, so I won't detain you long. I don't care where you were born or where you went to school, or what patent breakfast-food you eat. Tell me, are you going to build another railroad?"

"I hope so. I'm always building roads when my bids are low enough to secure the contracts; that's my business."

"Are you going to build one in Alaska?"

"Possibly! There seems to be an opportunity there— but Dan has probably told you as much about that as I am at liberty to tell. He's been over the ground."

She pursed her lips at him. "You know very well, or you ought to know, that Dan wouldn't tell me a thing while he's working for you. He hasn't said a word, but—Is that why you came in frowning like a thunder-cloud? Did you think he set me on your trail?"

"I think I do know that he wouldn't do anything really indiscreet." Murray regarded her with growing favor. There was something about this boyish girl which awakened the same spontaneous liking he had felt upon his first meeting with her brother. He surprised her by confessing boldly:

"I *am* building a railroad—to the interior of Alaska. I've been east and raised the money, my men are here; we'll begin operations at once."

"That's what Mr. Gordon told me about his scheme, but he hasn't done much, so far."

"My line will put his out of business, also that of the Trust, and the various wildcat promoters."

"Where does your road start from?"

"The town of Omar, on King Phillip Sound, near Hope and Cortez. It will run up the Salmon River and past the glaciers which those other men refused to tackle."

"If I weep, it is for joy," said the girl. "I don't like Curtis Gordon. I call him Simon Legree."

"Why?"

"Well, he impresses me as a real old-time villain—with the riding-boots and the whip and all that. 'Uncle Tom's Cabin' is my favorite play, it's so funny. This is a big story you've given me, Mr. O'Neil."

"I realize that."

"It has the biggest news value of anything Alaskan which has 'broken' for some time. I think you are a very nice person to interview, after all."

"Wait! I don't want you to use a word of what I've told you."

Miss Appleton's clearly penciled brows rose inquiringly. "Then why didn't you keep still?"

"You asked me. I told you because you are Dan Appleton's sister. Nevertheless, I don't want it made public."

"Let's sit down," said the girl with a laugh. "To tell you the truth, I didn't come here to interview you for my paper. I'm afraid I've tried your patience awfully." A faint flush tinged her clear complexion. "I just came, really, to get some news of Dan."

"He's perfectly well and happy, and you'll see him in a few days."

Miss Appleton nodded. "So he wrote, but I couldn't wait! Now won't you tell me all about him—not anything about his looks and his health, but little unimportant things that will mean something. You see, I'm his mother and his sister and his sweetheart."

O'Neil did as he was directed and before long found himself reciting the details of that trying trip up the Salmon River. He told her how he had sent the young engineer out to run the preliminary survey for the new railroad, and added: "He is in a fair way to realize his ambition of having you with him all the time. I'm sure that will please you."

"And it is my ambition to make enough money to have him with me," she announced. With an air of some importance she continued: "I'll tell you a secret: I'm writing for the magazines—stories!" She sat back awaiting his enthusiasm. When she saw that it was not forthcoming she exclaimed: "My! How you do rave over the idea!"

"I congratulate you, of course, but—"

"Now don't tell me that you tried it once. Of course you did. I know it's a harmless disease, like the measles, and that everybody has it when they're young. Above all, don't volunteer the information that your own life is full of romance and would make a splendid novel. They all say that."

Murray O'Neil felt the glow of personal interest that results from the discovery in another of a congenial sense of humor.

"I didn't suppose you had to write," he said. "Dan told me you had invested your fortune and were on Easy Street."

"That was poetic license. I fictionized slightly in my report to him because I knew he was doing so well."

"Then your investment didn't turn out fortunately?"

Miss Appleton hesitated. "You seem to be a kindly, trusting person. I'm tempted to destroy your faith in human nature."

"Please don't."

"Yes, I shall. My experience may help you to avoid the pitfalls of high finance. Well, then, it was a very sad little fortune, to begin with, like a boy in grammar-school—just big enough to be of no assistance. But even a boy's-size fortune looked big to me. I wanted to invest it in something sure—no national-bank stock, subject to the danger of an absconding cashier, mind you; no government bonds with the possibility of war to depreciate them; but something stable and agricultural, with the inexhaustible resources of nature back of it. This isn't my own language. I cribbed it from the apple-man."

"Apple-man?"

"Yes. He had brown eyes, and a silky mustache, and a big irrigation plan over east of the mountains. You gave him your money and he gave you a perfectly good receipt. Then he planted little apple trees. He nursed them tenderly for five years, after which he turned them over to you with his blessing, and you lived happily for evermore. At least that was the idea. You couldn't fail to grow rich, for the water always bubbled through his little ditch and it never froze nor rained to spoil things. I used to love apples. And then there was my name, which seemed a good omen. But lately I've considered changing 'Appleton' to 'Berry' or 'Plummer' or some other kind of fruit."

"I infer that the scheme failed." O'Neil's eyes were half closed with amusement.

"Yes. It was a good scheme, too, except for the fact that the irrigation ditch ran uphill, and that there wasn't any water where it started from, and that apples never had been made to grow in that locality because of something in the soil, and that Brown-eyed Betty's title to the land wouldn't hold water any more than the ditch. Otherwise I'm sure he'd have made a success and I'd have spent my declining years in a rocking-chair under the falling apple blossoms, eating Pippins and Jonathans and Northern Spies. I can't bear to touch them now. Life at my boarding-house is one long battle against apple pies, apple puddings, apple tapioca. Ugh! I hate the very word."

"I can understand your aversion," laughed O'Neil. "I wonder if you would let me order dinner for both of us, provided I taboo fruit. Perhaps I'll think of something more to tell you about Dan. I'm sure he wouldn't object—"

"Oh, my card is all the chaperon I need; it takes me

everywhere and renders me superior to the smaller conventionalities." She handed him one, and he read:

ELIZA V. APPLETON

The Review

"May I ask what the 'V' stands for?" He held up the card between his thumb and finger.

Miss Appleton blushed, for all the world like a boy, then answered, stiffly:

"It stands for Violet. But that isn't my fault, and I'm doing my best to live it down."

VIII   *In which We Come to Omar*

"Miss Appleton," said the editor of *The Review*, "would you like to take a vacation?"

"Is that your delicate way of telling me I'm discharged?" inquired Eliza.

"You know very well we wouldn't fire you. But you haven't had a vacation for three years, and you need a rest."

"I thought I was looking extremely well, for me."

"We're going to send you on an assignment—to Alaska —if you'll go."

"I'm thinking of quitting newspaper-work for good. The magazines pay better, and I'm writing a book."

"I know. Perhaps this will just fit in with your plans, for it has to do with your pet topic of conservation. Those forestry stories of yours and the article on the Water Power Combination made a hit, didn't they?"

"I judge so. Anyhow the magazine people want more."

"Good! Here's your chance to do something big for yourself and for us. Those Alaskan coal claimants have been making a great effort in Washington to rush their patents through, and there seems to be some possibility of their succeeding unless the public wakes up. We want to show up the whole fraudulent affair, show how the entries were illegal, and how the agents of the Trust are trying to put over the greatest steal of the century. It's the Heidlemanns that are back of it—and a few fellows like Murray O'Neil."

"O'Neil!"

"You know him, don't you?"

"Yes. I interviewed him a year ago last spring, when he started his railroad."

"He's fighting for one of the biggest and richest groups of claims. He's backed by some Eastern people. It's the psychological moment to expose both the railroad and the coal situation, for the thieves are fighting among themselves—Gordon, O'Neil, and the Heidlemanns."

"Mr. O'Neil is no thief," said the girl, shortly.

"Of course not. He's merely trying to snatch control of an empire, and to grab ten million dollars' worth of coal, for nothing. That's not theft, it's financial genius! Fortunately, however, the public is rousing itself—coming to regard its natural resources as its own and not the property of the first financier who lays hold of them. Call it what you will, but give us the true story of the Kyak coal and, above all, the story of the railroad battle. Things are growing bitter up there already, and they're bound to get rapidly worse. Give us the news and we'll play it up big through our Eastern syndicate. You can handle the magazine articles in a more dignified way, if you choose. A few good vigorous, fearless, newspaper stories, written by some one on the ground, will give Congress such a jolt that no coal patents will be issued this season and no Government aid will be given to the railroads. You get the idea?"

"Certainly! But it will take time to do all that."

"Spend a year at it if necessary. *The Review* is fighting for a principle; it will back you to any extent. Isn't it worth a year, two years, of hard labor, to awaken the American people to the knowledge that they are being robbed of their birthright? I have several men whom I could send, but I chose you because your work along this line has given you a standing. This is your chance, Eliza —to make a big reputation and to perform a real service to the country. It's a chance that may never come your way again. Will you go?"

"Of course I'll go."

"I knew you would. You're all business, and that's what makes a hit in this office. You're up against a tough proposition, but I can trust you to make good on it. You can't fail if you play one interest against the other, for they're all fighting like Kilkenny cats. The Heidlemanns are a bunch of bandits; Gordon is a brilliant, unscrupulous promoter; O'Neil is a cold, shrewd schemer with more brains and daring than any of the others—he showed that when he walked in there and seized the Salmon River cañon. He broke up all their plans and set the Copper Trust by the ears, but I understand they've got him bottled up at last. Here's your transportation—on Saturday's steamer." The editor shook Miss Appleton's hand warmly as she rose. "Good luck, Eliza! Remember, we won't balk, no matter how lively your stuff is. The hotter the better —and that's what the magazines want, too. If I were you, I'd gum-shoe it. They're a rotten crowd and they might send you back if they got wise."

"I think not," said Eliza, quietly.

The town of Omar lay drenched in mist as the steamer bearing the representative of *The Review* drew in at the dock. The whole region was sodden and rain-soaked, verdant with a lush growth. No summer sun shone here, to bake sprouting leaves or sear tender grasses. Beneath the sheltering firs a blanket of moss extended over hill and vale, knee-deep and treacherous to the foot. The mountain crests were white, and down every gully streamed water from the melting snows. The country itself lay on end, as if crumpled by some giant hand, and presented a tropical blend of colors. There was the gray of fog and low-swept clouds, the dense, dark green of the spruces, underlaid with the richer, lighter shades where the summer vegetation rioted. And running through it all were the shimmering, silent reaches of the sound.

Omar itself was a mushroom city, sprung up by magic, as if the dampness at its roots had caused it to rise overnight. A sawmill shrieked complainingly; a noisy switch-engine shunted rows of flat cars back and forth, tooting lustily; the rattle of steam-winches and the cries of stevedores from a discharging freighter echoed against the hillsides. Close huddled at the water-front lay the old cannery buildings, greatly expanded and multiplied now and glistening with fresh paint. Back of them again lay the town, its stumpy, half-graded streets terminating in the forest like the warty feelers of a stranded octopus. Everywhere was hurry and confusion, and over all was the ever-present shroud of mist which thickened into showers or parted reluctantly to let the sun peep through.

Dan Appleton, his clothing dewy from the fog, his cheeks bronzed by exposure, was over the rail before the ship had made fast, and had Eliza in his arms, crushing her with the hug of a bear.

"Come up to the house, Sis, quick!" he cried, when the first frenzy of greeting was over—"your house and mine!" His eyes were dancing, his face was alight with eagerness.

"But, Danny," she laughed, squeezing his arm tenderly, "you live with Mr. O'Neil and all those other men in a horrible, crawling bunk-house."

"Oh, do I? I'll have you know that our bunk-houses don't crawl. And besides—But wait! It's a s'prise."

"A s'prise?" she queried, eagerly. "For me?"

He nodded.

"Tell me what it is, quick! You know I never could wait for s'prises."

"Well, it's a brand-new ultra-stylish residence for just you and me. When the chief heard you were coming he had a cottage built."

"Danny! It was only five days ago that I cabled you!"

"That's really ten days for us, for you see we never sleep. It is finished and waiting, and your room is in white, and the paint will be dry to-morrow. He's a wonder!"

Remembering the nature of her mission, Eliza demurred. "I'm afraid I can't live there, Dan. You know" —she hesitated—"I may have to write some rather dreadful things about him."

"What?" Dan's face fell. "You are going to attack the chief! I had no idea of that!" He looked genuinely distressed and a little stern.

She laid a pleading hand upon his arm. "Forgive me, Dan," she said. "I knew how you would feel, and, to tell the truth, I don't like that part of it one bit. But it was my big chance—the sort of thing I have been waiting years for. I couldn't bear to miss it." There was a suspicion of tears in her eyes. "I didn't think it all out. I just came. Things get awfully mixed, don't they? Of course I wouldn't attack him unfairly, but I do believe in conservation—and what could I do but come here to you?"

Dan smiled to reassure her. "Perhaps you won't feel like excoriating him when you learn more about things. I know you wouldn't be unfair. You'd flunk the job first. Wait till you talk to him. But you can't refuse his kindness, for a time at least. There's nowhere else for you to stay, and Murray would pick you up and put you into the cottage, muck-rake and all, if I didn't. He had to go out on the work this morning or he'd have been here to welcome you. He sent apologies and said a lot of nice things, which I've forgotten."

"Well"—Eliza still looked troubled—"all right. But wait," she cried, with a swift change of mood. "I've made a little friend, the dearest, the most useless creature! We shared the same stateroom and we're sisters. She actually says I'm pretty, so of course I'm her slave for life." She hurried away in the midst of Dan's loyal protestations that she *was* pretty—more beautiful than the stars, more pleasing to the eye than the orchids of Brazil. A moment later she reappeared to present Natalie Gerard.

Dan greeted the new arrival with a cordiality in which there was a trace of shyness unusual with him. "We've made quite a change since you were up here, Miss Gerard," he remarked. "The ships stop first at Omar now, you see. I trust it won't inconvenience you."

"Not in the least," said Natalie. "I shall arrive at Hope quite soon enough."

"Omar Khayyam is out in the wilderness somewhere," Eliza informed her girl friend, "with his book of verses and his jug of wine, I suppose."

"Mr. O'Neil?"

"Yes. But he'll be back soon, and meanwhile you are to come up and see our paradise."

"It—looks terribly wet," Natalie ventured. "Perhaps we'd better wait until the rain stops."

"Please don't," Dan laughed. "It won't stop until autumn

and then it will only change to snow. We don't have much sunshine—"

"You must! You're tanned like an Indian," his sister exclaimed.

"That's rust! O'Neil wanted to get a record of the bright weather in Omar, so he put a man on the job to time it, but the experiment failed!"

"How so?"

"We didn't have a stop-watch in town. Now come! Nobody ever catches cold here—there isn't time."

He led the two girls ashore and up through the town to a moss-green bungalow, its newness attested by the yellow sawdust and fresh shavings which lay about. Amid their exclamations of delight he showed them the neatly furnished interior, and among other wonders a bedroom daintily done in white, with white curtains at the mullioned windows and a suite of wicker furniture.

"Where he dug all that up I don't know," Dan said, pointing to the bed and dresser and chairs. "He must have had it hidden out somewhere."

Eliza surveyed this chamber with wondering eyes. "It makes me feel quite ashamed," she said, "though, of course, he did it for Dan. When he discovers my abominable mission he'll probably set me out in the rain and break all my lead pencils. But—isn't he magnificent?"

"He quite overwhelms one," Natalie agreed. "Back in New York, he's been sending me American Beauties every week for more than a year. It's his princely way." She colored slightly, despite the easy frankness of her manner.

"Oh, he's always doing something like that," Dan informed them, whereupon his sister exclaimed:

"You see, Natalie! The man is a viper. If he let his beard grow I'm sure we'd see it was blue."

"You shall have an opportunity of judging," came O'Neil's voice from behind them, and he entered with hands outstretched, smiling at their surprise. When he had expressed his pleasure at Natalie's presence and had bidden both her and Eliza welcome to Omar, he explained:

"I've just covered eighteen miles on a railroad tricycle and my back is broken. The engines were busy, but I came, anyhow, hoping to arrive before the steamer. Now what is this I hear about my beard?"

It was Eliza's turn to blush, and she outdid Natalie.

"They were raving about your gallantry," said Dan with all a brother's ruthlessness, "until I told them it was merely a habit of mind with you; then Sis called you a Bluebeard."

O'Neil smiled, stroking his stubbly chin. "You see it's only gray."

"I—don't see," said Eliza, still flushing furiously.

"You would if I continued to let it grow."

"Hm-m! I think, myself, it's a sort of bluish gray," said Dan.

"You are still working miracles," Natalie told O'Neil, an hour later, while he was showing his visitors the few sights of Omar—"miracles of kindness, as usual."

Dan and his sister were following at a distance, arm in arm and chattering like magpies.

"No, no! That cottage is nothing. Miss Appleton had to have some place to stop."

"This all seems like magic." Natalie paused and looked over the busy little town. "And to think you have done it in a year."

"It was not I who did it; the credit belongs to those 'boys' of whom I told you. They are all here, by the way —Parker, McKay, Mellen, Sheldon, 'Doc' Gray—he has the hospital, you know."

"And Mr. Slater?"

"Oh, we couldn't exist without 'Happy Tom'! No, the only miracle about all this is the loyalty that has made it possible. It is that which has broken all records in railroad-building; that's what has pushed our tracks forward until we're nearly up to one of Nature's real miracles. You shall see those glaciers, one of these days. Sometimes I wonder if even the devotion of those men will carry us through the final test. But—you shall meet them all, to-night—my whole family."

"I can't. The ship leaves this afternoon."

"I've arranged to send you to Hope in my motor-boat, just as Mr. Gordon sent me on my way a year ago. You will stay with the Appletons to-night and help at the house-warming, then Dan will take you on in the morning. Women are such rare guests at Omar that we refuse to part with them. You agree?"

"How can I refuse? Your word seems to be law here. I'll send word to mother by the ship that I am detained by royal decree."

She spoke with a gaiety that seemed a little forced, and at mention of her departure a subtle change had come over her face. O'Neil realized that she had matured markedly since his last meeting with her; there was no longer quite the same effect of naïve girlishness.

"This was a very unhappy year for your loyal subject, Mr. O'Neil."

"I'm sorry," he declared with such genuine kindliness that she was moved to confide in him.

"Mother and I are ruined."

"Will you tell me about it?"

"It's merely—those wretched coal claims. I have a friend in the Land Office at Washington, and, remembering what you said, I asked him to look them up. I knew no other way to go about it. He tells me that something was done, or was not done, by us, and that we have lost all we put in."

"I urged Gordon to obey that ruling, last spring." Natalie saw that his face was dark with indignation, and the knowledge that he really cared set her heart to pounding gratefully. She was half tempted to tell about that other, that greater trouble which had stolen in upon her peace of mind and robbed her of her girlhood, but she shrank from baring her wounds—above all, a wound so vital and so personal as this.

"Does your mother know?" he queried.

"No, I preferred to tell her in Mr. Gordon's presence." Murray noticed that she no longer called the man uncle. "But now that the time has come, I'm frightened."

"Never allow yourself to be afraid. Fear is something false; it doesn't exist."

"It seems to me he was—unfaithful to his trust. Am I right?"

"That is something you must judge for yourself," he told her, gravely. "You see, I don't know anything about the reasons which prompted him to sacrifice your rights. He may have had very good reasons. I dare say he had. In building this railroad I have felt but one regret; that is the indirect effect it may have upon you and your mother.

Your affairs are linked closely with Gordon's and the success of my enterprise will mean the failure of his."

"You mustn't feel that way. I'm sure it won't affect us at all, for we have nothing more to lose. Sometimes I think his judgment is faulty, erratic, wonderful man though he is. Mother trusts him blindly, of course, and so do I, yet I hardly know what to do. It is impossible that he did worse than make a mistake."

Her dark eyes were bent upon Murray and they were eloquent with the question which she could not bring herself to ask. He longed to tell her frankly that Curtis Gordon was a charlatan, or even worse, and that his fairest schemes were doomed to failure by the very nature of his methods, but instead he said:

"I'm deeply distressed. I hope things are not as bad as you think and that Mr. Gordon will be able to straighten them out for you. If ever I can be of service you must be sure to call upon me."

Her thanks were conventional, but in her heart was a deep, warm gratitude, for she knew that he meant what he said and would not fail her.

Dan Appleton, eying Natalie and his chief from a distance, exclaimed, admiringly:

"She's a perfect peach, Sis. She registered a home run with me the first time at bat."

"She *is* nice."

"You know a fellow gets mighty lonely in a place like this. She'd make a dandy sister-in-law for you, wouldn't she?"

"Forget it!" said Eliza, sharply. "That's rank insubordination. Omar Khayyam snatched her from the briny and tried to die for her. He has bought her two acres of the most expensive roses and he remembers the date of her birthday. Just you keep your hands off."

"How does she feel about him?"

"Oh, she heroizes him, of course. I don't know just how deep the feeling goes, but I got the impression that it was pretty serious. Two women can't borrow hair-pins and mix powder puffs for a week and remain strangers."

"Then, as for Daniel Appleton, C.E., *good night!*" exclaimed her brother, ruefully. "If I were a woman I'd marry him myself, provided I could get ahead of the rush; but, being a male of the species, I suppose I shall creep out into the jungle and sulk."

"Right-o! Don't enter this race, for I'm afraid you'd be a bad loser! Personally I c ' see anything in him to rave about. What scares me ı the knowledge that I must tell him the wretched busıness that brings me here. If he strikes me, Danny, remember I'm still your sister."

When the big gong gave the signal for luncheon Appleton conducted Natalie and Eliza to the company messroom, where the field and office force dined together, and presented them to his fellow-lieutenants. At supper-time those who had been out on the line during the day were likewise introduced, and after a merry meal the whole party escorted the two girls back to the green bungalow.

"Why, here's a piano!" Eliza exclaimed upon entering the parlor.

"I borrowed it for the evening from the Elite Saloon," O'Neil volunteered. "It's a dissipated old instrument, and some of its teeth have been knocked out—in drunken brawls, I'm afraid—but the owner vouched for its behavior on this occasion."

"It knows only one tune—'I Won't Go Home until Morning,'" Dan declared.

McKay, however, promptly disproved this assertion by seating himself at the keyboard and rattling off some popular melodies. With music and laughter the long twilight fled, for O'Neil's "boys" flung themselves into the task of entertaining his guests with whole-souled enthusiasm.

So successful were their efforts that even "Happy Tom" appeared to derive a mild enjoyment from them, which was a testimonial indeed. His pleasure was made evident by no word of praise, nor faintest smile, but rather by the lightened gloom in which he chewed his gum and by the fact that he complained of nothing. In truth, he was not only entertained by the general gaiety, but he was supremely interested in Miss Appleton, who resembled no creature he had ever seen. He had met many girls like Natalie, and feared them, but Eliza, with her straightforward airs and her masculine mannerisms, was different. She affected him in a way at once pleasant and disagreeable. He felt no diffidence in speaking to her, for instance—a phenomenon which was in itself a ground for suspicion. Then, too, her clothes—he could not take his eyes off her clothes—were almost like Dan's. That seemed to show common sense, but was probably only the sign of an eccentric, domineering nature. On the other hand, the few words she addressed to him were gracious, and her eyes had a merry twinkle which warmed his heart. She must be all right, he reluctantly concluded, being Dan's sister and O'Neil's friend. But deep down in his mind he cherished a doubt.

At her first opportunity Eliza undertook to make that confession the thought of which had troubled her all the afternoon. Drawing O'Neil aside, she began with some trepidation, "Have you any idea why I'm here?"

"I supposed either you or Dan had achieved your pet ambition."

"Far from it. I have a fell purpose, and when you learn what it is I expect you to move the piano out—that's what always happens in the play when the heroine is dispossessed. Well, then, I've been sent by *The Review* to bare all the disgraceful secrets of your life!"

"I'm delighted to learn you'll be here so long. You can't possibly finish that task before next spring." His manner, though quizzical, was genuinely hearty.

"Don't laugh!" said the girl. "There's nothing funny about it. I came north as a spy."

"Then you're a Northern Spy!"

"Apples!" she cried. "You remembered, didn't you? I never supposed men like you could be flippant. Well, here goes for the worst." She outlined her conversation with the editor of her paper.

"So you think I'm trying to steal Alaska," he said when she had concluded.

"That seems to be the general idea."

"It's a pretty big job."

"Whoever controls transportation will have the country by the throat."

"Yet somebody must build railroads, since the Government won't. Did it ever occur to you that there is a great risk involved in a thing of this sort, and that capital must see a profit before it enters a new field? I wonder if you know how badly this country needs an outlet and how much greater the benefit in dollars and cents will be to the men in the interior than to those who finance the road. But I perceive that you are a conservationist."

"Rabid!" Eliza bridled a little at the hint of amused superiority in his voice. "I'm a suffragist, too! I dare say that adds to your disgust."

"Nonsense!" he protested. "I have no quarrel with conservation nor with 'votes for women.' Neither have I anything to conceal. I'm only afraid that, like most writers, you will be content with half-information. Incomplete facts are responsible for most misunderstandings. If you are in earnest and will promise to take the time necessary to get at all the facts, I'll make an agreement with you."

"I promise! Time and a typewriter are my only assets. I don't intend to be hurried."

Dan approached, drawn by the uncomfortable knowledge of his sister's predicament, and broke in:

"Oh, Sis has time to burn! She's going to write a book on the salmon canneries while she's here. It's bound to be one of the 'six best smellers'!"

O'Neil waved him away with the threat of sending him out among the mosquitoes.

"I'll agree to show you everything we're doing."

"Even to the coal-fields?"

"Even to them. You shall know everything, then you can write what you please."

"And when I've exposed you to the world as a commercial pickpocket, as a looter of the public domain—after Congress has appropriated your fabulous coal claims—will you nail up the door of this little cottage, and fire Dan?"

"No."

"Will you still be nice to me?"

"My dear child, you are my guest. Come and go when and where you will. Omar is yours so long as you stay, and when you depart in triumph, leaving me a broken, discredited wretch, I shall stand on the dock and wave you a bon voyage. Now it's bedtime for my 'boys,' since we rise at five o'clock."

"Heavens! Five! Why the sun isn't up at that time!"

"The sun shines very little here; that's why we want you to stay at Omar. I wish we might also keep Miss Natalie."

When the callers had gone Eliza told Natalie and Dan:

"He took it so nicely that I feel more ashamed than ever. One would think he didn't care at all. Do you suppose he does?"

"There's no denying that you appeared at an unfortunate time," said her brother.

"Why?"

"Well—I'm not sure we'll ever succeed with this project. Parker says the glacier bridge can be built, but the longer he studies it the graver he gets. It's making an old man of him."

"What does Mr. O'Neil say?"

"Oh, he's sanguine, as usual. He never gives up. But he has other things to worry him—money! It's money, money, all the time. He wasn't terribly rich, to begin with, and he has used up all his own fortune, besides what the other people put in. You see, he never expected to carry the project so far; he believed the Trust would buy him out."

"Well?"

"It hasn't and it evidently doesn't intend to. When it learned of his plan, its engineers beat it out to the glaciers and looked them over. Then they gave up their idea of building in from Cortez, but instead of making terms with us, they moved their whole outfit down to Kyak Bay, right alongside of the coal-fields, and now it has become a race to the glaciers, with Gordon fighting us on the side just to make matters lively. The Trust has the shorter route, but we have the start."

"Why didn't Mr. O'Neil take Kyak as a terminus, instead of Omar?"

"He says it's not feasible. Kyak is an open harbor, and he says no breakwater can be built there to withstand the storms. He still clings to that belief, although the Trust is actually building one. If they succeed we're cooked. Meanwhile he's rushing work and straining every nerve to raise more money. Now you come along with a proposal to advertise the whole affair to the public as a gigantic graft and set Congress against him. I think he treated you mighty well, under the circumstances."

"I won't act against my convictions," Eliza declared, firmly, "even if it means calamity to everybody."

Natalie spoke for the first time, her voice tuned to a

pitch of feeling that contrasted oddly with their conversational tones.

"If you hurt my Irish Prince," she said, "I shall hate you as long as I live."

IX   *Wherein Gordon Shows His Teeth*

Affairs at Hope were nearly, if not quite, as prosperous as those at Omar, for Curtis Gordon's advertising had yielded large and quick returns. His experiment, during the previous summer, of bringing his richest stockholders north, had been a great success. They had come, ostensibly at his expense, and once on the ground had allowed themselves to be fairly hypnotized. They had gone where he led, had seen what he pointed out, had believed what he told them. Their imaginations were fired with the grandeur of an undertaking which would develop the vast resources of the north country for the benefit of the struggling pioneers of the interior and humanity in general. Incidentally they were assured over and over again in a great variety of ways that the profits would be tremendous. Gordon showed them Hope and its half-completed mine buildings, he showed them the mountain behind. It was a large mountain. They noticed there were trees on the sides of it and snow on its top. They marveled. He said its heart was solid copper ore, and they gasped. Had he told them in the same impressive manner that the hill contained a vein three inches thick they would have exhibited the same astonishment. They entered the dripping tunnels and peered with grave approval at the drills, the rock-cars and the Montenegrin miners. They rambled over the dumps, to the detriment of shoe-leather and shins, filling their suit-cases with samples of perfectly good country rock. They confessed to each other, with admirable conservatism, that the proposition looked very promising, very promising indeed, and they listened with appreciation to Gordon's glowing accounts of his railroad enterprise, the physical evidence of which consisted of a mile or two of track which shrank along the steep shorefront and disappeared into a gulch as if ashamed of itself. He had a wonderful plan to consolidate the mining and railroad companies and talked of a giant holding corporation which would share in the profits of each. The details were intricate, but he seemed to see them all with perfect clearness, and his victims agreed.

He entertained them on a scale that was almost embarrassing, and when they returned to their homes they outdid one another in their praise of the financial genius who was leading them to the promised land of profits and preferred stock. As a matter of course they one and all advised their friends to buy, vouching for the fabulous richness of Hope Consolidated, and since their statements were backed by a personal examination of the property, subscriptions came pouring in.

All in all, the excursion had proven so profitable that Gordon had arranged for another, designed to accommodate new investors and promising "prospects." Preparations for their welcome were under way when Natalie arrived.

The girl and her mother talked late that evening, and Gordon saw on the following morning that Gloria, at least, had passed a trying night; but he gave himself no uneasiness. Emotional storms were not unusual; he always disregarded them as far as possible, and usually they passed off quietly. During breakfast he informed them:

"I received a letter from Miss Golden in yesterday's mail. She is to be one of the new party."

"Did you invite her to return this summer?" Mrs. Gerard inquired.

"Yes!"

"I remember her well," said Natalie—"too well, in fact. I thought her very bold."

"She is one of our largest investors, and she writes she would enjoy spending a fortnight here after the others go back."

"Will you allow it?"

"Allow it! My dear Gloria, I can't possibly refuse. In fact it would be the height of inhospitality not to urge her to do so. She is welcome to stay as long as she chooses, for these quarters are as much hers as ours. I hope you will be nice to her."

Mrs. Gerard made no answer, but later in the morning sought Gordon in his private office.

"I preferred not to discuss the Golden woman before Natalie," she explained, coldly, "but—you don't really intend to have her here, do you?"

"Most assuredly!"

"Then I shall have to tell her she is not welcome."

"You will do nothing of the sort, my dear: you will assume the duties of hostess, for which no one is more charmingly qualified."

Mrs. Gerard's lips were white with anger as she retorted:

"I shall not allow that woman under the same roof with Natalie."

"As usual, you choose the most inconvenient occasion for insisting upon your personal dislikes."

"My dislike has nothing to do with the matter. I overlooked her behavior with you last year—as I have overlooked a good many things in the past—but this is asking too much."

Gordon's coldness matched her own as he said:

"I repeat, this is no time for jealousy—"

"Jealousy! It's an insult to Natalie."

"Miss Golden is one of our largest stockholders."

"That's not true! I had Denny look up the matter."

"So!" Gordon flared up angrily. "Denny has been showing you the books, eh! He had no more right to do that than you had to pry into my affairs. While Miss Golden's investment may not be so large as some others', she has influential friends. She did yeoman service in the cause, and I can't allow your foolish fancies to interfere with my plans."

"Fancies!" cried the woman, furiously. "You behaved like a school-boy with her. It was disgraceful. I refuse to let her associate with my daughter."

"Aren't we drawing rather fine distinctions?" Gordon's lip curled. "In the first place, Natalie has no business here. Since she came, uninvited, for the second time, she must put up with what she finds. I warned you last summer that she might suspect—"

"She did. She does. She discovered the truth a year ago." Mrs. Gerard's usually impassive face was distorted and she voiced her confession with difficulty.

"The devil!" ejaculated Gordon.

The woman nodded. "She accused me last night. I tried to—lie, but—God! How I have lived through these hours I'll never know."

"Hm-m!" Gordon reflected, briefly. "Perhaps, after all, it's just as well that she knows; she would have found it out sooner or later, and there's some satisfaction in knowing that the worst is over."

Never before had his callous cynicism been so frankly displayed. It chilled her and made the plea she was about to voice seem doubly difficult.

"I wish I looked upon the matter as you do," she said, slowly. "But other people haven't the same social ideas as we. I'm—crushed, and she— Poor child! I don't know how she had the courage to face it. Now that she has heard the truth from my own lips I'm afraid it will kill her."

Gordon laughed. "Nonsense! Natalie is a sensible girl. Disillusionment is always painful, but never fatal. Sooner or later the young must confront the bald facts of life, and I venture to say she will soon forget her school-girl morality. Let me explain my views of—"

"Never!" cried the woman, aghast. "If you do I shall—" She checked herself and buried her face in her hands. "I feel no regrets for myself—for I drifted with my eyes open—but this—this is different. Don't you understand? I am a mother. Or are you dead to all decent feeling?"

"My dear, I'm the most tender-hearted of men. Of course I shall say nothing, if you prefer, for I am subservient to your commands in all things. But calm yourself. What is done cannot be undone."

In more even tones Mrs. Gerard said, "You seem to think the matter is ended, but it isn't. Natalie will never allow us to continue this way, and it isn't just to her that we should. We can't go on, Curtis."

"You mean I must marry you?"

She nodded.

He rose and paced the room before answering. "I always supposed you understood my views on that subject. Believe me, they are unalterable, and in no way the result of a pose."

"Nevertheless, for my sake and Natalie's you will do it.

I can't lose the one thing I love best in the world."

"It would seem that Natalie has filled your head with silly notions," he exclaimed, impatiently.

"She has awakened me. I have her life to consider as well as my own."

"We are all individuals, supreme in ourselves, responsible only to ourselves. We must all live our own lives; she cannot live yours, nor you hers."

"I am familiar with your arguments," Mrs. Gerard said, wearily, "but I have thought this all out and there is no other way."

He frowned in his most impressive manner and his chest swelled ominously.

"I will not be coerced. You know I can't be bullied into a thing. I deny that you have any right to demand—"

"I'm not demanding anything. I merely ask this—this favor, the first one I have ever asked. You see, my pride is crumbling. Don't answer now; let's wait until we are both calmer. The subject came up—at least she approached it, by asking about the coal claims. She is worried about them."

"Indeed?"

"She was told by a friend in the Land Office that our rights had been forfeited. I assured her—"

"I refused to heed the absurd rulings of the Department, if that is what she refers to."

"Then we—have lost?" Mrs. Gerard's pallor increased.

"Technically, yes! In reality I shall show that our titles were good and that our patents should issue."

"But"—the woman's bloodless fingers were tightly interlaced—"all I have, all Natalie has, is in those claims."

"Yes! And it would require another fortune the size of both to comply with the senseless vagaries of the Interior Department and to protect your interests. I grew weary of forever sending good hard-earned dollars after bad ones, merely because of the shifting whim of some theorist five thousand miles away."

"Then I am afraid—" Mrs. Gerard's voice trailed out miserably. "It is all we have, and you told me—"

Gordon broke in irritably: "My dear Gloria, spare me this painful faultfinding. If I can win for you, I shall do so, and then you will agree that I acted wisely. If I lose—it will merely be the luck of the average investor. We played for big returns, and of course the risks were great."

"But Mr. O'Neil told her his claims—"

Gordon's blazing eyes warned her. "O'Neil, eh? So, he is the 'friend in the Land Office'! No doubt he also gave Natalie the suggestion that led to her scene with you. Tell her to occupy herself less with affairs which do not concern her and more with her own conduct. Her actions with that upstart have been outrageous."

"What about your own actions with the Golden woman?" cried Mrs. Gerard, reverting with feminine insistence to the subject of their first difference. "What are you going to do about her?"

"Nothing."

"Remember, I refuse to share the same roof with her. You wouldn't ask it of your wife."

Now this second reference to a disagreeable subject was unfortunate. Gordon was given to the widest vagaries of temper, and this interview had exasperated him beyond measure, for he was strained by other worries. He exploded harshly:

"Please remember that you are not my wife! My ideas on matrimony will never change. You ought to know by this time that I am granite."

"I can't give up Natalie. I would give up much, for we women don't change, but—"

"A fallacy!" He laughed disagreeably. "Pardon me, Gloria, if I tell you that you do change; that you have changed; that time has left its imprint upon even you—a cruel fact, but true." He took a savage pleasure in her trembling, for she had roused all the devils in him and they were many.

"You are growing tired!"

"Not at all. But you have just voiced the strongest possible argument against marriage. We grow old! Age brings its alterations! I have ever been a slave to youth and beauty and the years bring to me only an increasing appreciation, a more critical judgment, of the beautiful. If I chose to marry—well, frankly, the mature charms of a woman of my own age would have slight attraction for me."

"Then—I will go," said Mrs. Gerard, faintly.

"Not by any wish of mine," he assured her. "You are quite welcome to stay. Things will run along in the usual way—more smoothly, perhaps, now that we have attained a complete understanding. You have no place to go, nor means with which to insure a living for yourself and Natalie. I would hate to see you sacrifice yourself and her to a Puritanical whim, for I owe you much happiness and I'm sure I should miss you greatly. Some one must rule, and since nature has given me the right I shall exercise it. We will have no more rebellion."

Mrs. Gerard left the room dazed and sick with despair.

"We must go! We must go!" she kept repeating, but her tragic look alarmed Natalie far more than her words.

"Yes, yes!" The girl took her in her arms and tried to still the ceaseless trembling which shook the mother's frame, while her own tears fell unheeded.

"We must go! Now!"

"Yes, dearest! But where?"

"You—love me still?" asked Gloria. "I suppose you need me, too, don't you? I hadn't thought of that."

"Every hour!" The round young arms pressed her closer. "You won't think of—of leaving me."

Mrs. Gerard shook her head slowly. "No! I suppose that must be part of the price. But— Penniless! Friendless! Where can we go?"

"Mr. O'Neil—my Irish Prince," faltered the daughter through her tears. "Perhaps he would take us in."

"Omar Khayyam," said Eliza Appleton, entering O'Neil's office briskly, "you are the general trouble man, so prepare to listen to mine."

"Won't the kitchen flue draw, or has a hinge come off the bungalow door?" Murray smiled. He was harassed by endless worries, a dozen pressing matters called for his instant attention; yet he showed no trace of annoyance. "If so, I'll be right up and fix it."

"The kitchen chimney has a draught that threatens to draw Dan's salary out with the smoke every time I cook a meal, and the house is dandy. This is a real man's-size tribulation, so of course I run to you. Simon Legree is at his tricks again."

"Legree!"

The girl nodded her blond head vigorously.

"Yes! He's stolen Mrs. St. Claire's slaves, and she and Little Eva are out in the cold."

"What the deuce are you talking about?"

"Gordon, of course, and the two Gerards, Natalie and Gloria—'Town Hall, To-night. Come one, Come all!'"

"Oh!" O'Neil's eyes brightened.

"There have been terrible goings-on over at Hope. I went up yesterday, in my official capacity, to reconnoiter the enemy's position and to give him a preliminary skirmish, but the great man was sulking in his tent and sent word by a menial for me to begone or look out for the bloodhounds. Isn't he the haughty thing? I don't like to 'begone'—I refuse to git when I'm told, so, of course, I paid my respects to Natalie and her mother. But what do you think I found? Mrs. St. Claire desolated, Eva dissolved in tears and her hair down."

"Will you talk sense?"

"Just try a little nonsense, and see. Well, the great eruption has taken place and the loss of life was terrible. Among those buried in the cinders are the dusky-eyed heroine and her friend mother. It seems Eva had a hand in the overseer's exposure—"

"Yes, yes! It's about those coal claims. I knew it was coming."

"She told her mother of the horrid treachery, and mother lugged the complaint to Gordon and placed it in his lap. Result, confession and defiance from him. Even the family jewels are gone."

"Is Gordon broke?"

"He's weltering in money, but the coal claims are lost, and he wants to know what they're going to do about it. The women are ruined. He magnanimously offers them his bounty, but of course they refuse to accept it."

"Hasn't he made any provision for them?"

"Coffee and cakes, three times a day. That's all! He won't even provide transportation, and the troupe can't walk home. They refuse to stay there, but they can't get away. I've cabled *The Review*, overdrawing my salary scandalously, and Dan is eager to help, but the worst of it is neither of those women knows how to make a living. Natalie wants to work, but the extent of her knowledge is the knack of frosting a layer cake, and her mother never even sewed on a button in all her life. It would make a lovely Sunday story, and it wouldn't help Curtis Gordon with his stockholders."

"You won't write it, of course!"

"Oh, I suppose not, but it's maddening not to be able to do something. Since there's a law against manslaughter, the pencil is my only weapon. I'd like to jab it clear through that ruffian." Eliza's animated face was very stern, her generous mouth was set firmly.

"You can leave out the personal element," he told her. "There's still a big story there, if you realize that it runs back to Washington and involves your favorite policy of conservation. Those claims belonged to Natalie and her mother. I happen to know that their locations were legal and that there was never any question of fraud in the titles, hence they were entitled to patents years ago. Gordon did wrong, of course, in refusing to obey the orders of the Secretary of the Interior even though he knew those orders to be senseless and contradictory, but the women are the ones to suffer. The Government froze them out. This is only one instance of what delay and indecision at headquarters has done. I'll show you others before we are through. As for those two— You say they want to do something?"

"It's not a question of wanting; they've *got* to do something—or starve. They would scrub kitchens if they knew how."

"Why didn't they come to me?"

"Do you need a cook and a dishwasher?"

Murray frowned. "Our new hotel is nearly finished; perhaps Mrs. Gerard would accept a position as—as hostess."

"*Hostess!* In a railroad-camp hotel! Who ever heard of such a thing?" Eliza eyed him incredulously.

O'Neil's flush did not go unnoticed as he said, quietly:

"It *is* unusual, but we'll try it. She might learn to manage the business, with a competent assistant. The salary will be ample for her and Natalie to live on."

Eliza laid a hand timidly upon his arm and said in an altered tone:

"Omar Khayyam, you're a fine old Persian gentleman! I know what it will mean to those two poor women, and I know what it will mean to you, for of course the salary will come out of your pocket."

He smiled down at her. "It's the best I can offer, and I'm sure you won't tell them."

"Of course not. I know how it feels to lose a fortune, too, for I've been through the mill— Don't laugh! You have a load on your shoulders heavier than Mr. Sinbad's, and it's mighty nice of you to let me add to the burden. I—I hope it won't break your poor back. Now I'm going up to your bungalow and lock myself into your white bedroom, and—"

"Have a good cry!" he said, noting the suspicious moisture in her eyes.

"Certainly not!" Eliza exclaimed, indignantly. "I'm not the least bit sentimental."

X *In which the Doctor Shows His Wit*

O'Neil's talk with Mrs. Gerard upon her arrival from Hope was short and businesslike. Neither by word nor look did he show that he knew or suspected anything of the real reason of her break with Gordon. Toward both her and Natalie he preserved his customary heartiness, and their first constraint soon disappeared. Mrs. Gerard had been plunged in one of those black moods in which it seems that no possible event can bring even a semblance of happiness, but it was remarkable how soon this state of mind began to give way before O'Neil's matter-of-fact cheerfulness. He refused to listen to their thanks and made them believe that they were conferring a real favor upon him by accepting the responsibility of the new hotel. Pending the completion of that structure he was hard pressed to find a lodging-place for them until Eliza and her brother insisted that they share the bungalow with them—a thing O'Neil had not felt at liberty to ask under the circumstances. Nor was the tact of the brother and sister less than his; they received the two unfortunates as honored guests.

Gradually the visitors began to feel that they were welcome, that they were needed, that they had an important task to fulfil, and the sense that they were really of service drove away depression. Night after night they lay awake, discussing the wonderful change in their fortunes and planning their future. Natalie at least had not the slightest doubt that all their troubles were at an end.

One morning they awoke to learn that O'Neil had gone to the States, leaving Dr. Gray in charge of affairs at Omar during his absence. The physician, who was fully in his chief's confidence, gravely discussed their duties with them, and so discreet was he that they had no faintest suspicion that he knew their secret. It was typical of O'Neil and his "boys" that they should show this chivalry toward two friendless outcasts; it was typical of them, also, that they one and all constituted themselves protectors of Natalie and her mother, letting it be known through the town that the slightest rudeness toward the women would be promptly punished.

While O'Neil's unexpected departure caused some comment, no one except his trusted lieutenants dreamed of the grave importance of his mission. They knew the necessities that hounded him, they were well aware of the trembling insecurity in which affairs now stood, but they maintained their cheerful industry, they pressed the work with unabated energy, and the road crept forward foot by foot, as steadily and as smoothly as if he himself were on the ground to direct it.

Many disappointments had arisen since the birth of the Salmon River & Northwestern; many misfortunes had united to retard the development of its builder's plans. The first obstacle O'Neil encountered was that of climate. During the summer, unceasing rains, mists, and fogs dispirited his workmen and actually cut their efficiency in half. He had made certain allowances for this, of course, but no one could have foreseen so great a percentage of inefficiency as later developed. In winter, the cold was intense and the snows were of prodigious depth, while outside the shelter of the Omar hills the winds howled and rioted over the frozen delta, chilling men and animals and paralyzing human effort. Under these conditions it was hard to get workmen, and thrice harder to keep them;

so that progress was much slower than had been anticipated.

Then, too, the physical difficulties of the country were almost insurmountable. The morass which comprised the Salmon River plain was in summer a bottomless ooze, over which nothing could be transported, yet in winter it became sheathed with a steel-hard armor against which piling splintered. It could be penetrated at that season only by the assistance of steam thawers, which involved delay and heavy expense. These were but samples of the obstacles that had to be met, and every one realized that the work thus far had been merely preparatory. The great obstruction, upon the conquest of which the success of the whole undertaking hinged, still lay before them.

But of all handicaps the most serious by far was the lack of capital. Murray had foreseen as inevitable the abandonment by the Trust of its Cortez route, but its change of base to Kyak had come as a startling surprise and as an almost crushing blow. Personally, he believed its present plan to be even more impracticable than its former one, but its refusal to buy him out had disheartened his financial associates and tightened their purse-strings into a knot which no argument of his could loose. He had long since exhausted his own liquid capital, he had realized upon his every available asset, and his personal credit was tottering. He was obliged to finance his operations upon new money—a task which became ever more difficult as the months passed and the Trust continued its work at Kyak. Yet he knew that the briefest flagging, even a temporary abandonment of work, meant swift and utter ruin. His track must go forward, his labor must be paid, his supplies must not be interrupted. He set his jaws and fought on stubbornly, certain of his ultimate triumph if only he could hold out.

A hundred miles to the westward was a melancholy example of failure in railroad-building, in the form of two rows of rust upon a weed-grown embankment. It was all that remained of another enterprise which had succumbed to financial starvation, and the wasted millions it represented was depressing to consider.

Thus far O'Neil's rivalry with the Trust had been friendly, if spirited, but his action in coming to the assistance of Mrs. Gerard and her daughter raised up a new and vigorous enemy whose methods were not as scrupulous as those of the Heidlemanns.

Gordon was a strangely unbalanced man. He was magnetic, his geniality was really heart-warming, yet he was perfectly cold-blooded in his selfishness. He was cool and calculating, but interference roused him to an almost insane pitch of passion. Fickle in most things, he was uncompromising in his hatreds. O'Neil's generosity in affording sanctuary to his defiant mistress struck him as a personal affront, and it fanned his dislike of his rival into a consuming rage. It was with no thought of profit that he cast about for a means of crippling O'Neil. He was quite capable of ruining himself, not to speak of incidental harm to others, if only he could gratify his spleen.

Denny, his trusted jackal, resisted stoutly any move against "The Irish Prince," but his employer would not listen to him or consent to any delay. Therefore, a certain plausible, shifty-eyed individual by the name of Linn was despatched to Omar on the first steamer. Landing at his destination, Mr. Linn quietly effaced himself, disappearing out the right-of-way, where he began moving from camp to camp, ostensibly in search of employment.

It was a few days later, perhaps a week after O'Neil's departure, that Eliza Appleton entered the hospital and informed Dr. Gray:

"I've finished my first story for *The Review*."

The big physician had a rapid, forceful habit of speech. "Well, I suppose you uncorked the vitriol bottle," he said, brusquely.

"No! Since you are now the fount of authority here, I thought I'd tell you that I have reserved my treachery for another time. I haven't learned enough yet to warrant real fireworks. As a matter of fact, I've been very kind to Mr. O'Neil in my story."

"Let me thank you for him."

"Now don't be sarcastic! I could have said a lot of nasty things, if he hadn't been so nice to me. I suppose it is the corrupting influence of his kindness."

"He really will be grateful," the doctor assured her, seriously. "Newspaper publicity of the wrong sort might hurt him a great deal just now. In every big enterprise there comes a critical time, when everything depends upon one man; strong as the structure seems, he's really supporting it. You see, the whole thing rests ultimately on credit and confidence. An ill-considered word, a little unfriendly shove, and down comes the whole works. Then some financial power steps in, reorganizes the wreckage, and gets the result of all the other fellow's efforts, for nothing."

"Dan tells me the affairs of the S. R. & N. are in just such a tottering condition."

"Yes. We're up against it, for the time being. Our cards are on the table, and you have it in your power to do us a lot of harm."

"Don't put it that way!" said Eliza, resentfully. "You and Mr. O'Neil and even Dan make it hard for me to do my duty. I won't let you rob me of my liberty. I'll get out and 'Siwash' it in a tent first."

The physician laughed. "Don't mistake leaf-mold for muck, that's all we ask. O'Neil is perfectly willing to let you investigate him."

"Exactly! And I could bite off his head for being so nice about it. Not that I've discovered anything against him, for I haven't—I think he's fine—but I object to the principle of the thing."

"He'll never peep, no matter what you do or say."

"It makes me furious to know how superior he is. I never detested a man's virtues as I do his. Gordon is the sort I like, for he needs exposing, and expects it. Wait until I get at him and the Trust."

"The Trust, too, eh?"

"Of course."

"Now what have the Heidlemanns done?"

"It's not what they have done; it's what they're going to do. They're trying to grab Alaska."

Dr. Gray shook his head impatiently, but before he could make answer Tom Slater entered and broke into the conversation by announcing:

"I've spotted him, Doc. His name is Linn, and he's Gordon's hand. He's at mile 24 and fifty men are quitting from that camp."

"That makes two hundred, so far," said the doctor.

"He's offering a raise of fifty cents a day and transportation to Hope."

Gray scowled and Eliza inquired quickly:

"What's wrong, Uncle Tom?"

"Don't call me 'Uncle Tom,'" Slater exclaimed, irritably; "I ain't related to you."

Miss Appleton smiled at him sweetly. "I had a dear friend once—you remind me of him, he was such a splendid big man," she said.

Tom eyed her suspiciously.

"He chewed gum incessantly, too, and declared that it never hurt anybody."

"It never did," asserted Slater.

"We pleaded, we argued, we did our best to save him, but—" She shook her blond head sadly.

"What happened to him?"

"What always happens? He lingered along for a time, stubborn to the last, then—" Turning abruptly to Dr. Gray, she asked, "Who is this man Linn, and what is he doing?"

"He's an emissary of Curtis Gordon and he's hiring our men away from us," snapped the physician.

"Why, Dan tells me Mr. O'Neil pays higher wages than anybody!"

"So he does, but Linn offers a raise. We didn't know what the trouble was till over a hundred men had quit. The town is full of them, now, and it's becoming a stampede."

"Can't you meet the raise?"

"That wouldn't do any good."

Tom agreed. "Gordon don't want these fellows. He's doing it to get even with Murray for those wo—" He bit his words in two at a glance from Gray. "What happened to the man that chewed gum?" he demanded abruptly.

"Oh yes! Poor fellow! We warned him time and again, but he was a sullen brute, he wouldn't heed advice. Why don't you bounce this man Linn? Why don't you run him out of camp?"

"Fine counsel from a champion of equal rights!" smiled Gray. "You forget we have laws and Gordon has a press bureau. It would antagonize the men and cause a lot of trouble in the end. What O'Neil could do personally, he can't do as the president of the S. R. & N. It would give us a black eye."

"We've got to do something dam' quick," said Slater, "or else the work will be tied up. That would 'crab' Murray's deal. I've got a pick-handle that's itching for Linn's head." The speaker coughed hollowly and complained: "I've got a bad cold on my chest—feels like pneumonia, to me. Wouldn't that be just my luck?"

"Do you have pains in your chest?" inquired the girl, solicitously.

"Terrible! But I'm so full of pains that I get used to 'em."

"It isn't pneumonia."

Slater flared up at this, for he was jealous of his sufferings.

"It's gumbago!" Eliza declared.

Dr. Gray's troubled countenance relaxed into a grin as he said:

"I'll give you something to rub on those leather lungs—harness-oil, perhaps."

"Is this labor trouble really serious?" asked the girl.

"Serious! It may knock us out completely. Go away now and let me think. Pardon my rudeness, Miss Appleton, but—"

Slater paused at the door.

"Don't think too long, Doc," he admonished him, "for there's a ship due in three days, and by that time there won't be a 'rough-neck' left on the job. It'll take a month to get a new crew from the States, and then it wouldn't be any good till it was broke in."

When he was alone the doctor sat down to weigh the news "Happy Tom" had brought, but the more squarely he considered the matter the more alarming it appeared. Thus far the S. R. & N. had been remarkably free from labor troubles. To permit them to creep in at this stage would be extremely perilous: the briefest cessation of work might, and probably would, have a serious bearing upon O'Neil's efforts to raise money. Gray felt the responsibility of his position with extraordinary force, for his chief's fortunes had never suffered in his hands and he could not permit them to do so now. But how to meet this move of Gordon's he did not know; he could think of no means of keeping these men at Omar. As he had told Eliza, to meet the raise would be useless, and a new scale of wages once adopted would be hard to reduce. Successful or unsuccessful in its effect, it would run into many thousands of dollars. The physician acknowledged himself dreadfully perplexed; he racked his brain uselessly, yearning meanwhile for the autocratic power to compel obedience among his men. He would have forced them back to their jobs had there been a way, and the fact that they were duped only added to his anger.

It occurred to him to quarantine the town, a thing he could easily do as port physician in case of an epidemic, but Omar was unusually healthy, and beyond a few surgical cases his hospital was empty.

His meditations were interrupted by Tom Slater, who returned to say:

"Give me that dope, Doc; I'm coughing like a switch engine." Gray rose and went to the shelves upon which his drugs were arranged, while the fat man continued, "That Appleton girl has got me worried with her foolishness. Maybe I *am* sick; anyhow, I feel rotten. What I need is a good rest and a nurse to wait on me."

The physician's eyes in running along the rows of bottles encountered one labeled "Oleum Tiglii," and paused there.

"You need a rest, eh?" he inquired, mechanically.

"If I don't get one I'll wing my way to realms eternal. I ain't been dried off for three months." Gray turned to regard his caller with a speculative stare, his fingers toyed with the bottle. "If it wasn't for this man Linn I'd lay off—I'd go to jail for him. But I can't do anything, with one foot always in the grave."

The doctor's face lightened with determination.

"Tom, you've been sent from heaven!"

"D'you mean I've been sent for, from heaven?" The invalid's red cheeks blanched, into his mournful eyes leaped a look of quick concern. "Say! Am I as sick as all that?"

"This will make you feel better." Gray uncorked the bottle and said, shortly, "Take off your shirt."

"What for?"

"I'm going to rub your chest and arms."

Slater obeyed, with some reluctance, pausing to inquire, doubtfully:

"You ain't stripping me down so you can operate?"

"Nonsense!"

"I'm feeling pretty good again."

"It's well to take these things early. They all look alike at the beginning."

"What things?"

"Grippe, gumbago, smallpox——"

"God'lmighty!" exclaimed Slater with a start. "I haven't got anything but a light cold."

"Then this liniment ought to be just the thing."

"Humph! It don't smell like liniment," Tom declared, after a moment, but the doctor had fallen to work on him and he submitted with resignation.

Perhaps an hour later Dr. Gray appeared at the Appleton bungalow and surprised Eliza by saying:

"I've come to you for some help. You're the only soul in Omar that I can trust."

"Have you gone raving mad?" she inquired.

"No. I must put an end to Linn's activity or we'll be ruined. These workmen must be held in Omar, and you must help me do it."

"They have the right to go where they please."

"Of course, but Gordon will let them out as soon as he has crippled us. Tell me, would you like to be a trained nurse?"

"No, I would not," declared Eliza, vehemently. "I'm neither antiseptic nor prophylactic."

"Nevertheless, you're going to be one—Tom needs you."

"Tom? What ails him?"

"Nothing at this moment, but—wait until tomorrow." The physician's eyes were twinkling, and when he had explained the cause of his amusement Eliza laughed.

"Of course I'll help," she said. "But it won't hurt the poor fellow, will it?"

"Not in the least, unless it frightens him to death. Tom's an awful coward about sickness; that's why I need some one like you to take care of him. He'll be at the hospital to-morrow at three. If you'll arrange to be there we'll break the news to him gently. I daren't tackle it alone."

Tom was a trifle embarrassed at finding Eliza in Dr. Gray's office when he entered, on the next afternoon. The boss packer seemed different than usual; he was much subdued. His cough had disappeared, but in its place he suffered a nervous apprehension; his cheeks were pale, the gloom in his eyes had changed to a lurking uneasiness.

"Just dropped in to say I'm all right again," he announced in an offhand tone.

"That's good!" said Gray. "You don't look well, however."

"I'm feeling fine!" Mr. Slater hunched his shoulders as if the contact of his shirt was irksome to the flesh.

"You'd better let me rub you. Why are you scratching yourself?"

"I ain't scratching."

"You were!" The doctor was sternly curious; he had assumed his coldest and most professional air.

"Well, if I scratched, I probably itched. That's why people scratch, ain't it?"

"Let me look you over."

"I can't spare the time, Doc—"

"Wait!" Gray's tone halted the speaker as he turned to leave. "I'm not going to let you out in this weather until I rub you."

This time there was no mistaking "Happy Tom's" pallor. "I tell you I feel great," he declared in a shaking voice. "I haven't felt so good for years."

"Come, come! Step into the other room and take off your shirt."

"Not on your life."

"What do you mean?"

"I don't want no more of your dam' liniment."

"Why?"

"Because I'm—because I don't."

"Then I suppose I'll have to throw and hog-tie you." The physician rose and laid a heavy hand upon his patient's arm, at which Tom exclaimed:

"Ouch! Leggo! Gimme the stuff and I'll rub myself."

"Tom!" The very gravity of the speaker's voice was portentous, alarming. Mr. Slater hesitated, his gaze wavered, he scratched his chest unconsciously.

Eliza shook her head pityingly; she uttered an inarticulate murmur of concern.

"You couldn't get my shirt off with a steam-winch. I tell you I'm feeling grand."

"Why *will* you chew the horrid stuff?" Miss Appleton inquired sadly.

"I'm just a little broke out, that's all."

"Ah! You're broken out. I feared so," said the doctor.

The grave concern in those two faces was too much for Slater's sensitive nature; his stubbornness gave way, his self-control vanished, and he confessed wretchedly:

"I spent an awful night, Doc. I'll bust into flame if this keeps up. What is it, anyhow?"

"Is there an eruption of the arms and chest?"

"They're all erupted to hell."

Dr. Gray silently parted the shirt over Slater's bosom. "Hm-m!" said he.

"Tell him what it is," urged Eliza, in whom mirth and pity were struggling for mastery.

"It has every appearance of—smallpox!"

The victim uttered a choking cry and sat down limply. Sweat leaped out upon his face, beads appeared upon his round bald head.

"I knew I was a sick man. I've felt it coming on for three months, but I fought it off for Murray's sake. Say it's chicken-pox," he pleaded.

"Never mind; it's seldom serious," Eliza endeavored to comfort the stricken man.

"You wanted a good rest—"

"I don't. I want to work."

"I'll have to quarantine you, Tom."

Slater was in no condition for further resistance; a complete collapse of body and mind had followed the intelligence of his illness. He began to complain of many symptoms, none of which were in any way connected with his fancied disease. He was racked with pains, he suffered a terrible nausea, his head swam; he spoke bravely of his destitute family and prepared to make his will. When he left the hospital, an hour later, it was on a stretcher between four straining bearers.

That evening a disturbing rumor crept through the town of Omar. It penetrated the crowded saloons where

the laborers who had quit work were squandering their pay,
and it caused a brief lull in the ribaldry; but the mere
fact that Tom Slater had come down with smallpox and
had been isolated upon a fishing-boat anchored in the
creek seemed, after all, of little consequence. Some of the
idlers strolled down the street to stare at the boat, and
upon their return verified the report. They also announced
that they had seen the yellow-haired newspaper woman
aboard, all dressed in white. It was considered high time
by the majority to leave Omar, for an epidemic was a
thing to be avoided, and a wager was made that the
whole force would quit in a body as soon as the truth
became known.

On the second day Dr. Gray undertook to allay the
general uneasiness, but, upon being pressed, reluctantly
acknowledged that his patient showed all the signs of the
dread disease. This hastened the general preparations for
departure, and when the incoming steamer hove in sight
every laborer was at the dock with his kit-bag. It excited
some idle comment among them to note that Dr. Gray had
gone down the bay a short distance to meet the ship,
and his efforts to speak to it were watched with interest and
amusement. Obviously it would have been much easier
for him to wait until she landed, for she came right on
and drew in toward the wharf. It was not until her bow
line was made fast that the physician succeeded in haling
the captain. Then the deserters were amazed to hear the
following conversation:

"I can't let you land, Captain Johnny," came from Dr.
Gray's launch.

"And why can't you?" demanded Brennan from the
bridge of his new ship. "Have you some prejudice against
the Irish?" The stern hawser was already being run out,
and the crowd was edging closer, waiting for the gangplank.

"There is smallpox here, and as health officer I've
quarantined the port."

There came a burst of Elizabethan profanity from the
little skipper, but it was drowned by the shout from shore
as the full meaning of the situation finally came home.
Then the waiting men made a rush for the ship. She had
not touched as yet, however, and the distance between

her and the pier was too great to leap. Above the confusion came Brennan's voice, through a megaphone, commanding them to stand back. Some one traitorously cast off the loop of the bow line, the ship's propellers began to thrash, and the big steel hull backed away inch by inch, foot by foot, until, amid curses and cries of rage, she described a majestic circle and plowed off up the sound toward Hope.

By a narrow margin the physician reached his hospital ahead of the infuriated mob, and it was well that he did so, for they were in a lynching mood. But, once within his own premises, he made a show of determined resistance that daunted them, and they sullenly retired. That night Omar rang with threats and deep-breathed curses, and Eliza Appleton, in the garb of a nurse, tended her patient cheerfully.

To the delegation which waited upon him the next morning, Dr. Gray explained the nature of his duties as health officer, informing them coolly that no living soul could leave Omar without incurring legal penalities. Since he could prevent any ships from landing, and inasmuch as the United States marshal was present to enforce the quarantine, he seemed to be master of the situation.

"How long will we be tied up?" demanded the spokesman of the party.

"That is hard to say."

"Well, we're going to leave this camp!" the man declared, darkly.

"Indeed? Where are you going?"

"We're going to Hope. You might as well let us go. We won't stand for this."

The physician eyed him coldly. "You won't? May I ask how you are going to help yourselves?"

"We're going to leave on the next steamer."

"Oh, no you're not!" the marshal spoke up.

"See here, Doc! There's over two hundred of us and we can't stay here; we'll go broke."

Gray shrugged his broad shoulders. "Sorry," he said, "but you see I've no choice in the matter. I never saw a case of smallpox that looked worse."

"It's a frame-up," growled the spokesman. "Tom hasn't got smallpox any more than I have. You cooked it to keep us here." There was an angry second to this, whereupon the doctor exclaimed:

"You think so, eh? Then just come with me."

"Where?"

"Out to the boat where he is. I'll show you."

"You won't show me no smallpox," asserted one of the committee.

"Then *you* come with me," the physician urged the leader.

"So you can bottle me up, too? No, thank you!"

"Get the town photographer with his flashlight. We'll help him make a picture; then you can show it to the others. I promise not to quarantine you."

After some hesitation the men agreed to this; the photographer was summoned and joined the party on its way to the floating pest-house.

It was not a pleasant place in which they found Tom Slater, for the cabin of the fishing-boat was neither light nor airy, but Eliza had done much to make it agreeable. The sick man was propped up in his bunk and playing solitaire, but he left off his occupation to groan as the newcomers came alongside.

When the cause of the visit had been made known, however, he rebelled.

"I won't pose for no camera fiend," he declared, loudly. "It ain't decent and I'm too sick. D'you take me for a bearded lady or a living skeleton?"

"These men think you're stalling," Dr. Gray told him.

"Who? Me?" Slater rolled an angry eye upon the delegation. "I ain't sick, eh? I s'pose I'm doing this for fun? I wish you had it, that's all."

The three members of the committee of investigation wisely halted at the foot of the companionway stairs where the fresh air fanned them; they were nervous and ill at ease.

Drawing his covers closer, Slater shouted:

"Close that hatch, you bone-heads! I'm blowing away!"

The photographer ventured to remonstrate.

"It's mighty close in here, Doc. Is it safe to breathe the bugs?"

"Perfectly safe," Gray assured him. "At least Miss Appleton hasn't suffered yet."

As a matter of fact the patient betrayed no symptoms of a wasting illness, for his cheeks were ruddy, he had eaten three hearty meals each day, and the enforced rest had done him good, so the committee saw nothing about him to satisfy their suspicions. But when Tom weakly called upon them for assistance in rising they shrank back and one of them exclaimed:

"I wouldn't touch you with a fish-pole."

Eliza came forward, however; she permitted her charge to lean upon her while she adjusted the pillows at his back; but when Dr. Gray ordered him to bare his breast and arms Slater refused positively. He blushed, he stammered, he clutched his nightrobe with a horny hand which would have required a cold chisel to loosen, and not until Eliza had gone upon deck would he consent to expose his bulging chest.

But Miss Appleton had barely left the cabin when she was followed by the most timid member of the delegation. He plunged up the stairs, gasping:

"I've saw enough! He's got it, and got it bad."

A moment later came the dull sound of the exploding flashlight, then a yell, and out of the smoke stumbled his two companions. The spokesman, it appeared, had also seen enough—too much—for with another yell he leaped the rail and made for shore. Fortunately the tide was out and the water low; he left a trail across the mud flat like that of a frightened hippopotamus.

When the two conspirators were finally alone upon the deck they rocked in each other's arms, striving to stifle their laughter. Meanwhile from the interior of the cabin came the feeble moans of the invalid.

That evening hastily made photographs of the sick man were shown upon the streets. Nor could the most skeptical deny that he presented a revolting sight and one warranting Dr. Gray's precautions. In spite of this evidence, however, threats against the physician continued to be made freely; but when Eliza expressed fears for his safety he only smiled grimly, and he stalked through the streets with such defiance written on his heavy features that no man dared raise a hand against him.

Day after day the quarantine continued, and at length some of the men went back to work. As others ex-

hausted their wages they followed. In a fortnight Omar
was once more free of its floating population and work
at the front was going forward as usual. Meanwhile the
patient recovered in marvelous fashion and was loud in
his thanks to the physician who had brought him through
so speedily. Yet Gray stubbornly refused to raise the
embargo.

Finally the cause of the whole trouble appeared at the
hospital and begged to be released.

"You put it over me," said Mr. Linn. "I've had enough
and I want to get out."

"I don't know what you're talking about," answered
the doctor. "No one can leave here now."

"I know it wasn't smallpox at all, but it worked
just the same. I'll leave your men alone if you'll let me
go out on the next Seattle steamer."

"But—I thought you came from Hope?" Gray said,
blandly.

Mr. Linn shifted his eyes and laughed uneasily. "I did,
and I'm going to keep coming from Hope. You don't
think I'd dare to go back after this, do you?"

"Why not?"

"Gordon would kill me."

"So! Mr. Gordon sent you?"

"You know he did. But—I've got to get out now. I'm
broke."

"I didn't think it of Gordon!" The doctor shook his
head sadly. "How underhanded of him!"

Linn exploded desperately: "Don't let's fourflush. You
were too slick for him, and you sewed me up. I've spent
the money he gave me and now I'm flat."

"You look strong. We need men."

Gordon's emissary turned pale. "Say! You wouldn't set
me to work? Why, those men would string me up."

"I think not. I've spoken to the shift boss at mile 30,
and he'll take care you're not hurt so long as you work
hard and keep your mouth shut."

An hour later Mr. Linn, cursing deeply, shouldered his
pack and tramped out the grade, nor could he obtain
food or shelter until he had covered those thirty weary
miles. Once at his destination, he was only too glad to
draw a numbered tag and fall to work with pick and

shovel, but at his leisure he estimated that it would take
him until late the following month to earn his fare to the
States.

XI   *The Two Sides of Eliza*
Violet Appleton

Dan Appleton entered the bungalow one evening, wet and
tired from his work, to find Eliza pacing the floor in
agitation.

"What's the matter, Sis?" he inquired, with quick concern.

His sister pointed to a copy of *The Review* which that
day's mail had brought.

"Look at that!" she cried. "Read it!"

"Oh! Your story, eh?"

"Read it!"

He read a column, and then glanced up to find her
watching him with angry eyes.

"Gee! That's pretty rough on the chief, Kid. I thought
you liked him," he said, gravely.

"I do! I do! Don't you understand, dummy? I didn't
write that! They've changed my story—distorted it. I'm—
furious!"

Dan whistled softly. "I didn't suppose they'd try anything
like that, but—they did a good job while they were at it.
Why, you'd think O'Neil was a grafter and the S. R. & N.
nothing but a land-grabbing deal."

"How *dared* they?" the girl cried. "The actual changes
aren't so many—just enough to alter the effect of the
story—but that's what makes it so devilish. For instance,
I described the obstacles and the handicaps Mr. O'Neil has
had to overcome in order to show the magnitude of his
enterprise, but Drake has altered it so that the physical
conditions here seem to be insuperable and he makes me
say that the road is doomed to failure. That's the way
he changed it all through."

"It may topple the chief's plans over; they're very in-
secure. It plays right into the hands of his enemies, too,

and of course Gordon's press bureau will make the most of it."

"Heavens! I want sympathy, not abuse!" wailed his sister. "It's all due to the policy of *The Review*. Drake thinks everybody up here is a thief. I dare say they are, but—How can I face Mr. O'Neil?"

Dan shook the paper in his fist. "Are you going to stand for this?" he demanded.

"Hardly! I cabled the office this morning, and here's Drake's answer." She read:

"'Stuff colorless. Don't allow admiration warp judgment.' Can you beat that?"

"He thinks you've surrendered to Murray, like all the others."

"I hate him!" cried Eliza. "I detest him!"

"Who? O'Neil or Drake?"

"Both. Mr. O'Neil for putting me in the position of a traitor, and Drake for presuming to rewrite my stuff. I'm going to resign, and I'm going to leave Omar before Murray O'Neil comes back."

"Don't be a quitter, Sis. If you throw up the job the paper will send somebody who will lie about us to suit the policy of the office. Show 'em where they're wrong; show 'em what this country needs. You have your magazine stories to write."

Eliza shook her head. "Bother the magazines and the whole business! I'm thinking about Mr. O'Neil. I—I could cry. I suppose I'll have to stay and explain to him, but—then I'll go home."

"No! You'll stay right here and go through with this thing. I need you."

"You? What for?"

"You can perform a great and a signal service for your loving brother. He's in terrible trouble!"

"What's wrong, Danny?" Eliza's anger gave instant place to solicitude. "You—you haven't *stolen* anything?"

"Lord, no! What put that into your head?"

"I don't know—except that's the worst thing that could happen to us. I like to start with the worst."

"I can't sulk in the jungle any more. I'm a rotten loser, Sis."

"Oh! You mean—Natalie? You—like her?"

"For a writer you select the most foolish words! Like, love, adore, worship—words are no good, anyway. I'm dippy; I'm out of my head; I've lost my reason. I'm deliriously happy and miserably unhappy. I—"

"That's enough!" the girl exclaimed. "I can imagine the rest."

"It was a fatal mistake for her to come to Omar, and to this very house, of all places, where I could see her every day. I might have recovered from the first jolt if I'd never seen her again, but—" He waved his hands hopelessly. "I'm beginning to hate O'Neil."

"You miserable traitor!" gasped Eliza.

"Yep! That's me! I'm dead to loyalty, lost to the claims of friendship. I've fought myself until I'm black in the face, but—it's no use. I must have Natalie!"

"She's crazy about O'Neil."

"Seems to be, for a fact, but that doesn't alter my fix. I can't live this way. You must help me or I'll lose my reason."

"Nonsense! You haven't any or you wouldn't talk like this. What can I do?"

"It's simple! Be nice to Murray and—and win him away from her."

Eliza stared at him as though she really believed him daft. Then she said, mockingly:

"Is that all? Just make him love me?"

Dan nodded. "That would be fine, if you could manage it."

"Why—you—you—I—" She gasped uncertainly for terms in which to voice her indignant surprise. "Idiot!" she finally exclaimed.

"Thanks for such glowing praise," Dan said, forlornly. "I feel a lot worse than an idiot. An idiot is not necessarily evil; at heart he may be likable, and pathetic, and merely unfortunate—"

"You simply can't be in earnest!"

"I am, though!" He turned upon her eyes which had grown suddenly old and weary with longing.

"You poor, foolish boy! In the first place, Mr. O'Neil will hate me for this story. In the second place, no man would look at me. I'm ugly—"

"I think you're beautiful."

"With my snub nose, and big mouth, and—"

"You can make him laugh, and when a woman can make a fellow laugh the rest is easy."

"In the third place I'm mannish and—vulgar, and besides—I don't care for him."

"Of course you don't, or I wouldn't ask it. You see, we're taking no risks! You can at least take up his attention and—and when you see him making for Natalie you can put out your foot and trip him up."

"It wouldn't be honorable, Danny."

"Possibly! But that doesn't make any difference with me. You may as well realize that I've got beyond the point where nice considerations of that sort weigh with me. If you'd ever been in love you'd understand that such things don't count at all. It's your chance to save the reason and happiness of an otherwise perfectly good brother."

"There is nothing I wouldn't do for your happiness— nothing. But— Oh, it's preposterous!"

Dan relapsed into gloomy silence, and they had a very uncomfortable meal. Unable to bear his continued lack of spirits, Eliza again referred to the subject, and tried until late in the evening to argue him out of his mood. But the longer they talked the more plainly she saw that his feeling for Natalie was not fanciful, but sincere and deep. She continued to scout his suggestion that she could help him by captivating O'Neil, and stoutly maintained that she had no attraction for men; nevertheless, when she went to her room she examined herself critically in her mirror. This done, she gave herself over to her favorite relaxation.

First she exchanged her walking-skirt, her prim shirt-waist and jacket, for a rose-pink wrapper which she furtively brought out of a closet. It was a very elaborate wrapper, all fluffy lace and ruffles and bows, and it had cost Eliza a sum which she strove desperately to forget. She donned silk stockings and a pair of tiny bedroom slippers; then seating herself once more at her dresser, she let down her hair. She invariably wore it tightly drawn back—so tightly, in fact, that Dan had more than once complained that it pulled her eyebrows out of place. On this occasion, however, she crimped it, she curled it, she brought it forward about her face in soft riotous puffs and strands, patting it into becoming shape with dexterous fingers until it formed a golden frame for her piquant features.

Now this was no unusual performance for her. In the midnight solitude of her chamber she regularly gave rein to the feminine side of her nature. By day she was the severe, matter-of-fact, businesslike Eliza Appleton, deaf to romance, lost to illusion, and unresponsive to masculine attention; but deep in her heart were all the instincts and longings of femininity, and at such times as this they came uppermost. Her bedroom had none of the Puritanical primness which marked her habit of dress; it was in no way suggestive of the masculine character which she so proudly paraded upon the street. On the contrary, it was a bower of daintiness, and was crowded with all the senseless fripperies of a school-girl. Carefully hidden away beneath her starched shirtwaists was much lingerie—bewildering creations to match the pink wrapper—and this she petted and talked to adoringly when no one could hear.

Eliza read much when she was unobserved—romances and improbable tales of fine ladies and gallant squires. There were times, too, when she wrote, chewing her pencil in the perplexities of vividly colored love scenes; but she always destroyed these manuscripts before the curious sun could spy upon her labors. In such ecstatic flights of fancy the beautiful heroine was a languorous brunette with hair of raven hue and soulful eyes in which slumbered the mystery of a tropic night. She had a Grecian nose, moreover, and her name was Violet.

From all this it may be gathered that Eliza Appleton was by no means the extraordinary person she seemed. Beneath her false exterior she was shamelessly normal.

In the days before O'Neil's return she suffered constant misgivings and qualms of conscience, but the sight of her brother reveling, expanding, fairly bursting into bloom beneath the influence of Natalie Gerard led her to think that perhaps she did have a duty to perform. Dan's cause was hers, and while she had only the faintest hope of aiding it, she was ready to battle for his happiness with every weapon at her command. The part she would have to play was not exactly nice, she reflected, but—the ties of sisterhood were strong and she would have made any sacrifice for Dan. She knew that Natalie was fond of him in a casual, friendly way, and although it was evident that the girl accorded him none of that hero-worship with which she favored his chief, Eliza began to think there still might be some hope for him. Since we are all prone to argue our consciences into agreement with our desires, she finally brought herself to the belief that O'Neil was not the man for Natalie. He was too old, too confirmed in his ways, and too self-centered to make a good husband for a girl of her age and disposition. Once her illusions had been rubbed away through daily contact with him, she would undoubtedly awaken to his human faults, and unhappiness would result for both. What Natalie needed for her lasting contentment was a boy her own age whose life would color to match hers. So argued Eliza with that supreme satisfaction which we feel in arranging the affairs of others to suit ourselves.

She was greatly embarrassed, nevertheless, when she next met O'Neil and tried to explain that story in *The Review*. He listened courteously and smiled his gentle smile.

"My dear," said he, finally, "I knew there had been some mistake, so let's forget that it ever happened. Now tell me about the smallpox epidemic. When I heard what Linn was doing with our men I was badly worried, for I couldn't see how to checkmate him, but it seems you and Doc were equal to the occasion. He cabled me a perfectly proper announcement of Tom's quarantine, and I believed we had been favored by a miracle."

"It wasn't a miracle at all," Eliza said in a matter-of-fact tone; "it was croton oil. Nobody has dared tell him the truth. He still believes he could smell the tuberoses."

O'Neil seemed to derive great amusement from her account of what followed. He had already heard Dr. Gray's version of the affair, but Eliza had a refreshing way of saying things.

"I brought you a little present," he said when she had finished.

She took the package he handed her, exclaiming with a slight flush of embarrassment, "A s'prise! Nobody but Dan ever gave me a present." Then her eyes darkened with suspicion. "Did you bring me this because of what I did?"

"Now don't be silly! I knew nothing about your part in

the comedy until Doc told me. You are a most difficult person."

Slowly she unwrapped the parcel, and then with a gasp lifted a splendidly embroidered kimono from its box.

"Oh-h!" Her eyes were round and astonished. "Oh-h! It's for *me!*"

It was a regal garment of heavy silk, superbly ornamented with golden dragons, each so cunningly worked that it seemed upon the point of taking wing. "Why, their eyes glitter! And—they'd breathe fire if I jabbed them. Oh-h!" She stared at the gift in helpless amazement. "Is it mine, *honestly?*"

He nodded. "Won't you put it on?"

"Over these things? Never!" Again Miss Appleton blushed, for she recalled that she had prepared for his coming with extraordinary care. Her boots were even stouter than usual, her skirt more plain, her waist more stiff, and her hair more tightly smoothed back. "It would take a fluffy person to wear this. I'll always keep it, of course, and—I'll worship it, but I'm not designed for pretty clothes. I'll let Natalie wear—"

"Natalie has one of her own, done in butterflies, and I brought one to her mother also."

"And you bought this for me after you had seen that fiendish story over my signature?"

"Certainly!" He quickly forestalled her attempted thanks by changing the subject. "Now then, Dan tells me you are anxious to begin your magazine-work, so I'm going to arrange for you to see the glaciers and the coal-fields. It will be a hard trip, for the track isn't through yet, but—"

"Oh, I'll take care of myself; I won't get in anybody's way," she said, eagerly.

"I intend to see that you don't, by going with you; so make your preparations and we'll leave as soon as I can get away."

When he had gone the girl said, aloud:

"Eliza Violet, this is your chance. It's underhanded and mean, but—you're a mean person, and the finger of Providence is directing you." She snatched up the silken kimono and ran into her room, locking the door behind her. Hurriedly she put it on, then posed before the mirror. Next down came her hair amid a shower of pins. She arranged it loosely about her face, and, ripping an artificial flower from her "party" hat, placed it over her ear, then swayed grandly to and fro while the golden dragons writhed and curved as if in joyous admiration. A dozen times she slipped out of the garment and, gathering it to her face, kissed it; a dozen times she donned it, strutting about her little room like a peacock. Her tip-tilted nose was red and her eyes were wet when at last she laid it out upon her bed and knelt with her cheek against it.

"Gee! If only I were pretty!" she sighed. "I almost believe he—likes me."

Tom Slater laboriously propelled himself up the hill to the bungalow that evening, and seated himself on the topmost step near where Eliza was rocking. She had come to occupy a considerable place in his thoughts of late, for she was quite beyond his understanding. She affected him as a mental gad-fly, stinging his mind into an activity quite unusual. At times he considered her a nice girl, though undoubtedly insane; then there were other moments when she excited his deepest animosity. Again, on rare occasions she completely upset all his preconceived notions by being so friendly and so sympathetic that she made him homesick for his own daughter. In his idle hours, therefore he spent much time at the Appleton cottage.

"Where have you been lately, Uncle Tom?" she began.

Slater winced at the appellation, but ignored it.

"I've been out on the delta hustling supplies ahead. Heard the news?"

"No."

"Curtis Gordon has bought the McDermott outfit in Kyak."

"That tells me nothing. Who is McDermott?"

"He's a shoe-stringer. He had a wildcat plan to build a railroad from Kyak to the coal-fields, but he never got farther than a row of alder stakes and a book of press clippings."

"Does that mean that Gordon abandons his Hope route?"

"Yep! He's swung in behind us and the Heidlemanns. Now it's a three-sided race, with us in the lead. Mellen just brought in the news half an hour ago; he was on his way down from the glaciers when he ran into a field party of Gordon's surveyors. Looks like trouble ahead if they try to crowd through the cañon alongside of us."

"He must believe Kyak Bay will make a safe harbor."

"Don't say it! If he's right, we're fried to a nice brown finish on both sides and it's time to take us off the stove. I'm praying for a storm."

" 'The prayers of the wicked are an abomination unto the Lord,' " quoted Eliza.

"Sure! But I keep right on praying just the same. It's a habit now. The news has set the chief to jumping sideways."

"Which, translated, I suppose means that he is disturbed."

"Or words to that effect! Too bad they changed that newspaper story of yours."

"Yes."

"It put a crimp in him."

"How—do you mean?"

"He had some California capitalists tuned up to put in three million dollars, but when they read that our plan was impracticable their fountain-pens refused to work."

"Oh!" Eliza gasped, faintly.

Slater regarded her curiously, then shook his head. "Funny how a kid like you can scare a bunch of hard-headed bankers, ain't it?" he said. "Doc Gray explained that it wasn't your fault, but—it doesn't take much racket to frighten the big fish."

"What will Mr. O'Neil do?"

"Oh, he'll fight it out, I s'pose. The first thing is to block Gordon. Say, I brought you a present."

"This is my lucky day," smiled Eliza as Tom fumbled in his pocket. "I'm sure I shall love it."

"It ain't much, but it was the best in the crate and I shined it up on my towel." Mr. Slater handed Eliza a fine red apple of prodigious size, at sight of which the girl turned pale.

"I—don't like apples," she cried, faintly.

"Never mind; they're good for your complexion."

"I'd die before I'd eat one."

"Then I'll eat it for you; my complexion ain't what it was before I had the smallpox." When he had carried out this intention and subjected his teeth to a process of vacuum-cleaning, he asked: "Say, what happened to your friend who chewed gum?"

"Well, he was hardly a friend," Miss Appleton said. "If he had been a real friend he would have listened to my warning."

"Gum never hurt anybody," Slater averred, argumentatively.

"Not ordinary gum. But you see, he chewed nothing except wintergreen—"

"That's what I chew."

Eliza's tone was one of shocked amazement. "Not *really?* Oh, well, some people would thrive on it, I dare say, but he had indigestion."

"Me too! That's why I chew it."

The girl eyed him during an uncomfortable pause. Finally she inquired:

"Do you ever feel a queer, gnawing feeling, like hunger, if you go without your breakfast?"

"Unh-hunh! Don't you?"

"I wouldn't alarm you for the world, Uncle Tom—"

"I ain't your uncle!"

"You might chew the stuff for years and not feel any bad effects, but if you wake up some morning feeling tired and listless—"

"I've done that, too." Slater's gloomy eyes were fixed upon her with a look of vague apprehension. "Is it a symptom?"

"Certainly! Pepsin-poisoning, it's called. This fellow I told you about was a charming man, and since we had all tried so hard to save him, we felt terribly at the end."

"Then he died?"

"Um-m! Yes and no. Remind me to tell you the story sometime— Here comes Dan, in a great hurry."

Young Appleton came panting up the hill.

"Good-by, Sis," he said. "I'm off for the front in ten minutes."

"Anybody hurt?" Slater asked quickly.

"Not yet, but somebody's liable to be. Gordon is trying to steal the cañon, and Murray has ordered me out with a car of dynamite to hold it."

"Dynamite! Why, Dan!" his sister exclaimed in consternation.

"We have poling-boats at the lower crossing and we'll be at the cañon in two days. I'm going to load the hillside with shots, and if they try to come through I'll set 'em off. They'll never dare tackle it." Dan's eyes were dancing; his face was alive with excitement.

"But suppose they should?" Eliza insisted, quietly.

"Then send Doc Gray with some stretchers. I owe one to Gordon, and this is my chance." Drawing her aside, he said in an undertone, "You've got to hold my ground with Natalie while I'm gone. Don't let her see too much of Murray."

"I'll do the best I can," she answered him, "but if he seems to be in earnest I'll renege, no matter what happens to you, Danny."

He kissed her affectionately and fled.

XII *How Gordon Failed in His Cunning*

The so-called cañon of the Salmon River lies just above the twin glaciers. Scenically, these are by far the more impressive, and they present a more complex engineering problem; yet the cañon itself was the real strategic point in the struggle between the railroad-builders. The floor of the valley immediately above Garfield glacier, though several miles wide, was partly filled with detritus which had been carried down from the mother range on the east, and this mass of debris had forced the stream far over against the westward rim, where it came roaring past the foot wall in a splendid cataract some three miles long. To the left of the river, looking up-stream at this point, the mountains slanted skyward like a roof, until lost in the hurrying scud four thousand feet above. To the right, however, was the old moraine, just mentioned, consisting of a desolate jumble of rock and gravel and silt overlaying the ice foot. On account of its broken character and the unstable nature of its foundation this bank was practically useless for road-building, and the only feasible route for steel rails was along the steep west wall.

O'Neil on his first reconnaissance had perceived that while there was room for more than one bridge across the Salmon between the upper and the lower ice masses, there was not room for more than one track alongside the rapids, some miles above that point. He knew, moreover, that once he had established his title to a right-of-way along the west rim of the cataract, it would be difficult for a rival to oust him, or to parallel his line without first crossing back to the east bank—an undertaking at once hazardous and costly. He had accordingly given Dan Appleton explicit instructions to be very careful in filing his survey, that no opportunity might be left open for a later arrival. The engineer had done his work well, and O'Neil rested secure in the belief that he held possession of the best and least expensive route through to the open valleys above. He had had no cause to fear a clash with the Heidlemann forces, for they had shown a strict regard for his rights and seemed content to devote themselves to developing their terminus before trying to negotiate the cañon. They were wise in taking this course, for their success would mean that O'Neil's project would fall of its own weight. Kyak was nearer Seattle, by many miles, than Omar; it was closer to the coal and copper fields, and the proven permanence of their breakwater would render useless further attempts to finance the S. R. & N.

But in the entrance of Curtis Gordon into the field O'Neil recognized danger. Gordon was swayed by no such business scruples as the Heidlemanns; he was evidently making a desperate effort to secure a footing at any cost. In purchasing the McDermott holdings he had executed a coup of considerable importance, for he had placed himself on equal footing with the Trust and in position to profit by its efforts at harbor-building without expense to himself. If, therefore, he succeeded in wresting from O'Neil the key to that upper passageway, he would be able to block his personal enemy and to command the consideration of his more powerful rival.

No one, not even the Trust, had taken the McDermott enterprise seriously, but with Curtis Gordon in control the "wildcat" suddenly became a tiger.

In view of all this, it was with no easy mind that O'Neil

despatched Appleton to the front, and it was with no small responsibility upon his shoulders that the young engineer set out in charge of those wooden boxes of dynamite. Murray had told him frankly what hung upon his success, and Dan had vowed to hold the survey at any cost.

Steam was up and the locomotive was puffing restlessly when he returned from his farewell to Eliza. A moment later and the single flat car carrying his party and its dangerous freight was being whirled along the shores of Omar Lake. On it rushed, shrieking through the night, out from the gloomy hills and upon the tangent that led across the delta. Ten minutes after it had rolled forth upon the trestle at the "lower crossing" the giant powder had been transferred to poling-boats and the long pull against the current had begun.

O'Neil had picked a crew for Dan, men upon whom he could depend. They were on double pay, and as they had worked upon the North Pass & Yukon, Appleton had no doubt of their loyalty.

The events of that trip were etched upon the engineer's mind with extraordinary vividness, for they surpassed in peril and excitement all his previous experiences. The journey resembled nothing but the mad scramble of a gold stampede. The stubborn boats with their cargoes which had to be so gently handled, the ever-increasing fury of the river, the growing menace of those ghastly, racing icebergs, the taut-hauled towing-lines, and the straining, sweating men in the loops, all made a picture hard to forget. Then, too, the uncertainty of the enterprise, the crying need of haste, the knowledge of those other men converging upon the same goal, lent a gnawing suspense to every hour. It was infinitely more terrible than that first expedition when he and Tom Slater and O'Neil had braved the unknown. It was vastly more trying than any of the trips which had followed, even with the winter hurricane streaming out of the north as from the mouth of a giant funnel.

Dan had faced death in various forms upon this delta during the past year and a half. He had seen his flesh harden to marble whiteness under the raging north wind; his eyes and lungs had been drifted full of sand in summer storms which rivaled those of the Sahara. With transit on his back he had come face to face with the huge brown grizzly. He had slept in mud, he had made his bed on moss which ran water like a sponge; he had taken danger and hardship as they came—yet never had he punished himself as on this dash.

Through his confusion of impressions, his intense preoccupation with present dangers and future contingencies, the thought of Natalie floated now and then vaguely but comfortingly. He had seen her for a moment, before leaving—barely long enough to explain the nature of his mission—but her quick concern, her unvoiced anxiety, had been very pleasant, and he could not believe that it was altogether due to her interest in the fortunes of O'Neil.

Dan knew that Mellen's crew was camped at the upper crossing, busied in drilling for the abutments and foundations of the bridge; but he reasoned that they would scarcely suspect the object of Gordon's party and that, in any case, they were not organized or equipped to resist it. Moreover, the strategic point was four miles above the bridge site, and the surveying corps would hardly precipitate a clash, particularly since there was ample room for them to select a crossing-place alongside.

It was after midnight of the second day when he and his weary boatmen stumbled into sight of the camp. Appleton halted his command and stole forward, approaching the place through the tangled alders which flanked it. He had anticipated that the rival party would be up to this point by now, if not even farther advanced, and he was both angered and relieved to sight the tops of other tents pitched a few hundred yards beyond Mellen's outfit. So they were here! He had arrived in time, after all! A feeling of exultation conquered the deathly fatigue that slowed his limbs. Although he still had to pass the invader's camp and establish himself at the cañon, the certainty that he had made good thus far was ample reward for his effort.

A dog broke into furious barking as he emerged from cover, and he had a moment's anxiety lest it serve as warning to the enemy; but a few quick strides brought him to the tent of Mellen's foreman. Going in, he roused the man, who was sleeping soundly.

"Hello!" cried the foreman, jumping up and rubbing his eyes. "I thought Curtis Gordon had taken possession."

"Hush! Don't wake them up," Dan cautioned.

"Oh, there's no danger of disturbing them with this infernal cannonading going on all the time." The night resounded to a rumbling crash as some huge mass of ice split off, perhaps two miles away.

"When did they arrive?"

"Night before last. They've located right alongside of us. Gee! We were surprised when they showed up. They expect to break camp in the morning." He yawned widely.

"Hm-m! They're making tracks, aren't they? Were they friendly?"

"Oh, sure! So were we. There was nothing else to do, was there? We had no orders."

"I have two dozen men and four boatloads of dynamite with me. I'm going to hold that mountainside."

"Then you're going to fight!" All vestige of drowsiness had fled from the man's face.

"Not if we can help it. Who is in charge of this crew?"

"Gordon himself."

"Gordon!"

"Yes! And he's got a tough gang with him."

"Armed?"

"Sure! This is a bear country, you know."

"Listen! I want you to tell him, as innocently as you can, that we're on the job ahead of him. Tell him we've been there for a week and have loaded that first rock shoulder and expect to shoot it off as soon as possible. You can tell him, too, that I'm up there and he'd better see me before trying to pass through."

"I've got you! But that won't stop him."

"Perhaps! Now have you any grub in camp?"

"No."

"We threw ours overboard, to make time. Send up anything you can spare; we're played out."

"It'll be nothing but beans, and they're moldy."

"We can fight on beans, and we'll eat the paper off those giant cartridges if we have to. Don't fail to warn Gordon that the hillside is mined, and warn him loud enough for his swampers to hear."

Appleton hastened back to his boats, where he found

his men sprawled among the boulders sleeping the sleep of complete exhaustion. They were drenched, half numbed by the chill air of the glacier, and it was well that he roused them.

"Gordon's men are camped just above," he told them. "But we must get through without waking them. No talking, now, until we're safe."

Silently the crew resumed their tow-lines, fitting them to their aching shoulders; gingerly the boats were edged out into the current.

It was fortunate that the place was noisy, and that the voice of the river and the periodic bombardment from the glaciers drowned the rattle of loose stones dislodged by their footsteps. But it was a trying half-hour that followed. Dan did not breathe easily until his party had crossed the bar and were safely out upon the placid waters of the lake, wtih the last stage of the journey ahead of them.

About mid-forenoon of the following day Curtis Gordon halted his party at the lower end of the rapids and went on alone. To his right lay the cataract and along the steep slope against which it chafed wound a faint footpath scarcely wide enough in places for a man to pass. This trail dipped in and out, wound back and forth around frowning promontories. It dodged through alder thickets or spanned slides of loose rock, until, three miles above, it emerged into the more open country back of the parent range. It had been worn by the feet of wild animals and it followed closely the right-of-way of the S. R. & N. To the left the hills rose swiftly in great leaps to the sky; to the right, so close that a false step meant disaster, roared the cataract, muddy and foam-flecked.

As Gordon neared the first bluff he heard, above the clamor of the flood, a faint metallic "tap-tap-tap," as of hammer and drill, and, drawing closer, he saw Dan Appleton perched upon a rock which commanded a view in both directions. Just around the shoulder, in a tiny gulch, or gutter from the slopes above, were pitched several tents, from one of which curled the smoke of a cookstove. Close at hand were moored four battered poling-boats.

"Look out!" Appleton shouted from on high.

Gordon flushed angrily and kept on, scanning the surroundings with practised eye.

"Hey, you!" Dan called, for a second time. "Keep back! We're going to shoot."

Still heedless of the warning, Gordon held stubbornly to his stride. He noted the heads of several men projecting from behind boulders, and his anger rose. How dared this whipper-snapper shout at him! He felt inclined to toss the insolent young scoundrel into the rapids. Then suddenly his resentment gave place to a totally different emotion. The slanting bank midway between him and Appleton lifted itself bodily in a chocolate-colored upheaval, and the roar of a dynamite blast rolled out across the river. It was but a feeble echo of the majestic reverberations from the glacier across the lake, but it was impressive enough to send Curtis Gordon scurrying to a place of safety. He wheeled in his tracks, doubling himself over, and his long legs began to thresh wildly. Reaching the shelter of a rock crevice, he hurled himself into it, while over his place of refuge descended a shower of dirt and rocks and debris. When the rain of missiles had subsided he stepped forth, his face white with fury, his big hands twitching. His voice was hoarse as he shouted his protest.

Appleton scrambled carefully down from his perch in the warm sunshine and approached with insolent leisure.

"Say! Do you want to get your fool self killed?" he cried; then in an altered tone: "Oh! Is it you, Gordon?"

"You knew very well it was I." Gordon swallowed hard and partially controlled his wrath. "What do you mean by such carelessness?" he demanded. "You ought to be hung for a thing like that." He brushed the dirt from his expensive hunting-suit.

"I yelled my head off! You must be deaf."

"You saw me coming! Don't say you didn't. Fortunately I wasn't hurt." In a tone of command he added, "You'll have to stop blasting until I go through with my party."

"Sorry! Every day counts with us." Appleton grinned. "You know how it is—short season, and all that."

"Come, come! Don't be an idiot. I have no time to waste."

"Then you'll have to go around," said Dan. "This isn't a public road, you know."

Gordon had come to argue, to pacify, to gain his ends by lying, if necessary, but this impudent jackanapes infuriated him. His plans had gone smoothly so far, and the unexpected threat of resistance momentarily provoked him beyond restraint.

"You scoundrel," he cried. "You'd have blown me into the river if you could. But I'll go through this cañon—"

"Go as far and as fast as you like," Dan interrupted with equal heat, "only take your own chances, and have a net spread at the lower end of the rapids to catch the remains."

They eyed each other angrily; then Gordon said, more quietly:

"This is ridiculous. You can't stop me."

"Maybe I can't and maybe I can. I'm under orders to rush this work and I don't intend to knock off to please you. I've planted shots at various places along our right-of-way and I'll set 'em off when it suits me. If you're so anxious to go upriver, why don't you cross over to the moraine? There's a much better trail on that side. You'll find better walking a few miles farther up, and you'll run no danger of being hurt."

"I intend to run a survey along this hillside."

"There isn't room; we beat you to it."

"The law provides—"

"Law? Jove! I'd forgotten there is such a thing. Why don't you go to law and settle the question that way? We'll have our track laid by the time you get action, and I'm sure Mr. O'Neil wouldn't place any obstacles in the way of your free passage back and forth. He's awfully obliging about such things."

Gordon ground his fine, white, even teeth. "Don't you understand that I'm entitled to a right-of-way through here under the law of common user?" he asked, with what patience he could command.

"If you're trying to get a legal opinion on the matter why don't you see a lawyer? I'm not a lawyer, neither am I a public speaker nor a piano-tuner, nor anything like that—I'm an engineer."

"Don't get funny. I can't send my men in here if you continue blasting."

"So it seems to me, but you appear to be hell bent on trying it."

Dan was enjoying himself and he deliberately added to the other's anger by inquiring, as if in the blinding light of a new idea:

"Why don't you bridge over and go up the other side?" He pointed to the forbidding, broken country which faced them across the rapids.

Gordon snorted. "How long do you intend to maintain this preposterous attitude?" he asked.

"As long as the powder lasts—and there's a good deal of it."

The promoter chewed his lip for a moment in perplexity, then said with a geniality he was far from feeling:

"Appleton, you're all right! I admire your loyalty, even though it happens to be for a mistaken cause. I always liked you. I admire loyalty—it's something I need in my business. What I need I pay for, and I pay well."

"So your man Linn told us."

"I never really discharged you. In fact, I intended to reemploy you, for I need you badly. You can name your own salary and go to work any time."

"In other words, you mean you'll pay me well to let you through."

"Fix your own price and I'll double it."

"Will you come with me up this trail a little way?" Dan inquired.

"Certainly."

"There's a spot where I'd like to have you stand. I'll save you the trouble of walking back to your men—you'll beat the echo."

There was a pause while Gordon digested this. "Better think it over," he said at length. "I'll never let O'Neil build his road, not if it breaks me, and you're merely laying yourself open to arrest by threatening me."

"Please come with me!" urged Appleton. "You'll never know what hit you."

With a curse the promoter wheeled and walked swiftly down the trail by which he had come.

"Get ready to shoot," Dan ordered when he had returned to his vantage-point. A few moments later he saw the invading party approach, but he withheld his warning shout until it was close at hand. Evidently Gordon did not believe. he would have the reckless courage to carry out his threat, and had determined to put him to the test.

The engineer gauged his distance nicely, and when the new-comers had fairly passed within the danger zone he gave the signal to fire.

A blast heavier than the one which had discouraged Gordon's advance followed his command, and down upon the new-comers rained a deluge which sent them scurrying to cover. Fortunately no one was injured.

An hour later the invaders had pitched camp a mile below, and after placing a trusted man on guard Appleton sent his weary men to bed.

It was Curtis Gordon himself who brought O'Neil the first tidings of this encounter, for, seeing the uselessness of an immediate attempt to overcome Dan's party by force, he determined to make formal protest. He secured a boat, and a few hours later the swift current swept him down to the lower crossing, where McKay put a locomotive at his disposal for the trip to Omar. By the time he arrived there he was quite himself again, suave, self-possessed, and magnificently outraged at the treatment he had received. O'Neil met him with courtesy.

"Your man Appleton has lost his head," Gordon began. "I've come to ask you to call him off."

"He is following instructions to the letter."

"Do you mean that you refuse to allow me to run my right-of-way along that hillside? Impossible!" His voice betokened shocked surprise.

"I am merely holding my own survey. I can't quit work to accommodate you."

"But, my dear sir, I must insist that you do."

O'Neil shrugged.

"Then there is but one way to construe your refusal —it means that you declare war."

"You saved me that necessity when you sent Linn to hire my men away."

Gordon ignored this reference. "You must realize,

O'Neal," said he, "that I am merely asking what is mine. I have the right to use that cañonside—the right to use your track at that point, in fact, if it proves impracticable to parallel it—under the law of common user. You are an experienced contractor; you must be familiar with that law."

"Yes. I looked it up before beginning operations, and I found it has never been applied to Alaska."

Gordon started. "That's a ridiculous statement."

"Perhaps, but it's true. Alaska is not a territory, it's a district, and it has its own code. Until the law of common user has been applied here you'll have to use the other side of the river."

"That would force me to bridge twice in passing the upper glacier. We shall see what the courts have to say."

"Thanks! I shall be grateful for the delay."

Gordon rose with a bow. The interview had been short and to the point. O'Neil put an engine at his service for the return trip, and after a stiff adieu the visitor departed, inwardly raging.

It was his first visit to Omar, and now that he was here he determined to see it all. But first another matter demanded his attention—a matter much in his mind of late, concerning which he had reached a more or less satisfactory decision during his journey.

He went directly to the new hotel and inquired for Gloria Gerard.

Beneath the widow's coldness when she came to meet him he detected an uncertainty, a frightened indecision which assured him of success, and he set himself to his task with the zest he always felt in bending another to his will.

"It has been the greatest regret of my life that we quarreled," he told her when their strained greeting was over. "I felt that I had to come and see with my own eyes that you are well."

"I am quite well."

"Two people who have been to each other as much as we have been cannot lightly separate; their lives cannot be divided without a painful readjustment." He paused, then reflecting that he could afford a little sentimental extravagance, added, "Flowers cannot easily be transplanted, and love, after all, is the frailest of blooms."

"I—think it is perennial. Have you—missed me?" Her dark eyes were strained and curious.

"My dear, you can never know how much, nor how deeply distressing this whole affair has been to me." He managed to put an affecting pathos into words sufficiently banal, for he was an excellent actor. "I find that I am all sentiment. Under the shell of the hard-headed business man beats the heart of a school-boy. The memory of the hours we have spent together, the places we have seen, the joys and discouragements we have shared, haunts me constantly. Memory can gleam but never renew: 'joy's recollection is no longer joy while sorrow's memory is sorrow still.' "

The spell of his personality worked strongly upon her. "Recollection is the only paradise from which we cannot be turned out," she said. "You read that to me once, but I didn't dream that my own happiness would some day consist of recollection."

"Why should it, Gloria? Hope is ready to welcome you. Your home stands open; my arms are outstretched."

"No!" she exclaimed, with a shake of her dark head. "There is some one besides myself to consider. Natalie is happy here; no one seems to know or to care what I have done."

"But surely you are not satisfied with this." He ran his eye critically over the garish newness of the little hotel parlor. It was flimsy, cheap, fresh with paint, very different from the surroundings he had given her at Hope. "I wonder that he presumed to offer you this after what you have had. A hotel-keeper! A landlady!"

"I was glad to get even this, for I have no pride now," she returned, coldly. "At least the house is honest, and the men who come here are the same. Mr. O'Neil is especially kind to Natalie, and she thinks a great deal of him."

"I presume he wants to marry her."

"I pray that he will. I don't intend her to make the mistake I did."

Gordon received this announcement with grim satisfaction. It was what he had suspected, and it fitted perfectly into his plans.

"I sha'n't allow this to continue, Gloria," he said. "Our difference has gone far enough, and I sha'n't permit O'Neil to put me in his debt. We have come to a final understanding, he and I. While my views on the holiness of the marriage relation have not changed in the least, still I am ready to follow your wishes."

"You—mean it?" she queried, breathlessly.

"I do. Come home, Gloria."

"Wait! I must tell Natalie." She rose unsteadily and left the room, while he reflected with mingled scorn and amusement upon the weakness of human nature and the gullibility of women.

A moment later mother and daughter appeared, arm in arm, both very pale.

"Is this true?" Natalie demanded.

"Quite true. You and Gloria seem to think I owe something; I never shirk a debt." Mrs. Gerard's fingers tightened painfully upon her daughter's arm as he continued: "There is only one condition upon which I insist: you must both return to Hope at once and have done with this—this man."

Natalie hesitated, but the look in her mother's eyes decided her. With some difficulty she forced herself to acquiesce, and felt the grip upon her arm suddenly relax. "When will the wedding take place?" she asked.

"At the earliest possible moment," Gordon declared, with well-feigned seriousness. "Once we return to God's country—"

"No!" cried Natalie. "We can't go back to Hope until she is married; it would be scandalous."

"Why more scandalous to accept my protection than that of a stranger? Do you care what these people think?" he demanded, with an air of fine scorn.

"Yes! I care very much."

"Is there any—reason for waiting?" Mrs. Gerard inquired.

"Many! Too many to enumerate. It is my condition that you both leave Omar at once."

Gloria Gerard looked at her daughter in troubled indecision, but Natalie answered firmly:

"We can't do that."

"So! You have your own plans, no doubt, and it doesn't trouble you that you are standing in the way of your mother's respectability!" His voice was harsh, his sneer open. "Bless my soul! Is the generosity to be all on my side? Or has this man O'Neil forbidden you to associate with me?"

"I don't trust you." Natalie flared up. "I'm afraid you are trying—"

"It is my condition, and I am adamant. Believe me, O'Neil knows of your disgrace, or will learn of it in time. It would be well to protect your name while you can." Turning to the other woman, he said loudly: "Gloria, the girl is ready to sacrifice you to her own ends."

"Wait!" Natalie's nerves were tingling with dislike of the man, but she said steadily: "I shall do exactly as mother wishes."

Be it said to the credit of Gloria Gerard that she did not hesitate.

"I shall be here when you are ready," she told him.

With an exclamation of rage Gordon rose and strode out of the room.

XIII   *We Journey to a Place of Many Wonders*

Curtis Gordon's men broke camp upon his return from Omar, and by taking the east bank of the Salmon River pressed through to the upper valley. Here they recrossed to the west side and completed their survey, with the exception of the three-mile gap which Dan Appleton held.

Gordon continued to smart under the sting of his defeat, however. O'Neil had gotten the better of him in argument, and Natalie's simplicity had proved more than a match for his powers of persuasion. At no time had he seriously considered making Mrs. Gerard his wife, but he had thought to entice the two women back under his own roof, in order to humble both them and their self-appointed protector. He felt sure that Natalie's return to

Hope and her residence there would injure her seriously in the eyes of the community, and this would be a stab to O'Neil. Although he had failed for the moment, he did not abandon the idea. His display of anger upon leaving the hotel had been due mainly to disappointment at the checkmate. But knowing well the hold he possessed upon the older woman, he laid it away for later use when the fight grew hot, and meanwhile devoted himself to devising further measures by which to harass his enemy and incidentally advance his own fortunes.

Gordon's business career had consisted of a series of brilliant manipulations whereby, with little to go upon, he had forced financial recognition for himself. No one knew better than he the unstable foundation beneath his Alaskan enterprises; yet more than once he had turned as desperate ventures into the semblance of success. By his present operations he sought not only to hamper O'Neil, but to create an appearance of opposition to both him and the Trust that could be coined into dollars and cents. There are in the commercial world money wolves who prey upon the weak and depend upon the spirit of compromise in their adversaries. Gordon was one of these. He had the faculty of snatching at least half a victory from apparent defeat, and for this reason he had been able to show a record sufficiently impressive to convince the average investor of his ability.

By purchasing for a song the McDermott rights at Kyak he had placed himself in position to share in the benefits of the Heidlemann breakwater, and by rapidly pushing his tracks ahead he made his rivalry seem formidable. As a means of attack upon O'Neil he adopted a procedure common in railroad-building. He amended his original survey so that it crossed that of the S. R. & N. midway between the lower bridge over the Salmon River and the glaciers, and at that point began the hasty erection of a grade.

It was at the cost of no little inconvenience that he rushed forward a large body of men and supplies, and began to lay track across the S. R. & N. right-of-way. If Appleton could hold a hillside, he reasoned, he himself could hold a crossing, if not permanently, at least for a sufficient length of time to serve his purpose.

His action came as a disagreeable surprise to Omar.

These battles for crossings have been common in the history of railroading, and they have not infrequently resulted in sanguinary affrays. Long after the ties are spiked and the heads are healed, the legal rights involved have been determined, but usually amid such a tangle of conflicting testimony and such a confusion of technicalities as to leave the justice of the final decision in doubt. In the unsettled conditions that prevailed in the Salmon River valley physical possession of a right-of-way was at least nine-tenths of the law, and O'Neil realized that he must choose between violence and a compromise. Not being given to compromise, he continued his construction work, and drew closer, day by day, to the point of contact.

Reports came from the front of his opponent's preparations for resistance. Gordon had laid several hundred yards of light rails upon his grade, and on these he had mounted a device in the nature of a "go-devil" or skip, which he shunted back and forth by means of a donkey-engine and steel cable. With this in operation across the point of intersection like a shuttle, interference would be extremely dangerous. In addition, he had built blockhouses and breastworks of ties, and in these, it was reported, he had stationed the pick of his hired helpers, armed and well provisioned.

Toward this stronghold Murray O'Neil's men worked, laying his road-bed as straight as an arrow, and as the intervening distance decreased anxiety and speculation at Omar increased.

Among those who hung upon the rumors of the approaching clash with greatest interest was Eliza Appleton. Since Dan's departure for the front she had done her modest best to act the part he had forced upon her, and in furtherance of their conspiracy she had urged O'Neil to fulfil his promise of taking her over the work. She felt an ever-growing curiosity to see those glaciers, about which she had heard so much; and she reflected, though not without a degree of self-contempt, that nothing could be more favorable to her design than the intimacy of several days together on the trail. Nothing breeds a closer relationship than the open life, nothing brings people more quickly into accord or hopeless disagreement. Although she had no faintest idea that Murray could or would ever care seriously for her, she felt that there was a bare possibility of winning his transient interest and in that way, perhaps, affording her brother time in which to attain his heart's desire. Of course, it was all utterly absurd, yet it was serious enough to Dan; and her own feelings—well, they didn't matter.

She was greatly excited when O'Neil announced one evening:

"I'm ready to make that trip to the front, if you are. I have business at Kyak; so after we've seen the glaciers we will go down there and you can take in the coal-fields."

"How long shall we be gone?"

"Ten days, perhaps. We'll start in the morning."

"I'm ready to leave at a moment's notice."

"Then perhaps you'd better help Natalie."

"Natalie!" exclaimed Eliza, seeing all her well-laid plans tottering. "Is she going?"

"Oh yes! It's an opportunity she shouldn't miss, and I thought it would be pleasanter for you if she went with us."

Eliza was forced to acknowledge his thoughtfulness, although it angered her to be sacrificed to the proprieties. Her newspaper training had made her feel superior to such things, and this of all occasions was one upon which she would have liked to be free of mere conventions. But of course she professed the greatest delight.

O'Neil had puzzled her greatly of late; for at times he seemed wrapped up in Natalie, and at other times he actually showed a preference for Eliza's own company. He was so impartial in his attentions that at one moment the girl would waver in her determination and in the next would believe herself succeeding beyond her hope. The game confused her emotions curiously. She accused herself of being overbold, and then she noted with horror that she was growing as sensitive to his apparent coldness as if she were really in earnest. She had not supposed that the mere acting of a sentimental rôle could so obsess her.

To counteract this tendency she assumed a very professional air when they set out on the following morning. She was once more Eliza Appleton the reporter, and O'Neil, in recognition of this fact, explained rapidly the difficulties of construction which he had met and over-come. As she began to understand there came to her a fuller appreciation of the man and the work he was doing. Natalie, however, could not seem to grasp the significance of the enterprise. She saw nothing beyond the even gravel road-bed, the uninteresting trestles and bridges and cuts and fills, the like of which she had seen many times before, and her comment was childlike. O'Neil, however, appeared to find her naïveté charming, and Eliza reflected bitterly:

"If my nose was perfectly chiseled and my eyebrows nice, he wouldn't care if my brain was the size of a rabbit's. Here am I, talking like a human being and really understanding him, while she sits like a Greek goddess, wondering if her hat is on straight. If ever I find a girl uglier than I am I'll make her my bosom friend." She jabbed her pencil viciously at her notebook.

The track by this time had been extended considerably beyond the lower crossing—a circumstance which rendered their boat journey to the glaciers considerably shorter than the one Dan had taken wtih his cargo of dynamite. When the engine finally stopped it was in the midst of a tent village beside which flowed one of the smaller branches of the Salmon. In the distance the grade stretched out across the level swamps like a thin, lately healed scar, and along its crest gravel-trains were slowly creeping. An army of men like a row of ants were toiling upon it, and still farther away shone the white sides of another encampment.

"Oh! That's Gordon's track," Eliza cried, quickly. "Why, you're nearly up to him. How do you intend to get across?"

O'Neil nodded at the long thin line of moiling men in the distance.

"There's a loose handle in each one of those picks," he said.

"Somebody will be killed in that kind of a racket."

"That rests with Gordon. I'm going through."

"Suppose he had said that when Dan stopped him at the cañon?"

"If he'd said it and meant it he'd probably have done it. He bluffs; I don't! I have to go on; he didn't. Now

lunch is served; and since this is our last glimpse of civiliza-
tion, I advise you to fortify yourselves. From here on
we shall see nothing but the wilderness."

He led them to a spotless tent which had been newly
erected at the edge of the spruce. It was smoothly stretched
upon a framework of timber, its walls and floor were
of dressed lumber, and within were two cots all in
clean linen. There were twin washstands also, and dressers
and rocking-chairs, a table and a stove. On the floor beside the beds lay a number of deep, soft bear-rugs. A
meal was spread amid glass and figured china and fresh
new napery.

"How cozy! Why, it's a perfect dear of a house!" exclaimed Natalie.

"You will leave anything but your necessaries here, for
we are going light," Murray told them. "You will stop
here on our way back to Kyak, and I'll warrant you'll
be glad to see the place by that time."

"You built this just for us," Eliza said, accusingly.

"Yes. But it didn't take long. I 'phoned this morning
that you were coming." He ran a critical eye over the place
to see that its equipment was complete, then drew out
their chairs for them.

A white-coated cook-boy served a luncheon in courses,
the quality of which astonished the visitors, for there
was soup, a roast, delicious vegetables, crisp salad, a
camembert which O'Neil had imported for his private use,
and his own particular blend of coffee.

The girls ate with appetites that rivaled those of the
men in the mess-tent near by. Their presence in the heart
of a great activity, the anticipation of adventure to
come, the electric atmosphere of haste and straining
effort on every hand excited them. Eliza began to be
less conscious of her secret intention, and Natalie showed
a gaiety rare in her since the shadow of her mother's
shame had fallen upon her life.

The boat crews were waiting when they had finished,
and they were soon under way. A mile of comparatively
slack water brought them out into one of the larger estu-
aries of the river, and there the long, uphill pull began.
O'Neil had equipped his two companions with high rubber
boots, which they were only too eager to try. As soon

as they got ashore they began to romp and play and splash
through the shallows quite like unruly children. They spat-
tered him mischievously, they tugged at the towing-ropes
with a great show of assistance, they scampered ahead
of the party, keeping him in a constant panic lest they
meet with serious accident.

It was with no little relief that he gave the order to
pitch camp some hours later. After sending them off to
pick wild currants, with a grave warning to beware of
bears, he saw to the preparations for the night. They
returned shortly with their hats filled and their lips stained;
then, much to his disgust, they insisted upon straightening
out his tent with their own hands. Once inside its low shelter, they gleefully sifted sand between his blankets and
replaced his pillow with a rock; then they induced the
cook to coil a wet string in his flapjack. When supper was
over and the camp-fires of driftwood were crackling mer-
rily, they fixed themselves comfortably where their feet
would toast, and made him tell them stories until his eyes
drooped with weariness.

It was late summer, and O'Neil had expected to find
the glaciers less active than usual, but heavy rains in the
interior and hot thawing weather along the coast had
swelled the Salmon until many bergs clogged it, while the
reverberations which rolled down the valley told him that
both Garfield and Jackson were caving badly. It was not
the safest time at which to approach the place, he reflected,
but the girls had shown themselves nimble of foot, and
he put aside his uneasiness.

Short though the miles had been and easy as the trip
had proved, Eliza soon found herself wondering that it
should be possible to penetrate this region at all. The
snarling river, the charging icebergs, the caving banks, and
the growing menace of that noisy gap ahead began to have
their effect upon her and Natalie; and when the party finally rounded the point where Murray and Dan had
caught their first glimpse of the lower glacier they paused
with exclamations of amazement. They stood at the upper
end of a gorge between low bluffs, and just across the
hurrying flood lay the lower limit of the giant ice-field.
The edge, perhaps six hundred feet distant, was sloping
and mud-stained, for in its slow advance it had plowed

a huge furrow, lifting boulders, trees, acres of soil upon
its back. The very bluff through which the river had cut
its bed was formed of the debris it had thrown off, and
constituted a bulwark protecting its flank. Farther up-
stream the slope became steeper, than changed to a
rugged perpendicular face showing marks of recent cleavage. This palisade extended on and on, around the nearest bend, following the contour of the Salmon as far as
they could see. The sun was reflected from its myriad
angles and facets in splendid iridescence. Mammoth caves
and caverns gaped. In spots the ice was white, opaque;
in other places it was a light cerulean blue which shaded
into purple. Ribbons and faint striations meandered
through it like the streaks in an agate. But what struck
the beholders with overwhelming force was the tremendous, the unbelievable bulk of the whole slowly moving
mass. It reared itself sheerly three hundred feet high,
and along its foot the river hurried, dwarfed to an insignificant trickle. Here and there it leaned outward threat-
eningly, bulging from the terrific weight behind; at other
points the muddy flood recoiled from vast heaps which
had slid downward and half dammed its current. Back
of these piles the fresh cleavage showed dazzlingly. On,
upward, back into the untracked mountains it ran through
mile upon mile of undulations, until at last it joined the
ice-cap which weighted the plateau. As far as the eye
could follow the river ahead it stood solidly. Across its
entire face it was dripping; a thousand little rills and
waterfalls ate into it, and over it swept a cool, dank
breath.

The effect of the first view was overwhelming. Nothing upon the earth compares in majesty and menace to
these dull-eyed monsters of bygone ages; nothing save the
roots of mountains can serve to check them; nothing
less than the ceaseless energy of mighty rivers can sweep
away their shattered fragments.

Murray O'Neil had seen Jackson Glacier many times, but
always he experienced the same feeling of awe, of personal insignificance, as when he first came stumbling
up that gorge more than a year before.

For a long time the girls stood gazing without a word.
They seemed to have forgotten his presence.

"Well?" he said at last.

"Isn't it *big?*" Natalie faltered, with round eyes. "Will it fall over on us?"

He shook his head. "The river is too wide for that, but when a particularly big mass drops it makes waves large enough to sweep everything before them. This bank on our right is sixty feet high, but I've seen it inundated."

Turning to Eliza, he inquired:

"What do you think of it?"

Her face as she met his was strangely glorified, her eyes were shining, her fingers tightly interlocked.

"I—I'd like to cry or—or swear," she said, uncertainly.

"Why, Eliza!" Natalie regarded her friend in shocked amazement, but Murray laughed.

"It affects people differently," he said. "I have men who refuse to make this trip. There's something about Jackson that frightens them—perhaps it is its nearness. You see, there's no other place on the globe where we pygmies dare come so close to a live glacier of this size."

"How can we go on?" Natalie asked.

"We must work our boats along this bank. If the ice begins to crack anywhere near us I want you both to scamper up into the alders as fast as your rubber boots will carry you."

"What will you do?" Eliza eyed him curiously.

"Oh, I'll follow; never fear! If it's not too bad, I'll stay with the boats, of course. But we're not likely to have much difficulty at this season."

Eliza noted the intensity with which the boatmen were scanning the passage ahead, and something in O'Neil's tone told her he was speaking with an assurance he did not wholly feel.

"You have lost some men here, haven't you?" she asked.

"Yes. But the greater danger is in coming down. Then we have to get out in the current and take our chances."

"I'd like to do that!" Her lips were parted, her eyes were glowing, but Natalie gave a little cry of dismay.

"It's an utterly new sensation," O'Neil admitted. "I've been thinking of sending you up across the moraine, but the trail is bad, and you might get lost among the alders—"

"And miss any part of this! I wouldn't do it for worlds."

Eliza's enthusiasm was irresistible, and the expedition was soon under way again.

Progress was more difficult now, for the river-shore was paved with smooth, round stones which rolled under foot, and the boats required extreme attention in the swift current. The farther they proceeded, the more the ice wall opposite increased in height, until at last it shut off the mountains behind. Then as they rounded the first bend a new prospect unfolded itself. The size of Jackson became even more apparent; the gravel bank under which they crept was steeper and higher also. In places it was undercut by the action of the waves which periodically surged across. At such points Murray sent his charges hurrying on ahead, while he and his men tracked the boats after them. In time they found themselves opposite the backbone of the glacier, where the Salmon gnawed at the foot of a frozen cliff of prodigious height. And now, although there had been no cause for apprehension beyond an occasional rumble far back or a splitting crack from near at hand, the men assumed an attitude of strained watchfulness and kept their faces turned to the left. They walked quietly, as if they felt themselves in some appalling presence.

At last there came a sound like that of a cannon-shot, and far ahead of them a fragment loosened itself and went plunging downward. Although it appeared small, a ridge promptly leaped out from beneath the splash and came racing down the river's bosom toward them.

"Better go up a bit," O'Neil called to his charges.

The men at the ends of the tow-lines scrambled part way up the shelving beach and braced themselves, then wrapped the ropes about their waists, like anchormen on a tug-of-war team. Their companions waded into the flood and fended the boats off the rocks.

The wave came swiftly, lifting the skiffs high upon the bank, then it sucked them back amid a tangle of arms and legs. A portion of the river-bottom suddenly bared itself and as suddenly was submerged again. The boats plunged and rolled and beat themselves upon the shore, wrenching the anchormen from their posts. They were half filled with water too, but the wave had passed and was scudding away down-stream.

Eliza Appleton came stumbling back over the rock-strewn bank, for during that first mad plunge she had seen O'Neil go down beneath one of the rearing craft. A man was helping him out.

"Nothing but my ankle!" he reassured her when she reached his side. "I was dragged a bit and jammed among the boulders." He sank down, and his lips were white with pain, but his gray eyes smiled bravely. The boatman removed his chief's boot and fell to rubbing the injury, while the girls looked on helplessly.

"Come, come! We can't stay here," Murray told them. He drew on the boot again to check the swelling.

"Can you walk?" they asked him, anxiously.

"Certainly! Two feet are really unnecessary. A man can get along nearly as well on one." He hurried his men back to their tasks, and managed to limp after them, although the effort brought beads of sweat to his lips and brow.

It was well that he insisted upon haste, for they had not gone far when the glacier broke abreast of the spot they had just left. There came a rending crack, terrifying in its loudness; a tremendous tower of ice separated itself from the main body, leaned slowly outward, then roared downward, falling in a solid piece like a sky-scraper undermined. Not until the arc described by its summit had reached the river's surface did it shiver itself. Then there was a burst as of an exploded mine. The saffron waters of the Salmon shot upward until they topped the main rampart, and there separated into a cloud of spray which rained down in a deluge. Out from the fallen mass rushed a billow which gushed across the channel, thrashed against the high bank, then inundated it until the alder thickets on its crest whipped their tips madly. A giant charge of fragments of every size flew far out across the flats or lashed the waters to further anger in its fall.

The prostrate column lay like a wing-dam, half across the stream, and over it the Salmon piled itself. Disintegration followed; bergs heaved themselves into sight and went rolling and lunging after the billow which was rushing downstream with the speed of a locomotive. They ground and clashed together in furious confusion as the river spun them; the greater ones up-ended themselves, casting off muddy cascades. From the depths of the flood came a grinding and crunching as ice met rock.

Spellbound, the girls watched that first wave go tearing out of sight, filling the river bank-full. With exclamations of wonder, they saw the imprisoned waters break the huge dam to pieces. Finally the last shattered fragment was hurried out of sight, the flood poured past unhampered, and overhead the glacier towered silent, unchanged, staring at them balefully like a blind man with filmed eyes. There remained nothing but a gleaming scar to show where the cataclysm had originated.

"If I'd known the river was so high I'd never have brought you," O'Neil told them. "It's fortunate we happened to be above that break. You see, the waves can't run up against the current." He turned to his men and spurred them on.

It was not until the travelers had reached the camp at the bridge site that all the wonders of this region became apparent. Then the two girls, in spite of their fatigue, spent the later afternoon sight-seeing. At this point they were able to gain a comprehensive view; for at their backs lay Jackson Glacier, which they had just passed, and directly fronting them, across a placid lake, was Garfield, even larger and more impressive than its mate. Thirty, forty miles it ran back, broadening into a frozen sea out of which scarred mountain peaks rose like bleak islands, and on beyond the range of vision was still more ice.

They were surrounded by ragged ramparts. The Salmon River ran through a broken chalice formed by the encircling hills, and over the rim of the bowl or through its cracks peered other and smaller ice bodies. The lake at its bottom was filled by as strange a navy as ever sailed the sea; for the ships were bergs, and they followed each other in senseless, ceaseless manœuvers, towed by the currents which swept through from the cataract at its upper end. They formed long battle-lines, they assembled into flotillas, they filed about the circumference of a devil's whirlpool at the foot of the rapids, gyrating, bobbing, bowing until crowded out by the pressure of their rivals. Some of them were grounded, like hulks defeated in previous encounters, and along the guardian bar which imprisoned them at the outlet of the lake others were huddled, a mass of slowly dissolving wreckage.

O'Neil was helped into camp, and when his boot had been cut away he sent news of his arrival to Dan, who came like an eager bridegroom.

XIV   *How the Truth Came to Eliza*

Appleton found his employer with one foot in a tub of hot water and his lap full of blueprints. O'Neil explained briefly the condition of affairs down the river.

"I want some one to make that crossing," he said.

"A volunteer?" asked Dan, with quickened pulses.

"Yes."

"Will I do?"

"I sent for you to give you the first chance—you've been chafing so at your idleness. We must have steel laid to this point before snow flies. Every hour counts. I daren't risk Mellen or McKay, for they might be disabled. I intended to take charge myself, but I won't be able to walk now for some time." He swore a little, and Dan nodded sympathetically. "I wouldn't send anybody where I'd refuse to go myself. You understand?"

"Of course."

"If either McKay or Mellen were hurt I couldn't build the bridge, and the bridge must be built."

"If Gordon stands pat somebody may be—hurt."

"I don't look for anything worse than a few broken heads, but of course I can't tell. I'll stand behind you with my last dollar, no matter what happens."

Dan laughed. "As I understand the situation you won't have a dollar unless we make the crossing."

"Right!" O'Neil smiled cheerfully. "The life of the S. R. & N. depends upon it. I'd give ten thousand dollars for your right ankle."

"You can have it for nothing, Chief. I'd amputate the

whole leg and present it to you," Dan declared, earnestly.

Murray took his hand in a hearty grip. "Perhaps I'll be able to serve you some time," he said, simply. "Anyhow, I'll look out for the chance. Now spend the evening with the girls, and leave in the morning. I'll be down as soon as I can travel, to watch the fight from the sidelines." O'Neil's voice was level, but his teeth were shut and his fingers were clenched with rage at his disability.

Dan hurried away highly elated, but when he told Eliza of the part he had undertaken she stormed indignantly.

"Why, the brute! He has no right to send you into danger. This isn't war."

"Sis, dear, it's my chance. He can't stand, and he daren't risk his right-hand men."

"So he sacrifices you! I won't permit it. Your life and safety are worth more than all his dollars. Let his old railroad go to smash!"

"Wait! More than my safety depends on this. He said he'd wait for a chance to pay me back. If I do this he'll owe me more than any man on the job, and when he learns that I love Natalie—"

"Dan!" exclaimed his sister.

"Oh, he'll make good!"

"Why, you're worse than he! The idea of suggesting such a thing!"

"Don't preach! I've had nothing to do lately but think of her; she's always in my mind. The loneliness up here has made me feel more than ever that I can't exist without her. The river whispers her name; her face looks at me from the camp-fire; the wind brings me her messages—"

"Fiddlesticks! She saves her messages for him. When a man reaches the poetical stage he's positively sickening. You'll be writing verses next."

"I've written 'em," Dan confessed, sheepishly; "oceans of mush."

"Fancy! Thank Heaven one of us is sane."

"Our dispositions were mixed when we were born, Eliza. You're unsentimental and hard-headed: I'm romantic. You'll never know what love means."

"If you are a sample, I hope not." Eliza's nose assumed an even higher tilt than usual.

"Well, if I knew I had no chance with Natalie I'd let Gordon's men put an end to me—that's how serious it is. But I have a chance—I know I have."

"Bosh! You've lived in railroad camps too long. I know a dozen girls prettier than she." Eying him with more concern, she asked, seriously, "You wouldn't really take advantage of a service to Murray O'Neil to—to tell him the nature of your insanity?"

"I might not actually tell him, but I'd manage it so he'd find out."

"Don't you think Natalie has something to say? Don't you think she is more than a piece of baggage waiting to be claimed by the first man who comes along?" sputtered Miss Appleton in fine disgust at this attitude. "She has more sense and determination than any girl, any pretty girl, I ever saw. That's one reason why I hate her so. There's no use trying to select a husband for her. When the time comes she'll do the selecting herself. She'll knock over all our plans and walk blushingly up to the altar with O'Neil, leaving us out on the sidewalk to cheer. I'm sorry I ever tried to help you! I'm going to quit and get back my self-respect."

"You'll do no such thing. You'll continue to help your poor red-headed brother to the finish. Say! When I'm alone I'm just bursting with optimism; when I'm with you I wither with despair; when I'm with Natalie I become as heavy and stupid as a frog full of buckshot—I just sit and blink and bask and revel in a sort of speechless bliss. If she ever saw how really bright and engaging I am—"

"You!" Eliza sniffed. "You're as uninteresting as I am."

"Now that you've pledged your undying support, here goes for some basking," said Dan; and he made off hastily in search of Miss Gerard.

Eliza had really made up her mind to wash her hands of the affair, but she wavered, and, as usual, she gave in. She did go to O'Neil to protest at Dan's selection for the post of danger, but after talking with him she began to see the matter in a new light, and her opposition weakened. He showed her that the S. R. & N. had an individuality of its own—an individuality greater than Murray O'Neil's, or Dan Appleton's, or that of any man connected with it. She began to understand that it was a living thing, and that O'Neil was merely a small part of it—a person driven by a power outside himself, the head servant of a great undertaking, upon whom rested a heavy responsibility. She saw for the first time that the millions invested in the project imposed upon those concerned with its management a sacred duty, and that failure to defend the company's rights would be the worst sort of treachery. She began to appreciate also how men may be willing to lay down their lives, if necessary, to pave the way for the march of commerce.

"I never looked at it in this way," she told him, when he had finished. "I—don't like to take that view of it, even now, but I suppose I must."

"Try not to worry about Dan," he said, sympathetically. "We'll start back as soon as I'm able to move around, and I'll do my best to see that he isn't hurt. It's—tough to be laid up this way."

"There's another sick man in camp, by the way."

"Who?"

"The Indian boy who helps the cook. He was hunting and shot himself in the arm."

"They told me he was doing well."

"Oh, he is, but the pain has kept the poor fellow awake until he's nearly out of his head. There are no drugs here."

"None this side of the end of the track."

"Can't we do something?"

"We can give Dan a note to 'Happy Tom' in the morning and have whatever you want sent up. Tom will be there, and perhaps if you ask him he'll despatch a man on foot at once."

Seizing pen and paper from the table, Eliza wrote a note, which she read aloud:

"DEAR UNCLE TOM,—There is a sick Indian here. Won't you please send up an opiate by special messenger, and receive the blessing of, Your affectionate, ELIZA."

"Better change the word 'opiate,'" O'Neil advised. "I don't think Tom is equal to that; he might send overalls!" So Eliza substituted "something to put him to sleep." This message Dan promised faithfully to deliver.

Murray had expected to begin the return journey within twenty-four hours after his arrival; but his injury mended slowly, and when the time came he was still unable to stand. This interval the girls spent in watching the glaciers, of which they never seemed to tire, and in spoiling many films.

It was late on the second day when a tired and sodden messenger bearing the marks of heavy travel appeared at O'Neil's tent and inquired for Miss Appleton. To her he handed a three-foot bundle and a note from Tom Slater which read:

DEAR MADAM,—Here is the best thing I know of to put an Indian to sleep. THOS. SLATER.

"There's some mistake, surely," said the girl, as she unrolled the odd-looking package; then she cried out angrily, and O'Neil burst into laughter. For inside the many wrappings was a pick-handle.

Eliza's resentment at "Happy Tom's" unsympathetic sense of humor was tempered in a measure by the fact that the patient had taken a turn for the better and really needed no further medical attention. But she was not accustomed to practical jokes, and she vowed to make Tom's life miserable if ever the occasion offered.

As the days wore on and Murray remained helpless his impatience became acute, and on the fourth morning he determined to leave, at whatever cost in pain or danger to the injury. He gave orders, therefore, to have a boat prepared, and allowed himself to be carried to it. The foreman of the bridge crew he delegated to guide the girls down across the moraine, where he promised to pick them up. The men who had come with him he sent on to the cataract where Dan had been.

"Aren't you coming with us?" asked Natalie, when they found him seated in the skiff with an oarsman.

"It's rough going. I'd have to be carried, so I prefer this," he told them.

"Then we'll go with you," Eliza promptly declared.

Natalie paled and shook her dark head. "Is it safe?" she ventured.

"No, it isn't! Run along now! I'll be down there waiting, when you arrive."

"If it's safe enough for you, it's safe enough for us," said Eliza. Climbing into the boat, she plumped herself down with a look which seemed to defy any power to remove her. Her blue eyes met O'Neil's gray ones with an expression he had never seen in them until this moment.

"Nonsense, child!" he said. "Don't be silly."

"Don't you try to put me out. I'll hang on and—kick. Don't you say 'please,' either," she warned him.

"I must," he protested. "Please don't insist."

She scowled like an angry boy, and seized the gunwales firmly. Her expression made him smile despite his annoyance, and this provoked her the more.

"I'm going!" she asserted, darkly.

This outing had done wonders for both girls. The wind and the sunshine had tanned them, the coarse fare had lent them a hearty vigor, and they made charming pictures in their trim short skirts and sweaters and leather-banded hats.

"Very well! If you're going, take off your boots," commanded O'Neil.

"What for?"

"We may be swamped and have to swim for it. You see the man has taken his off." Murray pointed to the raw-boned Norwegian oarsman, who had stripped down as if for a foot-race.

Eliza obeyed.

"Now your sweater."

Natalie had watched this scene with evident concern. She now seated herself upon a boulder and began to tug at her rubber boots.

"Here! Here! You're not going, too!" O'Neil exclaimed.

"Yes, I am. I'm frightened to death, but I won't be a coward." Her shaking hands and strained voice left no doubt of her seriousness.

"She can't swim," said Eliza; and O'Neil put an end to this display of heroism with a firm refusal.

"You'll think I'm afraid," Natalie expostulated.

"Bless you, of course we will, because you are! So am I, and so is Eliza, for that matter. If you can't swim you'd only be taking a foolish risk and adding to our danger. Besides, Eliza doesn't know the feel of cold water as we do."

Natalie smiled a little tremulously at recollection of the shipwreck.

"I'd much rather walk, of course," she said; and then to Eliza, "It—it will be a lovely ramble for us."

But Eliza shook her head. "This is material for my book, and I'll make enough out of it to—to—"

"Buy another orchard," Murray suggested.

Feeling more resigned now that the adventure had taken on a purely financial color, Natalie at length allowed herself to be dissuaded, and Eliza settled herself in her seat with the disturbing consciousness that she had made herself appear selfish and rude in O'Neil's eyes. Nevertheless, she had no notion of changing her mind.

When the other girl had gone the oarsman completed his preparations by lashing fast the contents of the skiff —a proceeding which Eliza watched with some uneasiness. O'Neil showed his resentment by a pointed silence, which nettled her, and she resolved to hold her seat though the boat turned somersaults.

Word was finally given, and they swung out into the flood. O'Neil stood as best he could on his firm leg, and steered by means of a sculling-oar, while the Norwegian rowed lustily.

Bits of drift, patches of froth, fragments of ice accompanied them, bobbing alongside so persistently that Eliza fancied the boat must be stationary until, glancing at the river-banks, she saw them racing past like the panoramic scenery in a melodrama. The same glance showed her that they were rushing directly toward the upper ramparts of Jackson Glacier, as if for an assault. Out here in the current there were waves, and these increased in size as the bed of the Salmon grew steeper, until the poling-boat began to rear and leap like a frightened horse. The gleaming wall ahead rose higher with every instant: it overhung, a giant, crumbling cliff, imposing, treacherous. Then the stream turned at right angles; they were swept along parallel with the ice face, and ahead of them for three miles stretched the gauntlet. The tottering wall seemed almost within reaching distance; its breath was cold and damp and clammy. O'Neil stood erect and powerful in the stern, swaying to the antics of the craft, his weight upon the sweep, his eyes fixed upon the Thing overhead. The Norwegian strained at his oars while the sweat ran down into his open shirt. The boat lunged and wallowed desperately, rising on end, falling with prodigious slaps, drenching the occupants with spray. It was splendid, terrifying! Eliza clung to her seat and felt her heartbeats smothering her. Occasionally the oarsman turned, staring past her with round, frightened eyes, and affording her a glimpse of a face working with mingled fear and exultation.

Thus far the glacier had not disputed their passage; it maintained the silence and the immobility of marble; nothing but the snarl of the surging flood re-echoed from its face. But with the suddenness of a rifle-shot there came a detonation, louder, sharper than any blast of powder. The Norwegian cursed; the helmsman dropped his eyes to the white face in the bow and smiled.

Half a mile ahead of them a mass of ice came rumbling down, and the whole valley rocked with the sound. Onward the little craft fled, a dancing speck beneath the majesty of that frozen giant, an atom threatened by the weight of mountains. At last through the opening of the gorge below came a glimpse of the flats that led to the sea. A moment later the boat swung into an eddy and came to rest, bumping against the boulders.

O'Neil sat down, wiping his wet face.

"Well, was it worth your trouble, Miss Kick-over-the-traces?" he asked.

"Oh, it was glorious! I'll never forget it." Eliza's cheeks were burning now, her aching hands relaxed their hold, and she drew a deep breath—the first of which she had been conscious since the start, fifteen minutes before.

"Now, on with your boots and your sweater. We'll have an hour's wait for Natalie."

She gave a cry of surprise and offered him a glimpse of a trim ankle and a dripping foot.

"See! They're wet, and I wriggled my toes right through my stockings. I *never* was so excited."

The boatman fastened the painter and resumed his outer clothing. O'Neil lit a cigar and asked:

"Tell me, why did you insist on coming?"

"I was afraid something might happen to you." He raised his brows, and she flushed. "Don't you understand? Dan would never have forgiven me, and—and—I just *had* to come, that's all. It's corking material for me—I thought you might upset, and I—I don't know why I insisted." She bent over her stubborn boots, hiding her face. She was flaming to the ears, for suddenly she knew the reason that had prompted her. It rushed upon her like a sense of great shame. She recalled the desperate grip at her heart when she had seen him ready to leave, the wildness of her longing to share his danger, the black fear that he might meet disaster alone. It had all come without warning, and there had been no time for self-consciousness, but now she realized the truth. The poignant pain of it made her fingers clumsy and sent that flood of scarlet to her neck and ears.

When Natalie arrived they cast off, and the remaining miles were made in a few hours.

Appleton joined them for lunch in the tent they remembered so well, and professed to be shocked at the report of his sister's foolhardiness. But whatever may have been Natalie's fear of ridicule, it promptly disappeared under his complete indorsement of her wisdom in refraining from such a mad adventure. As if to put her even more at ease, O'Neil was especially attentive to her; and Eliza reflected gloomily that men, after all, dislike bravado in women, that a trapeze artist or a lady balloonist inspires only a qualified admiration.

During O'Neil's absence work had progressed steadily. On his return he found the grade completed to within a few yards of Gordon's right-of-way. Although he was still unable to walk, he insisted upon going to the front, whither he was helped by Appleton and "Happy Tom."

Into the narrow space between the end of his embankment and that of his rival's a gravel-train was spilling its burden, and a hundred pick-and-shovel men were busy. The opposing forces also seemed hard at work, but their activity was largely a pretense, and they showed plainly that they were waiting for the clash. They were a hard-looking crew, and their employer had neglected no precaution. He had erected barricades for their protection until his grade looked like a military work.

"They haven't showed any guns yet, but I'm sure they're armed," Appleton told his chief.

"How is the place lighted by night?" O'Neil inquired.

"Oil torches," Slater answered. "Ah! We've been recognized. That comes from being fat, I s'pose."

As he spoke a donkey-engine at the right of the proposed crossing set up a noisy rattling, a thin steel cable whipped into view between the rails, and from the left there appeared a contrivance which O'Neil eyed curiously. It was a sort of drag, and rode back and forth upon the rails.

"Humph! They'd better not put much trust in that," Murray grunted, grimly.

"Don't fool yourself; it's no rubber-tired baby-carriage," said Slater. "Our men are afraid of it."

After watching the device scuttle back and forth for a few moments O'Neil said shortly:

"Post a notice at once, offering a thousand dollars for any man who cuts that cable."

"A thousand—" Appleton gasped. "Why, I'll do it. Let me—"

"No, you won't," Slater broke in. "I'll take that on myself."

"I spoke first. It's my first chance," Dan cried.

"It's my job! I'm going—"

"Wait a minute!" O'Neil silenced the two, who were glaring at each other angrily. "Don't let's have any fighting; there will be enough of that later."

"I spoke first," Dan repeated, stubbornly.

"I had my mouth puckered to spit, that's why," the fat man explained. "A fellow has to spit—"

"I'd rather you wouldn't volunteer, Dan," said O'Neil. "Why?"

"You might get hurt."

"Happy Tom" nodded his agreement. "Certainly! Never send a boy on a man's errand."

"And I don't want you to do it either, Tom, for the same reason."

Slater mumbled some sort of sour acquiescence, but Dan would not be denied.

"You made the offer, and I took it up," he told O'Neil. "Somebody has to make the first move, and I have a particular need for exactly one thousand dollars. If they start a rumpus, it will give us the excuse we're looking for. I've been studying that 'go-devil' through field-glasses for two days now, and I'll guarantee to put it out of commission before Gordon's men know what I'm about. Just forget the reward, if you like, and give me a chance."

"What's your plan?" Slater inquired, eagerly; but Appleton shook his head.

"No you don't, Tommy!" he said. "I'm wise to you."

Murray hesitated briefly, then gave his permission. "I'd rather you'd let one of the rough-necks take the chance, but if you insist—"

"I do."

"Then get your sister's consent—"

Slater swore mournfully, as if from a heart filled with black despair.

"Ain't that my luck? One cud of gum cost me a thousand dollars! Hell! It would take a millionaire to afford a habit like that." He expelled the gum violently and went grumbling off up the track.

"Sis won't object," said Dan, lightly. "She'd offer to do the trick herself, for she's getting the spirit of the work."

When O'Neil had managed to regain the camp he began preparations for an attack that very night, using the telephone busily. News of the coming affray quickly spread, and both the day and night shifts discussed it excitedly at supper-time.

Nor was the excitement lessened when a loaded gravel-train rolled in and Dr. Gray descended from it with his emergency kit and two helpers from the hospital at Omar.

Up to this point both Eliza and Natalie had hoped that the affair might not, after all, turn out to be very serious, but the presence of the grim-faced surgeon and the significant preparations he set about making boded otherwise. Eliza undertook to reason with her brother, but her words refused to come. As a matter of fact, deep down in her heart was a great rebellion at the fate which had made her a woman and thus debarred her from an active part in the struggle. Natalie, on the other hand, was filled with dread, and she made a much more vigorous attempt to dissuade Dan from his purpose than did his sister. But he refused to heed even her, and soon hurried away to finish his preparations.

After supper the camp settled itself to wait for darkness. Night was slow in coming, and long before Appleton signified his readiness speculation was rife. With the approach of twilight the torches along Gordon's grade began to glow brightly. Then Dan set his watch with "Happy Tom's," kissed Eliza, and made off across the tundra. He left the S. R. & N. at right angles and continued in that direction for a mile or more before swinging about in a wide circle which brought him well to the rear of Gordon's encampment. The gloom now covered his movements, and by taking advantage of an alder thicket he managed to approach very closely to the enemy's position. But the footing was treacherous, the darkness betrayed him into many a fall, and he was wet, muddy, and perspiring when he finally paused not more than two hundred feet from the scene of the proposed crossing.

XV   *The Battle of Gordon's Crossing*

Curtis Gordon was not in charge of his field forces, having left the command to his favorite jackal, Denny. Beneath his apparent contempt for the law there lurked a certain caution. He knew his rival's necessity, he appreciated his cunning, but, wishing to guard against the possibility of a personal humiliation, he retired to Kyak, where he was prepared to admit or to deny as much responsibility as suited him. Denny had not forgotten O'Neil's exposure of his dishonesty, and his zeal could be relied upon. He personally knew all the men under him, he had coached them carefully, and he assured Gordon of his ability to hold his ground.

Dan Appleton, from his covert, measured the preparations for resistance with some uneasiness, reflecting that if Denny had the nerve to use firearms he would undoubtedly rout O'Neil's men, who had not been permitted to carry guns. By the bright torchlight he could see figures coming and going along the grade like sentinels, and from within the barricades of ties he heard others talking. The camp itself, which lay farther to the left, was lighted, and black silhouettes were painted against the canvas walls and roofs. Some one was playing an accordion, and its wailing notes came to him intermittently. He saw that steam was up in the boiler which operated the "go-devil," although the contrivance itself was stationary. It was upon this that he centered his attention, consulting his watch nervously.

At last ten o'clock came, bringing with it a sound which startled the near-by camp into activity. It was a shrill blast from an S. R. & N. locomotive and the grinding of carwheels. The accordion ceased its complaint, men poured out of the lighted tents, Appleton moved cautiously out from cover.

He stumbled forward through the knee-deep mud and moss, bearing slightly to his right, counting upon the confusion to mask his approach. He timed it to that of the gravel-train, which came slowly creaking nearer, rocking over the uneven tracks, then down upon the half-submerged rails which terminated near the opposing grade. It stopped finally, with headlight glaring into the faces of

Denny and his troops, and from the high-heaped flat cars tumbled an army of pick-and-shovel men. During this hullabaloo Appleton slipped out of the marsh and climbed the gravel-bed in time to see the steel cable of the skip tighten, carrying the drag swiftly along the track. The endless cable propelling the contrivance ran through a metal block which was secured to a deadhead sunk between the ties, and up to this post Dan hastened. He carried a coldchisel and hammer, but he found no use for them, for the pulley was roped to the deadhead. Drawing his knife, he sawed at the manila strands. Men were all around him, but in their excitement they took no notice of him. Not until he had nearly completed his task was he discovered; then some one raised a shout. The next instant they charged upon him, but his work had been done. With a snap the ropes parted, the cable went writhing and twisting up the track, the unwieldy apparatus came to a stop.

Dan found himself beset by a half-dozen of the enemy, who, having singled him out of the general confusion as the cause of disaster, came at him headlong. But by this time O'Neil's men were pouring out of the darkness and overrunning the grade so rapidly that there was little opportunity for concerted action. Appleton had intended, as soon as he had cut the cable, to beat a hasty retreat into the marsh; but now, with the firm gravel road-bed under his feet and the battle breaking before his eyes, he changed his mind. He carried a light heart, and the love of trouble romped through his veins. He lowered his head, therefore, and ran toward his assailants.

He met the foremost one fairly and laid him out. He vanquished the second, then closed with a burly black man who withstood him capably. They went down together, and Dan began to repent his haste, for blows rained upon him and he became the target, not only of missiles of every kind, but of heavy hobnailed shoes that were more dangerous than horses' hoofs.

The engineer dearly loved a fair fight, even against odds, but this was entirely different: he was trampled, stamped upon, kicked; he felt himself being reduced to a pulp beneath the overpowering numbers of those savage heels. The fact that the black man received an equal share of the punishment was all that saved Dan. Over and over between the ties the two rolled, scorning no advantage, regarding no rules of combat, each striving to protect himself at the other's expense.

They were groveling there in a tangle of legs and arms when "Happy Tom" came down the grade, leading a charge which swept the embankment clean.

The boss packer had equipped his command with pick-handles and now set a brilliant example in the use of this, his favorite weapon. For once the apathetic Slater was fully roused; he was tremendous, irresistible. In his capable grasp the oaken cudgel became both armor and flail; in defense it was as active as a fencing-master's foil, in offense as deadly as the kick of a mule. Beneath his formless bulk were the muscles of a gladiator; his eye had all the quickness of a prize-fighter. There was something primeval, appallingly ferocious about the fat man, too: he fought with a magnificent enthusiasm, a splendid abandon. And yet, in spite of his rage, he was clear-headed, and his ears were sensitively strained for the sound of the first gunshot—something he dreaded beyond measure.

He was sobbing as much from anxiety as from the violence of his exertions when he tore Appleton from the clutch of the black man and set him on his feet.

"Are you hurt, son?" he gasped.

"Sure! I'm—hurt like hell." Dan spat out a mouthful of blood and sand. "Gimme a club."

"Go back yonder," Tom directed, swiftly. "Nail Denny before he gets 'em to shooting. Kill him if you have to. I'll take care of these fellers."

The younger man saw that the engagement at this end of the line was no longer general, but had become a series of individual combats, so he made what haste he could toward the scene of the more serious encounter to the right of the crossing. He judged that the issue was still in doubt there, although he could make out little in the confusion on account of the glaring headlight, which dazzled him.

As he ran, however, he discovered that the S. R. & N. forces were in possession of the middle ground, having divided the enemy's ranks like a wedge, and this encouraged him. Out of the darkness to right and left came shouts, curses, the sounds of men wallowing about in the knee-deep tundra. They were Gordon's helpers who had been routed from their positions.

Now that Appleton had time to collect himself he, too, grew sick with suspense, for he knew that arms had been stacked inside the barricades. Any instant might bring them into play. He began to wonder why Denny withheld the word to fire.

As a matter of fact, the explanation was simple, although it did not appear until later. Mr. Denny at that moment was in no condition to issue orders of any kind, the reason being as follows: when preparations for the advance were made, Dr. Gray, who understood perhaps more fully than any one else except O'Neil the gravity of the issue and the slender pivot upon which the outcome balanced, had taken his place in the vanguard of the attacking party instead of in the background, as befitted his calling. The first rush had carried him well into the fray, but once there he had shown his good judgment by refusing to participate in it.

Instead, he had selected Denny out of the opposing ranks and bored through the crowd in his direction, heedless of all efforts to stop him. His great strength had enabled him to gain ground; he had hurled his assailants aside, upsetting them, bursting through the press as a football-player penetrates a line; and when the retreat had begun he was close at the heels of his victim. He had overtaken Denny beside one of the barricades just as Denny seized a rifle and raised it. With one wrench he possessed himself of the weapon, and the next instant he had bent the barrel over its owner's head.

Then, as the fight surged onward, he had gathered the limp figure in his arms and borne it into the light of a gasolene-torch, where he could administer first aid. He was kneeling over the fellow when Appleton found him as he came stumbling along the grade.

But the decisive moment had come and gone now, and without a leader to command them Gordon's men seemed loath to adopt a more bloody reprisal. They gave way, therefore, in a half-hearted hesitation that spelled ruin to their cause. They were forced back to their encampment; over the ground they had vacated picks and shovels began to fly, rails were torn up and relaid, gravel rained from the flat cars, the blockhouses were razed, and above the rabble the locomotive panted and wheezed, its great yellow eye glaring through the night. When it backed away another took its place; the grade rose to the level of the intersection, then as morning approached it crept out beyond. By breakfast-time a long row of flats extended across the line which Curtis Gordon had tried to hold in defiance of the law.

Dan Appleton, very dirty, very tired, but happy, found Natalie and Eliza awaiting him when he limped up to their tent in the early morning light. One of his eyes was black and nearly closed, his lips were cut and swollen, but he grinned cheerfully as he exclaimed:

"Say! It was a great night, wasn't it?"

Eliza cried out in alarm at his appearance.

"You poor kid! You're a sight." She ran for hot water and soap, while Natalie said, warmly:

"You were perfectly splendid, Dan. I knew you'd do it."

"Did you?" He tried to smile his appreciation, but the effort resulted in a leer so repulsive that the girl looked dismayed. "You ought to have seen the shindy."

"Seen it! Maybe we didn't!"

"Honestly?"

"Did you think we could stay behind? We sneaked along with the cook-house gang, and one of them helped us up on the gravel-cars. He smelled of dish-water, but he was a hero. We screamed and cried, and Eliza threw stones until Mr. O'Neil discovered us and made us get down. He was awfully mean."

"He's a mean man."

"He isn't! He was jumping around on one leg like a crippled grasshopper."

"I made a thousand dollars," said Dan. "Guess what I'm going to do with it?"

"How can I guess?"

"I'm going to buy an engagement ring." Once more he leered repulsively.

"How nice!" said Natalie, coolly. "Congratulations!"

"Guess who it's for?"

"I couldn't, really."

"It's for you."

"Oh no, it isn't!" Natalie's voice was freezing. "You have made a mistake, a very great mistake, Dan. I like you, but—we won't even mention such things, if you please."

Eliza's entrance saved her further embarrassment, and she quickly made her escape. Dan groaned so deeply as his sister bathed his injuries that she was really concerned.

"Goodness, Danny," she said, "are you as badly hurt as all that?"

"I'm worse," he confessed. "I've just been shot through the heart. Slow music and flowers for me! Arrange for the services and put a rose in my hand, Sis."

"Nonsense! I'll put a beefsteak on your eye," she told him, unfeelingly.

Under Dr. Gray's attention O'Neil's ankle began to mend, and by the time the track had been laid far enough beyond the crossing to insure against further interference from Gordon he declared himself ready to complete the journey to Kyak, which he and the girls had begun nearly three weeks before.

During the interval Eliza had occupied herself in laying out her magazine stories, and now she was eager to complete her investigations so as to begin the final writing. Her

experience in the north thus far had given her an altered
outlook upon the railroad situation, but as yet she knew
little of the coal problem. That, after all, was the more
important subject, and she expected it to afford her the
basis for a sensational exposure. She had come to Alaska
sharing her newspaper's views upon questions of public
policy, looking upon Murray O'Neil as a daring promoter
bent upon seizing the means of transportation of a mighty
realm for his own individual profit; upon Gordon as an
unscrupulous adventurer; and upon the Copper Trust as a
greedy corporation reaching out to strangle competition
and absorb the riches of the northland. But she had found
O'Neil an honorably ambitious man, busied, like others,
in the struggle for success, and backing his judgment with
his last dollar. She had learned, moreover, to sympathize
with his aims, and his splendid determination awoke her
admiration. Her idea of the Trust had changed, likewise,
for it seemed to be a fair and dignified competitor. She
had seen no signs of that conscienceless, grasping policy
usually imputed to big business. In regard to Gordon alone,
her first conviction had remained unchanged. He was, in
truth, as evil as he had been reputed.

The readjustment of her ideas had been disappointing,
in a way, since it robbed her of a large part of her am-
munition; but she consoled herself with the thought that
she had not yet reached the big, vital story which most
deeply concerned the welfare of the north.

She was a bit afraid to pursue her inquiries into the
coal subject, for her ideas were fixed, and she feared that
O'Neil's activities merited condemnation. In his railroad-
building, she believed, he was doing a fine work, but the
coal was another matter. Obviously it belonged to the
people, and he had no right to lay hands upon their
heritage.

She wondered if it would not be possible to omit all
mention of him in her coal stories and center attention
upon the Trust. It was impossible for her to attack him
now, since she had come to understand her feelings toward
him. Even so, she reflected with horror that if her articles
created the comment she anticipated their effect would be
to rob him of his holdings. But she took her work very
seriously, and her sense of duty was unwavering. She was

one of the few who guide themselves by the line of principle, straight through all other considerations. She would write what she found true, for that was her mission in life. If Murray proved culpable she would grieve over his wrong-doing—and continue to love him.

O'Neil had recognized her sincerity, and on the broad subject of conservation he had done nothing to influence her views. He preferred to let her see the workings of the principle and, after actually meeting some of those who had suffered by it, form her own conclusions. It was for this reason mainly that he had arranged the trip to Kyak.

The journey in a small boat gave Eliza a longed-for opportunity to discuss with him the questions which troubled her. He was uncommunicative at first, but she persisted in her attempt, drawing him out in the hope of showing him the error of his ways. At last she provoked him to a vigorous defense of his views.

"Conservation is no more than economy," he declared, "and no one opposes that. It's the misapplication of the principle that has retarded Alaska and ruined so many of us. The situation would be laughable if it weren't so tragic."

"Of course you blame your troubles on the Government. That's one thing governments are for."

"Our ancestors blamed King George for their troubles, more than a hundred years ago, and a war resulted. But every abuse they suffered is suffered by the people of Alaska to-day, and a lot more besides. Certainly England never violated her contracts with the colonies half so flagrantly as our Government has violated its contracts with us."

"Of course you exaggerate."

"I don't. Judge for yourself. The law offers every citizen the chance—in fact, it invites him—to go upon the public domain and search for treasure. If he is successful it permits him to locate the land in blocks, and it agrees to grant him a clear title after he does a certain amount of work and pays a fixed price. Further, it says in effect: 'Realizing that you may need financial assistance in this work, we will allow you to locate not only for yourself, but also for your friends, through their powers of attorney, and thus gain their co-operation for your mutual advantage. These are the rules, and they are binding upon all parties to this agreement; you keep your part, we will keep ours.' Now then, some pioneers, at risk of life and health, came to Kyak and found coal. They located it, they did all the law required them to do—but did the Government keep its word? Not at all. It was charged that some of them hadn't conformed strictly to the letter of the agreement, and therefore *all* the claims were blacklisted. Because one man was alleged to have broken his contract the Government broke its contract with every man who had staked a coal claim, not only at Kyak, but anywhere else in Alaska. Guilty and innocent were treated alike. I was one of the latter. Was our money returned to us? No! The Government had it and it kept it, along with the land. We've been holding on now for years, and the Interior Department has tried by various means to shake us off. The law has been changed repeatedly at the whim of every theorist who happened to be in power. It has been changed without notice to us, even while we were out in the wilderness trying to comply with the regulations already imposed. You can see how it worked in the case of Natalie and her mother. The Government succeeded in shaking them off."

"That's only one side of the question," said Eliza. "You lose sight of the fact that this treasure never really belonged to you, but to the public. The coal-lands were withdrawn from entry because men like you and the agents of the Heidlemanns were grabbing it all up."

O'Neil shook his head, frowning. "That's what the papers say, but it isn't true. There are twenty millions acres of coal in Alaska, and not more than thirty thousand acres have been located. The law gave me the right to locate and buy coal claims, and I took advantage of it. Now it tells me that I have money enough, and takes back what it gave. If it did the right thing it would grant patents to those who located under the law as it then existed and withdraw the rest of the land from entry if advisable. This country needs two things to make it prosper—transportation and fuel. We are doing our best to supply the first in spite of hindrance from Washington; but the fuel has been locked away from us as if behind stone walls. Rich men must be brave to risk their dollars here under existing conditions, for they are not permitted to utilize the mines, the timber, or the water-power, except upon absurd and unreasonable terms. Why, I've seen timber lying four layers deep and rotting where it lies. The Government won't save it, nor will it allow us to do so. That's been its policy throughout. It is strangling industry and dedicating Alaska to eternal solitude. Railroads are the keys by which this realm can be unlocked; coal is the strength by which those keys can be turned. The keys are fitted to the lock, but our fingers are paralyzed. For eight years Alaska's greatest wealth has lain exposed to view, but the Government has posted the warning, 'Hands off! Some one among you is a crook!' Meanwhile the law has been suspended, the country has stagnated, men have left dispirited or broken, towns have been abandoned. The cost in dollars to me, for instance, has been tremendous. I'm laying my track alongside rich coal-fields, but if I picked up a chunk from my own claim to throw at a chipmunk I'd become a lawbreaker. I import from Canada the fuel to drive my locomotives past my own coal-beds—which I have paid for—and I pay five times the value of that fuel, forty per cent. of which is duty. I haul it two thousand miles, while there are a billion tons of better quality beneath my feet. Do you call that conservation? I call it waste."

"Fraud was practised at the start, and of course it takes time to find out just where it lay."

"That's the excuse, but after all these years no fraud has been proved. In administering the criminal law there is an axiom to the effect that it is better for ninety-nine guilty men to escape than for one innocent man to suffer, but the Land Office says that ninety-nine innocent Alaskans shall suffer rather than that one guilty man shall escape. The cry of fraud is only a pretense, raised to cover the main issue. There's something sinister back of it."

"What do you mean?"

"A conspiracy of the Eastern coal-operators and the transcontinental freight-lines."

"How ridiculous!" cried Eliza.

"You think so? Listen! Since all the high-grade coal of the Pacific coast must come from the East, who, then, would discourage the opening of local fields but those very interests? Every ton we burn means a profit to the Eastern miner and the railroad man. Yes, and twenty per cent. of the heat units of every ton hauled are consumed in transportation. Isn't that waste? Every two years it costs our navy the price of a battle-ship to bring coal to the Pacific fleet, while we have plenty of better fuel right here on the ground. Our coal is twenty-five hundred miles nearer to the Philippines than San Francisco, and twelve thousand miles nearer than its present source. If Alaskan coal-beds were opened up, we wouldn't have this yearly fight for battle-ship appropriations; we'd make ourselves a present of a first-class navy for nothing. No, our claims were disputed, and the dispute was thrown into politics to keep us out of competition with our Eastern cousins. We Alaskans sat in a game with high stakes, but after the cards were dealt the rules were changed."

"You argue very well," said Eliza, who was a bit dazed at this unexpected, forceful counter-attack, "but you haven't convinced me that this coal should be thrown open to the first person who comes along."

"I didn't expect to convince you. It's hard to convince a woman whose mind is made up. It would take hours to cover the subject; but I want to open your eyes to the effect of this new-fangled national policy. Any great principle may work evil if it isn't properly directed, and in Kyak you'll see the results of conservation ignorantly applied. You'll see how it has bound and gagged a wonderful country, and made loyal Americans into ragged, bitter traitors who would spit upon the flag they used to cherish."

"Is that the only reason why you came along—just to make sure that I saw all this?"

"No. I want to look at the Heidlemann breakwater. My fortune hangs upon it."

"It's as serious as that?"

O'Neil shrugged. "I'm waiting for the wind. My coal is in the hands of the bureaucracy at Washington, my railroad is in the hands of the wind god. Incidentally, I'd much rather trust the god than the Government."

Natalie, who had listened so far without the least sign of interest, now spoke up.

"If the storm doesn't come to your help, will you be ruined?" she asked.

Murray smiled cheerfully. "No man is ruined as long as

he keeps his dreams. Money isn't much, after all, and failure is merely a schooling. But—I won't fail. Autumn is here: the tempest is my friend; and he won't be long in coming now. He'll arrive with the equinox, and when he does he'll hold my fortune in his hand."

"Why, the equinoctial storm is due," said Eliza.

"Exactly! That's why I'm going to meet it and to bid it welcome."

The village of Kyak lay near the mouth of the most easterly outlet of the Salmon, and it was similar in most respects to Hope and to Omar, save that it looked out across a shallow, unprotected bay to the open reaches of the north Pacific. The shores were low; a pair of rocky islets afforded the only shelter to its shipping, and it was from these as a starting-point that the Copper Trust had built its breakwater. A trestle across the tide-flats connected the work with the mainland, and along this rock-trains crawled, adding their burdens to the strength of the barrier. Protected by this arm of steel and stone and timber lay the terminal buildings of the Alaska Northern, as the Heidlemann line was called, and there also lay the terminus of the old McDermott enterprise into which Curtis Gordon had infused new life. Both places showed plenty of activity when O'Neil and his two companions arrived, late one afternoon.

Kyak, they found, was inferior to Omar in its public accommodations, and Murray was at a loss to find shelter for the girls until his arrival was made known to the agents of the Alaska Northern. Then Mr. Trevor, the engineer in charge, looked him up and insisted upon sharing his quarters with the visitors. In Trevor's bearing was no suggestion of an enmity like Gordon's. He welcomed his rival warmly —and indeed the Trust had never been small in its opposition. O'Neil accepted the invitation gratefully.

After dinner he took Natalie with him to see the sights, while Eliza profited by the opportunity to interview Trevor. In her numerous tilts with O'Neil she had not been over-successful from the point of view of her magazine articles, but here at her hand was the representative of the power best known and best hated for its activities in the north-land, and he seemed perfectly willing to talk. Surely from him she would get information that would count.

"Understand, I'm on the side of your enemies," she warned him.

"So is everybody else," Mr. Trevor laughed; "but that's because we're misunderstood."

"The intentions of any Trust warrant suspicion."

He shrugged. "The Heidlemanns are just ordinary business men, like O'Neil, looking for investment. They heard of a great big copper-field hidden away back yonder in the mountains, and they bought what they considered to be the best group of claims. They knew the region was difficult of access, but they figured that a railroad from tidewater would open up not only their own properties, but the rest of the copper-belt and the whole interior country. They began to build a road from Cortez, when some 'shoe-stringer' raised the cry that they had monopolized the world's greatest copper supply, and had double-cinched it by monopolizing transportation also. That started the fuss. They needed cheap coal, of course, just as everybody else needs it; but somebody discovered the danger of a monopoly of that and set up another shout. Ever since then the yellow press has been screaming. The Government withdrew all coal-lands from entry, and it now refuses to grant patents to that which had been properly located. We don't own a foot of Alaskan coal-land, Miss Appleton. On the contrary, we haul our fuel from British Columbia, just like O'Neil and Gordon. Those who would like to sell local coal to us are prevented from doing so."

"It sounds well to hear you tell it," said Eliza. "But the minute the coal patents are issued you will buy what you want, then freeze out the other people. You expect to control the mines, the railroads, and the steamship lines, but public necessities like coal and oil and timber and water-power should belong to the people. There has been an awakening of the public conscience, and the day of monopolized necessities is passing."

"As long as men own coal-mines they will sell them. Here we are faced not by a question of what may happen, but of what has happened. If you agreed to buy a city lot from a real-estate dealer, and after you paid him his price he refused to give you a deed, you'd at least expect your money back, wouldn't you? Well, that's the case of Uncle Sam and the Alaskan miners. He not only refuses to deliver the lot, but keeps the money, and forces them to pay more every year. I represent a body of rich men who, because of their power, are regarded with suspicion; but if they did anything so dishonest as what our Government has done to its own people they would be jailed."

"No doubt there has been some injustice, but the great truth remains that the nation should own its natural resources, and should not allow favored individuals to profit by the public need."

"You mean railroads and coal-fields and such things?"

"I do."

Trevor shook his head. "If the people of Alaska waited for a Government railroad, they'd die of old age and be buried where they died, for lack of transportation. The Government owns telegraph-lines here, but it charges us five times the rates of the Western Union. No, Miss Appleton, we're not ready for Government ownership, and even if we were it wouldn't affect the legality of what has been done. Through fear that the Heidlemanns might profit this whole country has been made to stagnate. Alaska is being depopulated; houses and stores are closed; people are leaving despondent. Alaskans are denied self-government in any form; theories are tried at their expense, but they are never consulted. Not only does Congress fail to enact new laws to meet their needs, but it refuses to proceed under the laws that already exist. If the same policy had been pursued in the settlement of the Middle West that applies to this country, the buffalo would still be king of the plains and Chicago would be a frontier town. You seem to think that coal is the most important issue up here, but it isn't. Transportation is what the country needs, for the main riches of Alaska are as useless to-day as if hidden away in the chasms of the moon. O'Neil had the right idea when he selected the Salmon River route, but he made an error of judgment, and he lost."

"He hasn't lost!" cried Eliza, in quick defense of her friend. "Your breakwater hasn't been tested yet."

"Oh, it will hold," Trevor smiled. "It has cost too much money not to hold."

"Wait until the storms come," the girl persisted.

"That's what we're doing, and from present indications

we won't have much longer to wait. Weather has been breeding for several days, and the equinox is here. Of course I'm anxious, but—I built that breakwater, and it can't go out."

When O'Neil and Natalie returned they found the two still arguing. "Haven't you finished your tiresome discussions?" asked Natalie.

"Mr. Trevor has almost convinced me that the octopus is a noble creature, filled with high ideals and writhing at the thrusts of the muck-rakers," Eliza told them.

But at that the engineer protested. "No, no!" he said. "I haven't half done justice to the subject. There are a dozen men in Kyak to-night who could put up a much stronger case than I. There's McCann, for instance. He was a prospector back in the States until he made a strike which netted him a hundred thousand dollars. He put nearly all of it into Kyak coal claims and borrowed seventy thousand more. He got tired of the interminable delay and finally mined a few tons which he sent out for a test in the navy. It had better steaming qualities than the Eastern coal now being used, but six weeks later an agent of the Land Office ordered him to cease work until his title had been passed upon. That was two years ago, and nothing has been done since. No charges of irregularity of any sort have ever been filed against McCann or his property. The Government has had his money for five years, and still he can't get a ruling. He's broke now and too old to make a living. He's selling pies on the street—"

"He borrowed a dollar from me just now," said O'Neil, who was staring out of a window. Suddenly he turned and addressed his host. "Trevor, it's going to storm." His voice was harsh, his eyes were eager; his tone brought the engineer to his side. Together they looked out across the bay.

The southern sky was leaden, the evening had been shortened by a rack of clouds which came hurrying in from the sea.

"Let it storm," said Trevor, after a moment. "I'm ready."

"Have you ever seen it blow here?"

"The old-timers tell me I haven't, but—I've seen some terrible storms. Of course the place is unusual—"

"In what way?" Eliza inquired.

"The whole country back of here is ice-capped. This coast for a hundred miles to the east is glacial. The cold air inland and the warm air from the Japanese Current are always at war."

"There is a peculiar difference in air-pressures, too," O'Neil explained. "Over the warm interior it is high, and over the coast range it is low; so every valley becomes a pathway for the wind. But that isn't where the hurricanes come from. They're born out yonder." He pointed out beyond the islands from which the breakwater flung its slender arm. "This may be only a little storm, Trevor, but some day the sea and the air will come together and wipe out all your work. Then you'll see that I was right."

"You told me that more than a year ago, but I backed my skill against your prophecy."

O'Neil answered him gravely: "Men like you and me become over-confident of our powers; we grow arrogant, but after all we're only pygmies."

"If Nature beats me here, I'm a ruined man," said the engineer.

"And if you defeat her, I'm ruined." O'Neil smiled at him.

"Let's make medicine, the way the Indians did, and call upon the Spirit of the Wind to settle the question," Eliza suggested, with a woman's quick instinct for relieving a situation that threatened to become constrained. She and Natalie ran to Trevor's sideboard, and, seizing bottle and shaker, brewed a magic broth, while the two men looked on. They murmured incantations, they made mystic passes, then bore the glasses to their companions.

As the men faced each other Natalie cried:

"To the Wind!"

"Yes! More power to it!" Eliza echoed.

Trevor smiled. "I drink defiance."

"In my glass I see hope and confidence," said O'Neil. "May the storm profit him who most deserves help."

Despite their lightness, there was a certain gravity among the four, and as the night became more threatening they felt a growing suspense. The men's restlessness communicated itself to the girls, who found themselves listening with almost painful intentness to the voice of the wind and the rumble of the surf, which grew louder with every hour. By bed-time a torrent of rain was sweeping past, the roof strained, the windows were sheeted with water. Now and then the clamor ceased, only to begin with redoubled force. Trevor's guests were glad indeed of their snug shelter.

As Natalie prepared for bed she said: "It was fine of Mr. Trevor to treat Murray O'Neil so nicely. No one would dream that they were rivals, or that one's success means the other's ruin. Now Gordon—" She turned to see her friend kneeling at the bedside, and apologized quickly.

Eliza lifted her face and said simply, "I'm praying for the Wind."

Natalie slipped down beside her and bowed her dark head close to the light one. They remained there for a long time, while outside the rain pelted, the surf roared, and the wind came shrieking in from the sea.

XVI *The Fruit of the Tempest*

Neither O'Neil nor his host was in sight when the girls came to breakfast. The men had risen early, it seemed, and were somewhere out in the storm. A wilder day would be hard to imagine; a hurricane was raging, the rain was whirled ahead of it like charges of shot. The mountains behind Kyak were invisible, and to seaward was nothing but a dimly discernible smother of foam and spray, for the crests of the breakers were snatched up and carried by the wind. The town was sodden; the streets were running mud. Stove-pipes were down, tents lay flattened in the mire, and the board houses were shaking as if they might fly to pieces at any moment. The darkness was uncanny, and the tempest seemed to be steadily growing in violence.

When an hour or two had passed with no word from the men Eliza announced her intention of looking them up. She had spent the time at a window, straining her eyes through the welter, while Natalie had curled up cozily with a book in one of Trevor's arm-chairs.

"But, dearie, you'll be drenched." Natalie looked up in surprise. "Mr. O'Neil is all right."

"Of course he is. I'm not going out to spank him and bring him in. I want to look at the storm."

"So do I, but it won't do any good. I can't make it blow any harder by getting my feet wet."

"You read your novel and talk to Mr. Trevor when he comes back. He knows we're to blame for this storm, so you must be nice to him. I can't." She clad herself in raincoat, sou'wester, and boots, and hurried out. Walking was difficult enough, even in the shelter of the village, but not until she had emerged upon the beach did she meet the full strength of the gale. Here it wrapped her garments about her limbs until she could scarcely move. The rain came horizontally and blinded her; the wind fairly snatched her breath away and oppressed her lungs like a heavy weight. She shielded herself as best she could, and by clinging to stationary objects and watching her chance she managed to work her way onward. At last she caught sight of O'Neil, standing high above the surf, facing the wind defiantly, as if daring it to unfoot him. He saw her and came in answer to her signal; but to breast that wind was like stemming a rushing torrent, and when he reached her side he was panting.

"Child! What are you doing here?" he demanded.

"I couldn't wait any longer," she shouted back. "You've been out since daylight. You must be wet through."

He nodded. "I lay awake all night listening. So did Trevor. He's beginning to worry already."

"Already? If the breakwater stands this—"

"The storm hasn't half started! Come! We'll watch it together." He took her hand, and they lunged into the gale, battling their way back to his point of vantage. He paused at length, and with his arm about her pointed to the milk-white chaos which marked Trevor's handiwork. The rain pelted against their faces and streamed from their slickers.

The breakwater lay like a reef, and over it the sea was pounding in mighty wrath. High into the air the waters rose, only to disappear upon the bosom of the gale. They engulfed the structure bodily, they raced along it with thunderous detonations, bursting in a lather of rage. Out beyond, the billows appeared to be sheared flat by the force of the wind, yet that ceaseless upheaval of spume showed that the ocean was in furious tumult. For moments at a time the whole scene was blotted out by the scud, then the curtain would tear asunder and the wild scene would leap up again before their eyes.

Eliza screamed a question at her companion, but he did not seem to hear; his eyes roved back and forth along that lace-white ridge of rock on the weakness of which depended his salvation. She had never seen him so fierce, so hawklike, so impassive. The gusts shook him, his garments slatted viciously, every rag beneath his outer covering was sodden, yet he continued to face the tempest as indifferently as he had faced it since the dawn. The girl thrilled at thought of the issue these mighty forces were fighting out before her eyes, and of what it meant to the man beside her. His interests became hers; she shared his painful excitement. Her warm flesh chilled as the moisture embraced her limbs; but her heart was light, for O'Neil's strong arm encircled her, and her body lay against his.

After a long time he spoke. "See! It's coming up!" he said.

She felt no increase in the wind, but she noted that particles of sand and tiny pebbles from the beach were flying with the salt raindrops. Her muscles began to tremble from the constant effort at resistance, and she was relieved when Murray looked about for a place of refuge. She pointed to a pile of bridge timbers, but he shook his head.

"They'll go flying if this keeps up." He dragged her into the shelter of a little knoll. Here the blasts struck them with diminished force, the roaring in their ears grew less, and the labor of breathing was easier.

Rousing himself from his thoughts, the man said, gently: "Poor kid! You must be cold."

"I'm freezing. But—please don't send me back." The face that met his was supplicating; the eyes were bluer than a spring day. He patted her dripping shoulder.

"Not until you're ready."

"This is grander than our trip past the glacier. That was merely dangerous, but this—means something."

"There may be danger here if we expose ourselves. Look at that!"

High up beyond reach of the surf a dory had been

dragged and left bottom up. Under this the wind found a fingerhold and sent it flying. Over and over it rolled, until a stronger gust caught it and sent it in huge leaps, end over end. It brought up against the timber pile with a crash, and was held there as if by a mighty suction. Then the beams began to tremble and lift. The pile was disintegrated bit by bit, although it would have required many hands to move any one of its parts.

Even where the man and the woman crouched the wind harried them like a hound pack, but by clinging to the branches of a gnarled juniper bush they held their position and let the spray whine over their heads.

"Farther west I've seen houses chained to the earth with ships' cables," he shouted in her ear. "To think of building a harbor in a place like this!"

"I prayed for you last night. I prayed for the wind to come," said the girl, after a time.

O'Neil looked at her, curiously startled, then he looked out at the sea once more. All in a moment he realized that Eliza was beautiful and that she had a heart. It seemed wonderful that she should be interested in his fortunes. He was a lonely man; beneath his open friendliness lay a deep reserve, a curiously warm feeling of gratitude flamed through him now, and he silently blessed her for bearing him company in the deciding hour of his life.

Noon came, and still the two crouched in their half-shelter, drenched, chilled, stiff with exposure, watching Kyak Bay lash itself into a boiling smother. The light grew dim, night was settling; the air seemed full of screaming furies. Then O'Neil noticed bits of driftwood racing in upon the billows, and he rose with a loud cry.

"It's breaking up!" he shouted. "It's breaking up!"

Eliza lifted herself and clung to him, but she could see nothing except a misty confusion. In a few moments the flotsam came thicker. Splintered piling, huge square-hewn timbers with fragments of twisted iron or broken bolts came floating into sight. A confusion of wreckage began to clutter the shore, and into it the sea churned.

The spindrift tore asunder at length, and the watchers caught a brief glimpse of the tumbling ocean. The breakwater was gone. Over the place where it had stood the billows raced unhindered.

"Poor Trevor!" said O'Neil. "Poor Trevor! He did his best, but he didn't know." He looked down to find Eliza crying. "What's this? I've kept you here too long!"

"No, no! I'm just glad—so glad. Don't you understand?"

"I'll take you back. I must get ready to leave."

"Leave? Where—"

"For New York! I've made my fight, and I've won." His eyes kindled feverishly. "I've won in spite of them all. I hold the key to a kingdom. It's mine—mine! I hold the gateway to an empire, and those who pass through must pay." The girl had never seen such fierce triumph in a face. "I saw it in a dream, only it was more than a dream." The wind snatched O'Neil's words from his lips, but he ran on: "I saw a deserted fishing-village become a thriving city. I saw the glaciers part to let pass a great traffic in men and merchandise. I saw the unpeopled north grow into a land of homes, of farms, of mining-camps, where people lived and bred children. I heard the mountain passes echo to steam whistles and the whir of flying wheels. It was a wonderful vision that I saw, but my eyes were true. They called me a fool, and it took the sea and the hurricane to show them I was right." He paused, ashamed of his outburst, and, taking the girl's hand in his, went stumbling ahead of the storm.

Their limbs were cramped, their teeth chattered, they wallowed through mire, and more than once they fell. Nearing Trevor's house, they saw what the storm had done. Kyak was nearly razed. Roofs had been ripped off, chimneys were down, glass was out. None but the most substantial log cabins had withstood the assault, and men were busied in various quarters trying to repair the damage.

They found Natalie beside herself with anxiety for their safety, and an hour later Trevor came in, soaked to the skin. He was very tired, and his face was haggard.

"Well! She went out!" he said. "I saw a million dollars swallowed up in that sea."

They tried to comfort him, but the collapse of all his work had left him dazed.

"God! I didn't think it could blow like this—and it isn't over yet. The town is flat."

"I'm sorry. You understand I sympathize?" said Murray; and the engineer nodded.

"You told me it blew here, and I thought I knew what you meant, but nothing could withstand those rollers."

"Nothing."

"You'll go East and see our people, I suppose?"

"At once."

"Tell them what you saw. They'll never understand from my reports. They're good people. If there's anything I can do—"

O'Neil took his hand warmly.

Two days later Murray bade the girls good-by, and left, traveling light. They remained in Kyak so that Eliza might complete her investigations.

Of all those who suffered by the storm Curtis Gordon took his misfortune hardest. This had been a black season for him, indeed. Beginning with O'Neil's rivalry, everything had gone against him. He had dropped his coal interests at Kyak in favor of the copper-mine, because they failed to yield quick profits. Then he had learned that the mine was valueless, and realized that it could not serve him much longer as a means of raising funds. Still, he had trusted that by taking a vigorous part in the railroad struggle he would be able either to recoup his fortunes or at least to effect a compromise in the shadow of which his fiasco at Hope would be forgotten. As yet the truth about Hope Consolidated was not generally known to his stockholders, but a certain restlessness among them had become troublesome. The stream of money had diminished alarmingly, and it was largely because of this that he had bought the McDermott right-of-way and moved to Kyak. And now, just as he had his affairs in shape for another and a greater campaign of stock-flotation, the storm had come to ruin him.

The bitterest element in his defeat was the realization that O'Neil, who had bested him at every turn, was destined to profit by the very blow which crushed him. Defeat at the hands of the Copper Trust he would have accepted with a fairly good grace; but the mere thought that Murray O'Neil, whom he considered in every way his inferior, had gained the upper hand was intolerable. It was in keeping with Gordon's character that instead of blaming his own judgment he became furiously angry at the Trust for the mistake of its engineers, and held them responsible for his desperate situation. That it was truly desperate he very soon realized, since disaster to his railroad project meant that his stock-holders would be around his ears like a swarm of hornets, and once they understood the true state of affairs at Hope the complete collapse of his fortunes would surely follow.

During the days succeeding the storm he scarcely knew where to turn, so harassed was he; yet he never for a moment wavered in his resolve to make O'Neil pay for his interference and to exact a reckoning from Gloria Gerard.

Natalie's presence in Kyak confirmed his belief that O'Neil was interested in her, and he began to plan a stroke by which he could take revenge upon all three. It did not promise in any way to help him out of his financial straits, but at least it would give him a certain satisfaction.

He sent word to the girl that he would like to see her.

XVII *How the Prince Became*
a Man

Gordon found his erstwhile ward greatly improved by her recent life. She was brown, vigorous, healthy; her physical charms quickened his pulses.

"You must have a very good reason for coming to see me," she began. "I don't flatter myself that it is from affection."

"There you wrong me," he assured her, with the warm earnestness he so easily assumed. "I have always regarded you as a daughter."

"I have no faith in you."

"Exactly, and the knowledge distresses me. You and Gloria were a large part of my life; I can't bear to lose you. I hope—and I believe—that her regard for me has changed no more than mine for her. It remains for me to regain yours."

"That is impossible. You had the chance—"

"My dear, you can't know my reasons for acting as I did at Omar. But those reasons no longer exist."

"Just what—do you mean by that?" stammered Natalie.

"I mean what I say. I'm ready to marry your mother."

"When?"

"At once. You shall plead my cause for me. You shall add your voice to mine—"

"That isn't necessary. You know mother is only waiting for you. It means so much to her that she couldn't refuse."

"Doesn't it mean anything to you?"

Natalie nodded. "It means more to me than to any one else, perhaps. I have been carrying a great burden, almost more than I can bear. Sometimes I've wished I were a man —for just long enough to make you pay. Oh yes," she continued, as he started to protest. "Don't let us begin this new life with any false conceptions; you may as well know that I shall always hate you. We shall see very little of each other."

"Nonsense! I can't let you feel like that. I sha'n't rest until I win back your love and confidence."

She eyed him searchingly for a moment, then opened her lips to speak, but closed them.

"Well?" he prompted her. "Let us be frank with each other."

"I'm merely wondering how greatly your decision has been influenced by the storm and the fight at the railroad crossing. I understand how you feel toward Mr. O'Neil, and I know that he means to crush you."

"Oh!" Gordon's face lighted.

"Yes! He has never said so, but I can feel it. I wonder if you have snatched us up in your extremity as a defense."

"Ridiculous! Your suspicions are insulting. I have nothing to fear from him, for he is broken, his credit is gone, he is in desperate straits."

"Are you in any better condition? How long can you fool your people with that pretense of a mine?"

Gordon flushed, but affected scorn. "So! Have you and Gloria begun to balance my wealth against my love? If so—"

"You know she would marry you if you were penniless."

"I hope so—and, indeed, I can't believe her mercenary.

Well, I shall say good-by to Kyak, without idle regret, and we three shall return to Hope, where I can attack my problems with fresh courage. I can well afford my loss here, if by doing so I gain the woman of my desires."

"You want me to go with you?"

"Of course. You can't stay in Omar, knowing what you do about O'Neil. Remember, I shall be in the position of a father to you."

"Very well. It is the least I can do. Miss Appleton and I are returning to Omar in a few days. Will you go with us?"

"I shall be delighted, my dear." He smiled upon her in his most fatherly fashion, but she was far from feeling the assurance he meant to convey.

The eighteen-hour train from Chicago bore Murray O'Neil into New York on time, and he hastened directly to the Holland House, where the clerk greeted him as if he had run in from Yonkers instead of from the wilderness of the far northwest. His arrival was always the forerunner of great prosperity for the bell-boys, and there was the customary struggle for his baggage.

An hour later, having bathed and changed his linen, he was whizzing toward lower Broadway, with the roar of the subway in his ears. New York looked very good to O'Neil, for this time he came not as a suppliant, but as a conqueror, and a deep contentment rested in his heart. More than once during the last two years he had made this flying trip across an ocean and a continent, but heretofore he had been burdened with worries and responsibilities. Always he had needed to gather his wits for some supreme effort; always there had been the urgent necessity of raising money. As the S. R. & N. had grown his obligations had increased; and, while he had never returned empty-handed, no one but he knew at what cost of time and strength he had succeeded in financing his venture. Invariably he had left New York mentally and physically exhausted, and his days in the open had barely served to replenish his store of nervous energy for the next campaign.

As he looked back upon it all he was amazed at his daring in attempting to finance a railroad out of his own pocket. But he had won, and the Trust had met with a sharp reverse in attempting to beat him at his own game. He held the winning card, and he looked out upon the world through eyes which were strained and weary, but complacent.

Mr. Herman Heidlemann was expecting him.

"You have the most confident way of arranging appointments from the other side of the world," he began, as O'Neil entered his office. "Steamships and railroads appear to be your obedient servants."

"Not always. I find railroads very troublesome at times."

"Well, you're on time to the minute," said Heidlemann. "Now tell me about Kyak. Trevor cables that you were there during the storm which ruined us." The head of the copper syndicate did not look like a man facing ruin; in fact, he seemed more curious to hear of the physical phenomena of that hurricane than of its effect upon his fortune.

"Kyak was a great mistake," he admitted, when O'Neil had given him the particulars he asked for. "We're all agreed on that point. Some of our associates feel that the whole Alaskan enterprise has been a mistake—mines and all."

"Your mines are as good as they ever were, but Kyak is a long way from Wall Street, and you relied too much upon other people's judgment."

"We have to rely upon our experts."

"Of course. But that country must have a railroad."

"Must?" Heidlemann lifted his brows. "It has done very well without one so far. Our friends call us crazy for trying to build one, and our enemies call us thieves."

"You can't afford to give up."

"No. There's an element of pride in the matter, and I really believe the country does need transportation."

"You can't understand how badly it needs it."

"Yet it's a heavy load to carry," said Heidlemann, with conviction, "for a road will lose money for many years. We were willing to wait until the agriculture and the mining developed, even though the profit came only to our children; but—we have been misunderstood, abused by the press and the public. Even Congress is down on us. However, I suppose you came to tell me once more that Omar is the gateway and that we need it."

O'Neil smiled. "That's hardly necessary now, is it? I own every inch of water-front at that point, and there's no other harbor. My track will be laid to the glaciers by the time snow flies."

"Trevor reports that a bridge is possible, although expensive."

"It will cost two million dollars."

"I don't see how it can be built to withstand the ice."

"I'll guarantee to build it so it will hold."

"What is your proposition?" asked Heidlemann.

"I'll sell the S. R. & N. for five million dollars and contract to complete the road within two years on a ten-per-cent. commission."

"It has cost you about three million dollars, I believe. That would leave you a handsome profit."

"One million for me, one million for my associates."

"What will the remaining hundred miles cost?"

"About ten millions. That will give me another million profit as contractor. My force and equipment is on the ground. I can save you money and a year's time."

Mr. Heidlemann drummed upon the top of his desk for a moment.

"You're a high-priced man, O'Neil," he said, finally.

"You've had experience with the other kind."

"Counting the money we've already sunk, the road would stand us about twenty million dollars completed."

"It will cost thirty to build from Cortez, and take two years longer."

Mr. Heidlemann seemed to consider this for a moment. "We've had this matter before us almost constantly since the report of the storm," he said, at length, "and after deliberation our directors have voted to do nothing just yet."

O'Neil opened his eyes in amazement.

"I don't understand."

"It's this way. Our engineers first recommended Cortez as a starting-point, and we spent a fortune there. Then you attacked the other route, and we sent Trevor up to find if you were right and we were wrong. He recommended the Salmon River valley, and told us he could build a breakwater at Kyak. You know the result. We relied upon him, for he seemed to be the best man in the country, but as a matter of precaution we later sent other engineers. Their reports came in not three months ago, and, while all seemed confident that the breakwater could be built, none of them were certain about the bridge. One, in fact, condemned it absolutely. Now on the heels of their statements comes the news that the very work they united in declaring feasible has been undone. Naturally, we don't know where we are or whom to believe."

"They simply didn't know the conditions at Kyak," argued O'Neil, "and they evidently haven't studied the bridge as I have. But you'll have to go at the breakwater again or build in from Cortez or give up."

"No, we have decided to mark time until that crossing is proved feasible. Understand, I voice the sentiment of the majority."

"If I build that bridge you may find it more difficult to buy me out," said O'Neil, quietly.

"We'll have to take our medicine," Mr. Heidlemann replied, without heat. "We cannot afford another mistake."

"This is definite?"

"Oh, absolutely! We're going slow for a time."

A blow in the face could not have affected O'Neil more disagreeably than this statement. Fortune had seemed within his grasp when he entered the room; now ruin was more imminent than it had ever been before. The ground seemed to be slipping from beneath his feet; he discovered that he was dizzy. He felt himself utterly incapable of raising the two million dollars necessary to carry his road to a point where the Trust would consider a purchase, yet to fail meant the loss of all he had put in. He knew also that these men would never recede from a position once taken.

"Hasn't this public clamor had something to do with your determination?" he asked.

"A great deal. We had the best intentions when we started—we still have—but it's time to let the general sentiment cool. We thought we were doing a fine thing for the country in opening Alaska, but it seems we're regarded as thieves and grafters. One gets tired of abuse after a while."

"Will you take an option on the S. R. & N. conditional upon the building of the bridge?"

"We couldn't very well do that. Remember you are our rival." Heidlemann smiled in his recognition of the fact that the rivalry was friendly. "To do so would fan excitement at Washington to a white heat. We'd then be in the position they now accuse us of occupying, and that would have a serious bearing upon the coal situation. No, we can't help you, O'Neil, but rest assured we won't do anything to hinder you. You have treated us fairly; we will reciprocate. Once you have built your bridge we can discuss a purchase and the abandonment of our original enterprise, but meanwhile we must proceed cautiously. It is unfortunate for us all."

"Especially for me."

"You need money badly, don't you?"

"I'm worse than broke," O'Neil admitted.

"I'd really be sorry to take over the wreck of your enterprise," Heidlemann said, earnestly, "for you have made a good fight, and your ideas were better than ours. I'd much prefer to pay your price than to profit by your misfortune. Needless to say we don't feel that way about Gordon."

"There would be no uncertainty about the bridge if I had the money. With your means I could build a road to the moon, and double-track it."

Although Murray felt that further effort was useless, he continued to argue the matter from various angles, hoping against hope to sway Heidlemann's decision. But he gave up at last. Out in the marble hall which led to the elevators he discovered that all his vigor of an hour ago had passed. The spring was out of his limbs; he walked slowly, like an old man. A glimpse of his image in the mirrors of the car as he shot downward showed him a face grave and haggard. The crowds jostled him, but he was hardly conscious of them. The knowledge that his hardest fight was yet to come filled him with sickening apprehension. He was like a runner who toes the mark for a final heat knowing himself to be upon the verge of collapse.

The magnitude of the deal narrowed his field of operations alarmingly, and he had already learned what a serious effect upon capital the agitation about Alaska had pro-

duced. More than once he had found men who were willing to invest but feared the effect of public sentiment.
Popular magazines, newspapers like *The Review,* and writers like Eliza Appleton had been largely to blame for the
wrong. They had misunderstood the problem and misin-
terpreted the spirit of commercial progress. But, strangely
enough, he felt no bitterness at thought of Eliza. On the
contrary, his heart softened in a sort of friendly yearning
for her company. He would have liked to talk the matter
over with her.

Looking the situation squarely in the face, he realized
that he must face a crash or raise two million dollars
within the next month. That meant seventy thousand dollars a day. It was a man-sized task.

He bought himself a cigar at the corner, hailed a taxi-
cab, and was driven all the way up town to the Holland
House. Once there, he established himself in that corner
of the men's café which he always frequented.

The waiter who served him lingered to say:

"It's good to see you back in your 'office' again. You've
been a long time away, sir."

O'Neil smiled as he left a silver dollar on the tray.

"It's good to be back, Joe," he said. "This time I may
not leave."

XVIII   *How the Man Became a Prince Again*

O'Neil had the faculty of sleeping well, in spite of the
most tormenting worries. He arose on the morning after
his interview with Mr. Heidlemann, ready to begin the
struggle with all his normal energy and confidence. But
the day brought him only discouragement. He had a large
acquaintance, the mention of his name in quarters where
he was not personally known gained him respectful attention; but he found himself working in the shadow of the
Copper Trust, and its silent influence overcame his strongest arguments. One banker expressed the general attitude
by saying:

"If the Heidlemanns were not in the field we might help you, but it would be financial suicide to oppose them."

"There's no opposition about it," Murray assured him. "If I build that bridge they'll buy us out."

At this his hearer very naturally wished to know why, if the bridge were indeed feasible, the Heidlemanns delayed action; and O'Neil had to fall back upon a recital of the facts, realizing perfectly that they failed to carry conviction.

No one, it seemed, cared to risk even a semblance of rivalry with that monstrous aggregation of capital, for the interlacing of financial interests was amazingly intricate, and financiers were fearful of the least misstep. Everywhere O'Neil encountered the same disheartening timidity. His battle, it seemed, had been lost before it was begun.

Days passed in fruitless endeavors; evenings found O'Neil in his corner of the Holland House Café racking his brain for some way out of his perplexities. Usually he was surrounded by friends, for he continued to entertain in the lavish fashion for which he had gained a reputation; but sometimes he was alone, and then his solitude became more oppressive than it had ever been even in the farthest wastes of the northland. He was made to feel his responsibility with dreadful keenness, for his associates were in a panic and bombarded him with daily inquiries, vexatious and hard to answer. He had hoped that in this extremity they might give him some practical help, and they did make a few half-hearted attempts, only to meet the same discouragements as he. At last they left him to carry the burden alone.

A week, two weeks went by. He was in constant cable communication with Omar, but not even the faithful Dr. Gray knew the dire straits in which his chief was struggling. Work on the S. R. & N. was going forward as usual. The organization was running at its highest efficiency: rails were being laid; gangs of rock-workers were preparing the grade beyond the glaciers. Yet every day that passed, every pay-check drawn brought ruin closer. Nevertheless, O'Neil continued to joke and chat with the men who came to his table in the café and kept his business appointments with his customary cheerfulness. The waiters who attended him rejoiced in his usual princely tips.

One evening as he ran through his mail he found a letter in a woman's handwriting and, glancing at the signature, started. It was signed "Gloria Gordon." Briefly it apprised him of her marriage and of her and Natalie's return to Hope. Gloria thanked him perfunctorily for his many kindnesses, but she neither expressed nor implied an invitation for him to visit them. He smiled a little grimly—already her loyalty had veered to Gordon's side, and Natalie no doubt shared her feeling. Well, it was but natural, perhaps. It would be unreasonable to expect them to sacrifice their desires, and what they now seemed to consider their interests, to a business quarrel they could hardly be expected to understand. He could not help feeling hurt that the women should so readily exchange his friendship for the protection of his bitterest enemy, but—they were helpless and he had helped them; let it rest at that. He was really troubled, however, that they had been so easily deceived. If they had only waited! If he had only been able to advise them! For Gordon's intention was plain.

He was aroused from his train of thought by a stranger whom he found standing beside his table and looking down at him with wavering eye.

"Misser O'Neil, ain't it?" the fellow inquired. "Sure! Thought I knew you. I'm Bulker, of the old North Pass. Remember me?"

Mr. Bulker had been imbibing freely. He showed evidences of a protracted spree not only in his speech, but in the trembling hand which he extended. His eyes were bloodshot, and his good-natured face was purple.

O'Neil greeted him pleasantly, and, considering himself enthusiastically welcomed, the new-comer sat down suddenly, as if some one had tripped him.

"Been washing you for ten minutes."

"Washing me?"

"No! *Washing* you. Couldn't make you out—eyesight's getting bad. Too many bright lights in this town. Ha! Joke! Let's have a gill."

"Thank you, no."

"Must have a little dram for old time's sake. You're the only one of the North Pass crowd I'll drink with." Mr. Bulker gestured comprehensively at a group of waiters, and

Murray yielded. "You were my friend, O'Neil; you always treated me right."

"What are you doing now?" asked O'Neil, with the interest he could not refuse to any one who had ever worked with him. He remembered the fellow perfectly. He had come on from the East as auditor, and had appeared to be capable, although somewhat given to drink.

"I'm a broker. Wall Street's my habitat. Fine time to buy stocks, Misser O'Neil." Bulker assumed an expression of great wisdom. "Like to have a tip? No? Good! You're a wise man. They fired me from the North Pass. Wha'd you know about that? Fired me for drinking! Greatest injustice I ever heard of, but I hit running, like a turkey. That wasn't the reason they let me go, though. Not on your life!" He winked portentously, and strangely enough his eyelid failed to resume its normal position. It continued to droop, giving the appearance of a waggish leer. "I knew too mush! Isn't healthy to know too mush, is it?"

"I've never had a chance to find out," smiled Murray.

"Oh, don't be an ingénue; you savvied more than anybody on the job. I'll admit I took a nip now and then, but I never got pickled. Say! Who d'you s'pose I saw to-day? Old man Illis!"

O'Neil became suddenly intent. He had been trying to get in touch with Poultney Illis for more than a fortnight, but his cables to London had brought no response.

"When did he arrive?"

"Just lately. He's a game old rooster, ain't he? Gee, he's sore!"

"Sore about what?"

Bulker winked again, with the same lack of muscular control.

"About that North Pass deal, of course. He was blackmailed out of a cold million. The agreement's about up now, and I figure he's over here to renew it."

"You're talking Greek," said O'Neil; but his eagerness was manifest.

"I s'posed you knew. The North Pass has been paying blackmail to the Yukon steamboat companies for three years. When you built the line it practically put 'em out of the Dawson market, understand?"

"Of course."

Now that Mr. Bulker's mind was running along well-worn grooves, his intoxication became less apparent.

"Those Frisco steamboat men got together and started a rate war against the railroad; they hauled freight to Dawson by way of St. Michaels at a loss. Of course Illis and his crowd had to meet competition, and it nearly broke 'em the first two seasons. Gee, they were the mad ones! Finally they fixed up an agreement—had to or go bust—and of course the Native Sons put it over our English cousins. They agreed to restore the old rate, and each side promised to pay the other a royalty of ten dollars a ton on all the freight it hauled to Dawson and up-river points. You can guess the result, can't you? The steamboat companies let Illis haul all the freight and sat back on their haunches and took their profit. For every ton he hauled he slipped 'em ten round American dollars, stamped with the Goddess of Liberty. Oh, it was soft! When they had him fairly tied up they drydocked their steamboats, to save wear and tear. He paid 'em a thousand dollars a day for three years. If that ain't blackmail, it's a first cousin to it by marriage."

"Didn't the Interstate Commerce Commission get wise?"

"Certainly not. It looks wise, but it never *gets* wise. Oh, believe me, Poultney Illis is hopping mad. I s'pose he's over here now to renew the arrangement for another three years on behalf of his stock-holders. Let's have a dram." Bulker sat back and stared as through a mist at his companion, enjoying the effect of his disclosure.

O'Neil was indeed impressed—more deeply than his informant dreamed. Out of the lips of a drunken man had come a hint which set his nerves to tingling. He knew Illis well, he knew the caliber of the Englishman, and a plan was already leaping in his brain whereby he might save the S. R. & N.

It lacked an hour of midnight when O'Neil escaped from Bulker and reached his room. Once inside, he seized the telephone and rang up hotel after hotel, inquiring for the English capitalist, but without result. After a moment's consideration he took his hat and gloves and went out. The matter did not permit of delay. Not only were his own needs imperative, but if Poultney Illis had come from London to confer with his rivals there was little time to spare.

Remembering the Englishman's habits, O'Neil turned up the Avenue to the Waldorf, where he asked for the manager, whom he well knew.

"Yes, Mr. Illis is here," he was informed, "but he's registered under a different name. No doubt he'll be glad to see you, however."

A moment later Murray recognized the voice of Illis's valet over the wire and greeted him by name. Another brief delay, and the capitalist himself was at the 'phone.

"Come right up," he said; and O'Neil replaced the receiver with a sigh of relief.

Illis greeted him warmly, for their relations had been close.

"Lucky you found me," he said. "I'm going back on the next sailing."

"Have you signed up with the Arctic Navigation Company?" Murray inquired; and the other started.

"Bless me! What do you mean?"

His caller laughed. "I see you haven't. I don't think you will, either, after you've talked with me."

Without the tremor of an eyelash Illis exclaimed:

"My word! What are you driving at?"

"That agreement over freight rates, of course."

The Briton eyed him for a moment, then carefully closed the door leading from his sitting-room, and, seating himself, lit a cigar.

"What do you know about that matter?" he asked, quietly.

"About all there is to know—enough, at least, to appreciate your feelings."

"I flattered myself that my affairs were private. Where did you get your information?"

"I'll tell you if you insist, although I'd rather not. There's no danger of its becoming public."

Illis showed his relief. "I'm glad. You gave me a start. Rotten fix for a man to be in. Why, I'm here under an assumed name! Fancy! But—" he waved his hand in a gesture which showed his acceptance of the inevitable.

"You haven't made your new agreement?"

"I'm to meet Blum and Capron to-morrow."

"Why didn't you take the S. R. & N. when I cabled you last month?"

"I couldn't. But what has that to do with the matter?"

"Don't you see? It's so plain to me that I can't understand how you failed to realize the value—the necessity of buying my road."

"Explain, please."

"Gladly. The North Pass & Yukon is paying a fabulous blackmail to the river-lines to escape a ruinous rate war."

"Right! It's blackmail, as you say."

"Under the present agreement you handle the Dawson freight and keep out of the lower river; they take the whole Tanana valley and lower Yukon."

"Correct."

"Didn't it occur to you that the S. R. & N., which starts four hundred miles west of the North Pass and taps the Tanana valley, can be used to put the river steamers of that section out of business?"

"Let's have a look at the map." Mr. Illis hurried into an adjoining room and returned with a huge chart which he unrolled upon the table. "To tell you the truth, I never looked at the proposition from that angle. Our people were afraid of those glaciers and the competition of the Copper Trust. They're disgusted, too, with our treatment."

"The Trust is eliminated. Kyak harbor is wiped off the map, and I'm alone in the field."

"How about this fellow Gordon?"

"He'll be broke in a year. Incidentally, that's my trouble."

"But I'm told you can't pass the glaciers."

"I can. Parker says he'll have the bridge done by spring."

"Then I'd bank on it. I'd believe Parker if I knew he was lying. If you both agree, I haven't the slightest doubt."

"This is a bigger proposition than the North Pass, Mr. Illis. You made money out of that road, but this one will make more." He swiftly outlined the condition of affairs, even to the attitude assumed by the Heidlemanns; and Illis, knowing the speaker as he did, had no doubt that he was hearing the exact truth. "But that's not all," continued O'Neil. "The S. R. & N. is the club which will hammer your enemies into line. That's what I came to see you

about. With a voice in it you can control the traffic of all
central Alaska and force the San Francisco crowd to treat
the N. P. & Y. fairly, thereby saving half a million a
year."

"It's a big undertaking. I'm not sure our crowd could
swing it."

"They don't have to. There's a quick profit of two million to be had by selling to the Trust next spring. You can
dictate your own terms to those blackmailers to-morrow,
and then make a turn-over in nine months. It doesn't matter who owns the S. R. & N. after it's completed. The
steamboat men will see their profits cut. As it is now, they
can make enough out of their own territory to haul freight
into yours for nothing."

"I dare say you'll go to them if we don't take you up,
eh?"

"My road has its strategic value. I must have help. If
you don't come to my rescue it will mean war with your
line, I dare say."

Mr. Illis sat back, staring at the ceiling for a long time.
From the street below came the whir and clatter of taxi-
cabs as the midnight crowd came and went. The city's noc-
turnal life was at its height; men had put aside the worries
of the day and were devoting themselves to the more
serious and exhausting pastimes of relaxation. Still the
white-haired Briton weighed in his mind the matter of millions, while the fortunes of Murray O'Neil hung in the
balance.

"My people won't buy the S. R. & N.," Illis finally announced. "But I'll put it up to them."

"I can't delay action if there's a chance of a refusal. I'll
have to see Blum and Capron," said O'Neil.

"I'll cable full details within the hour. We'll have an
answer by to-morrow night."

"And if they refuse?" O'Neil lit a cigar with steady fingers.

"Oh, if they refuse I'll join you. We'll go over the matter carefully in the mean time. Two million you said,
didn't you?"

"Yes. There's two million profit for you in nine months."
His voice was husky and a bit uneven, for he had been
under a great strain.

"Good! You don't know how resentful I feel toward Blum and his crowd. I—I'm downright angry: I am that."

Illis took the hand which his caller extended, with an expressionless face.

"I'm glad I found you," confessed O'Neil. "I was on my last legs. Herman Heidlemann will pay our price when the last bridge-bolt is driven home, and he'll pay with a smile on his face—that's the sort of man he is."

"He won't pay if he knows I'm interested. We're not exactly friendly since I sold out my smelter interests. But he needn't know—nobody need know."

Illis called his valet and instructed him to rouse his secretary and ring for some cable blanks.

"I think I'll cable, too," Murray told him. "I have some 'boys' up there who are working in the dark with their teeth shut. They're waiting for the crash, and they'd like to hear the good news."

His fingers shook as he scrawled the name of Doctor Gray, but his eyes were bright and youth was singing in his heart once more.

"Now let's get down to business," said Mr. Illis. "We'll have to talk fast."

It was growing light in the east when O'Neil returned to the Holland House; but he felt no fatigue, and he laughed from the pure joy of living, for his dream seemed coming true.

XIX *Miss Appleton Makes a Sacrifice*

Tom Slater came puffing up the hill to the Appleton bungalow, plumped himself into a chair, and sighed deeply.

"What's the matter? Are you played out?" asked Eliza.

"No. I'm feeling like a colt."

"Any news from Omar Khayyam?"

"Not a word."

Eliza's brows drew together in a worried frown, for

none of Murray's "boys" had awaited tidings from him with greater anxiety than she.

It had been a trying month for them all. Dr. Gray, upon whom the heaviest responsibility rested, had aged visibly under the strain; Parker and Mellen and McKay had likewise become worn and grave as the days passed and they saw disaster approaching. Even Dan was blue; and Sheldon, the light-hearted, had begun to lose interest in his commissary duties.

After the storm at Kyak there had been a period of fierce rejoicing, which had ended abruptly with the receipt of O'Neil's curt cablegram announcing the attitude of the Trust. Gloom had succeeded the first surprise, deepening to hopeless despondency through the days that followed. Oddly enough, Slater had been the only one to bear up; under adversity he blossomed into a peculiar and almost offensive cheerfulness. It was characteristic of his crooked temperament that misfortune awoke in him a lofty and unshakable optimism.

"You're great on nicknames, ain't you?" he said to Eliza, regarding her with his never-failing curiosity. "Who's this Homer Keim you're always talking about?"

"He isn't any more: he *was*. He was a cheerful old Persian poet."

"I thought he was Dutch, from the name. Well! Murray's cheerful too. Him and me are alike in that. I'll bet he isn't worrying half so much as Doc and the others."

"You think he'll make good?"

"He never fails."

"But—we can't hold on much longer. Dan says that some of the men are getting uneasy and want their money."

Tom nodded. "The men are all right—Doc has kept them paid up; it's the shift bosses. I say let 'em quit."

"Has it gone as far as that?"

"Somebody keeps spreading the story that we're busted and that Murray has skipped out. More of Gordon's work, I s'pose. Some of the sore-heads are coming in this evening to demand their wages."

"Can we pay them?"

"Doc says he dassent; so I s'pose they'll quit. He should have fired 'em a week ago. Never let a man quit—always beat him to it. We could hold the rough-necks for another two weeks if it wasn't for these fellows, but they'll go back and start a stampede."

"How many are there?"

"About a dozen."

"I was afraid it was worse. There can't be much owing to them."

"Oh, it's bad enough! They've been letting their wages ride, that's why they got scared. We owe them about four thousand dollars."

"They must be paid," said Eliza. "It will give Mr. O'Neil another two weeks—a month, perhaps."

"Doc's got his back up, and he's told the cashier to make 'em wait."

Eliza hesitated, and flushed a little. "I suppose it's none of my business," she said, "but—couldn't you boys pay them out of your own salaries?"

Mr. Slater grinned—an unprecedented proceeding which lent his face an altogether strange and unnatural expression.

"Salary! We ain't had any salary," he said, cheerfully—"not for months."

"Dan has drawn his regularly."

"Oh, sure! But he ain't one of us. He's an outsider."

"I see!" Eliza's eyes were bright with a wistful admiration. "That's very nice of you men. You have a family, haven't you, Uncle Tom?"

"I have! Seven head, and they eat like a herd of stock. It looks like a lean winter for 'em if Murray don't make a sale—but he will. That isn't what I came to see you about; I've got my asking clothes on, and I want a favor."

"You shall have it, of course."

"I want a certificate."

"Of what?"

"Ill health. Nobody believes I had the smallpox."

"You didn't."

"Wh-what?" Tom's eyes opened wide. He stared at the girl in hurt surprise.

"It was nothing but pimples, Tom."

"Pimples!" He spat the word out indignantly, and his round cheeks grew purple. "I—I s'pose pimples gave me cramps and chills and backache and palpitation and swellings! Hunh! I had a narrow escape—narrow's the word. It was narrower than a knife-edge! Anything I get out of life from now on is 'velvet,' for I was knocking at death's door. The grave yawned, but I jumped it. It's the first sick spell I ever had, and I won't be cheated out of it. Understand?"

"What do you want me to do?" smiled the girl.

"You're a writer: write me an affidavit—"

"I can't do that."

"Then put it in your paper. Put it on the front page, where folks can see it."

"I've quit *The Review*. I'm doing magazine stories."

"Well, that'll do. I'm not particular where it's printed so long as—"

Eliza shook her head. "You weren't really sick, Uncle Tom."

At this Mr. Slater rose to his feet in high dudgeon.

"Don't call me 'Uncle,' " he exclaimed. "You're in with the others."

"It wouldn't be published if I wrote it."

"Then you can't be much of a writer." He glared at her, and slowly, distinctly, with all the emphasis at his command, said: "I had smallpox—and a dam' bad case, understand? I was sick. I had miseries in every joint and cartage of my body. I'm going to use a pick-handle for a cane, and anybody that laughs will get a hickory massage that 'll take a crooked needle and a pair of pinchers to fix. Thank God I've got my strength back! You get me?"

"I do."

He snorted irately and turned to go, but Eliza checked him.

"What about those shift bosses?" she asked.

Slater rolled his eyes balefully. "Just let one of 'em mention smallpox," he said, "and I'll fill the hospital till it bulges."

"No, no! Are you going to pay them?"

"Certainly not."

Eliza considered for a moment. "Don't let them see Dr. Gray," she said, at length. "He has enough to worry him. Meet them at the train and bring them here."

"What for? Tea?"

"You boys have done all you can; I think it's time Dan and I did something."

Tom stared. "Are *you* going to pay 'em?" he asked, gruffly.

"Yes. Mr. O'Neil needs time. Dan and I have saved four thousand dollars. I'd offer it to Dr. Gray——"

"He wouldn't take it."

"Exactly. Send Dan up here when you see him."

"It doesn't seem exactly right." Tom was obviously embarrassed. "You see, we sort of belong to Murray, and you don't, but——" He shook his head as if to rid himself of unwelcome emotion. "Women are funny things! You're willing to do that for the chief, and yet you won't write me a little affidavit!" He grunted and went away, still shaking his head.

When Eliza explained her plan to Dan she encountered an opposition that shocked and hurt her.

"I won't do it!" he said, shortly.

"You—*what?*"

"We can't build the S. R. & N. on four thousand dollars," he protested, bitterly. "I need my half."

"You'll get it back sometime."

"Oh! Will I? Well, I don't want it 'sometime'; I want it now. Why, the idea is ridiculous—just like a woman!"

"When was I ever 'just like a woman'?" cried Eliza. "Don't be ironic—it hurts. Never mind," she said, in answer to his look of bewilderment; "just listen. Mr. O'Neil will succeed. I'm sure he will. But he needs time—even a week may save him. You've risked your life for the road; you've suffered——"

"That's different!" said Dan, irritably. "That was part of my work. I earned my money, and I saved it. I need it now, for—you know—for Natalie. I can't afford to be penniless—I can't get along without her. If Murray goes bust, where will I land? Out in the street! I've been so lonesome since she left that I can't work—I thought you understood—I can't think; I can't sleep, nor eat!——"

"And what about him?" demanded the girl, with heat. "Do you think he's eating and sleeping any better than you? He made you, Dan! He took me in and treated me as a valued friend when he knew I was his enemy. He——"

"Yes, and made you love him, too," said Dan, roughly. "I can see that."

Eliza lifted her head and met his eyes squarely.

"That's true! But why not? Can't I love him? Isn't it my privilege to help if I want to? If I had two million dollars instead of two thousand I'd give it to him, and—and I wouldn't expect him to care for me, either. He'll never do that. He couldn't! But—oh, Danny, I've been miserable—"

Dan felt a certain dryness of the throat which made speech oddly difficult. "I don't see why he couldn't care for you," he said, lamely.

Eliza shook her head hopelessly. "I'm glad it happened," she said—"glad. In writing these articles I've tried to make him understood; I've tried to put my whole soul into them so that the people will see that he isn't, wouldn't be, a thief nor a grafter. I've described him as he is—big, honorable, gentle—"

"I didn't know you were writing fiction," said her brother, impatiently.

"I'm not. It's all true. I've cried over those articles, Dan. I've petted them, and I've kissed his name—oh, I've been silly!" She smiled at him through a sudden glimmer of tears.

Dan began to wonder if his sister, in spite of her exemplary conduct in the past, were after all going to have hysterics. Women were especially likely to, he reflected, when they demanded the impossible. At last he said, uncomfortably: "Gee, I thought I was the dippy member of the family!"

"It's our chance to help him," she urged. "Will you—?"

"No! I'm sorry, Sis, but my little bit wouldn't mean anything to him; it means everything to me. Maybe that's selfish—I don't care. I'm as mad over Natalie as you seem to be over him. A week's delay can't make any difference now—he played and lost. But I can't afford to lose. He'll make another fortune, that's sure—but do you think I'll ever find another Natalie? No! Don't argue, for I won't listen."

He left the house abruptly, and Eliza went into the white bedroom which O'Neil had fitted up for her. From the remotest corner of her lowest bureau drawer she drew a battered tin box, and, dividing the money it contained into two equal parts, placed one in the pockets of her mannish jacket.

It was dark when Tom Slater arrived, at the head of a group of soiled workmen whom he ushered into the parlor of the bungalow.

"Here's the bunch!" he announced, laconically.

As the new-comers ranged themselves uncomfortably about the wall Dan Appleton entered and greeted them with his customary breeziness.

"The pay-master is busy, and Doc Gray has a surgical case," he said, "so I'll cash your time-checks. Get me the box, will you, Sis?"

He had avoided Eliza's eyes upon entering, and he avoided them now, but the girl's throat was aching as she hurried into her bedroom and hastily replaced the rolls of greenbacks she had removed from the tin box.

When he had finished paying off, Dan said, brusquely:

"Now we mustn't have any loafing around town, understand?"

"We can't get back to-night," said one of the men.

"Oh yes, you can. I ordered an engine out."

"We hear—there's talk about quitting work," another ventured. "Where's O'Neil?"

"He's in the States buying a steamship," answered Dan, unblushingly. "We can't get stuff fast enough by the regular boats."

"Good! That sounds like business. We don't want to quit."

"Now hurry! Your parlor-car is waiting."

When he and Eliza were alone he turned to her with a flush of embarrassment. "Aren't we the darnedest fools, Sis? I wouldn't mind if we had done the chief any good, but we haven't." He closed the lid of the tin box, which was nearly empty now, and pushed it away from him, laughing mirthlessly. "Hide that sarcophagus where I can't see it," he commanded. "It makes me sick."

Eliza flung her arm about his neck and laid her cheek against his. "Poor Danny! You're a brick!"

"It's the bread-line for us," he told her.

"Never mind. We're used to it now." She laughed contentedly and snuggled her face closer to his.

It was on the following morning that O'Neil's cablegram announcing the result of his interview with Illis reached Omar. Dr. Gray brought the news to the Appleton bungalow while Dan and his sister were still at breakfast. "Happy Tom" came puffing and blowing at his heels with a highly satisfied I-told-you-so expression on his round features.

"He made it! The tide has turned," cried the doctor as he burst in waving the message on high. "Yes!" he explained, in answer to their excited questions. "Murray got the money and our troubles are over. Now give me some coffee, Eliza. I'm all shaky."

"English money!" commented Slater. "The same as we used on the North Pass."

"Then he interested Illis!" cried Dan.

"Yep! He's the white-winged messenger of hope. I wasn't worried for a minute," Tom averred.

The breakfast which followed was of a somewhat hysterical and fragmentary nature, for Eliza felt her heart swelling, and the faithful Gray was all but undone by the strain he had endured.

"That's the first food I've tasted for weeks," he confessed. "I've eaten, but I haven't tasted; and now—I'm not hungry." He sighed, stretched his long limbs gratefully, and eyed the Appletons with a kindly twinkle. "You were up in the air, too, weren't you? The chief will appreciate last night's affair."

Eliza colored faintly. "It was nothing. Please don't tell him." At the incredulous lift of his brows she hastened to explain: "Tom said you men 'belonged' to Mr. O'Neil and Dan was an outsider. That hurt me dreadfully."

"Well, he can't say that now; Dan is one of Murray's boys, all right, and you—you must be his girl."

At that moment Mellen and McKay burst into the bungalow, demanding the truth behind the rumor which had just come to their ears; and there followed fresh explanations and rejoicings, through which Eliza sat quietly, thrilled by the note of genuine affection and loyalty that pervaded it all. But, now that the general despondency had vanished and joy reigned in its place, Tom Slater relapsed into his habitual gloom and spoke forebodingly of the difficulties yet to be encountered.

"Murray don't say how *much* he's raised," he remarked. "It may be only a drop in the bucket. We'll have to go through all this again, probably, and the next time he won't find it so easy to sting a millionaire."

"We'll last through the winter anyhow—"

"Winter!" Slater shook his bald head. "Winter is hard on old men like me."

"We'll have the bridge built by spring, sure!" Mellen declared.

"Maybe! I hope so. I wish I could last to see it, but the smallpox undermined me. Perhaps it's a mercy I'm so far gone; nobody knows yet whether the bridge will stand, and—I'd hate to see it go out."

"It won't go out," said the engineer, confidently.

"Maybe you're right. But that's what Trevor said about his breakwater. His work was done, and ours isn't hardly begun. By the way, Murray didn't say he *had* the money; he just said he expected to get it."

"Go out and hang your crêpe on the roundhouse," Dan told him; "this is a jubilee. If you keep on rejoicing you'll have us all in tears." When the others had gone he turned to Eliza. "Why don't you want O'Neil to know about that money, Sis?" he asked, curiously. "When I'm a hero I like to be billed as one."

"Please!" She hesitated and turned her face away. "You —you are so stupid about some things."

On the afternoon of this very day Curtis Gordon found Natalie at a window staring out across the sound in the direction of Omar. He laid a warm hand upon her shoulder and said:

"My dear, confess! You are lonesome."

She nodded silently.

"Well, well! We mustn't allow that. Why don't you run over to Omar and see your friend Miss Appleton? She has a cheerful way with her."

"I'm afraid things aren't very gay over there," said Natalie, doubtfully.

"Quite probably. But the fact that O'Neil is on his last legs needn't interfere with your pleasure. A change will do you good."

"You are very kind," she murmured. "You have done everything to make me happy, but—it's autumn. Winter is coming. I feel dull and lonely and gray, like the sky. Are you sure Mr. O'Neil has failed?"

"Certainly. He tried to sell his holdings to the Trust, but they refused to consider it. Poor fellow!" he continued, unctuously. "Now that he's down I pity him. One can't dislike a person who has lost the power of working harm. His men are quitting: I doubt if he'll dare show his face in this country again. But never mind all that. There's a boat leaving for Omar in the morning. Go; have a good time, return when you will, and tell us how they bear up under their adversity." He patted her shoulder affectionately and went up to his room.

It was true enough that Natalie had been unhappy since returning to Hope—not even her mother dreamed how she rebelled at remaining here. She was lonely, uninterested, vaguely homesick. She missed the intimate companionship of Eliza; she missed Dan's extravagant courting and O'Neil's grave, respectful attentions. She also felt the loss of the honest good-fellowship of all those people at Omar whom she had learned to like and to admire. Life here was colorless, and was still haunted by the shadow of that thing from which she and her mother had fled.

Gordon, indeed, had been generous to them both. Since his marriage his attitude had changed entirely. He was polite, agreeable, charmingly devoted: no ship arrived without some tangible and expensive evidence of his often-expressed desire to make his wife and stepdaughter happy; he anticipated their slightest wish. Under his assiduous attentions Natalie's distrust and dislike had slowly melted, and she came to believe that she had misjudged him. There were times when he seemed to be overdoing the matter a bit, times when she wondered if his courtesy could be altogether disinterested; but these occasions were rare, and always she scornfully accused herself of disloyalty. As for Gloria, she was deeply contented—as nearly happy, in fact, as a woman of her temperament could be, and in this the daughter took her reward.

Natalie arrived at Omar in time to see the full effect of the good news from New York, and joined sincerely in the general rejoicing. She returned after a few days, bursting with the tidings of O'Neil's victory.

Gordon listened to her with keenest attention; he drew her out artfully, and when he knew what he had sent her to learn he gave voice to his unwelcome surprise.

"Jove!" he snarled. "That beggar hoodwinked the Heidlemanns, after all. It's their money. What fools! What fools!"

Natalie looked up quickly.

"Does it affect your plans?" she asked.

"Yes—in a way. It consolidates my enemies."

"You said you no longer had any ill feeling toward Mr. O'Neil."

Gordon had resumed his usual suavity. "When I say enemies," he qualified, "of course, I mean it only in a business sense. I heard that the Trust had withdrawn, discouraged by their losses, but, now that they re-enter the field, I shall have to fight them. They would have done well to consult me—to buy me off, rather than be bled by O'Neil. They shall pay well for their mistake, but— it's incredible! That man has the luck of the devil."

That evening he and Denny sat with their heads together until a late hour, and when they retired Gordon had begun to whip new plans into shape.

XX *How Gordon Changed His Attack*

O'Neil's return to Omar was triumphal. All his lieutenants gathered to meet him at the pier and the sincerity of their welcome stirred him deeply. His arrangements with Illis had taken time; he had been delayed at Seattle by bridge details and the placing of steel contracts. He had worked swiftly, and with such absorption that he had paid little heed to the rumors of Gordon's latest activities. Of the new venture which his own success had inspired he knew only the bare outline. He had learned enough, however, to arouse his curiosity, and as soon as the first confusion of his arrival at the front was over he asked for news.

"Haven't you read the papers?" inquired "Happy Tom."

He had attached himself to O'Neil at the moment of his stepping ashore, and now followed him to headquarters, with an air of melancholy satisfaction in mere physical nearness to his chief.

"Barely!" O'Neil confessed. "I've been working twenty hours a day getting that steel under motion."

Dr. Gray said with conviction: "Gordon is a remarkable man. It's a pity he's crooked."

"I think it's dam' lucky," declared Tom. "He's smarter than us, and if he wasn't handicapped by a total lack of decency he'd beat us."

"After the storm," explained Gray, "he moved back to Hope, and we thought he'd made his last bow, but in some way he got the idea that the Trust was back of us."

"So I judged from the little I read."

"Well, we didn't undeceive him, of course. His first move was an attack through the press in the shape of a broadside against the Heidlemanns. It fairly took our breaths. It appeared in the Cortez *Courier* and all over the States, we hear—a letter of defiance to Herman Heidlemann. It declared that the Trust was up to its old tricks here in Alaska—had gobbled the copper; had the coal tied up under secret agreements, and was trying to get possession of all the coast-range passes and defiles—the old story. But the man can write. That article caused a stir."

"I saw it."

"Naturally, the Cortez people ate it up. They're sore at the Trust for leaving their town, and at us for building Omar. Then Gordon called a mass-meeting, and some of us went up to watch the fireworks. I've never seen anything quite like that meeting; every man, woman, and child in the city was there, and they hissed us when we came in. Gordon knew what he was about, and he was in fine voice. He told them Cortez was the logical point of entry to the interior of Alaska and ought to have all the traffic. He fired their animosity toward the Trust, and accused us of basely selling out to it. Then he broached a project to build, by local subscription, a narrow-gauge electric line from Cortez, utilizing the waterfalls for power. The idea caught on, and went like wild-fire: the people cheered themselves hoarse, and pledged him over a hundred thousand dollars that night. Since then they have subscribed as much more, and the town is crazy. Work has actually begun, and they hope to reach the first summit by Christmas."

Slater broke in: "He's a spell-binder, all right. He made me hate the Heidlemanns and detest myself for five minutes. I wasn't even sure I liked *you*, Murray."

"It's a wild scheme, of course," continued the doctor, "but he's putting it over. The town council has granted him a ninety-nine-year lease covering every street; the road-bed is started, and things are booming. Lots have been staked all over the flats, property values are somersaulting, everybody is out of his head, and Gordon is a god. All he does is organize new companies. He has bought a sawmill, a wharf, a machine shop, acres of real estate. He has started a bank and a new hotel; he has consolidated the barber shops; and he talks about roofing in the streets with glass and making the town a series of arcades."

Slater half smiled—evidence of a convulsive mirth within.

"They've picked out a site for a university!" he said, bitterly. "Cortez is going to be a seat of learning and culture. They're planning a park and a place for an Alaskan World's Fair and a museum and a library. I've always wondered who starts public libraries—it's 'nuts.' But I didn't s'pose more than one or two people got foolish that way."

O'Neil drew from his pocket a newspaper five days old, which he unfolded and opened at a full-page advertisement, headed:

CORTEZ HOME RAILROAD

"This is running in all the coast papers," he said, and read:

OUR PLATFORM:

No promotion shares.	No construction profits.
No bonds.	No incompetence.
No high-salaried officials.	No monopoly.
No passes or rebates.	No graft.

OF ALASKA, BY ALASKA, FOR ALASKA.

There was much more of a similar kind, written to appeal to the quick-profit-loving public, and it was followed by a violent attack upon the Trust and an appeal to the people of Seattle for assistance, at one dollar per share.

"Listen to this," O'Neil went on:

Among the original subscribers are the following:	
Hotels and saloons of Cortez	$17,000
City Council	15,000
Prospectors	7,000
Ladies' Guild of Cortez	740
School-children of Cortez	420

Tom grew red in the face and gave his characteristic snort. "I don't mind his stringing the City Council and the saloons, and even the Ladies' Guild," he growled, "but when he steals the licorice and slate-pencils from the kids it's time he was stopped."

Murray agreed. "I think we are about done with Gordon. He has led his ace."

"I'm not sure. This is a kind of popular uprising, like a camp-meeting. If I went to Cortez now, some prattling school-girl would wallop me with her dinner-bucket. We can't shake Gordon loose: he's a regular splavvus."

"What is a splavvus, Tom?" inquired Dr. Gray.

"It's a real peculiar animal, being a cross between a bulldog and a skunk. We have lots of 'em in Maine!"

O'Neil soon found that the accounts he had received of Gordon's last attempt to recoup his fortunes were in no way exaggerated. Cortez, long the plaything of the railroad-builders, had been ripe for his touch: it rose in its wounded civic pride and greeted his appeal with frantic delight. It was quite true that the school-children had taken stock in the enterprise: their parents turned their own pockets inside out, and subscriptions came in a deluge. The price of real estate doubled, quadrupled, and Gordon bought just enough to establish the price firmly. The money he paid was deposited again in his new bank, and he proceeded to use it over and over in maintaining exorbitant prices and in advancing his grandiose schemes. His business took him often to Seattle, where by his whirlwind methods he duplicated his success in a measure: his sensational attack upon the money powers got a wide hearing, and he finally secured an indorsement of his scheme by the Businessmen's Association. This done, he opened splendid offices and began a wide-spread stock-flotation campaign. Soon the Cortez Home Railway became known as a mighty, patriotic effort of Alaskans to throw off the shackles of oppression.

Gordon perfectly understood that something more than vague accusations were necessary to bring the public to his support in sufficient numbers to sweep him on to victory, and with this in mind he laid crafty plans to seize the Heidlemann grade. The Trust had ceased active work on its old right-of-way and moved to Kyak, to be sure, but it had not abandoned its original route, and in fact had maintained a small crew at the first defile outside of Cortez, known as Beaver Cañon. Gordon reasoned shrewdly that a struggle between the agents of the Trust and the patriotic citizens of the town would afford him precisely the advertising he needed and give point to his charge of unfair play against the Heidlemanns.

It was not difficult to incite his victims to this act of robbery. On the contrary, once he had made the suggestion, he had hard work to restrain them until he had completed his preparations. These preparations were simple; they consisted in writing and mailing to every newspaper of consequence a highly colored account of the railroad struggle. These mimeographed stories were posted from Seattle in time for them to reach their destinations on the date set for the seizure of the grade.

It was an ingenious publicity move, worthy of a theatrical press-agent, and it succeeded beyond the promoter's fondest expectations—too well, in fact, for it drove the Trust in desperation to an alliance with the S. R. & N.

The day set for the demonstration came; the citizens of Cortez boldly marched into Beaver Cañon to take possession of the old Heidlemann workings, but it appeared that they had reckoned prematurely. A handful of grim-faced Trust employees warned them back: there was a rush, some rough work on the part of the aggressors, and then the guards brought their weapons into play. The result afforded Gordon far more sensational material than he had hoped for: one citizen was killed and five others were badly wounded. Cortez dazed and horror-stricken, arose in her wrath and descended upon the "assassins"; lynchings were planned, and mobs threatened the local jail, until soldiers were hurried thither and martial law was declared.

Of course, the wires were burdened with the accounts; the reading public of the States awoke to the fact that a bitter strife was waging in the north between honest miners and the soulless Heidlemann syndicate. Gordon's previously written and carefully colored stories of the clash were printed far and wide. Editorials breathed indignation at such lawlessness and pointed to the Cortez Home Railway as a commendable effort to destroy the Heidlemann throttle-hold upon the northland. Stock subscriptions came in a deluge which fairly engulfed Gordon's Seattle office force.

During this brief white-hot campaign the promoter had been actuated as much by his senseless hatred of O'Neil as by lust of glory and gain, and it was with no little satisfaction that he returned to Alaska conscious of having dealt a telling blow to his enemy. He sent Natalie to Omar on another visit in order that he might hear at first hand how O'Neil took the matter.

But his complacency received a shock when the girl returned. He had no need to question her.

"Uncle Curtis," she began, excitedly, "you ought to stop these terrible newspaper stories about Mr. O'Neil and the Trust."

"Stop them? My dear, what do you mean?"

"He didn't sell out to the Trust. He has nothing to do with it."

"What?" Gordon's incredulity was a challenge.

"He sold to an Englishman named Illis. They seem to be amused by your mistake over there at Omar, but I think some of the things printed are positively criminal. I knew you'd want the truth—"

"The truth, yes! But this can't be true," stammered Gordon.

"It is. Mr. O'Neil did try to interest the Heidlemanns, but they wouldn't have anything to do with him, and the S. R. & N. was going to smash when Mr. Illis came

along, barely in time. It was too exciting and dramatic
for anything the way Mr. O'Neil found him when he was
in hiding—"

"Hiding?"

"Yes. There was something about blackmail, or a secret
arrangement between Mr. Illis and the Yukon River lines
—I couldn't understand just what it was—but, anyhow,
Murray took advantage of it and saved the North Pass
and the S. R. & N. at the same time. It was really a perfectly wonderful stroke of genius. I determined at once
that you should stop these lies and correct the general
idea that he is in the pay of the Trust. Why, he went to
Cortez last week and they threatened his life!"

Mrs. Gordon, who had listened, said, quietly: "Don't
blame Curtis for that. That bloody affray at Beaver
Cañon has made Cortez bitter against every one connected
with the Heidlemanns."

"What about this blackmail?" said her husband, upon
whose ear the word had made a welcome impression.
"I don't understand what you mean by O'Neil's 'saving'
the North Pass and his own road at the same time—nor
Illis's being in hiding."

"Neither do I," Natalie confessed, "but I know you have
made a mistake that ought to be set right."

"Why doesn't he come out with the truth?"

"The whole thing is secret."

"Why?"

Natalie shrugged hopelessly, and Gordon lost himself
in frowning thought.

"This is amazing," he said, brusquely, after a moment.
"It's vital. It affects all my plans. I must know everything
at once."

"I'm sorry I paid so little attention."

"Never mind; try it again and be diplomatic. If O'Neil
won't tell you, question Appleton—you can wind him
around your fingers easily enough."

The girl eyed him with a quick change of expression.

"Isn't it enough to know that the Trust has nothing
to do with the S. R. & N.?"

"No!" he declared, impatiently. "I must know the whole
inside of this secret understanding—this blackmail, or
whatever it is."

"Then—I'm sorry."

"Come! Don't be silly. You can do me a great service."

"You said you no longer disliked Mr. O'Neil and that he couldn't harm you."

"Well, well! Must I explain the whys and wherefores of every move I make?"

"It would be spying if I went back. The matter is confidential—I know that."

"Will you do as I ask?" he demanded.

Natalie answered him firmly: "No! I told you what I did tell only so that you might correct—"

"You rebel, eh?" Gordon spoke out furiously.

It was their first clash since the marriage. Mrs. Gordon looked on, torn between loyalty to her husband and a desire to protect her daughter. She was searching her mind painfully for the compromise, the half-truth that was her remedy for every moral distress. At length she said, placatingly:

"I'm sure Natalie will help you in any way she can, Curtis. She isn't rebellious, she merely doesn't understand."

"She doesn't need to understand. It is enough that I direct her—" As Natalie turned and walked silently to the window he stifled an oath. "Have I no authority?" he stormed. "Do you mean to obey?"

"Wait!" Gloria laid a restraining hand on his arm. "Perhaps I can learn what you want to know. Mr. O'Neil was very kind—"

Her daughter whirled, with white face and flashing eyes.

"Mother!" she gasped.

"Our loyalty begins at home," said Gloria, feebly.

"Oh-h! I can't conceive of your—of such a thing. If you have no decency, I have. I'm sorry I spoke, but— if you *dare* to do such a thing I shall warn Mr. O'Neil that you are a spy." She turned a glance of loathing on Gordon. "I see," she said, quietly. "You used me as a tool. You lied about your feeling toward him. You meant harm to him all the time." She faced the window again.

"Lied!" he shouted. "Be careful—that's pretty strong language. Don't try me too far, or you may find yourself adrift once more. I have been too patient. But I have other ways of finding out what I wish to know, and I shall verify what you have told me." He strode angrily from the room, leaving Natalie staring out upon the bleak fall scene, her shoulders very straight, her breast heaving. Gloria did not venture to address her.

Fortunately for the peace of all concerned, Gordon left for Seattle on the next steamer. Neither of the women believed that Natalie's fragmentary revelation was the cause of his departure; but, once in touch with outside affairs, he lost no time in running down the clues he had gathered, and it was not long before he had learned enough to piece the truth together. Then he once more brought his mimeograph into use.

XXI *Dan Appleton Slips the Leash*

The first winter snows found O'Neil's track laid to the bridge site and the structure itself well begun. He had moved his office out to the front, and now saw little of Eliza, who was busied in writing her book. She had finished her magazine articles, and they had been accepted, but she had given him no hint as to their character.

One afternoon "Happy Tom" burst in upon his chief, having hastened out from Omar on a construction-train. Drawing a Seattle paper from his pocket, he began excitedly:

"Well, the fat's in the fire, Murray! Somebody has belched up the whole North Pass story."

O'Neil seized the newspaper and scanned it hurriedly. He looked up, scowling.

"Who gave this out?" he inquired, in a harsh voice.

Slater shrugged. "It's in the Cortez *Courier* too, so I s'pose it came from Gordon. Blessings come from one source, and Gordon's the fountain of all evil. I'm getting so I blame him for everything unpleasant. Sometimes I think he gave me the smallpox."

"Where did he learn the inside of Illis's deal? By God! There's a leak somewhere!"

"Maybe he uncovered it back there in the States."

Murray shook his head. "Nobody knows anything about it except you boys." He seized the telephone at his elbow and called Dr. Gray, while Tom listened with his shining forehead puckered anxiously. O'Neil hung up with a black face.

"Appleton!" he said.

Tom looked, if possible, a shade gloomier than usual. "I wouldn't be too sure it was Dan if I was you," he ventured, doubtfully.

"Where is he?" O'Neil ground out the words between his teeth.

"Surveying the town-site addition. If he let anything slip it was by mistake—"

"Mistake! I won't employ people who make mistakes of that kind. This story may bring the Canadian Government down on Illis and forfeit his North Pass charter—to say nothing of our authorities. That would finish us." He rose, went to the door, and ordered the recently arrived engine uncoupled. Flinging himself into his fur coat, he growled: "I'd rather have a crook under me than a fool. Appleton told us he talked too much."

Tom pursed his lips thoughtfully. "Gordon got it through the Gerard girl, I s'pose."

"Gordon! Gordon! Will there never be an end to Gordon?" His frown deepened. "He's in the way, Tom. If he balks this deal I'm afraid I'll—have to change ghosts."

"It would be a pious act," Slater declared. "And his ghost wouldn't ha'nt you none, either. It would put on its asbestos overshoes and go out among the other shades selling stock in electric fans or 'Gordon's Arctic Toboggan Slide.' He'd promote a Purgatory Development Company and underwrite the Bottomless Pit for its sulphur. I—I'd hate to think this came from Dan."

The locomotive had been switched out by this time, and O'Neil hurried to board it. On his way to Omar he had time thoroughly to weigh the results of this unexpected complication. His present desire was merely to verify his suspicion that Appleton had told his secret to Natalie; beyond that he did not care to think, for there was but one course open.

His anger reached the blazing-point after his arrival. As he stepped down from the engine-cab Gray silently handed him a code message from London which had arrived a few moments before. When its contents had been deciphered O'Neil cursed, and he was furious as he stumbled through the dark toward the green bungalow on the hill.

Swinging round the corner of the house, he came into a bright radiance which streamed forth from Eliza's window, and he could not help seeing the interior of the room. She was there, writing busily, and he saw that she was clad in the elaborate kimono which he had given her; yet it was not her personal appearance which arrested his angry eyes and caused his step to halt; it was, instead, her surroundings.

He had grown to accept her prim simplicity as a matter of course, and never associated her in his thoughts with anything feminine, but the room as it lay before him now was a revelation of daintiness and artful decoration. Tasteful water-colors hung on the walls, a warm rug was on the floor, and everywhere were rosy touches of color. The plain white bed had been transformed into a couch of Oriental luxury; a lace spread of weblike texture covered it, the pillows were hidden beneath billowing masses of ruffles and ribbons. He saw a typical woman's cozy corner piled high with cushions; there was a jar of burning incense sticks near it—everything, in fact, was utterly at variance with his notions of the owner. Even the girl herself seemed transfigured, for her hair was brought forward around her face in some loose mysterious fashion which gave her a bewilderingly girlish appearance. As he looked in upon her she raised her face so that the light shone full upon it; her brows were puckered, she nibbled at the end of her pencil, in the midst of some creative puzzle.

O'Neil's eyes photographed all this in a single surprised glance as he passed; the next moment he was mounting the steps to the porch.

Dan flung open the door, but his words of greeting froze, his smile of welcome vanished at sight of his chief's forbidding visage.

Murray was in no mood to waste words; he began roughly:

"Did you tell Miss Gerard that Poultney Illis is back-ing me?"

Dan stammered, "I—perhaps—I— What has gone wrong, Chief?"

"Did you tell her the inside—the story of his agree-ment with the steamboat people?"

Dan paled beneath his tan, but his eyes met Murray's without flinching. "I think I did—tell her something. I don't quite remember. But anything I may have said was in confi—"

"I thought so. I merely wished to make certain. Well, the whole thing is in the papers."

Appleton laid his hand upon the table to steady him-self.

"Then it—didn't come from her. She wouldn't—"

"Gordon has spread the story broadcast. It couldn't have come from any other source; it couldn't have reached him in any other way, for none of my boys has breathed a word." His voice rose despite his effort at self-control. "Illis's agreement was *illegal*," he said, savagely; "it will probably forfeit the charter of the North Pass or land him in court. I suppose you realize that! I discovered his secret and assured him it was safe with me; now you peddle it to Gordon, and the whole thing is public. Here's the first result." He shook the London cablegram in Dan's face, and his own was distorted with rage. There was a stir in Eliza's room which neither noticed. Appleton wiped his face with uncertain hand; he moistened his lips to say:

"I—I'm terribly sorry! But I'm sure Natalie wouldn't spy—I don't remember what I told her, or how I came to know about the affair. Doc Gray told me, I think, in the first excitement, but—God! She—wouldn't knowing-ly—"

"Gordon fired you for talking too much. I thought you had learned your lesson, but it seems you hadn't. Don't blame Miss Gerard for pumping you—her loyalty belongs to Gordon now. But I require loyalty, too. Since you lack it you can go."

O'Neil turned as Eliza's door opened; she stood before him, pale, frightened, trembling.

"I couldn't help hearing," she said. "You discharge us?"

He nodded. "I'm sorry! I've trusted my 'boys' so implicitly that the thought of betrayal by them never occurred to me. I can't have men close to me who make such mistakes as this."

"Perhaps there was—an excuse, or the shadow of one, at least. When a man is in love, you know—"

Murray wheeled upon Dan and demanded sharply:

"What's this?" Then in a noticeably altered tone he asked. "Do you love—Natalie?"

"Yes."

"Does she love you?"

"No, sir!"

O'Neil turned back to the girl, saying: "I told Dan, when I hired him, that he would be called upon to dare much, to suffer much, and that my interests must be his. He has disregarded them, and he must go. That's all. There's little difference between treachery and carelessness."

"It's—too bad," said the girl, faintly. Dan stood stiff and silent, wholly dazed by the sudden collapse of his fortunes.

"I'm not ungrateful for what you've done, Appleton," O'Neil went on. "I intend to pay you well for the help you gave me. You took a chance at the Cañon and at Gordon's Crossing. You'll get a check."

"I don't want your damned money," the other gulped. "I've drawn my wages."

"Nevertheless, I shall pay you well. It's highly probable that you've wrecked the S. R. & N. and ruined me, but I don't intend to forget my obligations to you. It's unfortunate. Call on the cashier in the morning. Good night."

He left them standing there unhappily, dumb and stiff with shame. Once outside the house, he plunged down the hill as if fleeing from the scene of some crime. He rushed through the night blindly, for he had loved his assistant engineer, and the memory of that chalk-faced, startled girl hurt him abominably.

When he came to the company office he was walking slowly, heavily. He found Gray inside and dropped into a chair: his face was grimly set, and he listened dully to the physician's rambling talk.

"I fired Appleton!" he broke out, at last. Gray looked up quickly. "He acknowledged that he—did it. I had no choice. It came hard, though. He's a good boy."

"He did some great work, Chief!"

"I know! That affair at the Crossing—I intend to pay him well, if he'll accept. It's not that—I like those kids, Stanley. Eliza took it harder than he. It wasn't easy for me, either," he sighed, wearily. "I'd give ten thousand dollars if it hadn't happened. She looked as if I'd struck her."

"What did they say?"

"Nothing. He has been careless, disloyal—"

"You told them so?"

O'Neil nodded.

"And they said nothing?"

"Nothing! What could they say?"

Gray answered gruffly: "They might have said a good deal. They might have told you how they paid off your men and saved a walk-out when I had no money."

O'Neil stared incredulously. "What are you talking about?" he demanded.

When he had the facts he rose with an exclamation of dismay.

"God! Why didn't you tell me? Why didn't they speak out? I—I—why, that's loyalty of the finest kind. All the money they had saved, too—when they thought I had failed! Jove! That was fine. Oh, I'm sorry! I wonder what they think of me? I can't let Dan go after that. I—" He seized his cap and hurried out of the building.

"It's hardly right—when things were going so well, too!" said Dan. He was sitting crumpled up in a chair, Eliza's arm encircling his shoulders. "I didn't mean to give up any secrets, but—I'm not myself when I'm with Natalie."

"We must take our medicine," his sister told him, gravely. "We deserve it, for this story may spoil all he's done. I didn't think it of her, though."

Dan groaned and bowed his head in his hands. "I don't know which hurts worse," he said—"his anger or her action. She—couldn't do such a thing, Sis; she just couldn't!"

"She probably didn't realize—she hasn't much sense,

you know. But after all he's suffered, to think that we should injure him! I could cry. I think I shall."

The door opened before a rough hand, and O'Neil strode into the room, huge, shaggy in his coonskin coat. They rose, startled, but he came to them swiftly, a look of mingled shame and gladness in his face.

"I've come back to apologize," he cried. "I couldn't wait. I've learned what you children did while I was gone, and I've come to beg forgiveness. It's all right— it's all right."

"I don't know what you mean," Dan gasped.

"Doc told me how you paid those men. That was real friendship; it was splendid. It touched me, and I—I want to apologize. You see, I hurried right back."

They saw that his eyes were moist, and at the sight Eliza gave a quivering cry, then turned swiftly to hide her face. She felt O'Neil's fur-clad arm about her shoulder; his hand was patting her, and he was saying gently: "You are a dear child. It was tremendously good of you both, and I—ought to be shot for acting as I did. I wonder if you can accept a wretched apology as bravely as you accepted a wrong accusation."

"It wasn't wrong; it was right," she sobbed. "Dan told her, and she told Gordon."

"There, there! I was to blame, after all, for letting any one know, and if Dan made a mistake he has more than offset it by his unselfishness—his sacrifices. It seems I forgot how much I really owe him."

"That affair with the shift bosses wasn't anything," said Dan, hastily, "and it was all Eliza's idea. I refused at first, but when she started to pay them herself I weakened." He stuttered awkwardly, for his sister was motioning him desperately to be silent; but he ran on: "Oh, he ought to know the whole truth and how rotten I acted, Sis. I deserve to be discharged."

"Please don't make this any harder for me than it is," Murray smiled. "I'm terribly embarrassed, for I'm not used to apologies. I can't afford to be unjust; I—have so few friends that I want to cherish them. I'm sorry you saw me in such a temper. Anger is a treacherous thing, and it always betrays me. Let's forget that I was here before and pretend that I just came to thank you for what you did." He drew Dan into the shelter of his other arm and pressed the two young people to him. "I didn't realize how deeply you kids care for each other and for me."

"Then I'm not fired?" Dan queried, doubtfully.

"Of course not. When I take time to think about discharging a man I invariably end by raising his salary."

"Dan isn't worth half what you're paying him," came Eliza's muffled voice. She freed herself from Murray's embrace and rearranged her hair with tremulous fingers. Surreptitiously she wiped her eyes. "You gave us an awful fright; it's terrible to be evicted in winter-time." She tried to laugh, but the attempt failed miserably.

"Just the same, when a man contemplates marriage he must have money."

"I don't want your blamed money," Dan blurted, "and it doesn't cost anything to contemplate marriage. That's all I'm doing—just looking at it from a distance."

"Perhaps I can help you to prevail on Miss Natalie to change her mind. That would be a real service, wouldn't it?" Under his grave glance Dan's heart leaped. "I can't believe she's indifferent to you, my boy. You're suited to each other, and there's no reason on earth why you shouldn't marry. Perhaps she doesn't know her own mind."

"You're mighty good, but—" The lover shook his head.

Murray smiled again. "I think you're too timid. Don't plead and beg—just carry her off. Be firm and masterful. Be rough—"

"The idea!" exclaimed Eliza. "She's no cavewoman!"

"Exactly. If she were, Dan would need to court her and send her bouquets of wild violets. She's over-civilized, and therefore he needs to be primitive."

Dan blushed and faltered. "I can't be firm with her, Murray; I turn to jelly whenever she looks at me." There was something so friendly and kind in his employer's attitude that the young fellow was tempted to pour out all his vexations; he had never felt so close to O'Neil as now; but his masculine reserve could not be overcome all in a moment, and he held his tongue.

When Murray had put the two young people fully at their ease he rose to go, but Eliza's eager voice made him turn with his hand on the door-knob.

"What can we do about this unfortunate Illis affair?" she asked. "Dan must try to—"

"Leave that to me. I'll straighten it out somehow. It is all my fault, and I'll have to meet it." He pressed their hands warmly.

When he had gone Dan heaved a great sigh of relief.

"I'm glad it happened just as it did, Sis," he announced. "He knows my secret now, and I can see that he never cared for Natalie. It's a load off my mind to know the track is clear."

"What a simpleton you are!" she told him. "Don't you see he's merely paying his debt?"

"I wonder—" Dan eyed her in amazement. "Gee! If that's so he *is* a prince, isn't he?"

The same ship which had brought the ominous news to O'Neil also brought Curtis Gordon north. He had remained in Seattle only long enough to see the Illis story in print, and then had hastened back to the front. But his satisfaction over the mischief he had done received a rude jolt when at his first moment of leisure he looked over the late magazines which he had bought before taking leave. In one which had appeared on the news-stands that very day he found, to his amazement, an article by Miss Eliza Appleton, in which his own picture appeared. He pounced upon it eagerly; and then, as he read, his eyes narrowed and his jaw stiffened. There, spread out to the public gaze, was his own record in full, including his initial venture into the Kyak coal-fields, his abandonment of that project in favor of Hope Consolidated, and an account of his connection with the latter enterprise. Eliza had not hesitated to call the mine worthless, and she showed how he, knowing its worthlessness from the first, had used it as a lure to investors. Then followed the story of his efforts to gain a foothold in the railroad struggle, his defeat at the Salmon River Cañon, his rout at the delta crossing, and his final death-blow at Kyak. His career stood out boldly in all its fraudulent colors; failure was written across every one of his undertakings. The naked facts showed him visionary, incompetent, unscrupulous.

Thus far he had succeeded in keeping a large part of his stock-holders in ignorance of the true condition of

Hope Consolidated, but he quailed at the inevitable result of this article, which had been flung far and wide into every city and village in the land. He dared not think of its effect upon his present enterprise, now so auspiciously launched. He had made a ringing appeal to the public, and its support would hinge upon its confidence in him as a man of affairs. Once that trust was destroyed the Cortez Home Railway would crumble as swiftly as had all his other schemes.

The worst of it was that he knew himself shut off from the world for five days as effectually as if he were locked in a dungeon. There was no wireless equipment on the ship, he could not start the machinery of his press bureau, and with every hour this damnable story was bound to gain momentum. He cursed the luck which had set him on this quest for vengeance and bound his hands.

Once he had gathered his wits, he occupied himself in the only possible way—by preparing a story of his own for the wire. But for the first time in his experience he found himself upon the defensive and opposing a force against which no bland persuasiveness, no personal magnetism could prevail. In the scattered nature of his support lay his greatest weakness, for it made the task of self-justification extremely difficult. Perhaps it was well for his peace of mind that he could not measure the full effect of those forces which Eliza Appleton's pen had set in motion.

In Omar, of course, the article excited lively interest. O'Neil felt a warm thrill of satisfaction as he read it on the morning after his scene with Eliza and Dan. But it deepened his feeling of obligation almost painfully; for, like all who are thoughtlessly prodigal of their own favors, he was deeply sensible of any kindness done himself. Eliza's dignified exposition of Alaskan affairs, and particularly the agreeable things she had written about him, were sure to be of great practical assistance, he knew, and he longed to make some real return. But so far as she was concerned there seemed to be nothing that he could do. With Dan, of course, it was quite different. Mere money or advancment, he admitted, seemed paltry, but there was a possibility of another kind of service.

Meanwhile Dan was struggling with his problem in his

own way. The possibility that Natalie had voluntarily betrayed him was a racking torture, and the remembrance of Eliza's words added to his suffering. He tried to gain some hint of his chief's feeling, but Murray's frank and friendly attitude baffled him.

When at last he received a brief note from Natalie asking him to call, he raced to Hope afraid, yet eager to hear what she might say. She met him on the dock as he left the S. R. & N. motor-boat and led him directly to the house.

Natalie went straight to the point. "I'm in dreadful trouble," she said, "and I sent for you to tell you that I had no idea of betraying confidences."

Dan uttered some inane platitude, but his eyes lighted with relief.

"When I saw in the papers what a stir that North Pass & Yukon story had made I was afraid I had done something dreadful. Tell me, is it so? Did I make trouble?"

"You certainly did. O'Neil was furious, and nobody knows yet what the result will be. It—it nearly cost me my head."

"Does he blame me?"

"N-no! He says you're on Gordon's side now. He blames me, or did, until he generously took it on himself."

"What does it all mean? I'm nearly distracted." Natalie's eyes were pleading. "Did you think I spied on you?"

Dan glowed with embarrassment and something more. "I didn't know what to think," he said. "I was wretchedly miserable, for I was afraid. And yet I knew you couldn't do such a thing. I told O'Neil I wasn't responsible for what I did or said when with you."

"Mr. Gordon sent me to Omar purposely. He sent me twice. It was I who brought him word that the road was saved. I told all I'd learned because I believed he no longer hated Mr. O'Neil. I was happy to tell all I knew, for he deceived me as he deceives every one. I learned the truth too late."

"Why do you stay here?" Dan demanded, hotly.

"Why? I—don't know. Perhaps because I'm afraid to leave. I'm alone—you see mother believes in him: she's completely under his sway, and I can't tell her the sort of man he is. She's happy, and her happiness is worth more to me than my own. But—I *shall* go away. I can't stand it here much longer."

"Where will you go?"

"Back to my old home, perhaps. Somewhere—anywhere away from Alaska."

"I suppose you know I can't get along without you."

"Please don't! You have been very good and sweet to me, but—" She shook her dark head. "You couldn't marry me—even if I cared for you in that way."

"Why? I intend to marry you whether you want to or not."

"Oh, Dan, it wouldn't do. You know—about—mother. I've nearly died of shame, and—it would be sure to come up. Somebody would speak of it, sometime."

Dan's blue eyes went cold and smoky as he said:

"It would take a pretty brave person to mention the subject in my presence. I don't care a whoop for anything Gordon or your family may say or do. I—"

There was a stir in the hall outside, and the speaker turned to behold Curtis Gordon himself in the doorway. The latter in passing had been drawn by the sound of voices and had looked into the library. Recognizing Natalie's caller, he frowned.

"What is this?" he inquired, coldly. "A proposal? Do I interrupt?"

"You do," said Dan; then, after a pause, "I'll finish it when you leave."

Gordon entered, and spoke to his stepdaughter.

"What is this man doing in my house?"

"He is here at my invitation," she replied.

"Tell him to leave. I won't have him here."

"Why don't *you* tell me?" cried Dan. "I don't need an interpreter."

"Young man, don't be rash. There is a limit to my patience. If you have the indecency to come here after what you have done, and after what your sister has said about me, I shall certainly—"

Dan broke in roughly: "I didn't come to see you, Gordon. You may be an agreeable sight to some people, but you're no golden sunset in my eyes. Eliza flattered you."

Natalie gave a little terrified cry, for the men were

glaring at each other savagely. Neither seemed to hear her.

"Did you read that article?"

"Read it? I wrote it!"

Gordon's face flamed suddenly with rage; he pointed to the door with trembling fingers, and shouted:

"Get out! I'll not have you here. I discharged you once. Get out!" His utterance was rapid and thick.

Dan smiled mirthlessly, dangerously. In a soft voice he said:

"I haven't finished proposing. I expect to be accepted. You'll pardon me, I know."

"Will you go, you—"

Dan turned to the girl, who, after that first outcry, had stood as if spellbound, her face pale, her eyes shining.

"Natalie dear," he said, earnestly, "you can't live in the same house with this beast. He's a cheat and a scoundrel. He's done his best to spoil your life, and he'll succeed if you stay, so come with me now. Eliza loves you and wants you, and I'll never cease loving you with all my heart. Marry me, and we'll go—"

Gordon uttered an inarticulate sound and came forward with his hands working hungrily.

"Don't interrupt!" warned Dan, over his shoulder, and his white teeth gleamed in sudden contrast with his tan. "No man could love you as I do, dear—" Gordon's clutch fell upon him and tightened. Dan stiffened, and his words ceased. Then the touch upon his flesh became unbearable. Whirling, he wrenched himself free. He was like a wild animal now; body and spirit had leaped into rebellion at contact with Gordon. His long resentment burst its bounds; his lean muscles quivered. His frame trembled as if it restrained some tremendous pressure from within.

"Don't do that!" he cried, hoarsely, and brushed the sleeve where his enemy's fingers had rested, as if it had been soiled.

Gordon snarled, and stretched out his hand a second time; but the younger man raised his fist and struck. Once, twice, again and again he flung his bony knuckles into that purple, distorted face, which he loathed as a thing unclean. He battered down the big man's guard:

right and left he rained blows, stepping forward as his victim fell back. Gordon reeled, he pawed wildly, he swung his arms, but they encountered nothing. Yet he was a heavy man, and, although half stunned by the sudden onslaught, he managed to retain his feet until he brought up against the heavy mahogany reading-table in the center of the room. His retreat ended there; another blow and his knees buckled, his arms sagged. Then Dan summoned all his strength and swung. Gordon groaned, lurched forward, and sprawled upon the warm red velvet carpet, face down, with his limbs twisted under him.

His vanquisher stood over him for an instant, then turned upon Natalie a face that was now keen and cruel and predatory.

"Come! We'll be married to-day," he said; and, crossing swiftly, he took her two hands in his. His voice was harsh and imperative. "He's down and out, so don't be frightened. Now hurry! I've had enough of this damned nonsense."

"I—I'm not frightened," she said, dazedly. "But—I—" Her eyes roved past him as if in quest of something.

"Here! This'll do for a wrap," Dan whipped his fur overcoat from a chair and flung it about her. "My hat, too!" He crushed his gray Stetson over her dark hair and, slipping his arm about her shoulders, urged her toward the hall.

"Mother! She'll never—"

"We'll call on her together. I'll do the talking for both of us." He jerked the front door open with a force that threatened to wrench it from its hinges and thrust his companion out into the bracing cold. Then, as Gordon's Japanese butler came running from the rear of the house, he turned.

"Hey, you!" he cried, sharply. "The boss has gone on a little visit. Don't stumble over him. And tell Mrs. Gordon that Mr. and Mrs. Appleton will call on her in a few days—Mr. and Mrs. Dan Appleton, of Omar!"

It was but a few steps to the pier; Dan felt that he was treading on air, for the fierce, unreasoning joy of possession was surging through his veins. His old indecision and doubt was gone, and the men he met recoiled before his hostile glance, staring after him in bewilderment.

But as he lifted Natalie down into the launch he felt her shaking violently, and of a sudden his selfish exultation gave way to a tender solicitude.

"There, there!" he said, gently. "Don't cry, honey. It's all right. It's all right!"

She raised her face to his, and his head swam, for he saw that she was radiant.

"I'm not crying; I'm laughing. I—I'm mad—insane with happiness."

He crushed her to him, he buried his face in her neck, mumbling her name over and over: and neither of them knew that he was rapturously kissing the coonskin collar of his own greatcoat. The launchman, motor crank in hand, paused, staring; he was still open-mouthed when Dan, catching sight of him, shouted:

"What's the matter, idiot? Is your back broken?"

"Yes— No, sir!" The fellow spun the flywheel vigorously; the little craft began to vibrate and quiver and then swung out from shore.

A moment later and the engineman yelled. He came stumbling forward and seized the steering-wheel as the boat grazed a buoy.

"That's right, you steer," Dan laughed, relaxing his hold. To Natalie he said, "There's a sky-pilot in Omar," and pressed her to him.

"It's a long way to Omar," she answered, then hid her face against his breast and said, meekly, "There's one in Cortez, too, and he's much nearer."

XXII *How the Hazard Was Played*

Eliza's greeting to the runaways was as warm as their hearts could wish. She divined the truth before they could speak, and took Natalie in her arms with a glad cry of welcome. The two girls kissed each other, wept, laughed, wept a little more, kissed again, and then the story came out.

Dan was plainly swollen with pride.

"I walloped him, Sis!" he told her. "I got even for the whole family, and I believe his eyes are closed even to the beauties of nature. He won't be able to read the wedding-notice."

Eliza hugged his arm and looked at him adoringly.

"It must have been perfectly splendid!"

Natalie nodded. "I was asleep," she said, "but Dan shocked me wide awake. Can you imagine it? I didn't know my own feelings until he went for—that brute. Then I knew all at once that I had loved him all the time. Isn't it funny? It came over me so suddenly! I—I can't realize that he's mine." She turned her eyes upon him with an expression that made his chest swell proudly.

"Gee!" he exclaimed. "If I'd known how she felt I'd have pitched into the first fellow I met. A man's an awful fool till he gets married."

There followed a recital of the day's incidents, zestful, full of happy digressions, endless; for the couple, after the manner of lovers, took it for granted that Eliza was caught up into the seventh heaven along with them. Dan was drunk with delight, and his bride seemed dizzied by the change which had overtaken her. She looked upon it as miraculous, almost unbelievable, and under the spell of her happiness her real self asserted itself. Those cares and humiliations which had reacted to make her cold and self-contained disappeared, giving place to an impetuous girlishness that distracted her newly made husband and delighted Eliza. The last lingering doubts that Dan's sister had cherished were cleared away.

It was not until the bride had been banished to prepare for dinner that Eliza thought to ask her brother:

"Have you told Mr. O'Neil?"

The triumph faded suddenly out of his face.

"Gee, no! I haven't told anybody."

They stared at each other, reading the thoughts they had no need to voice. "Well, I've done it! It's too late now," said Dan, defiantly.

"Maybe he'll fire us again. I would if I were he. You must tell him this very minute."

"I—suppose so," he agreed, reluctantly, and picked up his hat. "And yet—I—wonder if I'd better, after all.

Don't you think it would sound nicer coming from some one else?"

"Why?"

"Wouldn't it seem like crowing for me to—to— For instance, now, if you—"

"Coward!" exclaimed the girl.

He nodded. "But, Sis, you *do* have a nicer way of putting things than I have."

"Why, I wouldn't tell him for worlds. I couldn't. Poor man! We've brought him nothing but sorrow and bad luck."

"It's fierce!"

"Well, don't hesitate. That's what Gordon did, and he got licked."

Dan scowled and set his features in a brave show of moral courage. "She's mine, and he can't take her away," he vowed, "so—I don't care what happens. But I'd just as soon slap a baby in the face." He left the house like a man under sentence.

When he returned, a half-hour later, Eliza was awaiting him on the porch. She had been standing there with chattering teeth and limbs shaking from the cold while the minutes dragged.

"What did he say?" she asked, breathlessly.

"It went off finely. Thank Heaven, he was out at the front, so I could break it to him over the 'phone!"

"Did he—curse you?"

"No; I opened right up by saying I had bad news for him—"

"Oh, Dan!"

"Yes! I dare say I wasn't very tactful, now that I think it over, but, you see, I was rattled. I spilled out the whole story at once. 'Bad news?' said he. 'My dear boy, I'm delighted. God bless you both.' Then he made me tell him how it all happened, and listened without a word. I thought I'd faint. He pulled some gag about Daniel and the lion; then his voice got far away and the blamed wire began to buzz, so I hung up and beat it back here. I'm glad it's over."

"He'll probably send you a solid-silver dinner-set or raise your pay. That's the kind of man he is." Eliza's voice broke. "Oh, Danny," she cried, "he's the dearest, sweetest thing—" She turned away, and he kissed her sympathetically before going inside to the waiting Natalie.

Instead of following, Eliza remained on the porch, gazing down at the lights of the little city. An engine with its row of empty flats rolled into the yard, panting from its exertions; the notes of a piano came to her faintly from the street below. The lights of an incoming steamer showed far down the sound. O'Neil had made all this, she reflected: the busy town, the hopeful thousands who came and went daily owed their prosperity to him. He had made the wilderness fruitful, but what of his own life? She suspected that it was as bleak and barren as the mountain slopes above Omar. He, too, looked down upon this thriving intimate little community, but from a distance. Beneath his unfailing cheerfulness she felt sure there lurked a hunger which the mere affection of his "boys" could never satisfy. And now the thought that Dan had come between him and his heart's desire filled her with pity. He seemed suddenly a very lonely figure of a man, despite his material success. When his enemies were doing, had already done, so much to defeat him, it seemed unfair that his trusted friend should step between him and the fulfilment of his dearest ambition—that ambition common to all men, failure in which brings a sense of failure to a man's whole life, no matter what other ends are achieved. Of course, he would smile and swallow his bitterness—that was his nature—but she would know the truth.

"Poor Omar Khayyam," she thought, wistfully, "I wish there were love enough in the world for you. I wish there were two Natalies, or that—" Then she shook the dream from her mind and went into the house, for the night was cold and she was shaking wretchedly.

O'Neil behaved more handsomely even than Eliza had anticipated. He hurried into town on the following morning, and his congratulations were so sincere, his manner so hearty that Dan forgot his embarrassment and took a shameless delight in advertising his happiness. Nor did Murray stop with mere words: he summoned all his lieutenants, and Omar rang that night with a celebration such as it had never before known. The company chef had been busy all day, the commissary had been ransacked, and the wedding-supper was of a nature to interfere with office duties for many days thereafter. Tom Slater made a congratulatory speech—in reality, a mournful adjuration to avoid the pitfalls of matrimonial inharmony—and openly confessed that his digestion was now impaired beyond relief. Others followed him; there was music, laughter, a riotous popping of corks; and over it all O'Neil presided with grace and mellowness. Then, after the two young people had been made thoroughly to feel his good will, he went back to the front, and Omar saw him but seldom in the weeks that followed.

To romantic Eliza, this self-sought seclusion had but one meaning—the man was broken-hearted. She did not consider that there might be other reasons for his constant presence at the glaciers.

Of course, since the unwelcome publication of the North Pass & Yukon story O'Neil had been in close touch with Illis, and by dint of strong argument had convinced the Englishman of his own innocence in the affair. A vigorous investigation might have proved disastrous, but, fortunately, Curtis Gordon lacked leisure in which to follow the matter up. The truth was that after his public exposure at Eliza's hands he was far too busy mending his own fences to spare time for attempts upon his rival. Consequently, the story was allowed to die out, and O'Neil was finally relieved to learn that its effect had been killed. Precisely how Illis had effected this he did not know, nor did he care to inquire. Illis had been forced into an iniquitous bargain; and, since he had taken the first chance to free himself from it, the question of abstract right or wrong was not a subject for squeamish consideration.

It was at about this time that the sanguinary affray at Beaver Cañon began to bear fruit. One day a keen-faced, quiet stranger presented a card at Murray's office, with the name:

HENRY T. BLAINE

Beneath was the address of the Heidlemann building in New York, but otherwise the card told nothing. Something in Mr. Blaine's bearing, however, led Murray to treat him with more than ordinary consideration.

"I should like to go over your work," the stranger an-

nounced; and O'Neil himself acted as guide. Together they
inspected the huge concrete abutments, then were lowered into the heart of the giant caissons which protruded
from the frozen stream. The Salmon lay locked in its
winter slumber now, the glaciers stood as silent and inactive as the snow-mantled mountains that hemmed them
in. Down into the very bowels of the river the men descended, while O'Neil described the nature of the bottom,
the depth and character of his foundations, and the measure of his progress. He explained the character of that
bar which lay above the bridge site, and pointed out the
heavy layers of railroad iron with which his cement work
was reinforced.

"I spent nearly two seasons studying this spot before
I began the bridge," he continued. "I had men here, night
and day, observing the currents and the action of the
ice. Then I laid my piers accordingly. They are armored
and reinforced to withstand any shock."

"The river is subject to quick rises, I believe?" suggested Blaine.

"Twenty feet in a few hours."

"The volley of ice must be almost irresistible."

"Almost," Murray smiled. "Not quite. Our ice-breakers
were especially designed by Parker to withstand any weight.
There's nothing like them anywhere. In fact, there will
be nothing like this bridge when it's completed."

Blaine offered no comment, but his questions searched
to the depths of the builder's knowledge. When they were
back in camp he said:

"Of course you know why I'm here?"

"Your card told me that, but I don't need the Heidlemanns now."

"We are prepared to reopen negotiations."

"Why?"

"My people are human; they have feelings. You read
Gordon's lies about us and about that fight at Beaver
Cañon? Well, we're used to abuse, and opposition of a kind
we respect; but that man stirred public opinion to such
a point that there's no further use of heeding it. We're
ready to proceed with our plans now, and the public
can go to the devil till it understands us better. We have
several men in jail at Cortez, charged with murder: it

will cost us a fortune to free the poor fellows. First the Heidlemanns were thieves and grafters and looters of the public domain; now they have become assassins! If this route to the interior proves feasible, well and good; if not, we'll resume work at Cortez next spring. Kyak, of course, is out of the question."

"This route depends upon the bridge."

"Exactly."

"It's a two years' job."

"You offered to complete it this winter, when you talked with Mr. Herman Heidlemann."

"And—I can."

"Then we'll consider a reasonable price. But we must know definitely where we stand by next spring. We have a great deal of capital tied up in the interior; we can't wait."

"This delay will cost you something."

Mr. Blaine shrugged. "You made that point plain when you were in New York. We're accustomed to pay for our mistakes."

"Will you cover this in the shape of an option?"

"That's what I'm here for. If you finish your bridge and it stands the spring break-up, we'll be satisfied. I shall expect to stay here and watch the work."

O'Neil agreed heartily. "You're very welcome, Mr. Blaine. I like your brand of conversation. I build railroads; I don't run them. Now let's get down to figures."

The closing of the option required several weeks, of course, but the outcome was that even before mid-winter arrived O'Neil found himself in the position he had longed to occupy. In effect the sale was made, and on terms which netted him and his backers one hundred per cent. profit. There was but one proviso—namely, that the bridge should be built by spring. The Heidlemanns were impatient, their investment up to date had been heavy, and they frankly declared that failure to bridge the chasm on time would convince them that the task was hopeless. In a way this was unreasonable, but O'Neil was well aware that they could not permit delay—or a third failure: unless his route was proved feasible without loss of time they would abandon it for one they knew to be certain, even though more expensive. He did not argue that the task was of

unprecedented difficulty, for he had made his promise and
was ready to stand or fall by it. It is doubtful, however,
if any other contractor would have undertaken the work
on such time; in fact, had it been a public bridge it
would have required four years in the building. Yet O'Neil
cheerfully staked his fortune on completing it in eight
months.

With his option signed and the task squarely confront-
ing him, he realized with fresh force its bigness and the
weight of responsibility that rested upon his shoulders. He
began the most dramatic struggle of his career, a fight
against untried conditions, a desperate race against the
seasons, with ruin as the penalty of defeat.

The channel of the Salmon at this point is fifteen hundred feet wide and thirty feet deep. Through it boils a
ten-mile current; in other words, the waters race by with
the speed of a running man. Over this O'Neil expected
to suspend a structure capable of withstanding the might-
iest strains to which any bridge had ever been subjected.
Parker's plans called for seventeen thousand yards of cement work and nine million pounds of steel, every part
of which must be fabricated to a careful pattern. It was
a man-sized job, and O'Neil was thankful that he had prepared so systematically for the work; that he had gathered
his materials with such extraordinary care. Supplies were
arriving now in car-loads, in train-loads, in ship-loads:
from Seattle, from Vancouver, from far Pittsburgh they
came in a thin continuous stream, any interruption of
which meant confusion and serious loss of time. The
movement of this vast tonnage required the ceaseless attention of a corps of skilled men.

He had personally directed affairs up to this point, but
he now obliterated himself, and the leadership devolved
upon two others—Parker, small, smiling, gentle-mannered;
Mellen, tall, angular, saturnine. Upon them, engineer and
bridge-builder, O'Neil rested his confidence, serene in the
knowledge that of all men they were the ablest in their
lines. As for himself, he had all he could do to bring
materials to them and to keep the long supply-trail open.
Long it was, indeed; for the shortest haul was from Seattle,
twelve hundred miles away, and the steel bridge members
came from Pennsylvania.

The piers at Omar groaned beneath the cargóes that were belched from the big freighters—incidentally, "Happy Tom" Slater likewise groaned beneath his burdens as superintendent of transportation. At the glaciers a city as large as Omar sprang up, a city with electric lights, power-houses, machine shops, freight yards, and long rows of winter quarters. It lay behind ramparts of coal, of grillage timbers and piling, of shedded cement barrels, and tons of steel. Over it the winter snows sifted, the north winds howled, and the arctic cold deepened.

Here, locked in a mountain fastness more than a thousand miles from his base of supplies, O'Neil began the decisive struggle of his life. Here, at the focusing point of his enterprise, in the white heat of the battle, he spent his time, heedless of every other interest or consideration. The shifts were lengthened, wages were increased, a system of bonuses was adopted. Only picked men were given places, but of these there were hundreds: over them the grim-faced Mellen brooded, with the fevered eye of a fanatic and a tongue of flame. Wherever possible the men were sheltered, and steam-pipes were run to guard against the cold; but most of the labor was, of necessity, performed in the open and under trying conditions. At times the wind blew a hurricane; always there was the bitter cold. Men toiled until their flesh froze and their tools slipped from their fingers, then dragged themselves stiffly into huts and warmed themselves for further effort. They worked amid a boiling snow-smother that hid them from view, while gravel and fine ice cut their faces like knives; or again, on still, sharp days, when the touch of metal was like the bite of fangs and echoes filled the valley to the brim with an empty clanging. But they were no ordinary fellows—no chaff, to drift with the wind: they were men toughened by exposure to the breath of the north, men winnowed out from many thousands of their kind. Nor were they driven: they were led. Mellen was among them constantly; so was the soft-voiced, smiling Parker, not to mention O'Neil with his cheery laugh and his words of praise. Yet often it was hard to keep the work moving at all; for steam condensed in the cylinders, valves froze unless constantly operated, pipes were kept open only by the use of hot cloths: then, too, the snow crept upward steadily, stealthily, until it lay in heavy drifts which nearly hid the little town and changed the streets to miniature cañons.

Out of this snow-smothered, frost-bound valley there was but one trail. The army lay encamped in a *cul de sac;* all that connected it with the outside world were two slender threads of steel. To keep them clear of snow was in itself a giant's task; for as yet there were no snow-sheds, and in many places the construction-trains passed through deep cuts between solid walls of white. Every wind filled these level and threatened to seal the place fast; but furiously the "rotaries" attacked the choking mass, slowly it was whirled aside, and onward flowed that steady stream of supplies. No army of investment was ever in such constant peril of being cut off. For every man engaged in the attack there was another behind him fighting back the allied forces which swept down from either hand.

Only those who know that far land in her sterner moods can form any conception of the stupefying effect of continuous, unbroken cold. There is a point beyond which the power of reaction ceases: where the human mind and body recoils uncontrollably from exposure, and where the most robust effort results in a spiritless inactivity. It is then that efficiency is cut in half, then cut again. And of all the terrors of the Arctic there is none so compelling as the wind. It is a monstrous, deathly thing, a creature that has life and preys upon the agony of men. There are regions sheltered from it, of course; but in the gutters which penetrate the mountain ranges it lurks with constant menace, and of all the coast from Sitka westward the valley of the Salmon is the most evil.

In the throat of this mighty-mouthed funnel, joining the still, abysmal cold of the interior with the widely varying temperatures of the open sea, O'Neil's band was camped, and there the great hazard was played. Under such conditions it was fortunate indeed that he had field-marshals like Parker and Mellen, for no single man could have triumphed. Parker was cautious, brilliant, far-sighted; he reduced the battle to paper, he blue-printed it; with sliding-rule he analyzed it into inches and pounds and stresses and strains: Mellen was like a grim Hannibal, tireless, cunning, cold, and he wove steel in his fingers as a woman weaves her thread.

It was a remarkable alliance, a triumvirate of its kind unsurpassed. As the weeks crept into months it worked an engineering marvel.

XXIII *A New Crisis*

With the completion of the railroad to the glacier crossing there came to it a certain amount of travel, consisting mainly of prospectors bound to and from the interior. The Cortez winter trail was open, and over it passed most of the traffic from the northward mining-camps, but now and then a frost-rimed stranger emerged from the cañon above O'Neil's terminus with tales of the gold country, or a venturesome sledge party snow-shoed its way inland from the end of the track. Murray made a point of hauling these trailers on his construction-trains and of feeding them in his camps as freely as he did his own men. In time the wavering line of sled-tracks became fairly well broken, and scarcely a week passed without bringing several "mushers."

One day, as O'Neil was picking his way through the outskirts of the camp, he encountered one of his night foremen, and was surprised to see that the fellow was leading a trail-dog by a chain. Now these malamutes are as much a part of the northland as the winter snows, and they are a common sight in every community; but the man's patent embarrassment challenged Murray's attention: he acted as if he had been detected in a theft or a breach of duty.

"Hello, Walsh. Been buying some live stock?" O'Neil inquired.

"Yes, sir. I picked up this dog cheap."

"Harness too, eh?" Murray noted that Walsh's arms were full of gear—enough, indeed, for a full team. Knowing that the foreman owned no dogs, he asked, half banteringly:

"You're not getting ready for a trip, I hope?"

"No, sir. Not exactly, sir. The dog was cheap, so I—I just bought him."

As a matter of fact, dogs were not cheap, and Walsh should have been in bed at this hour. Murray walked on wondering what the fellow could be up to.

Later he came upon a laborer dickering with a Kyak Indian over the price of a fur robe, and in front of a bunkhouse he found other members of the night crew talking earnestly with two lately arrived strangers. They fell silent as he approached, and responded to his greeting with a peculiar nervous eagerness, staring after him curiously as he passed on.

He expected Dr. Gray out from Omar, but as he neared the track he met Mellen. The bridge superintendent engaged him briefly upon some detail, then said:

"I don't know what's the matter with the men this morning. They're loafing."

"Loafing? Nonsense! You expect too much."

Mellen shook his head. "The minute my back is turned they begin to gossip. I've had to call them down."

"Perhaps they want a holiday."

"They're not that kind. There's something in the air."

While they were speaking the morning train pulled in, and O'Neil was surprised to see at least a dozen townspeople descending from it. They were loafers, saloon-frequenters, for the most part, and, oddly enough, they had with them dogs and sleds and all the equipment for travel. He was prevented from making inquiry, however, by a shout from Dr. Gray, who cried:

"Hey, Chief! Look who's here!"

O'Neil hastened forward with a greeting upon his lips, for Stanley was helping Eliza and Natalie down from the caboose which served as a passenger-coach.

The young women, becomingly clad in their warm winter furs, made a picture good to look upon. Natalie had ripened wonderfully since her marriage, and added to her rich dark beauty there was now an elusive sweetness, a warmth and womanliness which had been lacking before. As for Eliza, she had never appeared more sparkling, more freshly wholesome and saucy than on this morning.

"We came to take pictures," she announced. "We want to see if the bridge suits us."

"Don't you believe her, Mr. O'Neil," said Natalie. "Dan told us you were working too hard, so Eliza insisted on taking you in hand. I'm here merely in the office of chaperon and common scold. You *have* been overdoing. You're positively haggard."

Gray nodded. "He won't mind me. I hope you'll abuse him well. Go at him hammer and tongs."

Ignoring Murray's smiling assertion that he was the only man in camp who really suffered from idleness, the girls pulled him about and examined him critically, then fell to discussing him as if he were not present.

"He's worn to the bone," said Eliza.

"Did you ever see anything like his wrinkles? He looks like a dried apple," Natalie declared.

"Dan says he doesn't eat."

"Probably he's too busy to chew his food. We'll make him Fletcherize—"

"And eat soup. Then we'll mend his underclothes. I'll warrant he doesn't dress properly."

"How much sleep does he get?" Natalie queried of the physician.

"About half as much as he needs."

"Leave him to us," said Eliza, grimly. "Now where does he live? We'll start in there."

O'Neil protested faintly. "Please don't! I hate soup, and I can't allow anybody to pry into my wardrobe. It won't stand inspection."

Miss Appleton pointed to his feet and asked, crisply: "How many pairs of socks do you wear?"

"One."

"Any holes?"

"Sometimes."

Natalie was shocked. "One pair of socks in this cold! It's time we took a hand. Now lead us to this rabbit-hole where you live."

Reluctantly, yet with an unaccustomed warmth about his heart, O'Neil escorted them to his headquarters. It was a sharp, clear morning, the sky was as empty and bright as an upturned saucepan; against it the soaring mountain peaks stood out as if carved from new ivory. The glaciers to right and left were mute and motionless in the grip of that force which alone had power to check them; the turbulent river was hidden beneath a case-hardened armor; the lake, with its weird flotilla of revolving bergs, was matted with a broad expanse of white, across which meandered dim sled and snow-shoe trails. Underfoot the paths gave out a crisp complaint, the sunlight slanting up the valley held no warmth whatever, and their breath hung about their heads like vapor, crystallizing upon the fur of their caps and hoods.

O'Neil's living-quarters consisted of a good-sized room adjoining the office-building. Pausing at the door, he told his visitors:

"I'm sorry to disappoint you, but your zeal is utterly misplaced. I live like a pasha, in the midst of debilitating luxuries, as you will see for yourselves." He waved them proudly inside.

The room was bare, damp, and chill; it was furnished plentifully, but it was in characteristically masculine disorder. The bed was tumbled, the stove was half filled with cold ashes, the water pitcher on the washstand had frozen. In one corner was a heap of damp clothing, now stiff with frost.

"Of course, it's a little upset," he apologized. "I wasn't expecting callers, you know."

"When was it made up last?" Eliza inquired, a little weakly.

"Yesterday, of course."

"Are you sure?"

"Now, see here," he said, firmly; "I haven't time to make beds, and everybody else is busier than I am. I'm not in here enough to make it worthwhile—I go to bed late, and I tumble out before dawn."

The girls exchanged meaningful glances. Eliza began to lay off her furs.

"Not bad, is it?" he said, hopefully.

Natalie picked up the discarded clothing, which crackled stiffly under her touch and parted from the bare boards with a tearing sound.

"Frozen! The idea!" said she.

Eliza poked among the other garments which hung against the wall and found them also rigid. The nail-heads behind them were coated with ice. Turning to the table, with its litter of papers and the various unclassified accumulation of a bachelor's house, she said:

"I suppose we'll have to leave this as it is."

"Just leave everything. I'll get a man to clean up while you take pictures of the bridge." As Natalie began preparing for action he queried, in surprise, "Don't you like my little home?"

"It's awful," the bride answered, feelingly.

"A perfect bear's den," Eliza agreed. "It will take us all day."

"It's just the way I like it," he told them; but they resolutely banished him and locked the door in his face.

"Hey! I don't want my things all mussed up," he called, pounding for readmittance; "I know right where everything is, and—" The door opened, out came an armful of papers, a shower of burnt matches, and a litter of trash from his work-table. He groaned. Eliza showed her countenance for a moment to say:

"Now, run away, little boy. You're going to have your face washed, no matter how you cry. When we've finished in here we'll attend to you." The door slammed once more, and he went away shaking his head.

At lunch-time they grudgingly admitted him, and, although they protested that they were not half through, he was naïvely astonished at the change they had brought to pass. For the first time in many days the place was thoroughly warm and dry; it likewise displayed an orderliness and comfort to which it had been a stranger. From some obscure source the girls had gathered pictures for the bare walls; they had hung figured curtains at the windows; there were fresh white covers for bed, bureau, and washstand. His clothes had been rearranged, and posted in conspicuous places were written directions telling him of their whereabouts. One of the cards bore these words: "Your soup! Take one in cup of hot brandy and water before retiring." Beneath were a bottle and a box of bouillon tablets. A shining tea-kettle was humming on the stove.

"This is splendid," he agreed, when they had completed a tour of inspection. "But where are my blue-prints?"

"In the drafting-room, where they belong. This room is

for rest and sleep. We want to see it in this condition when
we come back."

"Where did you find the fur rug?" He indicated a thick
bearskin beside the bed.

"We stole it from Mr. Parker," they confessed, shamelessly. "He had two."

Eliza continued complacently: "We nearly came to
blows with the chef when we kidnapped his best boy.
We've ordered him to keep this place warm and look after
your clothes and clean up every morning. He's to be your
valet and take care of you."

"But—we're dreadfully short-handed in the mess-
house," O'Neil protested.

"We've given the chef your bill of fare, and your man
Ben will see that you eat it."

"I won't stand for soup. It—"

"Hush! Do you want us to come again?" Natalie demanded.

"Yes! Again and again!" He nodded vigorously. "I dare
say I was getting careless. I pay more attention to the
men's quarters than to my own. Do you know—this is the
first hint of home I've had since I was a boy? And—it's
mighty agreeable." He stared wistfully at the feminine
touches on all sides.

The bride settled herself with needle and thread, saying:

"Now take Eliza to the bridge while the light is good;
she wants to snap-shoot it. I'm going to sew on buttons and
enjoy myself."

O'Neil read agreement in Eliza's eyes, and obeyed. As
they neared the river-bank the girl exclaimed in surprise;
for up out of the frozen Salmon two giant towers of concrete thrust themselves, on each bank were massive abutments, and connecting them were the beginnings of a com-
plicated "false-work" structure by means of which the
steel was to be laid in place. It consisted of rows upon
rows of piling, laced together with an intricate pattern of
squared timbers. Tracks were being laid upon it, and along
the rails ran a towering movable crane, or "traveler,"
somewhat like a tremendous cradle. This too was nearing
completion. Pile-drivers were piercing the ice with long
slender needles of spruce; across the whole river was weav-
ing a gigantic fretwork of wood which appeared to be

geometrically regular in design. The air was noisy with the cries of men, and a rhythmic thudding, through which came the rattle of winches and the hiss of steam. Over the whole vast structure swarmed an army of human ants, feeble pygmy figures that crept slowly here and there, regardless of their dizzy height.

"Isn't it beautiful?" said the builder, gazing at the scene with kindling eyes. "We're breaking records every day in spite of the weather. Those fellows are heroes. I feel guilty and mean when I see them risking life and limb while I just walk about and look on."

"Will it—really stand the break-up?" asked the girl. "When that ice goes out it will be as if the solid earth were sliding down the channel. It frightens me to think of it."

"We've built solid rock; in fact, those piers are stronger than rock, for they're laced with veins of steel and anchored beneath the river-bed."

But Eliza doubted. "I've seen rivers break, and it's frightful; but of course I've never seen anything to compare with the Salmon. Suppose—just suppose there should be some weak spot—"

O'Neil settled his shoulders a little under his coat. "It would nearly kill Mellen—and Parker, too, for that matter."

"And you?"

He hesitated. "It means a great deal to me. Sometimes I think I could pull myself together and begin again, but —I'm getting old, and I'm not sure I'd care to try." After a pause he added a little stiffly, as if not quite sure of the effect of his words: "That's the penalty of being alone in life, I suppose. We men are grand-stand players: we need an audience, some one person who really cares whether we succeed or fail. Your brother, for instance, has won more in the building of the S. R. & N. than I can ever hope to win."

Eliza felt a trifle self-conscious, too, and she did not look at him when she said: "Poor, lonely old Omar Khayyam! You deserve all Dan has. I think I understand why you haven't been to see us."

"I've been too busy; this thing has kept me here every hour. It's my child, and one can't neglect his own child, you know—even if it isn't a real one." He laughed apologetically. "See! there's where we took the skiff that day we ran Jackson Glacier. He's harmless enough now. You annoyed me dreadfully that morning, Eliza, and—I've never quite understood why you were so reckless."

"I wanted the sensation. Writers have to live before they can write. I've worked the experience into my novel."

"Indeed? What is your book about?"

"Well—it's the story of a railroad-builder, of a fellow who risked everything he had on his own judgment. It's—you!"

"Why, my dear!" cried O'Neil, turning upon her a look of almost comic surprise. "I'm flattered, of course, but there's nothing romantic or uncommon about me."

"You don't mind?"

"Of course not. But there ought to be a hero, and love, and—such things—in a novel. You must have a tremendous imagination."

"Perhaps. I'm not writing a biography, you know. However, you needn't be alarmed; it will never be accepted."

"It should be, for you write well. Your magazine articles are bully."

Eliza smiled. "If the novel would only go as well as those stories I'd be happy. They put Gordon on the defensive."

"I knew they would."

"Yes. I built a nice fire under him, and now he's squirming. I think I helped you a little bit, too."

"Indeed you did—a great deal! When you came to Omar I never thought you'd turn out to be my champion. I—" He turned as Dr. Gray came hurrying toward them, panting in his haste.

The doctor began abruptly:

"I've been looking for you, Murray. The men are all quitting."

O'Neil started. "All quitting? What are you talking about?"

"There's a stampede—a gold stampede!"

Murray stared at the speaker as if doubting his own senses.

"There's no gold around here," he said, at last.

"Two men came in last night. They've been prospecting over in the White River and report rich quartz. They've got samples with 'em and say there are placer indications everywhere. They were on their way to Omar to tell their friends, and telephoned in from here. Somebody over-heard and—it leaked. The whole camp is up in the air. That's what brought out that gang from town this morn-ing."

The significance of the incidents which had troubled him earlier in the day flashed upon O'Neil; it was plain enough now why his men had been gossiping and buying dogs and fur robes. He understood only too well what a general stampede would mean to his plans, for it would take months to replace these skilled iron-workers.

"Who are these prospectors?" he inquired, curtly.

"Nobody seems to know. Their names are Thorn and Baker. That gang from Omar has gone on, and our people will follow in the morning. Those who can't scrape up an outfit here are going into town to equip. We won't have fifty men on the job by to-morrow night."

"What made Baker and Thorn stop here?"

Gray shrugged. "Tired out, perhaps. We've got to do something quick, Murray. Thank God, we don't have to sell 'em grub or haul 'em to Omar. That will check things for a day or two. If they ever start for the interior we're lost, but the cataract isn't frozen over, and there's only one sled trail past it. We don't need more than six good men to do the trick."

"We can't stop a stampede that way."

Dr. Gray's face fell into harsh lines. "I'll bend a Win-chester over the first man who tries to pass. Appleton held the place last summer; I'll guarantee to do it now."

"No. The men have a right to quit, Stanley. We can't force them to work. We can't build this bridge with a chain-gang."

"Humph! I can beat up these two prospectors and ship 'em in to the hospital until things cool down."

"That won't do, either. I'll talk with them, and if their story is right—well, I'll throw open the commissary and outfit every one."

Eliza gasped; Gray stammered.

"You're crazy!" exclaimed the doctor.

"If it's a real stampede they'll go anyhow, so we may

as well take our medicine with a good grace. The loss of even a hundred men would cripple us."

"The camp is seething. It's all Mellen can do to keep the day shift at work. If you talk to 'em maybe they'll listen to you."

"Argument won't sway them. This isn't a strike; it's a gold rush." He turned toward the town.

Eliza was speechless with dismay as she hurried along beside him; Gray was scowling darkly and muttering anathemas; O'Neil himself was lost in thought. The gravity of this final catastrophe left nothing to be said.

Stanley lost little time in bringing the two miners to the office, and there, for a half-hour, Murray talked with them. When they perceived that he was disposed to treat them courteously they told their story in detail and answered his questions with apparent honesty. They willingly showed him their quartz samples and retailed the hardships they had suffered.

Gray listened impatiently and once or twice undertook to interpolate some question, but at a glance from his chief he desisted. Nevertheless, his long fingers itched to lay hold of the strangers and put an end to this tale which threatened ruin. His anger grew when Murray dismissed them with every evidence of a full belief in their words.

"Now that the news is out and my men are determined to quit, I want everybody to have an equal chance," O'Neil announced, as they rose to go. "There's bound to be a great rush and a lot of suffering—maybe some deaths —so I'm going to call the boys together and have you talk to them."

Thorn and Baker agreed and departed. As the door closed behind them Gray exploded, but Murray checked him quickly, saying with an abrupt change of manner: "Wait! Those fellows are lying!"

Seizing the telephone, he rang up Dan Appleton and swiftly made known the situation. Stanley could hear the engineer's startled exclamation.

"Get the cable to Cortez as quickly as you can," O'Neil was saying. "You have friends there, haven't you? Good! He's just the man, for he'll have Gordon's pay-roll. Find out if Joe Thorn and Henry Baker are known, and, if so, who they are and what they've been doing lately. Get it quick, understand? Then 'phone me." He slammed the receiver upon its hook. "That's not Alaskan quartz," he said, shortly; "it came from Nevada, or I'm greatly mistaken. Every hard-rock miner carries specimens like those in his kit."

"You think Gordon—"

"I don't know. But we've got rock-men on this job who'll recognize ore out of any mine they ever worked in. Go find them, then come back here and hold the line open for Dan."

"Suppose he can't locate these fellows in Cortez?"

"Then— Let's not think about that."

XXIV *Gordon's Fall*

The news of O'Neil's attitude spread quickly, and excitement grew among the workmen. Up through the chill darkness of early evening they came charging. They were noisy and eager, and when the gong summoned them to supper they rushed the mess-house in boisterous good humor. No attempt was made to call out the night crew: by tacit consent its members were allowed to mingle freely with their fellows and plan for the morrow's departure. Some, envious of the crowd from Omar which had profited by an early start, were anxious to be gone at once, but the more sober-minded argued that the road to White River was so long that a day's advantage would mean little in the end, and the advance party would merely serve to break trail for those behind.

These men, be it said, were not those who had struck, earlier in the season, at the behest of Gordon's emissary, Linn, but fellows whose loyalty and industry were unquestioned. Their refusal to stampede at the first news was proof of their devotion, yet any one who has lived in a mining community knows that no loyalty of employee to employer is strong enough to withstand for long the feverish excitement of a gold rush. These bridge-workers were the aristocracy of the whole force, men inured to hardship and capable of extreme sacrifice in the course of their work; but they were also independent Americans who believed themselves entitled to every reward which fortune laid in their paths. For this reason they were even harder to handle than the unskilled, unimaginative men farther down the line.

Long before the hour when O'Neil appeared the low-roofed mess-house was crowded.

Natalie and Eliza, knowing the importance of this crisis, refused to go home, and begged Murray to let them attend the meeting. Mr. Blaine, who also felt the keenest concern in the outcome, offered to escort them, and at last with some difficulty he managed to wedge them inside the door, where they apprehensively scanned the gathering.

It was not an ideal place for a meeting of this size, but tables and benches had been pushed aside, and into the space thus cleared the men were packed. Their appearance was hardly reassuring: it was a brawny, heavy-muscled army with which O'Neil had to deal—an army of loud-voiced toilers whose ways were violent and whose passions were quick. Nevertheless, the two girls were treated with the greatest respect, and when O'Neil stepped to a bench and raised himself above their heads his welcome was not unduly boisterous. Outside, the night was clear and cold; inside the cramped quarters the air was hot and close and fetid.

Murray had no skill as a public speaker in the ordinary sense; he attempted no oratorical tricks, and addressed his workmen in a matter-of-fact tone.

"Boys," he began, "there has been a gold strike at the head of the White River, and you want to go. I don't blame you; I'd like to go myself, if there's any chance to make money."

"You're all right, boss!" shouted some one; and a general laugh attested the crowd's relief at this acceptance of the inevitable. They had expected argument, despite the contrary assurances they had received.

"Now we all want an even break. We want to know all there is to know, so that a few fellows won't have the advantage of the rest. The strike is three hundred miles away; it's winter, and—you know what that means. I talked with Baker and Thorn this afternoon. I want them to tell you just what they told me. That's why I called this meeting. If you decide to go you won't have to waste time going to Omar after your outfits, for I'll sell you what you want from my supplies. And I'll sell at cost."

There was a yell of approval, a cheer for the speaker; then came calls for Baker and Thorn.

The two miners were thrust forward, and the embarrassed Thorn, who had acted as spokesman, was boosted to a table. Under Murray's encouragement he stammered out the story of his good fortune, the tale running straight enough to fan excitement into a blaze. There was no disposition to doubt, for news of this sort is only too sure of credence.

When the speaker had finished, O'Neil inquired:

"Are you an experienced quartz-miner? Do you know ore when you see it?"

"Sure! I worked in the Jumbo, at Goldfield, Nevada, up to last year. So did Baker."

"When did you go into the White River country?"

"August."

"How did you go in?"

"We packed in. When our grub ran out, we killed our horses and cachéd the meat for dog-feed."

"Is there any other dog-feed there?"

"No, sir."

"Any people?"

"Not a soul. The country is open to the first comers. It's a fine-looking country, too: we seen quartz indications everywhere. I reckon this speaks for itself." Thorn significantly held up his ore samples. "We've made our locations. You fellows is welcome to the rest. First come, first served."

There was an eager scramble for the specimens on the part of those nearest the speaker. After a moment Murray asked them:

"Did you fellows ever see any rock like that?"

One of his workmen answered:

"*I* have."

"Where?"

"In the Jumbo, at Goldfield. I 'high-graded' there in the early days."

There was a laugh at this. Thorn flushed angrily. "Well,"

he rejoined, "we've got the same formation over there in the White River. It's just like Goldfield. It'll be the same kind of a camp, too, when the news gets out."

O'Neil broke in smoothly, to say:

"Most of our fellows have no dogs. It will take them three weeks to cover the trail. They'll have to spend three weeks in there, then three weeks more coming out— over two months altogether. They can't haul enough grub to do them." He turned to his employees and said gravely: "You'd better think it over, boys. Those who have teams can make it but the rest of you will get left. Do you think the chance is worth all that work and suffering?"

The bridge-workers shifted uncomfortably on their feet. Then a voice exclaimed:

"Don't worry, boss. We'll make it somehow."

"Thorn says there's nobody over there," Murray continued; "but that seems strange, for I happen to know of half a dozen outfits at the head of the White River. Jack Dalton has had a gang working there for four years."

Dalton was a famous character in the north—one of the most intrepid of the early pioneers—and the mention of his name brought a hush. A large part of the audience realized the truth of O'Neil's last statement, yet resented having it thrust upon them. Thorn and Baker were scowling. Gray had just entered the room and was signaling to his chief, and O'Neil realized that he must score a triumph quickly if he wished to hold the attention of his men. He resumed gravely:

"If this strike was genuine I wouldn't argue, but—it isn't." A confusion of startled protests rose; the two miners burst out indignantly; but O'Neil, raising his voice for the first time, managed to make himself heard. "Those jewelry samples came from Nevada," he cried. "I recognized them myself this afternoon, and here's another fellow who can't be fooled. Thorn told you he used to work in Goldfield. You can draw your own conclusions."

The temper of the crowd changed instantly: jeers, groans, hisses arose; the men were on their feet now, and growing noisier every moment; Baker and Thorn were glaring balefully at their accuser. But Gray succeeded in shouldering his way forward, and whispered to O'Neil, who turned suddenly and faced the men again.

"Just a minute!" he shouted. "You heard Thorn say he and Baker went prospecting in August. Well, we've just had Cortez on the cable and learn that they were working for Gordon until two weeks ago." A sudden silence fell. Murray smiled down at the two strangers. "What do you say to that?"

Thorn flew into a purple rage: "It's a damned lie! He's afraid you'll quit work, fellows." Viciously he flung himself toward the door, only to feel the grasp of the muscular physician upon his arm.

"Listen to this message from the cashier of the Cortez Home Bank!" bellowed Gray, his big voice dominating the uproar. Undisturbed by his prisoner's struggles, he read loudly:

Joe Thorn and Henry Baker quit work fifteenth, leaving for Fairbanks over winter trail, with five dogs—four gray and white malamutes, black shepherd leader. Thorn medium size, thirty-five, red hair. Baker dark, scar on cheek.

WILSON, *Cashier.*

The doctor's features spread into a broad grin. "You've all seen the dog-team, and here's the red hair." His fingers sunk into his prisoner's fiery locks with a grip that threatened to leave him a scalp for a trophy. Thorn cursed and twisted.

The crowd's allegiance had been quick to shift, but it veered back to O'Neil with equal suddenness.

"Bunco!" yelled a hoarse voice, after a brief hush.

"Lynch 'em!" cried another; and the angry clamor burst forth anew.

"Don't be foolish," shouted Murray; "nobody has been hurt."

"We'd have been on the trail to-morrow. Send 'em down the river barefoot!"

"Yes! What about that gang from Omar?"

"I'm afraid they'll have to take care of themselves," O'Neil said. "But these two men aren't altogether to blame; they're acting under orders. Isn't that right?" he asked Thorn.

The miner hesitated, until the grip in his hair tightened; then, evidently fearing the menace in the faces on every side, he decided to seek protection in a complete confession.

"Yes!" he agreed, sullenly. "Gordon cooked it up. It's all a fake."

O'Neil nodded with satisfaction. "This is the second time he's tried to get my men away from me. The other time he failed because Tom Slater happened to come down with smallpox. Thank God, he recovered!"

A ripple of laughter spread, then grew into a bellow, for the nature of "Happy Tom's" illness had long since become a source of general merriment, and O'Neil's timely reference served to divert the crowd. It also destroyed most of its resentment.

"You fellows don't seem able to protect yourselves; so Doc and I will have to do it for you. Now listen," he continued, more gravely. "I meant it when I said I'd open the commissary and help you out if the strike were genuine, but, nevertheless, I want you to know just what it would have meant to me. I haven't enough money to complete the S. R. & N., and I can't raise enough, but I have signed an option to sell the road if the bridge is built by next spring. It's really a two years' job, and some engineers don't believe it can be built at all, but I know it can if you'll help. If we fail I'm ruined; if we succeed"—he waved his hands and smiled at them cheerfully—"maybe we'll build another railroad somewhere. That's what this stampede meant. Now, will you stick to me?"

The answer roared from a hundred throats:

"You bet we'll stick!"

At the rear of the room, whence they had witnessed the rapid unfolding of this drama, the two girls joined in the shout. They were hugging each other and laughing hysterically.

"He handled them just right," said Blaine, with shining eyes; "just right—but I was worried."

Walsh, the night foreman, raised his voice to inquire:

"Does anybody want to buy a dog-team cheap?"

"Who wants dogs now?" jeered some one.

"Give 'em to Baker and Thorn!"

O'Neil was still speaking in all earnestness.

"Boys," he said; "we have a big job on our hands. It means fast work, long hours, and little sleep. We picked you fellows out because we knew you were the very best bridge-workers in the world. Now the life of the S. R. & N. lies with you, and that bridge *must be built* on time. About these two men who tried to stampede us: I think it's enough punishment if we laugh at them. Don't you?" He smiled down at Thorn, who scowled, then grinned reluctantly and nodded his head.

When general good feeling was restored Murray attempted to make his way out; but his men seemed determined to thank him one by one, and he was delayed through a long process of hand-shaking. It pleased him to see that they understood from what hardships and disappointments he had saved them, and he was doubly grateful when Walsh rounded up his crew and announced that the night shift would resume work at midnight.

He escaped at last, leaving the men grouped contentedly about huge pans of smoking doughnuts and pots of coffee, which the cook-boys had brought in. Liquor was taboo in the camp, but he gave orders that unlimited cigars be distributed.

When he reached his quarters he was completely fagged, for the crisis, coming on top of his many responsibilities, had taken all his vitality.

His once cheerless room was warm and cozy as he entered: he found Natalie sleeping peacefully on his bed and Eliza curled up in his big chair waiting. She opened her eyes drowsily and smiled up at him, saying:

"You were splendid, Omar Khayyam. I'm *so* glad."

He laid a finger on his lips and glanced at the sleeping Natalie.

"Sh-h!"

"Where are you going to put us for the night?"

"Right here, of course."

"Those men will do anything for you now. I—I think I'd die, too, if anything happened to the bridge."

He took her hand in his and smiled down into her earnest eyes a little wearily. "Nothing will happen. Now go to bed—and thank you for making a home for me. It really is a home now. I'll appreciate it to-morrow."

He tiptoed out and tramped over to Parker's quarters for the night.

The news of the White River fiasco reached Curtis Gor-

don in Seattle, whither he had gone in a final attempt to
bolster up the tottering fortunes of the Cortez Home Railway. His disappointment was keen, yet O'Neil from the
beginning had met his attacks with such uniform success
that new failure did not really surprise him; it had been a
forlorn hope at best. Strangely enough, he had begun to
lose something of his assurance of late. Although he
maintained his outward appearance of confidence with all
his old skill, within himself he felt a growing uneasiness, a
lurking doubt of his abilities. Outwardly there was reason
enough for discouragement, for, while his co-operative
railroad scheme had begun brilliantly, its initial success
had not been sustained. As time passed and Eliza Appleton's exposure remained unrefuted he had found it ever
more difficult to enlist support. His own denials and explanations seemed powerless to affect the public mind, and
as he looked back he dated his decline from the appearance of her first article. It had done all the mischief he
had feared. Not only were his old stock-holders dissatisfied, but wherever he went for aid he found a disconcert-
ing lack of response, a half-veiled skepticism that was
maddening.

Yet his immediate business worries were not all, nor
the worst of his troubles: his physical powers were wan-
ing. To all appearances he was as strong as ever, but a
strange bodily lassitude hampered him; he tired easily,
and against this handicap he was forced to struggle con-
tinually. He had never rightly valued his amazing equipment of energy until now, when some subtle ailment had
begun to sap it. The change was less in his muscular
strength than in his nerves and his mental vigor. He
found himself growing peculiarly irritable; his failures excited spasms of blind fury which left him weak and spent;
he began to suffer the depressing tortures of insomnia.
At times the nerves in his face and neck twitched unac-
countably, and this distressing affection spread.

These symptoms had first manifested themselves after
his unmerciful drubbing at the hands of Dan Appleton:
but they were not the result of any injury; they were due
to some deeper cause. When he had recovered his senses,
after the departure of Dan and Natalie, he had fallen into
a paroxysm of anger that lasted for days; he had raged and

stormed like a madman, for, to say nothing of other humiliations, he prided himself extravagantly on his physical prowess. While the marks of the rough treatment he had suffered were disappearing he remained indoors, plunged in such abysmal fury that neither Gloria nor the fawning Denny dared approach him. The very force of his emotions had permanently disturbed his poise, or perhaps effected some obscure lesion in his brain. Even when he showed himself again in public he was still abnormally choleric. His fits of passion became almost apoplectic in their violence; they caused his associates to shun him as a man dangerous, and in his calmer moments he thought of them with alarm. He had tried to regain his nervous control, but without success, and his wife's anxiety only chafed him further. Gradually he lost his mental buoyancy, and for the first time in his life he really yielded to pessimism. He found he could no longer attack a problem with his accustomed certainty of conquering it, but was haunted by a foreboding of inevitable failure. All in all, when he reached the States on his critical mission he knew that he was far from being his old self, and he had deteriorated more than he knew.

A week or two of disappointments should have shown him the futility of further effort; at any other time it would have set him to putting his house in order for the final crash, but now it merely enraged him. He redoubled his activity, launching a new campaign of publicity so extravagant and ill-timed as to repel the assistance he needed. He had lost his finesse; his nicely adjusted financial sense had gone.

The outcome was not long delayed; it came in the form of a newspaper despatch to the effect that his Cortez bank had suspended payment because of a run started by the dissatisfied employees of the railroad. Through Gordon's flamboyant advertising his enterprises were so well known by this time that the story was featured despite his efforts to kill it. His frantic cables to Cortez for a denial only brought assurances that the report was true and that conditions would not mend unless a shipment of currency was immediately forthcoming.

Harassed by reporters, driven on by the need for a show of action, he set out to raise the money, but the support he had hoped for failed him when it transpired that his bank's assets consisted mainly of real estate at boom prices and stock in his various companies which had been inflated to the bursting-point. Days passed, a week or more; then he was compelled to relinquish his option on the steamship line he had partly purchased, and to sacrifice all that had been paid in on the enterprise. This, too, made a big story for the newspapers, for it punctured one of the most imposing corporations in the famous "Gordon System." It likewise threatened to involve the others in the general crash. Hope Consolidated, indeed, still remained, and Gordon's declaration that the value of its shares was more than sufficient to protect his bank met with some credence until, swift upon the heels of the other disasters, came an application for a receiver by the stockholders, coupled with the promise of a rigorous investigation into his various financial manipulations. Then at last Gordon acknowledged defeat.

Ruin had come swiftly; the diversity of his interests made his situation the more hopeless, for so cunningly had he interlocked one with another that to separate them promised to be an endless task.

He still kept up a fairly successful pretense of confidence, and publicly he promised to bring order out of chaos, but in secret he gave way to the blackest despair. Heretofore, failure had never affected him deeply, for he had always managed to escape with advantage to his pocket and without serious damage to his prestige, but out of the present difficulty he could find no way. His office force stopped work, frightened at his bearing; the bellboys of his hotel brought to the desk tales of such maniacal violence that he was requested to move.

At last the citizens of Cortez, who up to this time had been like putty in his fingers, realized their betrayal and turned against him. Creditors attached the railway property, certain violent-tempered men prayed openly and earnestly to their gods for his return to Alaska in order that they might exact satisfaction in frontier fashion. Eastern investors in Hope Consolidated appeared in Seattle: there was talk of criminal procedure.

Bewildered as he was, half crazed with anxiety, Gordon knew that the avalanche had not only wrecked his fortunes, but was bearing him swiftly toward the penitentiary. Its gates yawned to welcome him, and he felt a chilling terror such as he had never known.

One evening as Captain Johnny Brennan stood on the dock superintending the final loading of a cargo for the S. R. & N. he was accosted by a tall, nervous man with shifting eyes and twitching lips. It was hard to recognize in this pitiable shaken creature the once resplendent Gordon, who had bent the whole northland to his ends. Some tantalizing demons inside the man's frame were jerking at his sinews. Fear was in his roving glance; he stammered; he plucked at the little captain's sleeve like a frightened woman. The open-hearted Irishman was touched.

"Yes," said Johnny, after listening for a time. "I'll take you with me, and they won't catch you, either."

Gordon chattered: "I'll pay you well, handsomely. I'm a rich man. I have interests that demand attention, so—accept this money. Please! Keep it all, my good fellow."

Brennan stared at the bundle Gordon had thrust into his hand, then regarded the speaker curiously.

"Man dear," he said, "this isn't money. These are stock certificates."

"Eh? Stock? Well, there's money in stocks, big money, if you know how to handle them." The promoter's wandering eye shifted to the line of stevedores trundling their trucks into the hold, then up to the crane with its straining burden of bridge material. Every package was stenciled with his rival's name, but he exclaimed:

"Bravo, Captain! We'll be up to the summit by Christmas. 'No graft! No incompetence! The utmost publicity in corporate affairs!'—that's our platform. We're destined for a glorious success. Glorious success!"

"Go aboard and lie down," Brennan said, gently. "You need a good sleep." Then, calling a steward, he ordered, "Show Mr. Gordon to my cabin and give him what he wants."

He watched the tall figure stumble up the gangplank, and shook his head:

" 'The utmost publicity,' is it? Well, it's you that's getting it now. And to think that you're the man with the mines and the railroads and the widow! I'm afraid you'll be in irons when she sees you, but—that's as good a finish as you deserve, after all."

XXV   *Preparations*

The building of the Salmon River bridge will not soon be forgotten by engineers and men of science. But, while the technical features of the undertaking are familiar to a few, the general public knows little about how the work was actually done; and since the building of the bridge was the pivotal point in Murray O'Neil's career, it may be well to describe in some detail its various phases—the steps which led up to that day when the Salmon burst her bonds and put the result of all his planning and labor to the final test.

Nowhere else in the history of bridge-building had such conditions been encountered; nowhere on earth had work of this character been attended with greater hazards; never had circumstances created a situation of more dramatic interest. By many the whole venture was regarded as a reckless gamble; for more than a million dollars had been risked on the chance not alone that O'Neil could build supports which the ice could not demolish, but that he could build them under the most serious difficulties in record-breaking time. Far more than the mere cost of the structure hinged upon his success: failure would mean that his whole investment up to that point would be wiped out, to say nothing of the twenty-million-dollar project of a trunk-line up the valley of the Salmon.

Had the Government permitted the Kyak coal-fields to be opened up, the lower reaches of the S. R. & N. would have had a value, but all activity in that region had been throttled, and the policy of delay and indecision at headquarters promised no relief.

Careful as had been the plans, exhaustive and painstaking as had been the preparations, the bridge-builders met with unpreventable delays, disappointments, and disasters; for man is but a feeble creature whose brain tires and whose dreams are brittle. It is with these hindrances and accidents and with their effect upon the outcome that we have to deal.

Of course, the greatest handicap, the one ever-present obstacle, was the cold, and this made itself most troublesome in the sinking of the caissons and the building of the concrete piers. It was necessary, for instance, to house in all cement work, and to raise the temperature not only of the air surrounding it, but of the materials themselves before they were mixed and laid. Huge wind-breaks had to be built to protect the outside men from the gales that scoured the river-bed, and these were forever blowing down or suffering damage from the hurricanes. All this, however, had been anticipated: it was but the normal condition of work in the northland. And it was not until the middle of winter, shortly after Eliza's and Natalie's visit to the front, that an unexpected danger threatened, a danger more appalling than any upon which O'Neil and his assistants had reckoned.

In laying his plans Parker had proceeded upon the assumption that, once the cold had gripped the glaciers, they would remain motionless until spring. All available evidence went to prove the correctness of this supposition, but Alaska is a land of surprises, of contrasts, of contradictions: study of its phenomena is too recent to make practicable the laying down of hard and fast rules. In the midst of a season of cruelly low temperatures there came a thaw, unprecedented, inexplicable. A tremendous warm breath from the Pacific rolled northward, bathing the frozen plains and mountain ranges. Blizzards turned to rains and weeping fogs, the dry and shifting snow-fields melted, water ran in the courses. Winter loosed its hold; its mantle slipped. Nothing like this had ever been known or imagined. It was impossible! It was as if the unhallowed region were bent upon living up to its evil reputation. In a short time the loosened waters that trickled through the sleeping ice-fields greased the foundations upon which they lay. Jackson Glacier roused itself, then began to glide forward like a ship upon its ways. First there came the usual premonitory explosions—the sound of subterranean blasts as the ice cracked, gave way, and shifted to the weight above; echoes filled the sodden valley with memories of the

summer months. It was as if the seasons had changed, as
if the zodiacal procession had been thrown into confusion.
The frozen surface of the Salmon was inundated; water
four feet deep in some places ran over it.

The general wonder at this occurrence changed to consternation when it was seen that the glacier acted like a
battering-ram of stupendous size, buckling the river ice in
front of it as if ice were made of paper. That seven-foot
armor was crushed, broken into a thousand fragments,
which threatened to choke the stream. A half-mile below
the bridge site the Salmon was pinched as if between two
jaws; its smooth surface was rapidly turned into an inde-
scribable jumble of up-ended cakes.

When a fortnight had passed O'Neil began to fear that
this movement would go on until the channel had been
closed as by a huge sliding door. In that case the rising
waters would quickly wipe out all traces of his work. Such
a crumpling and shifting of the ice had never occurred
before—at least, not within fifty years, as the alder and
cottonwood growth on the east bank showed; but nothing
seemed impossible, no prank too grimly grotesque for
Nature to play in this solitude. O'Neil felt that his own
ingenuity was quite unequal to the task of combating this
peril. Set against forces so tremendous and arbitrary human invention seemed dwarfed to a pitiable insignificance.

Day after day he watched the progress of that white
palisade; day after day he scanned the heavens for a sign
of change, for out of the sky alone could come his deliverance. Hourly tests were made at the bridge site, lest the
ice should give way before the pressure from below and
by moving up-stream destroy the intricate pattern of piling which was being driven to support the steelwork. But
day after day the snows continued to melt and the rain to
fall. Two rivers were now boiling past the camp, one hidden deep, the other a shallow torrent which ran upon a
bed of ice. The valley was rent by the sounds of the
glacier's snail-like progress.

Then, without apparent cause, the seasons fell into order again, the mercury dropped, the surface-water disappeared, the country was sheeted with a glittering crust
over which men walked, leaving no trace of footprints.
Jackson became silent: once again the wind blew cold

from out of the funnel-mouth and the bridge-builders threshed their arms to start their blood. But the glacier face had advanced four hundred feet from its position in August; it had narrowed the Salmon by fully one-half its width.

Fortunately, the bridge had suffered no damage as yet, and no one foresaw the effect which these altered conditions were to have.

The actual erection of steelwork was impossible during the coldest months; Parker had planned only to rush the piers, abutments, and false-work to completion so that he could take advantage of the mild spring weather preceding the break-up. The execution of this plan was in itself an unparalleled undertaking, making it necessary to hire double crews of picked men. Yet, as the weeks wore into months the intricate details were wrought out one by one, and preparations were completed for the great race.

Late in March Dan Appleton went to the front, taking with him his wife and his sister, for whom O'Neil had thoughtfully prepared suitable living-quarters. The girls were as hungry as Dan to have a part in the deciding struggle, or at least to see it close at hand, for the spirit of those engaged in the work had entered them also. Life at Omar of late had been rather uneventful, and they looked forward with pleasure to a renewal of those companionable relations which had made the summer months so full of interest and delight. But they were disappointed. Life at the end of the line they found to be a very grim, a very earnest, and in some respects an extremely disagreeable affair: the feverish, unceasing activity of their friends left no time for companionship or recreation of any sort. More and more they, too, came to feel the sense of haste and strain pervading the whole army of workers, the weight of responsibility that bore upon the commander.

Dan became almost a stranger to them, and when they saw him he was obsessed by vital issues. Mellen was gruff and irritable: Parker in his preoccupation ignored everything but his duties. Of all their former comrades O'Neil alone seemed aware of their presence. But behind his smile they saw the lurking worries; in his eyes was an abstraction they could not penetrate, in his bearing the fatigue of a man tried to the breaking-point.

To Eliza there was a certain joy merely in being near the man she loved, even though she could not help being hurt by his apparent indifference. The long weeks without sight of him had deepened her feeling, and she had turned for relief to the writing of her book—the natural outlet for her repressed emotions. Into its pages she had poured all her passion, all her yearning, and she had written with an intimate understanding of O'Neil's ambitions and aims which later gave the story its unique success as an epic of financial romance.

Hers was a nature which could not be content with idleness. She took up the work that she and Natalie had begun, devoting herself unobtrusively yet effectively to making O'Neil comfortable. It was a labor of love, done with no expectation of reward; it thrilled her, filling her with mingled sadness and satisfaction. But if Murray noticed the improvement in his surroundings, which she sometimes doubted, he evidently attributed it to a sudden access of zeal on the part of Ben, for he made no comment. Whether or not she wished him to see and understand she could hardly tell. Somehow his unobservant, masculine acceptance of things better and worse appealed to the woman in her. She slipped into O'Neil's quarters during his absence, and slipped out again quietly; she learned to know his ways, his peculiarities; she found herself caressing and talking to his personal belongings as if they could hear and understand. She conducted long conversations with the objects on his bureau. One morning Ben entered unexpectedly to surprise her in the act of kissing Murray's shaving-mirror as if it still preserved the image of its owner's face, after which she banished the cook-boy utterly and performed his duties with her own hands.

Of course, discovery was inevitable. At last O'Neil stumbled in upon her in the midst of her task, and, questioning her, read the truth from her blushes and her incoherent attempts at explanation.

"So! You're the one who has been doing this!" he exclaimed, in frank astonishment. "And I've been tipping

Benny for his thoughtfulness all this time! The rascal has made enough to retire rich."

"He seemed not to understand his duties very well, so I took charge. But you had no business to catch me!" The flush died from Eliza's cheeks, and she faced him with thoroughly feminine indignation.

"I can't let you go on with this," said Murray. "*I* ought to be doing something for *you*."

But the girl flared up defiantly. "I love it. I'll do it, no matter if you lock me out. I'm not on the pay-roll, you know, so you have no authority over me—none at all!"

His eyes roved around the room, and for the first time he fully took in the changes her hands had wrought.

"My dear child, it's very nice to be spoiled this way and have everything neat and clean, but—it embarrasses me dreadfully to have you saddled with the sordid work—"

"It isn't sordid, and—what brought you home at this hour, anyhow?" she demanded.

O'Neil's smile gave place to an anxious frown.

"The ice is rising, and—"

"Rising?"

"Yes. Our old enemy Jackson Glacier is causing us trouble again. That jam of broken ice in front of it is backing up the water—there's more running now, and the ice is lifting. It's lifting the false-work with it, pulling the piles out of the river-bottom like splinters out of a sore hand."

"That's pretty bad, isn't it?"

"It certainly is. It threatens to throw everything out of alignment and prevent us from laying the steel if we don't check it."

"Check it!" cried Eliza. "How can you check a thing like that?"

"Easily enough, if we can spare the hands—but cutting away the ice where it is frozen to the piles, so that it won't lift them with it. The trouble is to get men enough—you see, the ice is nine feet thick now. I've set every man to work with axes and chisels and steam-points, and I came up to telephone Slater for more help. We'll have to work fast, night and day."

"There's nobody left in Omar," Eliza said, quickly.

"I know. Tom's going to gather all he can at Cortez and Hope and rush them out here. Our task is to keep the ice cut away until help arrives."

"I suppose it's too late in the season to repair any serious damage?"

"Exactly. If you care to go back with me you can see what we're doing." As they set off for the bridge site Murray looked down at Eliza, striding man-like beside him, with something of affectionate appreciation in his eyes, and said humbly: "It was careless of me not to see what you have been doing for me all this time. My only excuse is that I've been driven half mad with other things. I—haven't time to think of myself."

"All housekeepers have a thankless task," laughed Eliza.

When they reached the river-bank she saw everything apparently just as when she had last seen it. "Why, it's not as bad as I imagined!" she exclaimed. "I thought I'd find everything going to smash."

"Oh, there's nothing spectacular about it. There seldom is about serious mishaps in this business. The ice has risen only an inch or more so far, but the very slowness and sureness of it is what's alarming. It shows that the water is backing up, and as the flow increases the rise of the ice will quicken. If it starts to move up or down stream, we're lost."

There was ample evidence that the menace was thoroughly understood, for the whole day shift was toiling at the ice, chopping it, thawing it, shoveling it away, although its tremendous thickness made their efforts seem puerile. Everywhere there was manifested a frantic haste, a grim, strained eagerness that was full of ominous meaning.

All that day Eliza watched the unequal struggle, and in the evening Dan brought her reports that were far from reassuring. The relentless movement showed no sign of ceasing. When she retired that night she sought ease from her anxiety in a prayer that was half a petition for O'Neil's success and half an exceedingly full and frank confession of her love for him. Outside, beneath the glare of torches and hastily strung incandescents, a weary army toiled stubbornly, digging, gouging, chopping at the foot of the towering wall of timbers which stretched across the

Salmon. In the north the aurora borealis played brilliantly as if to light a council of the gods.

On the following day "Happy Tom" arrived with fifty men.

"I got the last mother's son I could find," he explained, as he warmed himself at O'Neil's stove.

"Did you go to Hope?"

"I did, and I saw the splavvus, himself."

"Gordon?"

"He's worse than we thought." Tom tapped his shining forehead significantly. "Loft to let!"

"What—insane?"

"Nothing but echoes in his dome. The town's as empty as his bonnet too, and the streets are full of snow. It's a sight!"

"Tell me about Mrs. Gordon."

"She's quite a person," said Slater, slowly. "She surprised me. She's there, alone with him and a watchman. She does all the work, even to lugging in the wood and coal—he's too busy to help—but she won't leave him. She told me that Dan and Natalie wanted her to come over here, but she couldn't bring herself to do it or to let them assist in any way. Gordon spends all his time at his desk, promoting, writing ads and prospectuses. He's got a grand scheme. He's found that 'Hope Consolidated' is full of rich ore, but the trouble is in getting it out; so he's working on a new process of extraction. It's a wonderful process—you'd never guess what it is. He *smokes* it out! He says all he needs is plenty of smoke. That bothered him until he hit on the idea of burning feathers. Now he's planning to raise ducks, because they've got so much down. Isn't that the limit? She'll have to fit him into a padded cell sooner or later."

"Poor devil!" said O'Neil. "I'm sorry. He had an unusual mind."

Slater sniffed. "I think it's pretty soft for him, myself. He's made better than a stand-off—he lost his memory, but he saved his skin. It's funny how some men can't fall: if they slip on a banana-peel somebody shoves a cushion under 'em before they 'light. *I* never got the best of anything. If I dropped asleep in church my wife would divorce me and I'd go to the electric chair. Gordon robs widows and orphans, right and left, then ends up with a loving woman to take care of him in his old age. Why, if I even robbed a blind puppy of a biscuit I'd leave a thumb-print on his ear, or the dog's mother would turn out to be a bloodhound. Anyhow, I'd spend *my* declining years nestled up to a rock-pile, with a mallet in my mitt, and a low-browed gentleman scowling at me from the top of a wall. He'd lean on his shotgun and say, 'Hurry up, Fatty; it's getting late and there's a ton of oakum to pick.' It just goes to show that some of us is born behind the game and never get even, while others, like Gordon, quit winner no matter how much they lose." Having relieved himself of this fervid homily, "Happy Tom" unrolled a package of gum and thrust three sticks into his mouth. "Speaking of bad luck," he continued, "when are you going to get married, Murray?"

O'Neil started. "Why—never. It isn't the same kind of proposition as building a bridge, you know. There's a little matter of youth and good looks that counts considerably in the marriage business. No woman would have an old chap like me."

Slater took a mournful inventory of his chief's person, then said doubtfully: "You *might* put it over, Murray. I ain't strictly handsome, myself, but I did."

As O'Neil slipped into his fur coat, after the fat man had slouched out, he caught sight of himself in the glass of his bureau and paused. He leaned forward and studied the care-worn countenance that peered forth at him, then shook his head. He saw that the hair was growing grayer; that the face was very plain, and—yes, unquestionably, it was no longer youthful. Of course, he didn't feel old, but the evidence that he was so admitted of no disproof, and it was evidence of a sort which no woman could disregard. He turned from the glass with a qualm of disgust at his weakness in allowing himself to be influenced in the slightest by Tom's suggestion.

For a week the ice rose slowly, a foot a day, and in spite of the greatest watchfulness it took the false-work with it here and there. But concentrated effort at the critical points saved the structure from serious injury. Then the jam in front of Jackson Glacier went out, at least in part, and the ice began to fall. Down it settled, smoothly, swiftly, until it rested once more upon the shores. It was still as firm as in midwinter, and showed no sign of breaking; nor had it moved down-stream a hair's breadth. O'Neil gathered his forces for the final onslaught.

XXVI The Race

On April 5th the last of the steel for Span Number One reached the front, and erection was begun. The men fell to with a vim and an enthusiasm impossible to describe. With incredible rapidity the heavy sections were laid in place; the riveters began their metallic song; the towering three bent traveler ran smoothly on its track, and under it grew a webwork of metal, braced and reinforced to withstand, in addition to ordinary strains, the pressure of a hundred-mile-an-hour wind. To those who looked on, the structure appeared to build itself, like some dream edifice; it seemed a miracle that human hands could work that stubborn metal so swiftly and with so little effort. But every piece had been cut and fitted carefully, then checked and placed where it was accessible.

Now that winter had broken, spring came with a rush. The snows began to shrink and the drifts to settle. The air grew balmier with every day; the drip from eaves was answered by the gurgling laughter of hidden waters. Here and there the boldest mountainsides began to show, and the tops of alder thickets thrust themselves into sight. Where wood or metal caught the sun-rays the snow retreated; pools of ice-water began to form at noon.

The days were long, too, and no frozen winds charged out of the north. As the daylight lengthened, so did the working-hours of the toilers.

On April 18th the span was completed. In thirteen days Mellen's crew had laid four hundred feet of the heaviest steel ever used in a bridge of this type. But there was no halt; the material for the second section had been assembled, meanwhile, and the traveler began to swing it into place.

The din was unceasing; the clash of riveters, the creak
and rattle of hoists, the shouts of men mingled in a per-
sistent, ear-splitting clamor; and foot by foot the girders
reached out toward the second monolith which rose from
the river-bed. The well-adjusted human machine was running smoothly; every man knew his place and the duties
that went with it; the hands of each worker were capable
and skilled. But now the hillsides were growing bare, rills
gashed the sloping snow-fields, the upper gullies began to
rumble to avalanches—forerunners of the process that
would strip the earth of snow and ice and free the river
in all its fury. In six days three hundred feet more of steel
had been bolted fast to the complete section, and Span
Two was in place. But the surface of the Salmon was no
longer white and pure; it was dirty and discolored now,
for the debris which had collected during the past winter
was exposing itself. The icy covering was partially inundated also; shallow ponds formed upon it and were rip-
pled by the south breeze. Running waters on every side
sang a menace to the workers.

Then progress ceased abruptly. It became known that a
part of the material for the third span had gone astray in
its long journey across the continent. There had been a
delay at the Pittsburgh mills, then a blockade in the Sier-
ras; O'Neil was in Omar at the end of the cable straining
every nerve to have the shipment rushed through. Mellen
brooded over his uncompleted work: Parker studied the
dripping hills and measured the melting snows. He still
smiled; but he showed his anxiety in a constant nervous
unrest, and he could not sleep.

At length news came that Johnny Brennan had the steel
aboard his ship and had sailed. A record run was predicted, but meanwhile the south wind brought havoc on
its breath. The sun shone hotly into the valley of the Salmon, and instead of warmth it brought a chill to the
hearts of those who watched and waited.

Twelve endless, idle days crawled by. Winter no longer
gave battle; she was routed, and in her mad retreat she
threatened to overwhelm O'Neil's fortunes.

On May 6th the needed bridge members were assembled, and the erection of Span Three began. The original
plan had been to build this section on the cantilever princi-

ple, so as to gain independence of the river ice, but to do so would have meant slow work and much delay—an expenditure of time which the terms of the option made impossible. Arrangements had been made, therefore, to lay it on false-work as the other spans had been laid, risking everything upon the weather.

As a matter of precaution the southern half of the span was connected to the completed portion; but before the connection could be fully made the remainder of the jam in front of Jackson Glacier, which had caused so much trouble heretofore, went out suddenly, and the river ice moved down-stream about a foot, carrying with it the whole intricate system of supporting timbers beneath the uncompleted span. Hasty measurements showed that the north end of the steel then on the false-work was thirteen inches out of line.

It was Mr. Blaine who brought the tidings of this last calamity to Eliza Appleton. From his evident anxiety she gathered that the matter was of graver consequence than she could well understand.

"Thirteen inches in fifteen hundred feet can't amount to much," she said, vaguely.

Blaine smiled in spite of himself. "You don't understand. It's as bad as thirteen feet, for the work can't go on until everything is in perfect alignment. That whole forest of piles must be straightened."

"Impossible!" she gasped. "Why, there are thousands of them."

He shook his head, still smiling doubtfully. "Nothing is impossible to Mellen and Parker. They've begun clearing away the ice on the up-stream side and driving new anchor-piles above. They're going to fit tackle to them and yank the whole thing up-stream. I never heard of such a thing, but there's no time to do anything else." He cast a worried look at the smiling sky. "I wonder what will happen next. This is getting on my nerves."

Out on the river swift work was going on. Steam from every available boiler was carried across the ice in feed-pipes, the night shift had been roused from sleep, and every available man was busied in relieving the pressure. Pile-drivers hammered long timbers into the river-bed above the threatened point, hydraulic jacks were put in place, and steel cables were run to drum and pully. The men worked sometimes knee-deep in ice-water; but they did not walk, they ran. In an incredibly short time the preparations were completed, a strain was put upon the tackle, and when night came the massive false-work had been pulled back into line and the traveler was once more swinging steel into place. It was a magnificent feat, yet not one of those concerned in it could feel confident that the work had not been done in vain; for the time was growing terribly short, and, although the ice seemed solid, it was rotting fast.

After the southern half of the span had been completed the warmth increased rapidly, therefore the steel crew lengthened its hours. The men worked from seven o'clock in the morning until eleven o'clock at night.

On the 13th, without warning of any sort, Garfield Glacier began moving forward. It had lain inactive even during the midwinter thaw which had started its smaller brother, but that warm spell had evidently had its effect upon the giant, for now he shook off his lethargy and awoke. He stirred, gradually at first and without sound, as if bent upon surprising the interlopers; then his speed increased. As the glacier advanced it thrust the nine-foot blanket of lake ice ahead of it, and this in turn crowded the river ice down upon the bridge. The movement at the camp site on the first day was only two inches, but that was sufficiently serious.

The onset of Garfield at this time was, of course, unexpected; for no forward motion had ever been reported prior to the spring break-up. The action of the ice heretofore had been alarming; but now consternation spread, a panic swept the ranks of the builders, for this was no short-lived phenomenon, this was the annual march of the glacier itself which promised to continue indefinitely. A tremendous cutting-edge, nine feet in thickness, like the blade of a carpenter's plane, was being driven against the bridge by an irresistible force.

Once again the endless thawing and chopping and gouging of ice began, but the more rapidly the encroaching edge was cut away the more swiftly did it bear down. The huge mass began to rumble; it "calved," it split, it detonated, and, having finally loosened itself from its bed, it acquired increased momentum. As the men with chisels and steam-points became exhausted others took their places, but the structural gang clung to its perch above, augmenting the din of riveters and the groaning of blocks and tackle. Among the able-bodied men sleep now was out of the question, for the ice gained in spite of every effort. It was too late to remove the steel in the uncompleted span to a place of safety, for that would have required more time than to bridge the remaining gap.

Piling began to buckle and bend before that irresistible push; the whole nicely balanced mass of metal was in danger of being unseated. Mellen cursed the heavens in a black fury; Parker smiled through white lips; O'Neil ground his teeth and spurred his men on.

This feverish haste brought its penalty. On the evening of the 14th, when the span was more than three-quarters finished, a lower chord section fouled as it was lifted, and two loading-beams at the top of the traveler snapped.

On that day victory had been in sight; the driving of the last bolt had been but a question of hours, a race with the sliding ice. But with the hoisting apparatus out of use work halted. Swiftly, desperately, without loss of a moment's time, repairs began. No regrets were voiced, no effort was made to place the blame, for that would have caused delay, and every minute counted. Eleven hours later the broken beams were replaced, and erection had recommenced.

But now for those above there was danger to life and limb. During the pause the ice had gained, and no effort could relieve the false-work of its strain. All knew that if it gave way the workmen would be caught in a chaos of collapsing wood and steel.

From the morning of May 14th until midnight of the 16th the iron-workers clung to their tasks. They dropped their tools and ran to their meals; they gulped their food and fled back to their posts. The weaker ones gave out and staggered away, cursed and taunted by their companions. They were rough fellows, and in their deep-throated profanity was a prayer.

The strong ones struggled on, blind with weariness, but upheld by that desperate, unthinking courage that animates a bayonet charge. It seemed that every moment must see the beginning of that slow work of demolition which would send them all scurrying to safety; but hour after hour the piling continued to hold and the fingers of steel to reach out, foot by foot, for the concrete pier which was their goal.

At midnight of the 16th the last rivet was driven; but the ice had gained to such an extent that the lower chord was buckled down-stream about eight inches, and the distance was growing steadily. Quickly the traveler was shifted to the false-work beyond the pier, and the men under Mellen's direction fell to splitting out the blocking.

As the supports were chopped away the mass began to crush the last few wedges; there was a great snapping and rending of wood; and some one, strained to the breaking-point, shouted:

"Look out! There she goes!"

A cry of terror arose, the men fled, trampling one another in their panic. But Mellen charged them like a wild man, firing curses and orders at them until they rallied. The remaining supports were removed; the fifteen hundred tons of metal settled into place and rested securely on its foundations.

O'Neil was the last man ashore. As he walked the completed span from Pier Three the barricade of piling beneath him was bending and tearing; but he issued no orders to remove it, for the river was doing that. In the general haste pile-drivers, hoists, boilers, and various odds and ends of machinery and material had been left where they stood. They were being inundated now; many of them were all but submerged. There was no possibility of saving them at present, for the men were half dead from exhaustion.

As he lurched up the muddy, uneven street to his quarters Murray felt his fatigue like a heavy burden, for he had been sixty hours without sleep. He saw Slater and Appleton and the rest of his "boys"; he saw Natalie and Eliza, but he was too tired to speak to them, or to grasp what they said. He heard the workmen cheering Mellen and Parker and himself. It was very foolish, he thought, to cheer, since the river had so nearly triumphed and the final test was yet to come.

He fell upon his bed, clothed as he was; an hour later the false-work beneath Span Three collapsed.

Although the bridge was not yet finished, the most critical point of its construction had been passed, for the fourth and final portion would be built over shallow water, and no great difficulties were to be expected even though the ice went out before the work was finished. But Murray had made his promise and his boast to complete the structure within a stated time, and he was determined to live up to the very letter of his agreement with the Trust. As to the result of the break-up, he had no fear whatever.

For once Nature aided him: she seemed to smile as if in approval of his steadfastness. The movement of the channel ice became irregular, spasmodic, but it remained firm until the last span had been put in place.

Of this dramatic struggle Eliza Appleton had watched every phase with intensest interest; but when at last she knew that the battle was won she experienced a peculiar revulsion of feeling. So long as O'Neil had been working against odds, with the prospect of ruin and failure forever imminent, she had felt an almost painful sympathy, but now that he had conquered she felt timid about congratulating him. He was no longer to be pitied and helped; he had attained his goal and the fame he longed for. His success would inevitably take him out of her life. She was very sorry that he needed her no longer.

She did not watch the last bridge-member swung, but went to her room, and tried to face the future. Spring was here, her book was finished, there was the need to take up her life again.

She was surprised when Murray came to find her.

"I missed you, Eliza," he said. "The others are all down at the river-bank. I want you to congratulate me."

She saw, with a jealous twinge, that exultation over his victory had overcome his weariness, that his face was alight with a fire she had never before seen. He seemed young, vigorous, and masterful once more.

"Of course," he went on, "the credit belongs to Parker, who worked the bridge out in each detail—he's marvelous —and to Mellen, who actually built it, but I helped a little. Praise to me means praise to them."

"It is all over now, isn't it?"

"Practically. Blaine has cabled New York that we've won. Strictly speaking, we haven't as yet, for there's still the break-up to face; but the bridge will come through it without a scratch. The ice may go out any minute now, and after that I can rest." He smiled at her gladly. "It will feel good to get rid of all this responsibility, won't it? I think you've suffered under it as much as I have."

A little wistfully she answered: "You're going to realize that dream you told me about the day of the storm at Kyak. You have conquered this great country—just as you dreamed."

He acquiesced eagerly, boyishly. "Yes. Whirring wheels, a current of traffic, a broad highway of steel—that's the sort of monument I want to leave."

"Sometime I'll come back and see it all completed and tell myself that I had a little part in making it."

"Come back?" he queried. "Why, you're going to stay till we're through, aren't you?"

"Oh no! I'm going south with the spring flight—on the next boat, perhaps."

His face fell; the exultant light gradually faded from his eyes.

"Why—I had no idea! Aren't you happy here?"

She nodded. "But I must try to make good in my work as you have in yours."

He was looking at her sorrowfully, almost as if she had deserted him. "That's too bad, but—I suppose you must go. Yes; this is no place for you. I dare say other people need you to bring sunshine and joy to them just as we old fellows do, but—I've never thought about your leaving. It wouldn't be right to ask you to stay here among such people as we are when you have so much ahead of you. Still, it will leave a gap. Yes—it certainly will—leave a gap."

She longed desperately to tell him how willingly she would stay if he only asked her, but the very thought shocked her into a deeper reserve.

"I'm going East to sell my book," she said, stiffly. "You've given me the climax of the story in this race with the seasons."

"Is it a—love story?" he asked.

Eliza flushed. "Yes. It's mostly love."

"You're not at all the girl I thought you when we first met. You're very—different. I'm sure I won't recognize myself as the hero. Who—or what is the girl in the story?"

"Well, she's just the kind of girl that would appeal to a person like you. She's tall and dark and dashing, and—of course, she's remarkably beautiful. She's very feminine, too."

"What's her name?"

Miss Appleton stammered: "Why—I called her Violet —until I could think of a better—"

"What's wrong with Violet? You couldn't think of a better name than that. I'm fond of it."

"Oh, it's a good book-name, but for real life it's too— delicate." Eliza felt with vexation that her face was burning. She was sure he was laughing at her.

"Can't I read the manuscript?" he pleaded.

"Heavens! No! I—" She changed the subject abruptly. "I've left word to be called the minute the ice starts to go out. I want to see the last act of the drama."

When O'Neil left her he was vaguely perplexed, for something in her bearing did not seem quite natural. He was forlorn, too, at the prospect of losing her. He wondered if fathers suffered thus, or if a lover could be more deeply pained at a parting than he. Somehow he seemed to share the feelings of both.

XXVII   *How a Dream Came True*

Early on the following morning Eliza was awakened by a sound of shouting outside her window. She lay half dazed for a moment or two, until the significance of the uproar made itself apparent; then she leaped from her bed.

Men were crying:

"There she goes!"

"She's going out!"

Doors were slamming, there was the rustle and scuff of

flying feet, and in the next room Dan was evidently throwing himself into his clothes like a fireman. Eliza called to him, but he did not answer; and the next moment he had fled, upsetting some article of furniture in his haste. Drawing her curtains aside, the girl saw in the brightening dawn men pouring down the street, dressing as they went. They seemed half demented; they were yelling at one another, but she could not gather from their words whether it was the ice which was moving or—the bridge. The bridge! That possibility set her to dressing with tremulous fingers, her heart sick with fear. She called to Natalie, but scarcely recognized her own voice.

"I—don't know," came the muffled reply to her question. "It sounds like something—terrible. I'm afraid Dan will fall in or—get hurt." The confusion in the street was growing. *"Eliza!"* Natalie's voice was tragic.

"What is it, dear?"

"H-help me, quick!"

"How?"

"I can't find my other shoe."

But Eliza was sitting on the floor, lacing up her own stout boots, and an instant later she followed her brother, pursued by a wail of dismay from the adjoining chamber. Through the chill morning light she hurried, asking many questions, but receiving no coherent reply from the racing men; then after endless moments of suspense she saw with relief that the massive superstructure of the bridge was still standing. Above the shouting she heard another sound, indistinct but insistent. It filled the air with a whispering movement; it was punctuated at intervals by a dull rumbling and grinding. She found the river-bank black with forms, but like a cat she wormed her way through the crowd until the whole panorama lay before her.

The bridge stood as she had seen it on the yesterday—slender, strong, superb in the simplicity of its splendid outline; but beneath it and as far as her eyes could follow the river she saw, not the solid spread of white to which she had become accustomed, but a moving expanse of floes. At first the winter burden slipped past in huge masses, acres in extent, but soon these began to be rent apart; irregular black seams ran through them, opened, closed, and threw up ridges of ice-shavings as they ground together. The floes were rubbing against the banks, they came sliding out over the dry shore like tremendous sheets of cardboard manipulated by unseen hands, and not until their nine-foot edges were exposed to view did the mind grasp the appalling significance of their movement. They swept down in phalanxes upon the wedge-like ice-breakers which stood guard above the bridge-piers, then they halted, separated, and the armored cutting-edges sheared through them like blades.

A half-mile below, where the Salmon flung itself headlong against the upper wing of Jackson Glacier, the floating ice was checked by the narrowed passageway. There a jam was forming, and as the river heaved and tore at its growing burden a spectacular struggle went on. The sound of it came faintly but impressively to the watchers—a grinding and crushing of bergs, a roar of escaping waters. Fragments were up-ended, masses were rearing themselves edgewise into the air, were overturning and collapsing. They were wedging themselves into every conceivable angle, and the crowding procession from above was adding to the barrier momentarily. As the passageway became blocked the waters rose; the river piled itself up so swiftly that the eye could note its rise along the banks.

But the attention of the crowd was divided between the jam and something far out on the bridge itself. At first glance Eliza did not comprehend; then she heard a man explaining:

"He was going out when we got here, and now he won't come back."

The girl gasped, for she recognized the distant figure of a man, dwarfed to puny proportions by the bulk of the structure in the mazes of which he stood. The man was O'Neil; he was perched upon one of the girders near the center of the longest span, where he could watch the attack upon the pyramidal ice-breakers beneath him.

"He's a fool," said some one at Eliza's back. "That jam is getting bigger."

"He'd better let the damned bridge take care of itself."

She turned and began to force her way through the press of people between her and the south abutment. She arrived there, disheveled and panting, to find Slater, Mellen, and Parker standing in the approach. In front of them extended the long skeleton tunnel into which Murray had gone.

"Mr. O'Neil is out there!" she cried to Tom.

Slater turned and, reading the tragic appeal in her face, said reassuringly:

"Sure! But he's all right."

"They say—there's danger."

"Happy Tom's" round visage puckered into a doubtful smile. "Oh, he'll take care of himself."

Mellen turned to the girl and said briefly:

"There's no danger whatever."

But Eliza's fear was not to be so easily quieted.

"Then why did he go out alone? What are you men doing here?"

"It's his orders," Tom told her.

Mellen was staring at the jam below, over which the Salmon was hurling a flood of ice and foaming waters. The stream was swelling and rising steadily; already it had nearly reached the level of the timber-line on the left bank; the blockade was extending upstream almost to the bridge itself. Mellen said something to Parker, who shook his head silently.

Dan Appleton shouldered his way out of the crowd, with Natalie at his heels. She had dressed herself in haste: her hair was loose, her jacket was buttoned awry; on one foot was a shoe, on the other a bedroom slipper muddy and sodden. Her dark eyes were big with excitement.

"Why don't you make Murray come in?" Dan demanded sharply.

"He won't do it," muttered Slater.

"The jam is growing. Nobody knows what'll happen if it holds much longer. If the bridge should go—"

Mellen whirled, crying savagely: "It won't go! All hell couldn't take it out."

From the ranks of the workmen came a bellow of triumph, as an unusually heavy ice-floe was swept against the breakers and rent asunder. The tumult of the imprisoned waters below was growing louder every moment: across the lake came a stentorian rumble as a huge mass was loosened from the front of Garfield. The channel of the Salmon where the onlookers stood was a heaving, churning caldron over which the slim bridge flung itself defiantly.

Eliza plucked at her brother's sleeve imploringly, and he saw her for the first time.

"Hello, Sis," he cried. "How did you get here?"

"Is he in—danger, Danny?"

"Yes—no! Mellen says it's all right, so it must be, but —that dam—"

At that moment Natalie began to sob hysterically, and Dan turned his attention to her.

But his sister was not of the hysterical kind. Seizing Tom Slater by the arm, she tried to shake him, demanding fiercely:

"Suppose the jam doesn't give way! What will happen?"

"Happy Tom" stared at her uncomprehendingly. Her voice was shrill and insistent. "Suppose the water rises higher. Won't the ice sweep down on the bridge itself? Won't it wreck everything if it goes out suddenly? Tell me—"

"It *can't* hold. Mellen says so." Slater, like the others, found it impossible to keep his eyes from the river where those immeasurable forces were at play; then in his peculiar irascible manner he complained: "I told 'em we was crazy to try this. It ain't a white man's country; it ain't a safe place for a bridge. There's just one God-awful thing after another—" He broke into a shout, for Eliza had slipped past him and was speeding like a shadow out across the irregularly spaced ties upon which the bridge track was laid.

Mellen whirled at the cry and made after her, but he might as well have tried to catch the wind. As she ran she heard her brother shout in sudden alarm and Natalie's voice raised in entreaty, but she sped on under an impulse as irresistible as panic fear. Down through the openings beneath her feet she saw, as in a nightmare, the sweeping flood, burdened with plunging ice chunks and flecked with foam. She seemed to be suspended above it; yet she was running at reckless speed, dimly aware of the consequences of a misjudged footstep, but fearful only of being overtaken. Suddenly she hated her companions; her mind was in a furious revolt at their cowardice, their indecision, or whatever it was that held them like a group of wooden figures safe on shore while the man whose life was worth all theirs put together exposed himself to needless peril. That he was really in danger she felt sure. She knew that Murray was apt to lose himself in his dreams; perhaps some visionary mood had blinded him to the menace of that mounting ice-ridge in front of the glacier, or had he madly chosen to stand or fall with this structure that meant so much to him? She would make him yield to her own terror, drag him ashore, if necessary, with her own hands.

She stumbled, but saved herself from a fall, then gathered her skirts more closely and rushed on, measuring with instinctive nicety the length of every stride. It was not an easy path over which she dashed, for the ties were unevenly spaced; gaping apertures gave terrible glimpses of the river below, and across these ghastly abysses she had to leap.

The hoarse bursts of shouting from the shore ceased as the workmen beheld her flitting out along the steel causeway. They watched her in dumb amazement.

All at once O'Neil saw her and hurried to meet her.

"Eliza!" he cried. "Be careful! What possessed you to do this?"

"Come away," she gasped. "It's dangerous. The jam— Look!" She pointed down the channel.

He shook his head impatiently.

"Yes!" she pleaded. "Yes! Please! They wouldn't come to warn you—they tried to stop me. You must go ashore." The frightened entreaty in her clear, wide-open eyes, the disorder that her haste had made affected O'Neil strangely. He stared at her, bewildered, doubtful, then steadied her and groped with his free hand for support. He could feel her trembling wretchedly.

"There's no danger, none whatever," he said, soothingly. "Nothing can happen."

"You don't know. The bridge has never been tried. The ice is battering at it, and that jam—if it doesn't burst—"

"But it will. It can't last much longer."

"It's rising—"

"To be sure, but the river will overflow the bank."

"Please!" she urged. "You can do no good here. I'm afraid."

He stared at her in the same incredulous bewilderment; some impulse deep within him was struggling for expres-

sion, but he could not find words to frame it. His eyes were
oddly bright as he smiled at her.

"Won't you go ashore?" she begged.

"I'll take you back, of course, but I want to stay and
see—"

"Then—I'll stay."

"Eliza!" Her name burst from his lips in a tone that
thrilled her, but with it came a sudden uproar from the
distant crowd, and the next instant they saw that the ice-
barrier was giving way. The pressure had become irresistible. As the Salmon had risen the ice had risen also, and
now the narrow throat was belching its contents forth.
The chaos of up-ended bergs was being torn apart; over
it and through it burst a deluge which filled the valley
with the roar of a mighty cataract. Clouds of spray were
in the air; broken masses were leaping and somersaulting;
high up on the shore were stranded floes and fragments,
left in the wake of the moving body. Onward it coursed,
clashing and grinding along the brittle face of the glacier;
over the alder tops beyond the bend they could see it
moving faster and faster, like the crest of a tidal wave.
The surface of the river lowered swiftly beneath the bridge;
the huge white pans ground and milled, shouldered aside
by the iron-sheathed pillars of concrete.

"See! See! It's gone already. Once it clears a passageway we'll have no more gorges, for the freshets are coming. The bridge didn't even tremble—there wasn't a tremor,
not a scratch!" Eliza looked up to find O'Neil regarding her
with an expression that set her heart throbbing and her
thoughts scattering. She clasped a huge, cold bolt-head
and clung to it desperately, for the upheaval in her soul
rivaled that which had just passed before her eyes. The
bridge, the river, the valley itself were gyrating slowly,
dizzily.

"Eliza!" She did not answer. "Child!" O'Neil's voice was
shaking. "Why did you come to me? Why did you do this
mad thing? I saw something in your face that I can't believe—that I—can't think possible. It—it gives me courage. If I don't speak quickly I'll never dare. Is it—true?
Dear girl, can it be? I'm so old—such a poor thing—you
couldn't possibly care, and yet, *why did you come?*" The

words were torn from him; he was gripped and shaken by a powerful emotion.

She tried to answer, but her lips were soundless. She closed her eyes, and Murray saw that she was whiter than the foam far beneath. He stared into the colorless face upturned to his until her eyelids fluttered open and she managed to voice the words that clung in her throat.

"I've always—loved you like this."

He gave a cry, like that of a starving man; she felt herself drawn against him. But now he, too, was speechless; he could only press her close while his mind went groping for words to express that joy which was as yet unbelievable and stunning.

"Couldn't you see?" she asked, breathlessly.

He shook his head. "I'm such a dreamer. I'm afraid it —can't be true. I'm afraid you'll go away and—leave me. You won't ever—will you, Eliza? I couldn't stand that." Then fresh realization of the truth swept over him; they clung to each other, drunk with ecstasy, senseless of their surroundings.

"I thought you cared for Natalie," she said, softly, after a while.

"It was always you."

"Always?"

"Always!"

She turned her lips to his, and lifted her entwining arms.

The breakfast-gong had called the men away before the two figures far out upon the bridge picked their way slowly to the shore. The Salmon was still flooded with hurrying masses of ice, as it would continue to be for several days, but it was running free; the channel in front of the glacier was open.

Blaine was the first to shake O'Neil's hand, for the members of Murray's crew held aloof in some embarrassment. "It's a perfect piece of work," said he. "I congratulate you."

The others echoed his sentiments faintly, hesitatingly, for they were abashed at what they saw in their chief's face and realized that words were weak and meaningless.

Dan dared not trust himself to speak. He had many

things to say to his sister, but his throat ached miserably. Natalie restrained herself only by the greatest effort.

It was Tom Slater who ended the awkward pause by grumbling, sarcastically:

"If all the young lovers are safely ashore, maybe us old men who built the bridge can go and get something to eat."

Murray smiled at the girl beside him.

"I'm afraid they've guessed our secret, dear."

"Secret!" Slater rolled his eyes. "There ain't over a couple thousand people beside us that saw you pop the question. I s'pose she was out of breath and couldn't say no."

Eliza gasped and fled to her brother's arms.

"Sis! Poor—little Sis!" Dan cried, and two tears stole down his brown cheeks. "Isn't this—just great?" Then the others burst into a noisy expression of their gladness.

"Happy Tom" regarded them all pessimistically. "I feel bound to warn you," he said at length, "that marriage is an awful gamble. It ain't what it seems."

"It is!" Natalie declared. "It's better, and you know it."

"It turned out all right for me," Tom acknowledged, "because I got the best woman in the world. But"—he eyed his chief accusingly—"I went about it in a modest way; I didn't humiliate her in public."

He turned impatiently upon his companions, still pouring out their babble of congratulations.

"Come along, can't you," he cried, "and leave 'em alone. I'm a dyspeptic old married man, but I used to be young and affectionate, like Murray. After breakfast I'm going to cable Mrs. Slater to come and bring the kids with her and watch her bed-ridden, invalid husband build the rest of this railroad. I'm getting chuck full of romance."

"It has been a miraculous morning for me," said Murray, after a time, "and the greatest miracle is—you, dear."

"This is just the way the story ended in my book," Eliza told him happily—"our book."

He pressed her closer. "Yes! Our book—our bridge—our everything, Eliza."

She hid her blushing face against his shoulder, then with thumb and finger drew his ear down to her lips. Summoning her courage, she whispered:

"Murray dear, won't you call me—Violet?"

THE FLYING NORTH

Jean Potter

When the first Jenny plane rose from the forbidding terrain of Alaska, the real conquest of two of man's last frontiers—the American far north and the unknown sky above it—began This is the story of that conquest and of the famed flying heroes, the "bush pilots" of Alaska.

"Exceptional! An arresting and important chapter in the history of aviation."

New York Herald Tribune

$2.25

A COMSTOCK EDITION

To order by mail, send price of book plus 35¢ for handling to Dept. CS, Comstock Editions, 3030 Bridgeway, Sausalito, CA 94965.